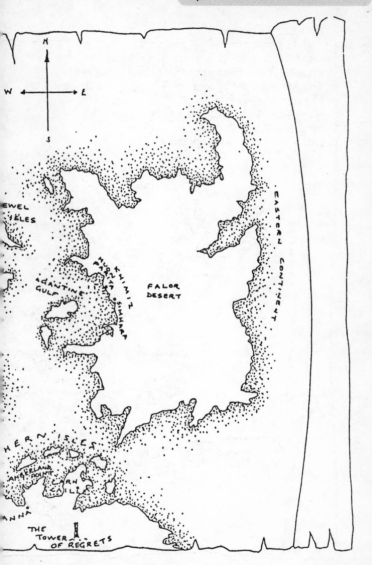

By the same author

The Initiate – Book 1 of the Time Master trilogy
The Outcast – Book 2 of the Time Master trilogy
The Master – Book 3 of the Time Master trilogy
Mirage
Nemesis – Book 1 of Indigo
Inferno – Book 2 of Indigo
Infanta – Book 3 of Indigo

NOCTURNE

Book 4 of

INDIGO

LOUISE COOPER

UNWIN
PAPERBACKS

LONDON SYDNEY WELLINGTON

First published in Great Britain by Unwin® Paperbacks, an imprint
of Unwin Hyman Limited, in 1989

UNWIN HYMAN LIMITED
15–17 Broadwick Street, London W1V 1FP

Allen & Unwin Australia Pty Ltd
8 Napier Street, North Sydney, NSW 2060, Australia

Allen & Unwin New Zealand Pty Ltd with the Port Nicholson Press
Compusales Building, 75 Ghunzee Street, Wellington, New Zealand

British Library Cataloguing in Publication Data
Cooper, Louise, *1952–*
   Nocturne.
   I. Title   II. Series
823'.914[F]

ISBN 0-04-440392-5

Set in 10 on 10½ point Times by Computape (Pickering) Ltd,
North Yorkshire
and printed in Great Britain by
Cox & Wyman Ltd, Reading

Night and silence – who is here?
> *Shakespeare: 'A Midsummer Night's Dream'*

For Lorna
– who is eminently qualified to be a Brabazon Fairplayer!

Prologue

In the cold southernmost region of the Earth, bordering the great ice cliffs that guard the polar wastes, Cathlor Ryensson rules peaceably over his small kingdom from the great and ancient stronghold of Carn Caille. In Carn Caille's hall, the face of Cathlor's father smiles down from the portrait which since his death five years ago has hung in the place of honour above the king's chair: and beside the portrait hangs another, its pigments a little faded by the salt air and the smoke of fires, which depicts a family group. This painting is particularly fine; so lifelike that it would be easy to imagine the four figures within the canvas rising, stretching their arms and stepping down from the frame to cross the dais and take their places at the royal table.

But King Kalig, Imogen his queen, and his son and daughter, Kirra and Anghara, are all long dead; struck down by the fever, now commemorated only in story and ballad, that came like a plague to the Southern Isles more than a quarter of a century ago.

Or so the world believes.

Many of those who pass through the hall these days have no memories of Kalig and his family. Their concern is with the new dynasty founded by Ryen and now continuing through his son; and though some might pause occasionally to gaze at the painting in admiration and respect, few now can recall Imogen's gracious voice, or Kalig's hearty laugh.

And no one, least of all King Cathlor, guesses even in their strangest dreams that one of Kalig's family still lives, and that to see her now would be to see again, unaged and unchanged, the face of the serious, amber-haired girl who sits at her father's feet in the old portrait.

The Princess Anghara did not die with her kin; though

many times down the long years she has wished it could be otherwise. She, alone among humanity, knows the true nature of the plague that slew her loved ones; for it was by her hand, and through her foolish, reckless curiosity, that an age-old law was broken, and seven demons were released shrieking and laughing into the world to set their curse upon mankind.

One single moment, one wild and rebellious impulse; now Anghara bears a burden of guilt and remorse that has haunted her, waking and sleeping, since the day when she lost her name and her home, and left the Southern Isles to begin a new and bitter life as a wanderer. For she alone has the power to make reparation for her crime, by seeking out and slaying the seven demons unshackled by her hand. Until that task is done there can be no rest for her, and no return to her homeland.

Anghara is forgotten now. But Indigo – the new name she chose for herself, which is also the colour of mourning among her people – lives on, and sometimes, in far-flung corners of the Earth, others have cause to know and remember her. She has fought with fire and she has fought with water; two demons have died by her hand, and the ghosts of many innocent souls walk in her wake. Memories crowd her mind and her uneasy dreams; and when she thinks now of her home and her kinfolk, it is with a sadness that is distanced, if not diminished, by the long years of her exile.

But, immortal and ageless though she might be, Indigo is not entirely alone in her quest. With her travels a friend who, though not human, understands what it is to be an outcast among her own kind and has chosen to share both Indigo's curse and her obligation. Close behind them both travels an implacable and eternal enemy – Nemesis. Nemesis stalks Indigo like a malign shadow wherever she goes for it is a part of herself, created from the blackest depths of her own soul and grown to independent life: the deadliest of all adversaries, a smiling child who lurks in every shadow; a tempter, a seducer, a deceiver. While Indigo lives, Nemesis will thrive – and its existence is the greatest threat of all.

Now, guided by the lodestone which was the Earth

Goddess's gift to her, Indigo journeys through the sprawl of the great western continent. For a while she has found a kind of peace, a calm hiatus in the storm of her life. But the hiatus cannot last, and she knows that soon she must take up the threads of her dark tapestry once more. The clouds are gathering: the auguries are growing stronger. And amid the shadow of a land which is not what it seems, among friends and foes who may be interchangeable, Indigo must face the third, and perhaps the most perilous, of her trials . . .

Chapter I

Temperance Brabazon shook his hair, soaked by the persistent drizzle, from his eyes, and listened for the distant whistle that would tell him the quarry were heading in his direction. His clothes were sodden – the short hide cloak that covered them hadn't been designed to keep out this sort of wet – and his feet and hands were growing stiff from inactivity and cold. He flexed his toes, sending a scatter of loose shale sliding away from the ledge where he perched above the valley floor, and cursed frayed ropes and straying ponies and the filthy autumn weather.

Suddenly the signal he'd been waiting for rang shrilly from the far end of the valley, slicing through the wet mist and carrying more emphatically than any shout. Temperance leaned forward, peering into the murk, and in the distance was just able to make out the smudge of his brother Courage's bright red hair against the fells' indeterminate grey-green. Cour whistled again; a sequence of four sharp notes that in the fellmen's code meant *be ready*: Temperance heard hoofbeats, then three riderless ponies galloped into view, led by the little chestnut stallion who was snorting like a racehorse and kicking up clods of turf with his shaggy hooves. A second later two more ponies – carrying riders this time – appeared in their wake, while what looked like a large, grey dog ran along the valley's gentler flank to deter the stallion and his small entourage from any thought of escape by that route.

Temperance jumped down from the ledge as the ponies raced towards the narrow neck of the valley, and stepped into their path, shouting and waving his arms. The stallion slithered to a halt, rearing and tossing his head, but his defiance was a sham; he knew he was cornered, and as Temperance approached him he whickered a friendly greeting and began to search the boy's hands and pockets with his muzzle, looking for tidbits. Taking their cue from him the mares dropped their heads and began to snatch at the lush grass, their tails switching nonchalantly.

The two mounted ponies came up behind the little group, and their riders slid to the ground. Forthright, who at nineteen was the eldest of the Brabazon brothers, approached the stallion and slipped a halter over its head, then looked up and grinned at Temperance through his sodden auburn forelock.

'Well done, Rance. I thought for a moment he was going to run you down.'

'Not him.' Rance glanced at the stallion, who eyed him back wickedly. 'He's all wind, that one; a rabbit could beat him in a kicking match. Where are the other ponies?'

'Cour's bringing 'em.' Forth looked over his shoulder to where his fellow rider, a tall young woman dressed in a hide coat and wool riding-breeches and with her long hair in a single, practical braid, was haltering the two mares. The grey animal had come trotting down from the slope to sit near her, panting, and Forth crossed over to the creature and bent down to rub the top of its brindled head.

'Eh, Grimya! That was a good run, uh?'

Grimya showed her fangs in a canine laugh, and her tail wagged with pleasure. Anyone not native to these south-western lands might have been excused for assuming that she was a domestic dog, despite her size and feral appearance. The Brabazons, though, knew better; in their years of travelling they had become well enough acquainted with wild creatures to distinguish a forest wolf from its domestic cousins. And in the past ten months, since their first meeting with her and her mistress, Grimya had become as close a friend of the family as any human.

Forth straightened, and met the young woman's gaze as she turned her head to smile at him. 'Thanks, Indigo.

If they'd got out of the valley the Harvest Lady alone knows how long we'd have spent chasing them.'

'Three days,' Rance put in. 'That was what it took last time they chewed through their tethers, remember? I keep telling Da we need new ropes, but he says it isn't worth it.'

'He's right. After next market day, they'll be someone else's problem.'

Rance still looked disgruntled, but before he could argue the point further Forth straightened and stared along the valley. 'Here comes Cour with the other ponies. Stop complaining, Rance, and let's get back to the vans before this rain drowns us all!'

The small cavalcade set off a few minutes later. Forth led the stallion while Cour and Rance took a mare apiece, and behind the brothers the young woman whom Forth had addressed as Indigo allowed her pony to pick its own way on the narrow fell path. The weather was worsening as the morning wore on; in the last few minutes the drizzle had increased to solid, steady rain, and tattered shreds of darker grey scudded under the lowering belly of the cloud-mass that stretched from horizon to horizon. Visibility was down to a few yards; anything beyond that was hidden in wet murk, and somewhere off to her right Indigo could hear the chatter of a swollen stream.

Grimya, who was trotting a few paces ahead of her, looked back over her shoulder, and a voice spoke in Indigo's mind.

I am glad we caught the ponies so quickly. This is a day for firesides, not for running.

Indigo smiled at the observation, and projected a silent reply. *We'll be back at the fireside soon enough, love. I only hope that Charity has saved us some breakfast!*

The Brabazons were unaware, she knew, of the extraordinary exchange between herself and the wolf; the mutation that enabled Grimya to understand human speech, and the strange telepathic link that the two of them shared, were part of an old and closely-kept secret between them. For a quarter of a century Indigo and Grimya had been companions on a journey that had

7

taken them across the face of the Earth, and whose end lay in a distant and unknown future. The unlikely bond between a human woman, born a king's daughter in the Southern Isles, and a mutant animal whose 'affliction' had made her an outcast among her own kind, concealed a stranger and deeper secret; for through those long and often turbulent years together, Indigo and Grimya had borne the stigma of immortality. To Grimya, it was a boon, granted at her own request by the great Earth Goddess; but to Indigo, the knowledge that she would not age, would not change, was an almost unbearable burden – for it lay at the heart of the curse that her own foolishness had brought on herself and on the world. And until her journey and her quest were over, she would have no release from it.

A quarter of a century . . . she blinked rain from her eyelashes and looked at the three red-haired figures riding ahead of her. In the year that Forth, the eldest, was born, she and Grimya had been in the blazing lands far to the north, facing a corrupt and deadly adversary whose memory could still bring her screaming and sweating from monstrous nightmares. As Rance learned to toddle, they had begun their long sojourn in eastern Khimiz, trapped by the deceits of the Serpent-Eater. And now, it seemed, the cycle was beginning again.

With a gesture that over the years had become as familiar as breathing, Indigo reached up and touched a small leather pouch that hung from a thong about her neck. The leather was old and cracked; inside, she felt the hard contours of the small pebble that she'd carried with her since her journey began: the lodestone, gift of the Earth Mother, which guided her unerringly and unceasingly in her quest. For the third time the golden pinpoint which lay at the stone's centre had awakened, to pulse like a tiny, living heart and show her that the next battle she must face was close at hand.

She let her arm drop back to the saddle pommel, staring down at the pony's wet, shaggy withers as it plodded stoically on. Time and again since the lodestone had shown her its clear message she had prayed that the Brabazons would not become embroiled in whatever lay in store for her on this particular road. They had been first saviours and then staunch friends to her and to Grimya since their first, chance meeting, and it would be a bitter irony to repay their kindness by leading them into danger. Enough innocents had died to further her cause: she wanted there to be no more.

For a while the procession trudged on in silence. Grimya, though she was aware of Indigo's uneasy thoughts, knew also that they would pass in their own good time and so said nothing; no one else felt inclined to talk, and even the little stallion's exuberance was defeated by the weather. The path was leading them towards the top of a gentle escarpment, where a small flock of sheep huddled disconsolately, pale blurs in the downpour. They reached the crest of the rise – and suddenly Forth held up a hand, signalling the others to halt. He stood in his stirrups, looking down the far slope, then turned back and beckoned urgently for his companions to join him. As they gathered round, he pointed down over the edge.

'Look.' His voice was low-pitched, quiet. 'There's another of them.'

Fifty feet or so below their vantage point a drove road wound along the foot of the scarp. On the road was a solitary horseman, uncloaked, hatless and seemingly oblivious to the rain that pelted down on his head and shoulders. He held his horse on an unnaturally tight rein, and stared directly, unswervingly ahead of him, as though following some lure which only he could see.

Cour whistled softly between his teeth, but Rance drew back, looking uneasily at his eldest brother. 'He might not be one of them, Forth. The others we saw were going northwards, not east.'

'You weren't with Cour and Esty and me when we saw the third one,' Forth said. 'She was heading south-west. We told you about it, remember? I don't think the direction's got much to do with it.'

'All the same, he might – '

'There's one way to find out,' Cour cut in. 'Hail him, Forth. Let's see if he responds.'

Forth glanced inquiringly at Rance, who shrugged.

'All right,' Forth said, and turned again in his saddle, cupping both hands to his mouth.

'*Ho-la!*' The ponies jumped, startled, as the shout rang out. 'Stranger! Up here!'

The call bounced and echoed back from the fells, but though the horse below them tossed its head uneasily, its rider didn't respond. Forth shouted again and the horse whickered; but the man only tightened the reins still further, forcing it onward.

Rance reached out and touched Forth's shoulder. 'Best leave it, Forth. There's nothing we can do.'

'No.' Forth shook his head. 'I'm going to go down, intercept him and see if I can find out what's to do.'

'You can go alone, then.'

Forth looked at the others. 'Cour? Indigo?'

'I'll come with you.' Indigo was still watching the solitary rider. Though she shared Rance's unease, her curiosity was aroused. And at the back of her mind lurked a less pleasant feeling; an intuitive sensation that told her there was more significance to this than any of them yet knew.

Grimya, picking up the thought, spoke silently to her. *I think you may be right. Let us go and see.*

Cour elected to stay behind with Rance, and so Forth handed over the little stallion and told his brothers to take the easier path and meet him and Indigo at the crossroads a mile on. The others moved away, setting their ponies at the scarp's edge and leaning back in the saddles for the steep descent. As the ponies slipped and slithered down the slope, Indigo watched the rider below them and recalled the previous bizarre encounters to which Forth had referred. She had seen two of the other travellers for herself – the first had been an elderly man, on foot, who had passed the Brabazons' camp four days ago as a sullen dusk was falling. She and Charity had been tending the cooking fire and, following the local custom of hailing strangers to show they meant no threat, had called out a greeting. The man ignored them, and walked on with an odd, stiff-legged gait. In the gathering gloom Indigo had noticed that his face had a ghastly pallor. Two days later, Forth, Cour and their

10

sister Esty had encountered a second lonely walker, a woman this time, with the same dead-whiteness to her skin, who again seemed to be oblivious to her surroundings; and that same evening the third traveller had passed the camp on horseback, moving with the steady but mindless determination of a sleepwalker or a man in a trance. They had all looked more like apparitions than living human beings, and the chill, silent aura that hung about them had turned Indigo's stomach queasy. Who they were, where they were going or why, she couldn't begin to imagine. And despite her curiosity, she had the unpleasant conviction that she didn't want to know the answer.

They were almost level with the road now. Grimya, more sure-footed than the ponies, had bounded down ahead of them; seeing her approach, the stranger's horse shied and tried to sidle off the road, and again the rider jerked fiercely but reflexively at its head, though he gave no sign that he too was aware of the interlopers.

Forth's pony scrambled the last few feet to the valley floor and broke into a canter, intercepting the solitary rider and turning square into his path. Forth held up a hand, palm outward in the universal sign of peaceable greeting.

'Good day to you, sir!'

The horse came on. Indigo, catching up with Forth, wheeled her own pony across the road and stared through the rain at the rider. He was a middle-aged man, well-dressed, but in clothes better suited to a warm hearth than to travelling the country in a downpour. His face was deathly pale, as were the hands that gripped the reins; his eyes, glazed and unseeing, stared through and beyond her. She had seen such a look before, that dreadful air of purpose that hinted at an obsession strong enough to have brought this man – and at least three others before him – from home and family, out into the cold, sodden day on some unimaginable errand.

'I was right.' Forth, too, was gazing at the rider, steadying his pony which began to grow nervous as the strange horse drew closer. 'That makes four, Indigo. Four, in as many days. I don't like it.'

11

'Best leave him be,' she counselled. 'There's nothing we can do to make him acknowledge us.'

'Oh, I don't know. Maybe we shouldn't let this one go by as we did the others.'

'Forth, don't be – ' But before she could say it, he had wheeled his pony about and was heading towards the oncoming rider.

'Sir!' Forth drew alongside and reached out to lay a hand on the stranger's arm. 'Sir, stop! I would – '

Indigo had a sharp twinge of premonition, and shouted a warning. '*Forth!*'

The rider turned. The white, rigid face stared down at Forth for a single instant – though it seemed that the man's mind still didn't register what his eyes took in – then, so fast that Forth had no time to evade it, a short-thonged whip cracked through the air and caught him on the shoulder. Forth yelled with pain and outrage; his pony squealed and made a violent, stiff-legged jump to one side and he tumbled out of the saddle to sprawl full-length in the road as the stranger and his horse swept past.

Forth seemed dazed, but only for a moment. He raised himself to his knees, spitting gravel – then, uttering a basic and furious oath, he scrambled to his feet, reaching for the wicked, curved knife he wore at his belt.

'Forth!' Indigo dismounted and ran towards him. 'No!' She grabbed his arm, twisting it up as he made to start after the departing horseman.

'Let go of me!' He struggled to free himself but, though she was slighter than he was, Indigo was the more skilled fighter; she twisted his arm a little further, applied pressure, and the knife spun from his hands.

Forth stumbled away from her, holding his wrist and grimacing. 'Why did you do that?' He was breathing hard, his temper barely under control.

'Because you won't solve anything by attacking him!'

'He attacked *me*!'

'He didn't know what he was doing! You saw him, Forth – you saw the look on his face. He wasn't even aware of your existence!'

Slowly the indignant fire died from Forth's eyes. His

12

shoulders relaxed, and at last he turned his head away, muttering an imprecation under his breath.

'All right, all right. I'll let him go.' He transferred his attention from his wrist to rub at his stinging shoulder and glared venomously after the stranger, who was now no more than an indistinct shape through the rain. 'But if it wasn't for this weather, and the others waiting for us, I'd follow him and see just where it is he's going.'

Privately Indigo was tempted to agree, but she thought better of saying so. Forth was impulsive, and she had a strong instinct that to track the stranger, armed as they were only with knives, might not be a wise move, though she couldn't rationalise the feeling.

Partly to distract Forth and partly to give another focus to her own disquiet, she said, 'He looked ill. Did you notice?'

'Unh. Just like the others – white as a dead fish. As if something had sucked all the life out of him.' Forth laughed, but edgily. 'This land's rife with legends of ghosties and were-beasts and suchlike. Perhaps our friend's been got at by a ghoul. Or a vampire.' He saw Indigo's expression, and forced a smile. 'I'm joking, Indigo. At least, I think I am.'

She caught his meaning, the reference to the unpleasant coincidence that they had noted before. 'I hope you are, Forth.' She gathered up her pony's reins and prepared to remount. 'We'd best be on our way, or we'll keep the others waiting.'

They set off, urging their mounts into a steady trot. When the solitary horseman loomed into view once more ahead of them, Indigo guided her pony off the road to pass him at a prudent distance and was relieved when Forth followed suit without argument. As the rider fell behind, Forth drew level with her once more and gestured towards the land that stretched away to their left. Here grapevines grew in neat, terraced rows, scrambling up the side of a relatively gentle south-facing slope. The autumn harvest was imminent, but the rain had battered the vines to a sorry, dripping tangle. A few days of hot weather before the picking began would put that to rights, but it was another and more insidious kind of

13

damage that had commanded Forth's attention and which he pointed out to Indigo.

'About half way up, towards the far end of that terrace.' He raised his voice to be heard above the hiss of rain and the noise of the ponies' hooves. 'See it?'

She narrowed her eyes, and saw. A whole group of vines appeared to have withered, losing their rich colour and turning to a sickly grey-white that reminded her disconcertingly of the pallor in the strange horseman's skin.

'I see,' she called back. 'Then it is spreading, as the rumours say.'

'But in isolated patches like that? It isn't natural. Little wonder the farmers hereabouts are getting worried!' Forth checked his pony as it stumbled in a rut. 'I've heard it's affecting the apple orchards too; and in the valleys the hop harvest gave only a shadow of its usual yield. And always the same thing. No obvious signs: no rotting, no mildew. Just fading and withering – '

'As if something had sucked all the life out of them.' Indigo finished the sentence for him.

'Yes,' Forth said darkly. 'Exactly like our friend on the road, and the others we saw.'

They both fell silent but Indigo knew that their thoughts ran on an unpleasant parallel course. A blight, formless and apparently sourceless, afflicting the harvest at this crucial time of year. And strange, solitary wanderers who seemed to be caught in some form of trance, oblivious to the world around them, walking or riding on their lonely way with that unnerving air of purpose. On the surface there could be no link between the two peculiar events; but Forth wasn't the only one to have noted the disturbing similarity between the white and withering crops and the dessicated look of the zombie-like travellers.

The crossroads came in sight ahead of them. Cour and Rance were already waiting with the other ponies, and when he and Indigo joined them Forth described the encounter, omitting, Indigo noticed with dry amusement, any reference to his own thwarted show of outrage. Cour listened soberly, then said:

14

'We should reach Bruhome within two or three days. If anyone knows what this is all about, the townsfolk there will. And there'll also be plenty of outlanders coming in for the harvest festival. *Someone* must be able to tell us what's afoot.'

The others agreed and nothing more was said of the incident. But as they set off on the last mile back to the camp, Indigo looked back over her shoulder uneasily. The road behind them was empty – the solitary rider hadn't yet caught up – and she quelled a shiver that had nothing to do with the rain's chill. Cour was right: in Bruhome, which was the hub of trade and festivity for farmers, sheepherders and vintners alike, they would learn the answers to their questions, if there were answers to be found.

And she knew, with an unerring instinct, that her own quest and the conundrum of the blighted crops and the blighted travellers were mysteriously but inextricably linked.

Chapter II

Two days later, the three caravans that were the pivot of the Brabazon family's itinerant life trundled over the bridge marking the town boundary of Bruhome an hour before sunset. Others crossing the bridge made way, pausing to stare at the spectacle: the vans, each drawn by a pair of stoical, soft-eyed oxen – less excitable and therefore more reliable, the family's father declared, than horses – were high-roofed wooden structures carried on four great wheels apiece, highly decorated and painted in a motley of brilliant colours. Pennants streamed cheerfully from short poles set on either side of the driver's boxes, and in huge, curlicued yellow script on the side of the leading van was emblazoned the legend: BRABAZON FAIRPLAYERS.

Steadfast Brabazon, father of Forthright, Courage, Temperance and their ten brothers and sisters, sat high on the driving box of the first van, flourishing a whip adorned with multicoloured ribbons and grinning widely at the world about them. He was a short man, as broad and solid as an oak tree, with a crown of fiery red curls that were only just beginning to grey and recede at the temples. For all his fifty years, like his father and grandfather before him, he had been a travelling showman. His nuptial bed had been this caravan, his children had all been born on the roads between one town and the next, and in the six years since his turbulent but adored wife had died giving birth to their youngest daughter, he had managed both his chaotic family and his business with an irresistible combination of fearsome sternness and all-embracing good humour. In the late winter of this year, while travelling south-westwards from the Inland Sea to entertain the visitors at an

16

ox-racing festival, Steadfast and his tribe had come upon a stranger with a pet wolf, living on her wits and her crossbow and making a poor show of it. Indigo and Grimya had suffered a hard winter in a country where outlanders – especially those unable to speak the local tongue fluently – received short shrift: for four months Indigo had found neither paid work nor anyone willing to offer her transport into the kinder western lands, and with game in short supply due to the season and no hope but to tramp the roads on foot, both she and her companion had grown thin and weak almost to the point of emaciation. The Brabazons had taken them in, fed them, nurtured them; and almost before they knew it Indigo and Grimya had become honorary members of the family – and an integral part of the showman's entourage.

Stead's delight at learning that Indigo was a musician and singer was eclipsed only by his excitement when he discovered that her tame wolf – in itself enough of a rarity to draw the crowds, he said – appeared to understand every word addressed to her and act accordingly. When Indigo first played her lap-harp for him at their campfire one night he had sat in the flamelight with tears streaming down his face and declared that such music could make a statue weep. Mother Earth had smiled upon him this day, he said, and filled his cup to overflowing. Such friends and talents to have discovered – a lovely girl whose songs could melt the hardest heart, and a performing animal to bring wonder and laughter after the tears! He was a man blessed, a king thrice-crowned, to have had such a boon placed in his lap and he nothing but a poor, unworthy fairplayer who strove humbly to bring a little entertainment to the good folk of his homeland. Indigo, trying not to laugh, had grasped the core of the rhetoric and gravely replied that she and Grimya would both consider themselves honoured to be offered a place in the Brabazon entourage. So, much to their own surprise, they had begun a new life as travelling players.

And thus far it had been a good life. They journeyed from place to place, town to town, and at every stop they presented one of the shows known in the region as 'fairplays': a lively mixture of music and song and theatrics. Every member of the family, from Stead himself down to six-year-old Piety, had some particular talent or skill, and the Brabazons were in demand wherever they went; even in those districts where itinerants were looked upon with deepest suspicion. They knew nothing of Indigo's quest, nor of the lodestone which had set her on a path that, fortunately coincided (at least for the time being) with their own travels. And for her part Indigo had grown fiercely fond of her new friends, and hoped that, though the time for parting must inevitably come, that time lay in the distant future.

She sat now beside Stead on the driver's box, gazing at the unfamiliar sights unfolding before her as they rolled on into the town. Bruhome lay between two small rivers that divided the spectacular sheep- and goat-farming fell country from the lusher and lower arable lands: here, the farmers, brewers and vintners who drew their livelihoods from the soil came to sell the fruits of their labours, to elect leaders, pay taxes and argue politics; and to enjoy their leisure. People in this region needed only the barest excuse for a festival – and now with the hop-harvest in, the livestock fattened on good fell grass and ready for market, and the grape- and apple-picking season getting under way, it was time for the annual Autumn Revels to begin. The Brabazon Fairplayers had become frequent and popular visitors to Bruhome over the years and Stead had regaled Indigo with descriptions of the festivities, which went on for seven days and were the locals' way of giving thanks to the Harvest Mother for Her bounty. The first casks of wine from the previous year's grape vintage would be breached; there would be processions, speeches, singing and dancing, games and sports; and anyone who could entertain a lively audience would be assured of a welcome.

Indigo liked Bruhome on sight. Most of its buildings were made of wood; some thatched, others tiled, and though its layout was untidy somehow the cheerful jumble of houses and taverns and public halls, interspersed by a maze of narrow, winding streets, struck a note of order rather than of chaos. Brightly-painted shutters flanked almost every window, while carved figures and murals adorned the steep, gabled roofs; with the festival about to begin, the lanes were decorated with bunting and garlands of meadow flowers which added an extra touch to the vivid atmosphere.

The rain had finally given way to kinder weather, and the last, mellow sunlight of a glorious day slanted across the scene. Now and then, as they made their way through the town, Stead was hailed by people who clearly knew the family of old. But though he waved and smiled to each one, Indigo thought she detected a lessening of his usual exuberance; and twice, when he thought she wasn't looking, a faint, disquieted frown crossed his face. No one else seemed to be aware of anything amiss: Forth, inside the caravan with Grimya, was leaning out of a side window, enthusiastically greeting all and sundry, and from one of the following vans Indigo could hear the rhythm of a tambourine and the voices of Charity, Modesty and Harmony, the three eldest Brabazon girls, practising a popular song.

She glanced towards Stead again. Something *was* wrong, she was sure; but she couldn't guess its cause. She could see nothing untoward in the town: far from it. But Stead was uneasy, and that wasn't like him.

She touched his arm. 'Stead? Is something amiss?'

He looked at her, the frown appearing once more. 'You've noticed it?'

'Noticed what?'

His gaze roved over the scene before them. Then he sighed, a hissing sound through teeth clamped tightly shut. 'I don't know. Maybe I'm wrong. Maybe it's just been a long day and we all need some sleep.' He reached over and patted her knee in a fond, avuncular manner. 'We'll talk about it later and see what's what. Come on, now; smile for the people. They're tomorrow's audience, and our bread and meat.'

Partly to placate townsfolk nervous at such a great influx of newcomers, and partly so that any potential troublemakers could be more easily watched, a piece of ground on the town's western flank had been set aside to

accommodate the motley assortment of itinerant enter-
tainers arriving to take part in the revels. Here, where one
of the rivers spread out into a flat, lazy meander, there
was space for two dozen or more wagons and good
grazing for the animals that pulled them, and a cheer
went up from the Brabazon caravans as they rolled
through the open gate and on to the lush turf beyond.

Dusk was falling; stars had begun to wink in the east,
and one or two campfires were already blazing in the
pasture. Forth and Cour set about unharnessing the oxen
and tethering them and the riding ponies, while Stead
strolled off across the meadow to see if there were any old
friends or enemies among the groups already encamped.
Travellers, as he'd often explained to Indigo, were as
mixed a bunch as a sackful of stage props, and a festival
such as this was bound to attract a lot of curdled milk as
well as the cream of the profession. Mingling with the
genuine players, he said, would be any number of thieves,
pickpockets and vagabonds, and they as much as the
good townsfolk of Bruhome would do well to watch their
purses and their backs.

While he was gone, Indigo and two of the younger
children took wood from the great basket carried at the
back of one of the vans and built their own small blaze.
Everyone was too tired to explore Bruhome's taverns
tonight; instead they would eat around the fire then bed
down under the stars or in the caravans to be fresh for the
morning.

Charity, the eldest of Stead's thirteen children, was in
charge of the cooking. She had recently celebrated her
twentieth birth-anniversary, and had cast herself in the
role of substitute mother to her younger siblings; a
responsibility which she took very seriously. She was a
tall, willowy girl with waist-length auburn hair – every
Brabazon, father and child alike, had hair that was one
shade or another of red – which she wore in braids
wound around her head; the dreamy nature she had
inherited from her grandmother was tempered by a firm
thread of practicality. Stead might be the foundation
stone of the Brabazons, but Charity was his invaluable
lieutenant, and Indigo often wondered what would

20

happen when – as it surely must – Charity's quiet charm and beauty captivated some young man and she chose to leave her brothers and sisters for a husband and hearth of her own. It was hard to imagine Modesty, the flamboyant and inaptly-named next-eldest sister, stepping into her shoes, and the other girls were as yet too young for such a responsibility.

Charity was singing in her warm contralto as she set a battered and well-seasoned cauldron on the fire and began to put herbs, scrubbed root vegetables and some jointed pieces of meat into the simmering water. Cooking was a holy mystery to most of the Brabazons, and Indigo's own skills were limited; but as the stew began to bubble in earnest, and Charity thrust some tubers skewered on peeled sticks into the fire's embers to roast, the others began to drift in ones and twos towards the fire, lured by the rich aroma. As they settled down, their faces were cast into dramatic shadow by the flamelight; chestnut hair, copper hair and fire-orange hair glinted; talk was warm and comfortable. Only Stead was missing: Indigo thought she could glimpse his distinctive head among a group of men who were talking by one of the other fires.

'What's to eat?' Rance asked as he sat down on the grass.

'Mutton,' Charity told him.

'The same one that Forth and Cour – ?'

'Yes; and don't let me catch you saying anything about it to anyone in Bruhome!' Charity admonished, then frowned at the two eldest boys. 'Sheep stealing – I'm ashamed of the pair of you!'

Forth grinned. 'Not too ashamed to eat the spoils though, eh, Chari?'

She tossed her head. 'What's done can't be undone. Now keep still and let me make sure everyone's here.' She began to count: it was an unnecessary but familiar ritual. 'Forthright, Courage, Modesty, Temperance, Fortitude, Harmony, Honesty, Truth, Gentility, Moderation, Duty, Piety. Then Indigo, Grimya and me – that's everyone except for Da.' Satisfied, she started to ladle stew into bowls.

'Da's over there with some of the other travellers,' Cour volunteered, pointing. 'Burgher Mischyn's there, too; I think he's making some sort of speech.'

'Better not disturb him, then.' Deftly Chari speared a tuber out of the embers and prodded it to see if it was cooked through. 'Forth, get some ale, please.' She handed a brimming bowl to Indigo.

For a while then there was a comfortable silence as everyone turned their attention to the food. Indigo was savouring her last tuber, which she'd soaked in the stew gravy, when a footfall announced Stead's return. He lowered his bulk down between his two eldest sons, and grunted thanks as Charity filled another bowl and passed it to him.

Forth studied Stead's expression for a moment, then frowned. 'Da? What's amiss?'

Stead spooned up a mouthful of stew and washed it down with ale before replying. 'You might as well know now as later,' he said gloomily. 'The Autumn Revels have been cut short. Just three days, starting tomorrow, and it'll all be over.'

Only Duty and Piety, who were too young to grasp the significance of Stead's words, failed to react. The rest were appalled.

'*Three days*? That's hardly time to do anything!'

'What sort of takings can we hope to get in just three days?'

'We've been preparing for Bruhome for months – '

'We'd relied on it to keep us in coin through the winter – '

And Forth's voice, cutting through the others with the question that mattered most of all. 'But *why*, Da? What's happened?'

'It's the harvests.' Stead took another swig of beer; he seemed to have lost interest in the food. 'You know the rumours we've been hearing about the blight? Well, they're true. Burgher Mischyn's been telling us the whole tale.'

Glances were exchanged. Cour said, softly, 'Those withered vines we saw . . . '

'It isn't just the vines,' Stead told him. 'It's the hops,

22

the apples – even the pastureland's getting affected. And no one knows what's causing it. The plants just turn pale, then white, then wither and die. The farmers hereabouts have already lost half their hop harvest, and now it looks as if the grapes and apples are following suit. And it's happening to some of the stock beasts, too, where they've been grazed on afflicted pastures. There's new reports of it coming in every day, Burgher Mischyn says. So nobody feels much like celebrating.'

Modesty leaned forward, twisting her hands together. 'But surely it can't last, Da? Maybe there'll be a bad year, but come winter the disease is sure to die off along with everything else. Why should they cut the revels short? People want cheering!'

'If it was just the harvest, Esty lass, I'd agree,' Stead said. 'But it seems there's been other rum happenings in the district.'

'What sort of happenings?'

Stead pursed his lips. 'To begin with, there's an illness going about the town. Like a kind of sleeping sickness, Mischyn says. Those who get it just fall asleep and won't wake up.'

Charity looked at him in alarm. 'Da, we might catch it!'

'It isn't the catching kind. Mischyn should know: his own son's down with it, and his goodwife's been tending the boy day and night without any ill effect on her. But it's like the crop blight – they don't know what it is or where it comes from.'

'There must be a town physician,' Indigo put in. 'What does he say?'

'He's in no position to say anything. He's got the sickness – been asleep for nine days now. Ach, what was the word Mischyn used?' Stead snapped his fingers, searching for inspiration. 'C. . . something . . . '

'Coma?'

'That's it. Coma. But they've no idea why. And then, as if that wasn't enough, there's been people disappearing.'

Silence fell and astonished faces stared at him around the circle of firelight. At last, Rance said: '*Disappearing*?'

Stead nodded. 'Here one day, gone the next. Shepherd went up on the fells, didn't come back that evening. They sent searchers but they didn't find him. Man set out to meet friends at a tavern: didn't arrive at the tavern, hasn't been seen since. Another man went to bed with his wife one night and woke up next morning to find her gone, with nothing but a shawl missing from among her clothes.' He shrugged eloquently. 'Gone, all of them. Just gone.'

Indigo felt tension crawling through her. She glanced obliquely in Forth's direction and saw that he, too, was disquieted. She guessed what he was thinking, and a silent communication from Grimya confirmed it.

He, too, is remembering the horseman we saw on the road, I think, the she-wolf said. *Could there be a link between them?*

It's possible. She recalled the dead-white face, the blank eyes that seemed to stare uncomprehendingly into another world. And the purpose. Above all, the dreadful aura of purpose.

Stead was speaking again. 'Whatever's afoot here, it's more than anyone knows how to cope with. I've known Burgher Mischyn since before you three youngest were born, when he'd only just succeeded to his own da's brewery, and in all those years I've never seen him in such a taking as he is now. He's frightened.' He looked at Indigo and raised an ironic eyebrow. 'You asked me earlier, lass, what was amiss when we came through the town. Now you know – and if you'd been to Bruhome before today, you'd have seen the difference in the people's mood. They're *all* frightened. And I can't hardly blame them.'

'So what are we to do?' Cour asked.

'What we always meant to do, so far as we can. The revels are still to take place even if they're subdued, so, like Esty said, we must do our best to cheer the good folk and help 'em forget their troubles for a while.'

'And hope we can earn enough to see us by,' Charity added.

'Exactly.' Stead stared down at his bowl of stew. It had grown cold and begun to congeal, and he set it aside,

24

refilling his ale mug instead. 'You younger ones should be abed. And the rest of us'd do well to get a good night's rest. In the morning we'd best look at the show we planned to do and see whether there's changes ought to be made. Wouldn't do, would it, to perform something that might offend the townsfolk's sensibilities with all this going on?'

It was a tacit dismissal, and although the older Brabazons seemed disposed to argue, something in Stead's demeanour made them think better of it. Slowly, reluctantly, they all rose and went to attend their last chores: Harmony, the third eldest girl, chivvied her younger sisters towards the second caravan where all the women slept, and Indigo helped Chari and Esty to wash bowls and spoons at the river and then stamp out the fire.

As the last embers died and the camp circle sank into starlit darkness, Chari looked up at the sky. 'I think we'd best sleep in tonight,' she said thoughtfully. 'When there's no cloud, the small hours can get cold this time of year.'

That wasn't her only reason for seeking the security of the caravan, and Indigo knew it; but she made no comment, only nodded agreement. They started towards the van, Grimya padding at Indigo's side, and had almost reached the steps when a hand came out of the gloom and touched Indigo's arm.

'Indigo – before you sleep.' It was Forth. He drew her aside, ignoring Chari's exasperated look as she walked on, and dropped his voice to a whisper. 'You were thinking the same as me, weren't you? When Da told us about those people vanishing.' He paused, scrutinising her face. 'Well? *Do* you reckon those benighted souls we saw on the road might be the ones who disappeared?'

Indigo hesitated, then nodded. 'Yes, Forth; I do.' She glanced towards the van. Chari had gone inside. 'But I don't think we should say anything about it to the others.'

'Cour and Rance have already worked it out for themselves. Esty too, if I know her. And Da. It was written all over his face.'

'Nonetheless – '

25

'I know; I know. Look, I'll say nothing to anyone else unless they say it to me first. But I think we should keep our eyes and ears open in the town tomorrow. And in particular, watch for anyone who looks too pale for their own good.'

It was a sensible enough suggestion. 'Yes,' Indigo said. 'I agree.'

She would have started on towards the van, but Forth seemed reluctant to end the conversation. Suddenly, he said:

'About the sickness – there was a word for it; you knew what it was . . . '

'Coma.'

'Yes. What does it mean?'

'It's like a very deep sleep,' she told him. 'A kind of trance. The victims still live, but it's as though their minds are in a kind of limbo.'

'Ah.' Forth chewed his lower lip. 'You mean, they're not aware of anything around them – just like those travellers?'

Indigo's pulse had quickened to a discomfortingly rapid beat. 'Yes,' she said. 'Exactly like those travellers.'

The night was peaceful, and the caravan's interior dark and warm; but Indigo couldn't sleep. She lay at the edge of the tangle of cushions and rough blankets spread across the floor to form the bed she shared with the six Brabazon sisters, watching the infinitesimally slow wheeling of the stars across the sky beyond the open half-door. At her back, Esty snored softly; Gentility and Piety, the two youngest girls, had whispered and giggled for a while before a sleepy but sharp admonition from Chari silenced them; now there was no sound but Esty's throaty, rhythmic breathing.

Indigo couldn't stop thinking about what Forth had said, and about the link between the vanishing towns-folk, four entranced travellers on the road, and the mysterious illness. Forth was right: *coma* was the key word, and a disquietingly apposite description of the oblivious, unswervable wanderers.

She turned on to her back, staring up at the van's

26

painted ceiling. Blighted crops and pastures, looking as though the very stuff of life had been leached from them. Animals, suffering a similar fate. Human beings, bleached, drained, walking or riding the roads as if in a trance. Disappearances. A sleeping sickness. It was a progression, she thought; each stage leading to the next in an awful parade.

And her subconscious mind was crying out that, somewhere behind this increasingly convoluted mystery, lay the hand of a demon.

The pattern of star-shadows on the ceiling shifted suddenly, and Indigo looked behind her to see that Grimya had raised her head and was watching her. In the dark, the wolf's eyes were faintly lambent.

Indigo? Are you awake?

I can't sleep, she communicated. *I can't stop thinking, Grimya. My thoughts won't let me alone.*

Is it what Forth was saying?

That, yes. And more.

Grimya rose quietly to her feet, a silhouette against the square of the door. Raising her muzzle, she sniffed the air. *It is a good night. No wind, and I can hear the river talking. Why don't we walk for a while?*

Aren't you tired?

No. You know I love the dark hours.

Indigo glanced over her shoulder at the soundly sleeping Esty, then carefully eased herself out from under the blanket that covered her. Quietly, she unlatched the lower half of the door and followed Grimya down the steps and out into the night.

The scents of extinguished fires, grass, animal dung and the river mingled in her nostrils as she stretched her arms to loosen muscles cramped from lying still. The air had an autumnal chill, but her knee-length robe was protection enough, and the grass beneath her bare feet was soft and pleasant. They skirted the wagons and tents where other travellers slept and walked down the gentle slope to the river's broad, shallow bank. In the vegetation at the water's edge something rustled and splashed; a water-fowl paddled away, complaining briefly. Grimya's ears pricked with a hunter's instinct

27

before the bird swam out of reach, and she subsided. Indigo sat down on a reedy tussock and stretched her toes to the water, watching the ripples glint in the starlight as they spread out into the slow current.

For a few minutes they sat in companionable silence; until Grimya spoke. Long ago the she-wolf had determined, through an odd but somehow dignified sense of pride, that she would use her talent to speak aloud (however guttural and halting) whenever there was no one but Indigo to hear her.

Voicing the question that Indigo had not wanted to ask herself, she said: 'Have you ll. . .*ooked* at the lodestone?'

'No.' She smiled, but a little bleakly. 'I haven't been able to summon the courage. We know it was leading us towards Bruhome, but now . . . '

'You th-ink it may show that we have reached our d. . .destination?'

'It's what I fear. And I don't want to involve the Brabazons, Grimya. They've been true friends to us, and I remember all too well what's befallen those who befriended me in the past.'

'These have been good times,' Grimya said sombrely. 'It is s-sad to think that they must end.'

'I know; and that's another part of it.' Indigo looked out at the slow-moving river.

'Per-haps they need not; at least not yet,' Grimya suggested. 'We don't know for sure what the stone says. Not until we look.'

Indigo was reluctant to look: she knew what the lodestone's answer to her question would be. But Grimya's gentle admonition was fair: the moment couldn't be postponed for ever.

She raised a hand to her neck and drew out the leather pouch on its thong. The stone – small, smooth and unremarkable – fell into her upturned palm. Even in the dark the tiny golden pinpoint within was clearly visible: after a few moments she held it out for Grimya to see. Her face was expressionless.

Grimya looked, and said, 'Ah . . . '

The tiny gold eye was no longer pointing westward.

Instead, it had settled at the stone's exact centre.

They had reached the end of their journey.

For a long time neither of them spoke. Grimya watched her friend with troubled eyes, reading her thoughts but unable to say anything that would be of any comfort. The tracking was done and the hunt was about to begin: here in this peaceable rural backwater something dark and evil was waiting for them, and they must turn their backs on the quiet idyll of the recent past and, once again, face a new manifestation of the horror that Indigo had released from the Tower of Regrets so long ago. The third of the seven demons was stirring. And, no matter what the cost, it must be found and destroyed.

Something glinted on Indigo's cheek, and Grimya saw that she was crying. But there was neither anger nor despair in her tears; they were simply a release, an acknowledgement and acceptance of her destiny and a wistful regret for the quiet interlude that must now come to an end. The wolf blinked, trying to think of some words of sympathy, but before she could speak Indigo wiped her eyes with the back of one hand.

'I'm all right, Grimya. Don't fret.' She looked at the moisture on her skin, noting abstractedly that the starlight made it gleam like silver. Silver – the colour of her own weakness, the sign of the flaw within her that was, perhaps, the greatest danger of all. She shut her eyes for a moment, trying to banish the unwonted image of a face she had seen all too often in her dreams. A child's features, cat's teeth like pearls in the small, cruelly-smiling mouth, silver hair a soft nimbus, silver eyes calculating and mocking. It had been a long time since the creature she called Nemesis, the unholy symbiote born of her own dark nature and released to independent life, had crossed her path. Her last glimpse of it had been from the deck of the *Pride of Simhara* as she sailed away from the great eastern land of Khimiz, and she could still remember the hatred in the creature's eyes and the sense of silent promise that that encounter would not be their last. Nemesis lived only to thwart her quest and lure her from her resolve, for with the destruction of the last demon it, too, would die. And Nemesis's touchstone was silver . . .

Suddenly the night felt cold, and the sleepy river flowing so smoothly between its banks seemed to take on a faint tinge of menace. A little way off, the reeds rustled; Indigo started to turn her head, then stopped, half-afraid that if she looked, her tired mood might translate the sound and movement into something less innocent than the caprices of the breeze. Silver stars in the sky; silver reflections on the water. She shivered, and reached out to bury her hand in the rough, comforting warmth of Grimya's fur.

'Let's go back,' she said.

Grimya understood. They rose, and walked slowly past the dead fires and unlit wagons to the Brabazon encampment. A faint and pleasant smell of woodsmoke lingered on the air; at the caravan Indigo looked back across the field. Nothing stirred, and with the she-wolf at her heels she climbed the steps and returned to the peace and security of her sleeping companions.

Chapter III

'Indigo, I can't find my *mask*! Oh, help me, please!'

Indigo was sitting on one of the costume-chests, head bent over her harp as she made adjustments to the tuning. On the raised platform beyond the screen that formed a cramped and makeshift preparation area for the Revels performers a troupe of acrobats were nearing the end of their routine; there was a good deal of noise in the square and it was almost impossible to hear the notes her fingers were plucking, so she set the harp aside – she'd have time for a final check later – and went to answer Honesty's wailing plea.

'Which mask have you lost, Honi?'

'The one for the Drover's Dance.' Honesty was holding a lantern over a wooden box with one hand and rummaging frantically through its contents with the other. 'I know I don't need it yet, but I've *got* to have it ready; there won't be time to look later.'

A gleam of yellow satin among a pile of cloaks caught Indigo's eye, and she reached out. 'This one?'

'Ohh!' Honesty put a hand to her heart and made a mock show of rolling her eyes up as though about to faint. '*Thank* you!'

Stead appeared around the screen. He paused, casting a professional eye over the seeming chaos, then said:

'Everybody ready? The acrobats are finishing.'

A scatter of applause, mixed with a few cheers and good-natured catcalls, sounded from the square, and Forth looked up from lacing seven-year-old Duty's leggings.

'What about the audience, Da? Is it as bad as we feared?'

'Could be better, but then again it could be worse,'

31

Stead told him. 'There's no shortage of numbers, at least; a lot more have come in since sunset and they're packing the square like kits at a milk-saucer. But there's far too many doleful faces for my liking.'

'Well, we'll just have to make extra efforts to cheer 'em.' Forth stood up, his task completed, and Duty flexed his legs experimentally. There was a sudden flurry of activity as the acrobats – small people from the far south-west with pale skins and near-white hair – came running round the edge of the screen. Their leader smiled and bowed to Stead, then the group flopped breathlessly down on the ground and began to chatter in their own unintelligible tongue.

'Right,' Forth said. 'This is us, then. Got your pipe, Chari? And you young ones – line up, now.'

Stead swore. 'Damn me, I almost forgot, Forth – we're going to have to cut out the Tree Spirits Masque.'

'What?' Forth stared at him. 'Why, in the Harvest Mother's name? It's one of our best acts!'

'I know. But there's a new rumour going about – I heard it just now from the landlord of the Apple-Barrel Inn. Seems people are talking about some kind of forest that's sprung up where there wasn't one before.'

'Eh?'

Stead shook his head. 'Don't ask me what it's all about. All I heard was some garble about black forests and trees that move. It sounds like someone got carried away in his cups and started seeing things, but the story's spreading like a grass fire. So if we don't want to upset the good townsfolk, we'd better leave out that masque.'

Forth said something that made Chari look at him in sharp disapproval. 'All right. But what can we put in its place?'

'See how it goes, and we'll discuss it during the interval,' his father said. 'The way things are, it might be as well to make our act shorter than usual anyway.'

Piety, who had poked her carrot-red head round the screen, said, 'Come *on*. They're waiting for us,' and Stead waved Forth away.

'Go on, boy. Mustn't keep the crowd waiting.'

Rance picked up a hide drum and, still hidden behind

the screen, began to beat a smart, formal rhythm. Esty joined in on a tambourine while Forth and Chari stood ready with their reed-pipes: at a nod from Stead they launched into a lively tune, and the four youngest Brabazons, with Piety in the lead, marched in single file round the screen and up the rickety wooden steps to the platform.

There was a ripple of warm applause, and Indigo saw a faint smile crease Stead's face. He knew the wisdom of opening his entertainment with an item from this little quartet. Piety, who hadn't quite lost her babyhood lisp, was perfect for the central role: the sight of that pretty, winsome child with her freckles and vivid curls was guaranteed to touch an audience's hearts and put them in a receptive mood.

The procession halted in the middle of the stage, then Gentility, Moderation and Duty spread out in a line, so that Piety stood alone before them. The light of the flamboys on long poles which illuminated the platform made her hair gleam like a newly-minted gold coin, and from a group of old women who had gaggled together in one section of the crowd came a soft, affectionate sigh. The music stopped on a last, crisp beat, and Piety held out her skirt and curtsied deeply to the assembled throng before striking a dramatic pose.

'Good people all, we bring you greeting,' she piped, with the confidence of a lifelong trouper, 'and welcome you to this night's meeting. Gather round, all grief forsaking – And join us in our merrymaking!'

The three older children linked hands, and all four chanted in chorus:

'For we can dance and we can sing,
'And so to you our gifts we bring,
'With mirth and music, jest and play
'To wish you joy this Revel day!'

Forth, Chari and Rance struck up again, this time a lively skip-tune. On the stage, the children began to dance. The boards thumped and creaked alarmingly, but no one seemed to notice; behind the screen Stead picked up his fiddle and Cour his hurdy-gurdy as the others jostled into order. Indigo took her harp – she'd have no chance now to finish tuning, but it didn't matter; any sour notes would be lost in the general cheerful noise – and abruptly the music of the pipes was augmented, swelling into full flood as Stead led the rest of his players on to the stage.

Esty, Honi and Harmony swung immediately into the dance, flourishing tambourines as they spun in a swirl of bright-coloured skirts. Two of their brothers also joined in, while the musicians lined up behind the whirling dancers. There was a gasp from the crowd as Grimya, exactly on cue, ran in a wide circle around the stage and up to Piety; then the gasp changed to applause as the she-wolf made a good imitation of a bow to the little girl and they circled each other, looking for all the world as if they were dancing together.

At the back of the stage, Indigo smiled at her friend's antics and the crowd's reaction. The energy of the music and the excitement of being on stage once again were already banishing her unhappy thoughts of the previous night, and in spite of the problems afflicting Bruhome the audience seemed ready to put aside their troubles and enjoy the entertainment.

The dance ended to enthusiastic applause, and as the younger children ran off, Piety waving and blowing impudent kisses, the older ones hurried to set the scene for the one-act play that followed. Prudently, Stead had decided on 'The Dame and Her Indiscretion' a comic melodrama with ample room for overacting and an abundance of innuendo and salacious jokes. Indigo had no part in the play, and so retired behind the screen to keep watch on the little ones and listen to the play's progress, which was punctuated with roars of laughter from the townsfolk. Esty, who had great natural comic talent, was in fine fettle as the Dame of the title, while Stead as her cuckolded husband and Cour and Rance as her two constantly squabbling would-be swains supported her with gusto. There was cheering as well as clapping when they took their bow; a sure sign that the Fairplayers' skills, together with the wine and ale now freely circulating in the square, were working their own brand of magic.

34

After the play came a medley of songs, followed by the Drovers' Dance, and lastly more singing, this time popular melodies in which the audience was encouraged to join, before a half-hour break for the players to refresh themselves. During this interval, Indigo – fortified by a spiced harvest-cake and mug of apple ale – joined Esty and Cour to walk about the crowded square and look at the floral decorations. The aromas of food and drink mingled with the more basic smells of humanity and the stink of pitch from the blazing flamboys; studying faces and overhearing snatches of conversation, Indigo detected few signs of the troubles that beset Bruhome. People talked of mundane matters: the weather, the latest domestic scandal, the shortcomings of this new apprentice or that tavern landlord. Only once or twice did a sour note interpose – the words '*dark forest*' as one voice stood out momentary from the general hubbub; another voice, shocked, '*three more stricken since this morning, so I've heard*'; a whispered, inaudible but clearly urgent conversation between two women whose faces were drawn with worry. Indigo didn't know if her companions were aware of the tenuous, uneasy thread weaving through the atmosphere, and thought better of drawing their attention to it. Stead, with his more intimate knowledge of the town and its leading citizens, would find out what more there was to know in good time. Until then, she thought, it was best to forget this undercurrent and concentrate on the night's happier aspects.

With the interval over, what Cour ruefully referred to as the real hard work of the evening began. The second half of the Brabazon Fairplayers' show consisted almost entirely of music and dance: by this time, it was reasoned, the audience would be too lively, or too drunk (or both) to want their powers of concentration taxed by plays and recitations. They wanted only to roar their way through the simple old songs that everyone knew, and – with some encouragement from the Brabazons themselves – to take part in the final dance sets.

Indigo's hands ached from harping; beside her Cour was hunched over the hurdy-gurdy, fingers flying as the wooden drone-wheel spun, while Stead's fiddle and

Forth's reed-pipe threaded a rapid, complex melody through their thrumming background. The girls had jumped down from the platform and were inviting men in the crowd to partner them; the boys, taking their cue, approached a group of giggling women and bowed to them, holding out their hands. As suspicion and self-consciousness broke down, and more and more people started to join in the dancing, Indigo glanced sidelong at Stead and saw the quick, worried frown of the previous day cross his face once more. It didn't last – he was too intent on his playing to be distracted for more than a moment – but she had a shrewd idea of its cause.

At long last the final set came to an end. The Brabazon dancers left their partners with kisses and light-hearted promises that wouldn't be kept, and made a last circuit of the stage, waving to the crowd. The musicians stepped forward, surreptitiously flexing tired fingers as they smiled and bowed. Light-headed with exhilaration, relieved and sad that the evening's revels were over, Indigo followed the others back behind the screen: but when she looked at Stead again, she saw the uneasiness returning.

'My body and soul for a mug of beer!' Cour pleaded, dumping the hurdy-gurdy on the ground and flapping his hands to loosen their tension.

Esty, who was sitting on an upturned box unlacing her shoes, looked up. 'You started the dance sets early, Da,' she said to Stead. 'Another few minutes and my feet would've caught fire – we danced more than an hour, d'you know that?'

Some of the others concurred with her protest, and Stead scowled. 'Better that than lose our audience, my girl. They were getting restive; they wanted to be part of what was going on, to take their minds off other things.'

'But – '

'Never mind "but". When you've been about as long as I have, you'll know how to read the signs if you've any wits at all.' He glanced at his eldest son. 'Forth knows what I'm talking about.'

Forth nodded. 'We had to work hard to get them to join in at all. Usually the men'll fight over who gets to dance with the girls, but this time . . .' He let an expressive shrug finish the point for him.

'So that's why you had to dance for so long.' Stead glowered at Esty. 'Satisfied now, miss? Any more complaints?'

Esty looked away. Her eyes were still mutinous but she knew better than to argue.

Forth started to pack their gear into its boxes and chests in readiness for the trek back to the caravans. 'What about tomorrow, Da?' he asked. 'Can't do the same show twice running. If tonight's anything to go by we'll need to make some more changes.'

'We'll talk about that in the morning.' Stead scrubbed at his eyes. 'Right now, I'm dry as a bone and I want nothing more than a taste of a decent brew. Anyone else coming to the Apple Barrel for a few mugs?'

Forth, Cour, Rance and Esty immediately elected to go with him. Chari, a little primly, said no, and Indigo shook her head with a smile.

'Thanks, Stead, but I slept poorly last night. Grimya and I'll go back to the vans with the others.'

'As you like. Leave what you can't carry and we'll bring it later. The town militia are watching to see nothing gets stolen.'

The party split up and went their separate ways. A few people still lingered in the square and its surrounding streets, and light and noise spilled from all the taverns, but for most of Bruhome's inhabitants the evening was over. A fresh breeze had sprung up, and the sky was clear and dark as velvet. Last night there had been no moon; tonight it was a thin, glimmering crescent, hanging low on the eastern horizon as it began its nocturnal voyage.

'The wind's blowing from the moon tonight,' Chari said softly as the riverside encampment came in sight.

She and Indigo were carrying the largest of the costume-chests between them, and Indigo looked across at the tall girl in curiosity. 'Is that significant?' she asked.

Chari smiled. 'Oh, it's just an old superstition. They say that when the wind blows from the point where a new moon rises, it heralds great change.'

'For good or ill?'

37

'It can be either.'

'Then let's hope it's good this time.'

'Yes.' In the dark, Chari's face looked like a pale mask. 'Let's hope it is.'

To everyone's surprise, Stead and his companions returned an hour later. Many people in the meadow were still awake; banked-down fires glowed here and there, and the occasional murmur of subdued voices drifted across the lea. The four youngest Brabazons were abed and asleep, but the others, enlivened a little by the walk back from the town, had gathered in the main caravan to drink hot mulled ale and talk idly over the evening's events. The clump of booted feet on the steps alerted them, and they looked up to see Stead framed in the doorway.

'Well,' Stead said with rancorous humour. 'It looks like there's more enjoyment to be had under our own roof than in any of Bruhome's taverns tonight!'

They squeezed into the cramped space and Chari fetched more mugs. 'What's amiss, Stead?' Indigo asked. 'Surely they haven't all closed their doors?'

'No; but they might as well do for all the pleasure there is to be had. We went to the Apple Barrel; then – let me see,' Stead counted on his fingers. 'The Fleece, the Hop Pickers and the Five Vines, and everywhere it was the same. Long faces and frightened eyes.' He shook his head sorrowfully. 'I've never seen the like of it.'

'And the talk,' Cour put in. 'Rumour piling up on rumour. This tale about a moving forest's all over the town now.'

Grimya's ears pricked, and Indigo said uneasily, 'Then the story's true?'

'People are behaving as though it is,' Stead told her. 'More and more claim to have seen it with their own eyes. Black trees, they say, with thorns long as a man's arm growing on them. And dense as the strongest wall ever built.'

'But if there really is something there, Da, we'd have seen it on our way here,' Chari objected. 'Or if we

38

hadn't, some of the other travellers would, and we'd have heard of it from them by now.'

Stead patted her hand. 'I know, lass, I know. It doesn't make any sense. But people hereabouts are starting to believe the tale.'

'And that's not all,' Forth added grimly. 'Five more people went down with the mysterious sickness today, and another two have disappeared.'

Stead gave him an angry look. 'I told you not to say that. Not in front of the younger ones.'

Forth shrugged. 'If they don't find out from us they'll hear it from someone else soon enough.'

'Da, this place isn't healthy,' Rance said. 'I think we should go, before it gets any worse.'

Forth snorted contemptuously, but Stead held up a hand. 'No, Forth. I've been thinking along much the same lines and I reckon I've decided what to do. We'll put on another show tomorrow, just like we planned; but after that we'll make our farewells to Bruhome and move on.'

'And miss the end of the Revels?'

'Yes. For what little that's going to be worth now.' Stead gazed in turn at each of their faces. 'Well?'

There were murmurs, shuffles. Harmony said, 'You know best, Da,' and several others voiced agreement. Forth continued to scowl, but for the most part the feeling seemed to be one of relief. Though everyone pretended to be unaffected by the blight that hung over Bruhome there was no doubt that the town's unquiet atmosphere had made its mark.

But while her friends seemed glad of Stead's decision, Indigo felt as though a cold, leaden weight had lodged beneath her ribs. She looked at Grimya and knew that the she-wolf shared her apprehension. One more day, and the Brabazon Fairplayers would be moving on. She would have to break the news that she and Grimya would no longer be travelling with them.

She'd known from the first that it must eventually come to this, but had put the knowledge as far from her mind as possible, telling herself that there was no point in fretting over it before the time arrived. And now that the time *had* arrived she didn't know how she would find the words to say goodbye. They wouldn't understand – they'd think she had grown tired of them, had been merely using them; for she'd never be able to explain the truth . . .

'Indigo?'

She raised her head and saw Chari looking at her with grave concern.

'Are you all right?' Chari asked. 'You look . . . well, *strange.*'

'I'm – fine. Really, there's nothing . . . '

Indigo. Grimya spoke gently, sadly in her mind. *I think you must tell them. They know something is wrong, and the moment will have to come soon anyway. Tell them, Indigo. It will be kinder for us all.*

Perhaps Grimya was right. If she prevaricated, her courage might fail her, and then where would she be? Chari was still watching her, unconvinced by her assurance, and Indigo took a deep breath.

'Stead,' she said. 'Everyone. There's something I have to tell you.'

Silence fell. They were all looking at her now, and suddenly the speech she was struggling to build in her mind collapsed.

'Hey now, lass.' Stead leaned over and squeezed her arm. 'What is it, eh? Come on; you can tell us. Aren't we your good friends?'

It was the worst thing he could have said, however unwitting, and Indigo felt stifling pain in the back of her throat. She opened her mouth, forcing herself to speak; started to say, 'Stead, I – '

And the words turned into a shocked oath as a distant, hideous and utterly unhuman wail rang out across the lea.

Mugs crashed to the caravan floor and only Rance's instinctive reflex stopped the little wood-stove from being toppled as everyone sprang to their feet.

'Harvest Mother!' The hair on Forth's scalp rose. 'What was *that*?' He started towards the door, but Stead grabbed his arm.

'Wait, boy! Let me look.' He shouldered past and flung

40

the top of the door wide open. As he did so, the terrible sound began again; thin, eldritch, like the voice of a soul in monstrous torment. Chari moaned and tried to block her ears; Harmony and Honesty clung to each other, and Truth forgot his twelve-year-old bravado and stumbled across the floor to clutch at Indigo's hand. As the ghastly sound died away again they heard shouts from other parts of the meadow; figures were silhouetted against the fires' embers as other travellers scrambled up. Grimya, bristling, began to growl defensively – then for the third time the awful voice wailed out of the night, and from somewhere closer to the river bank a woman screamed.

'It's coming from somewhere across the river.' Stead wrenched open the lower door and raced down the caravan steps, Forth, Cour and Esty at his heels. Before Indigo could call her back, Grimya had run after them, and all five were hurrying across the grass towards the bank.

'Da!' Charity called, her voice stark with fear. 'Da, be careful!'

Grimya's excited mental voice cut through the chaos in Indigo's mind. The wolf had bounded ahead of the slower humans and had already reached the bank, where she stood with her muzzle raised to the wind. *I can hear where the dreadful sound comes from*, she said. *It is a long way off, far across the river in the hills. And I can scent something; I can – Indigo!* and Grimya's voice broke into the physical world as she howled aloud.

'Great Mother!' Indigo leaped down the steps. As she ran towards the river bank she heard a frightened wail from one of the other caravans as the two smallest girls woke, but she couldn't stop to attend to them. She had felt the stunning mental surge of sheer terror that burst from Grimya's mind as she howled, and an answering panic was rising in her own psyche.

On the bank, Grimya was crouched low, ears back and snarling. Stead had tried to calm her but didn't dare go too close, and as Indigo ran towards him he looked up in relief.

'Damn my eyes, Indigo, she's as frightened as any of us!'

41

'Grimya!' Indigo dropped to her knees, hugging the wolf's brindled head. 'Hush! It's all right!' And silently she added the urgent question, *What did you sense?*

Grimya was shivering; she licked Indigo's hand then nuzzled hard against her. *I ... don't know. But I was afraid of it!*

'She's all right,' Indigo told Stead, who was still watching her.

'Then she's the only one among us who is!' Stead's face was ashen. The night was quiet again, but in the silence the echoes of the terrible wailing seemed to linger. More people were emerging from vans and tents and cautiously approaching the bank; a horse whinnied and gradually voices began to break the hiatus. A child grizzled; there were whisperings, questions, shadowy figures clustering in small groups to debate and point across the river. Somewhere in the background more than one person was sobbing, a reflexive reaction to fear and shock.

Stead stared out across the water. Softly, through clenched teeth, he hissed: 'What in the names of a thousand curses is out there?'

Cour shook his head emphatically. He, too, was white-faced. 'Don't ask, Da. Better not to know.'

'No,' Forth interjected fiercely. 'We *should* know.' He gestured wildly at the smooth, sliding water. 'There's something ugly over the river, Da, and I'd take any wager that it's got some bearing on what's going on in Bruhome! We shouldn't just sit here like a flock of sheep – we should go after it, and find out what it is!'

'Don't be a dumb ox, boy,' Stead retorted angrily. 'Whatever that thing is, it's beyond our understanding!'

'How do we know that unless we look?' Forth persisted. 'Da, listen to me! If we take the ponies – you and me and Cour, and maybe even Temp if he's got the stomach for it – and Indigo and Grimya; they're both more than equal to most men; we can go and see for ourselves what's to do!'

Grimya said silently, but with terrible emphasis, *No.* And suddenly Indigo knew what the she-wolf had been trying to tell her but couldn't articulate. She got to her feet.

42

'No, Forth.'

Forth turned, startled, and Stead stopped on the verge of a furious rebuttal. Neither of them had ever heard Indigo speak with such authority, and Forth scowled, annoyed by her intervention.

'What d'you mean, no?' he demanded. 'How else are we going to find out what's out there? Or do you expect us to sit here and do nothing?'

'Yes,' Indigo said. 'If you've any wit, that's exactly what I expect.'

Stead started to say, 'Look, lass – ' but Forth interrupted him, angry now.

'You listen to me, Indigo – '

'No, Forth, *you* listen to *me*!' Her tone was sharply aggressive. 'And for once, have the sense not to argue with those who know better than you do!' She paused. 'None of you – *none* of you – should go in pursuit of whatever it is that's out there. Not tonight, not tomorrow or any other night. *Leave it alone*. Do you understand me?'

Forth was visibly taken aback. Others close enough to have overheard were watching them curiously, and to cover his chagrin he tried to make light of it. 'Look, Indigo, I don't blame you for being afraid, but – '

'Yes, I'm afraid.' She cut across him. 'And I'm ready to admit it – which makes me less of a fool than you!' And before he could respond, she turned on her heel and stalked away, back towards the caravans.

Forth swore and, determined that she shouldn't have the last word in such a way, made to start in pursuit – then stopped again, his stomach turning to water as the thin, eerie wailing rose again out of the night. This time it seemed that not one but fifty voices were moaning in desolate harmony; people cried out fearfully, backing away from the water's edge – and the wailing subsided, fading until only one stark, tortured voice remained. For a moment a single note of deep agony echoed from the distant fells; then it, too, shivered away into nothing and was gone.

Nearby, two men hugged themselves and bowed their heads in silent, fervent prayer. Forth and Stead met each other's gazes, but neither could speak. Cour and Esty were holding tightly to each other's hands, mute. At last, Stead broke the silence.

'Go back to the vans.' There was a quiet authority in his voice that none of them would dare to flout. 'Maybe none of us will sleep tonight, but we'll bar the doors and keep the night at bay.' Esty and Cour started to move away and Forth would have followed them, but Stead held him back.

'Forth.' His eyes were intense, and troubled. 'I don't like to see quarrelling.'

Forth flushed angrily. 'She started it! Talking to me as if I was no better than a harvest-dance dumdolly – '

'Maybe she overstepped the mark, but she thought she had good reason,' Stead said soberly. 'She was only trying to act for the best; and for all any of us knows, she might be right. Make your peace with her, Forth, and don't bear a grudge.'

Forth hesitated, then nodded reluctantly. 'Yes, Da.'

'Good lad.' Stead looked back over his shoulder to where the river flowed, smooth and peaceful. He couldn't explain it, but he felt a strong conviction that there would be no more phantom voices: at least, not tonight. But as for tomorrow . . .

'This has made up my mind for good and all,' he said quietly.

'About leaving Bruhome?'

'Yes. One more show, and we'll be on our way.'

There was a long pause. Then Forth said: 'I'm glad, Da. I know I was the one who spoke against it, but . . . ' He, too, looked at the river and suppressed a shiver. 'Between you and me, I'm glad.'

Chapter IV

The mood in the meadow encampment was deeply subdued the next morning. People greeted each other warily and seemed anxious to avoid meeting a gaze directly; certainly no one was willing even to mention the events of the night, though the memory hung about the encampment like smoke.

In Bruhome itself, however, the atmosphere was very different. The townsfolk, too, had heard the phantasmic sounds echoing out of the fells, but unlike the outsiders they made no secret of their fear. When Indigo, Chari and Cour arrived at the morning market to buy provisions for the caravan they found it thronged with people, talking, questioning and speculating. It seemed as if every man, woman and child in Bruhome had taken to the streets, seeking comfort and security in the company of their fellows. Or rather, Indigo amended grimly, every man, woman and child not yet afflicted by the sickness. Rumour had it that nine more had been stricken during the night; what had begun as an isolated phenomenon was threatening to become an epidemic, and the events of the night gave an extra, ugly dimension to the townsfolk's terror. Some said – and the whisper was growing, creeping through the town – that the dreadful wailing had been the voices of disembodied souls, lost and wandering among the fells: the tortured spirits, perhaps, of the poor creatures who had vanished from their hearthsides since the blight began.

Listening to the rumours, the tales, the fearful murmurings, Indigo tried not to think about the clash she had had with Forth at the river bank. Both Forth and Stead – and Cour and Esty – had made no further reference to the incident, but the memory still struck a

45

sour note in Indigo's mind, and the talk rife in the town did nothing to diminish it. She hadn't meant to belittle Forth; but at that moment, with Grimya's warning resounding in her head and the after-echoes of that ghastly wailing still tainting the air, she had been frightened; and with good reason.

Something dire and unclean had come to Bruhome. Indigo believed that she knew its essence if not its form, and she was determined that the Brabazons should be shielded from it at all costs. Forth's reckless bravado was no match for this thing, and curiosity was a deadly trap. They *had* to move on. They had to leave her and Grimya behind and get away from Bruhome before they became embroiled in something beyond their ability to understand, let alone control.

' . . . do you think?' Cour's voice broke into her mind. 'Indigo?'

She looked up blankly and realised that he'd asked her a question, but it hadn't registered.

'What?'

Cour grinned. 'Where were you? Behind the moon?'

'I'm sorry.' She looked about her at the slightly faded festival garlands adorning walls and posts and awnings; suppressed a shiver. 'I was looking at the flowers.'

Cour raised his eyebrows. 'I asked how much oatmeal you think we'll need. One sack, or two? I don't know how long it keeps.'

Indigo struggled to drag herself back to mundane matters, but her brain wouldn't respond. 'I . . . don't know, Cour. Best ask Chari.'

He frowned. 'Eh, what's wrong? You look as if you're in a trance!' His expression grew alarmed. 'Indigo, you're not going down with the sickness?'

'No,' she assured him. 'No, Cour.' She knew instinctively that Bruhome's sickness wouldn't afflict her. Another, greater effort, and this time her mind cleared and the real world came back. 'I'm all right.'

'Ach, it's the mood in this place.' Cour gestured helplessly about him. 'It's getting to us all, Indigo. I'm beginning to think Da ought to forget tonight's show and move out now. I know it sounds unkind, because these

46

people need cheering; but . . . well, sometimes you have to put yourself first, don't you?' He watched her face, anxious for approbation, and Indigo nodded.

'I agree with you, Cour. In fact I'd speak to your father about it myself if I thought it'd make any difference.'

'It might. Da's more likely to listen to you than to anyone else, except maybe Chari.'

Indigo scanned the faces milling around them, telling herself not to think about that, not to think about what it would mean; not yet . . . 'Where is Chari, anyway?'

Cour turned, looking back. 'She was over there a minute ago, at the ironmonger's stall. Said she wanted a new rivet for the big ladle; the handle's coming off. But I can't see her now. Chari?' He raised his voice. 'Cha-RI!'

A few people glanced up, but Chari was nowhere to be seen. Cour said something under his breath and started into the crowd, then stopped and pointed, grinning.

'There she is. On the bench outside that tavern, resting her feet if you please, the lazy cat! Chari! Over here!'

A suspicion, no more: but Indigo's stomach contracted . . .

'Chari?' Suddenly Cour's expression changed. He began to move, shoving past surprised and indignant townsfolk as he hastened towards his sister. '*Chari!*'

Chari was slumped on a wooden settle that fronted the limewashed wall of one of Bruhome's many alehouses. Her hemp bag, on the ground beside her, had tipped over and her purchases were spilling out, but she was oblivious to it: her head lolled at a drunken angle, strands of bright hair falling over her face, and her hands flapped weakly, helplessly, beyond her control.

'Chari!' Cour reached her in a skidding slide, dropping to his knees and grabbing hold of her arms. 'Chari, what is it? What's amiss?'

Indigo, catching up with him, bent over Chari and took her face between cupped hands, forcing the girl's head up. Utterly empty eyes met her shocked gaze, and she knew, *knew*, before logic could take control, what it was.

Chari's face was deathly white. For a moment she

47

stared unseeingly at Indigo, then her mouth curved downwards in a look of ineffable sorrow.

'So sad,' she said, and there was deep wonder in her voice, a terrible, childlike innocence. 'Ohh . . . so very *sad* . . . ' And her body keeled sideways off the settle as consciousness fled.

Cour caught her. 'Chari!' He called her name harshly, desperately, shaking her. '*Chari!*'

'Don't!' Indigo reached out to stop him as he seemed about to crack Chari's skull against the wall in his frantic urgency. 'Cour, it's no use! She – '

She stopped, abruptly aware of the people gathering around them, of the curious faces and, as fear changed to certainty, of the shock and sympathy and tide of fellow feeling.

' . . . *Just like Goodwife Frenc's girl* . . . '

' . . . *so sudden, no one can ever predict when* . . . '

'*Burgher Mischyn's little boy; you recall how he* . . . '

'Cour – ' Amid the rising murmur Indigo heard her own voice and barely recognised it. 'Go back to the meadow – fetch your father; *run!*' And when it seemed that he was too stunned to comprehend fully, 'Cour, don't you understand? *She's got the sickness!*'

'What has she done to deserve it? Answer me that – what has my little girl ever done to deserve to be struck down in the bloom of her youth, at the height of her beauty, at – '

'Da; Da, *please*.' Forth, who had come running with his father from the meadow, gripped his shoulders and shook him very gently, trying to stem the babbling flow of words. 'Chari didn't do anything. It's just . . . ' He looked up helplessly at the ring of concerned onlookers; Burgher Mischyn, brought from his nearby house by the commotion, shook his head sadly and others stared at the ground beneath their feet. 'It's bad luck, Da,' Forth finished miserably. 'Just bad luck.'

'*Bad luck?*' Stead sprang to his feet, furious. 'The Brabazons don't have bad luck! *Good* luck, that's what's always attended us! Even when your thrice-blessed mother was taken from us that wasn't bad luck, that was the will of the Great Goddess and a reward for her after years of toil! We don't *have* bad luck – not until now; not until we came to this forsaken midden of a town, with its blights and its sicknesses and – '

'Da, stop it!' Forth shook him again, harder this time. 'You don't mean that, and you know you don't! This isn't Bruhome's fault; they're suffering as much as we are!'

Stead's face was almost purple. Tears ran down his cheeks and for a moment it seemed as if he would strike Forth; but after a moment a grain of reason struggled to the surface and he looked away, blinking.

'You don't understand,' he mumbled. 'You don't understand what it is to have children, and to love them and try to protect them, and – '

'Steadfast, my good friend,' Burgher Mischyn stepped forward and put an arm about the distraught man's shoulders. 'There are many people here who *do* understand, and who sympathise with your suffering.' He sighed heavily. 'If I had thought for one moment that this sickness might spread to our guests, then I would never have allowed the Revels to take place; I would have quarantined the town, I would have done anything . . . Stead, I am at fault, and I grieve for it!'

Stead's shoulders heaved and he swallowed. His self-control had returned now and he nodded, taking care not to look at Chari's still, pale figure laid out on the settle.

'Forgive me, Mischyn. The shock; the worry – ' He made a helpless gesture. 'I didn't mean . . .'

'Of course you didn't. And I assure you that everything possible will be done for your daughter. We'll take her to my own house, and – '

'No,' Stead interrupted. 'I'll carry her back to the caravans.'

'As you wish, of course. But – '

'No,' Stead said again, mulishly. 'She'll go to her own home. That's where she wants to be; I know my girl. And then we're leaving.' He looked quickly at Forth and Cour, daring them to argue. 'I'm taking my little Chari to a physician, and I'm getting her *cured*!'

No one spoke, but a few heads nodded gravely.

49

Brushing aside Forth's attempts to help him Stead gathered Chari's limp form into his arms, then gave the assembled company one last, unhappy glare before striding away back towards the lea. Forth looked at Burgher Mischyn but could think of nothing to say; instead he made an apologetic gesture and, with Cour beside him, hastened off in Stead's wake.

Indigo watched the three Brabazons disappear with their burden into the crowd, but made no attempt to follow them. Since Stead's arrival she had stayed in the background; in the ensuing confusion they had forgotten her, and she had had no wish to intrude. But, watching the dismal little scenario outside the tavern, she had suddenly and painfully come face to face with the cold reality of her own conscience. Whatever anyone else might think or say, she felt that she alone was to blame for the ill fortune which had befallen the Brabazons. She should have warned them the moment she had realised that her goal lay in Bruhome; she should have used every wile she could find to persuade them not to stay in the town. Better still, she should have refused to give way to weakness and left the troupe, with or without an explanation, when her intuition had first warned her of what might lie ahead. But no: she had chosen instead to put off the moment, hiding behind a complacent illusion and promising herself that she could continue in her hiatus for a little longer, just a little longer, without endangering her friends. If she'd been honest, she thought bitterly, she would have acknowledged the truth long ago, and Chari and her family wouldn't now be suffering for her selfishness.

She wished Grimya were here. She needed the wolf's support, her advice and her down-to-earth wisdom to help her decide what to do for the best. But Grimya had stayed at the camp, preferring to play with the younger children rather than trail about the market: and besides, Indigo didn't need to ask her in order to know what she would say. Grimya would tell her what she already knew; that she must part from the Brabazons now, and see them safe away from Bruhome before anything worse could befall them. However much the parting hurt on either side, it had to be done. There could be no more excuses.

Charity's overturned bag had been forgotten in the chaos, and still lay beside the now empty bench. Indigo bent to gather the spilled contents and pack them back inside, then straightened and looked through the mill of townsfolk in the direction Stead and the others had taken. A cold, dark sense of premonition moved within her, like something unclean awakening. Then she hefted the bag, slipped the strap over her shoulder, and set off across the square.

All the way back to the meadow Indigo silently rehearsed what she would say to the Brabazons, how she would break the news that she wouldn't be coming with them when they left Bruhome. The words were inadequate and fell far short of the whole truth, but they were the best she could find and, whatever they might think of her, would have to suffice.

But when the camp came in sight, she realised immediately that something else was amiss. She'd expected to see a flurry of activity, the vans being loaded, the oxen harnessed, the ponies marshalled into tethered lines behind the last caravan. Instead, she saw the family – those who weren't in the girls' van attending to Chari – gathered around the leading wagon. Voices were raised in agitated argument, and suddenly Grimya emerged from the group. She had sensed Indigo's arrival, and came running to meet her.

Grimya? Indigo spoke silently to the she-wolf. *What's to do?*

I am not sure, Grimya told her. *Something is wrong with Chari, and there was talk of leaving the town. I couldn't understand all that was said. But now it seems that one of the caravans can't move. The axle is broken, Stead says.*

Indigo's dark premonition abruptly deepened into something uglier. She quickened her pace towards the vans, and Grimya, trotting beside her, said, *Indigo, what happened to Chari? I thought you were with her in the market, but when you didn't come back with the others –*

51

*I was with them. Chari . . . Grimya, she has the sickness.
The sleeping sickness that is plaguing the town.*

Her communication conveyed far more than words,
and Grimya sensed instantly the painful self-
recrimination underlying the message. Loyally she
started to protest, to argue that Indigo couldn't have
predicted such a twist of events, but before she could
form more than a few emphatic words, Forth looked up,
saw them and came hurrying over. His face was haggard.

'The ill luck's all running our way, Indigo,' he told her
tersely.

'What's happened?'

'Crossbar on the axle's split. The Mother alone knows
how it could've happened, but we can't move until it's
mended.'

'How long will that take?'

'Hard to say. There's a good wheelwright in the town,
thanks be. Provided he hasn't fallen sick or disappeared,
it might – '

'Forth!'

Forth broke off as his father shouted to him from
where he crouched by the stricken van. Stead got to his
feet and came towards them. He was sweating, but his
face under its tan was pallid.

Nodding a quick, curt greeting to Indigo, he said, 'It'll
take half a day's work to set this right. I'm not waiting
that long; not while my Chari's lying in there like the
dead.' He wiped his forehead with grimy hands; the day
was hot and threatening to become oppressive. 'Listen,
boy: I want you to take the best pony, and ride ahead of
us. There's a town thirty miles north that's big enough to
have its own physician; you find him, and you start back
here with him and meet us on the road.'

'Right, Da.' Forth looked relieved, thankful to have
something practical and positive to do. 'I'll take the
stallion; he's wilful but he's fast and he's got the stamina.'
He made to hurry off towards the tethered ponies, and
suddenly Indigo said:

'Forth – I'll come with you.'

He looked at her. For a moment she saw a glimmer of
resentment, as though, recalling their clash of the pre-

52

vious night, Forth thought she was implying that he needed protection, and quickly she added, 'There's nothing I can do here, and I want to help Chari.'

Stead said, 'Thank you, lass. Thank you!' and Forth relented.

'All right. Come on; there's no point wasting time.'

As they ran towards the ponies, Indigo wondered if she'd made a wise decision. It had been pure impulse, fuelled by an intuitive feeling that, while the Brabazons were forced to remain in Bruhome, they might be safer if she wasn't in their midst. There was no logic to the conviction, but she'd learned through hard experience that instinct was often a surer guide than logic – and besides, any help she could give now might be some small recompense for the troubles she had brought on the family. Damn the lodestone and its instructions, she thought: her business in Bruhome could wait a while.

Forth saddled two ponies while Indigo filled water-skins and gathered a small parcel of basic rations. She also took a moment to fetch the short-shafted but powerful crossbow that she'd bought several years before in Davakos, after sailing on the *Pride of Simhara* from Khimiz to the western continent. She'd learned to use a bow at an early age and was an excellent shot; her skill together with Forth's knife-fighting expertise and Grimya's presence should give them all the protection they could need on the journey.

Grimya accepted her decision to accompany Forth without question or comment. The wolf merely said that she preferred activity to waiting, and Indigo had a suspicion that she, too, would feel happier to be away from the caravans. She also agreed with Indigo's second intention, which was to speak to Forth on the ride and explain as best she could why she would be returning to Bruhome rather than continuing on with the vans. It would be easier, she thought, to say what she had to say to one person alone at first rather than face the protests and persuasions of the whole Brabazon family. Forth, perhaps more than any of the others, might at least try to understand her reasons and help her to face the others when the time came.

They set off without lengthy farewells, and as the ponies turned out of the meadow Indigo looked back for her last view of the encampment. She saw Stead and three of his sons crouched beside the stricken caravan with Esty and Honi nearby; they were absorbed and hardly aware of the riders' departure. Only Esty looked up briefly and waved to them before turning her attention back to the others, and Indigo felt misery clutch at her.

The lea fell behind them, and Forth turned on to the road that would lead them away from the town. Indigo blinked back moisture that clung tenaciously to her eyelashes, then resolutely set her back to the camp and her friends, and urged her pony into a rapid trot.

For the best part of an hour Indigo and Forth rode without speaking. Forth set a rapid pace, wanting to cover as much ground as possible while the ponies were fresh, and there was little opportunity for conversation: nonetheless Indigo was aware of a residual tension between them which told her that, while Forth might have forgiven her harsh words of the previous night, he'd by no means forgotten them. And she was acutely aware that the barrier which had sprung up between them would make what she had to say to him all the harder. But for the moment there was little she could do to bridge the gulf, so she made herself concentrate instead on the landscape around them.

The road north from Bruhome ran between two distinctly different kinds of country which merged together in a vista typical of this land. To the west was the gradually rising green sweep of the fells, broken here and there by the starker grey of a rocky outcrop or scarp; while eastwards the gentler spread of low-lying orchards and hop fields stretched away to a hazy horizon. The day was unusually hot even for the unpredictable autumn: there wasn't a breath of wind, and as the morning wore on the sky was losing its clarity and taking on a brassy overcast. The travellers' shadows were no longer visible on the road, and Indigo surmised that it wouldn't be long before the good weather broke. If there was to be a storm, she hoped they'd reach their destination before it arrived.

Shortly after noon they reached a shallow ford where one of the numerous fell streams crossed the road, and stopped for a while to rest and eat, and to water the ponies. Grimya wandered off alone to explore rabbit-holes at the edge of the fells, while Indigo took some bread and cheese from her supplies. Forth – perhaps deliberately – sat at a distance from Indigo that made idle conversation impossible, and she realised that if she waited for the tension between them to fade of its own accord what she had to say to him might never be said. She couldn't procrastinate any longer.

She got up and, trying to seem casual, walked a little way along the edge of the ford before turning and coming back to where Forth sat. He didn't look at her, but continued to stare along the road ahead of them, chewing slowly on a hunk of bread.

She said: 'Forth, I need to talk to you.'

This time he did look up, and made an expansive gesture. 'Of course.' But there was a touch of wary hostility in his voice.

'When we reach the town – when we've found a physician – ' She hesitated. 'Forth, I . . . that is, when – ' Damn, she thought, *damn* her cowardice. It *had* to be said.

'Forth, listen.' She dropped to a crouch in front of him. 'When we've found a physician and brought him back to meet the others on the road, I won't be travelling on with you.'

At last the words were out. And Forth was staring at her, his expression uncomprehending. 'What?'

'I'm trying to say that the time has come for me to leave the Brabazon Fairplayers.'

There was an acute silence while what she had said registered fully in Forth's mind. Then he said, in an utterly changed tone, '*Why?*'

All trace of hostility had suddenly vanished, resentment transformed into unhappy bewilderment. Indigo stared at the ground between her feet. 'I'm sorry. I didn't want to say it so bluntly; but there doesn't seem

55

much point in couching it in flowery phrases. I have to leave. It's – '

He interrupted her before she could finish. 'Indigo, what have we done?'

'Done?' Indigo looked up at him, and realised that he'd misinterpreted her meaning. 'Nothing! It isn't – '

'It's me, isn't it? Last night, when we . . . Indigo, I swear to the Great Mother that I didn't mean to quarrel with you! All right; I was angry then. I thought you were trying to tell me how I should behave and I didn't think you had the right, but – '

'Forth.' She put out a hand and gripped his arm. 'It isn't that. Last night had nothing to do with it.'

He clearly didn't believe her. 'Indigo, you can't let something so trivial turn you against us – it isn't fair! Whatever you think about me, it isn't fair on the others!'

'Forth, please *listen*! It's *not* because of you. It's nothing to do with *any* of you.' Indigo's throat was tight with emotion, but she fought to keep it under control. 'I don't want to leave you at all – '

'Then – '

'But I *have* to. I've known that since the day your father took me in, though I didn't have the courage to tell you before now. Believe me, I wish it could be otherwise, but there's nothing I can do to change it.'

'I don't understand! You're talking as if . . . I don't know; as if there's some *compulsion* on you.'

Indigo shook her head vehemently. 'I can't explain, Forth. Perhaps if there'd been more time I could have found the right words, but as things are, I can only ask you to try not to think too badly of me.'

Forth considered this for a few moments. Then, with slow deliberation, he said: 'So you're going. And whatever this is, whatever's taking you away from us, you can't tell us about it, and you won't change your mind.'

'I can't change my mind. I only wish I could.'

'Yes. I see.' Forth's expression had grown oddly thoughtful. Then he met her eyes again. '*Where* will you be going?'

She paused. In theory it would do no harm to tell

56

him, but caution, and her knowledge of Forth, warned her against it. 'I can't say.'

'Don't you trust me?'

'Oh, Forth . . . ' He was too close to the truth for comfort, but she couldn't admit it to him. 'It isn't like that.'

'No. No, of course not. Well . . . there's nothing more I can say, then, is there?' Forth swayed backwards and got to his feet in one movement. He narrowed his eyes, looking out towards the fells that rose away to the west. 'The sky's getting angry. If it doesn't storm before nightfall, I'll be surprised.'

Indigo, too, rose. 'Forth – '

'No.' He turned back towards her. 'There's no point talking about it any more. If you're rested, we ought to be on our way.' For a moment, bitterness showed in his eyes. 'Unless you want to go back and collect your things now, and forget about Chari?'

'No.' Indigo felt shame colour her face. 'I'll ride with you. That is, if you'll allow me to.'

Forth shrugged. 'It's up to you.' And he strode away towards his pony.

They set off again in painful silence. Grimya returned at Indigo's mental call: she had hunted successfully and was still licking the last taste of rabbit from her jowls. Indigo communicated the gist of her conversation with Forth, and the wolf looked sadly at the young man's stiff-backed figure riding some yards ahead of them.

I am sorry that he's taken the news so badly, she said. *But I think you did the only thing you could. He had to know, and this was the easiest way.*

Yes; but I feel so guilty, Grimya. As if I've betrayed their trust and kindness.

You haven't, Grimya argued firmly. *Not to tell them would have been a far greater betrayal. So: when we meet the caravans again, then we will make our farewells and leave?*

Yes; and return to Bruhome.

I hope the storm has passed by then, Grimya observed. *I sense it will be a very heavy one. The air is already beginning to smell strongly of it.*

57

Indigo glanced westward. Above the fells the sky now looked like tarnished bronze, and humidity was increasing with the heat so that there seemed to be insufficient air to breathe. Odd breaths of wind were striking occasionally from the east, against the march of the overcast, and she estimated that they'd have no more than a few hours before the heavens opened.

She touched her heels to the pony's flanks and spurred it into a trot, calling out to Forth. Even voices sounded peculiar in the unnatural stillness; too clear, too carrying: Forth turned his head and she gestured towards the creeping cloud-bank, starting to speak. But Forth was looking beyond her, out towards the fells.

'Just a moment – ' He raised a warning hand and craned, staring, suddenly tense. Then: 'Look! Over there!'

A flicker of something paler moved among the green in the distance. Instinctively Indigo unslung her crossbow, reaching behind her for a bolt, but before she could load the weapon Forth swore softly.

'It's another of them!'

'Another – ' Then abruptly she realised what he meant, and shaded her eyes against the brazen sky to see better.

A solitary figure was trudging towards the crest of a steep rise. From here she couldn't tell whether it was male or female, young or old – but its air of mindless purpose was unmistakable.

She and Forth exchanged a look, the rift between them suddenly forgotten. 'Do you think – ' Indigo started to say.

'Can't be anything else, can it? And he's heading in the same direction as us.' Forth scanned the road ahead of them. Perhaps a hundred yards on, the fells' edge bulged out in a steep escarpment around which the track curved. Whatever lay beyond that point was out of sight, but it was clear that the solitary walker's path must cross their own on the far side of that same hill.

Forth shortened his reins, making the stallion toss his head with anticipation. 'Come on,' he said tersely. 'Let's see where he's going!'

The stallion sprang away before Indigo could argue, and she urged her own pony in pursuit. Grimya ran with her, then called eagerly, *Indigo, I am faster than your horses on this rough ground – I'll run ahead and find out what lies beyond!*

Yes, but be wary!

I shall. Grimya streaked ahead, overtaking Forth, and disappeared around the turn in the road. An instant later Indigo felt the flare of silent shock and alarm from her mind, then the she-wolf reappeared, ears flat to her head, racing back towards them.

Forth, seeing her, had the presence of mind to rein his pony to a halt, and Grimya ran to Indigo.

Indigo! On the other side – there is – Confusion roiled from her mind and she finished desperately, *You must see for yourself!*

'What's frightened her?' Forth asked agitatedly.

'I don't know. We'd best go on, but slowly – be very careful.'

The ponies had sensed their unease and snorted, jinking, as Indigo and Forth cajoled them on. They rounded the escarpment – and Forth's shocked curse was echoed by a cry of horror from Indigo as they saw what barred the road ahead.

The forest rose out of the ground before them, towering against the moody sky. Vast black trees had smashed up through earth and rock, their alien, evilly twisted branches tangling together to form an impenetrable barrier that repelled the brassy daylight and seemed to reflect an intense inner darkness of its own. Black leaves, thick and waxy with a malignant sheen, rustled without a breath of wind to stir them, the sound horribly redolent of whispering, conspiratorial voices. And, though no living creature could have hoped to break through their wall, the trees seemed to beckon, to lure, as though they would enfold and devour anything that came within their reach.

Forth looked wildly to left and right. The unnatural forest spread away in both directions, stretching into the distance until it was swallowed by the deepening haze. For a moment the sight seemed to freeze Forth's mind;

then he twisted in his saddle and stared uncomprehendingly at Indigo.

'It wasn't there before!' His voice was stark, horrified.
'Before we reached the turn in the road – we'd have *seen*
it, we couldn't have missed it. But it wasn't *there*!'

Indigo didn't answer him. She was staring at the
malevolent trees, her eyes wide, her face rigid. Forth said,
'Indigo – ' but she continued to look fixedly ahead and
didn't even hear him.

Thorns. Thorns like knives, like sword-blades: she
could see them, vicious and deadly against the sinuous
movements of the leaves. Thorns that could impale a
man, pierce him and pin him and trap him like a fly in a
spider's web, to bleed his life slowly away in agony . . .
The memory which had haunted her nightmares for so
long, which she had learned so slowly and so painfully to
banish from her waking mind, came searing back to grip
her in its monstrous hand. She had seen this place, these
trees, before. They had no place on the mortal Earth, but
were things of another world, a world of demons.

The world into which, a quarter of a century ago, her
own love Fenran had been taken, broken and bleeding,
to suffer the torments of the living death from which she
alone might one day free him.

Forth was calling out to her, urgently now, alarmed by
the paralysis that made her deaf and blind to his presence. Grimya was backing away from the trees, snarling,
the hair along her spine bristling. The pony beneath her
trembled, stiff-legged, its eyes rolling as it fought the bit:
but Indigo was aware of nothing but the forest, and the
images that her mind was superimposing upon the deadly
black branches.

Suddenly an awful sound broke from her throat: pain
and horror and fear mingling in a wordless, croaking cry.
She snatched at her reins, jerking the pony's head about,
and the animal's hooves slipped and scrabbled as she
kicked it into a standing gallop, flying down the track
that would take her back to Bruhome.

Chapter V

'I'm all right.' Indigo pulled her arms back out of Forth's grasp and pushed hair from her eyes with a nervous, self-conscious movement. 'Truly, Forth. I'm all right now.'

Forth sighed, letting his shoulders relax and the air seep back into his lungs. Grimya hadn't been able to catch Indigo, and Forth had chased her for the best part of two miles before the chestnut stallion's greater stamina began to assert itself and he'd been able to overtake her, reach perilously across the gap between them to grab her pony's bridle and force her to a halt. Unbalanced, Indigo had fallen from the saddle, and as Forth went to help her up, to his chagrin she had burst into tears. He'd never seen her cry before: despite the fact that she was – or so Forth believed – only a few years his senior, somehow he'd always felt like a child by comparison; and to see her sobbing as bitterly as one of his little sisters when something hurt or frightened them was bewildering. He'd tried to comfort her, but knew his efforts were gauche and clumsy, and he was relieved when at last she regained her self-control and the tears ceased.

Indigo wiped her eyes. Grimya stood gazing worriedly up at her, knowing what was wrong but not knowing what to do, and after a few moments Indigo felt able to look at Forth directly.

'I'm sorry,' she said in a small voice. 'I shouldn't have ridden off like that.'

'That place was enough to unman anyone,' Forth replied with considerable feeling. 'But – what was it that *really* upset you, Indigo? It just isn't like you to be so . . .' He faltered, unable to find the right word, and Indigo smiled ruefully.

61

'Frightened? Don't try to be kind to me, Forth; it's true. I was *terrified*. But I don't know how to explain why.' For a moment her eyes unfocused, as though she was seeing something else, something invisible to him, overlaid on the landscape before her. Then it passed with a small shiver, and when she looked at him again her full composure had returned.

'Well,' she said. 'What now?'

Forth understood her meaning. The road beyond the distant escarpment was impassable: whatever the nature or origin of that evil forest they could no more break through the barrier it presented than fly over it. Nor, he admitted to himself, did he want to risk venturing anywhere near it again. There was, it seemed, only one choice open to them.

'We'd best go back to Bruhome. There's no point trying to find another route, not with the storm so close. We'll have to return, and wait till it passes.' Despite his fear and uncertainty, and increasing worry for Chari's plight, his mouth couldn't help but twitch in a wry smile. 'It seems you won't be rid of us quite as easily as you'd thought.'

Indigo hung her head. 'Oh, Forth . . . '

'Come on, now.' Afraid that she might cry again, he patted her shoulder awkwardly and guided her back towards the waiting ponies. 'Better hurry, or it'll be on us. Don't want a dose of the rain-ague to add to our troubles, do we?'

Indigo said nothing, only nodded, and they remounted and continued on southward. Grimya, loping alongside Indigo's pony, was silent for a while, but at last she communicated a tentative message.

Indigo. That forest. We have seen it before, haven't we?

Indigo didn't reply, but the she-wolf felt the quick stab of pain that emanated from her mind. *It comes from the world of demons*, Grimya persisted. *The twisted world, where we ventured once before and were almost lost. Does this mean that we will have to enter that world again?*

Indigo didn't know the answer to that question. It might be that the form the black forest had taken was nothing more than an evil coincidence. Or it might be that somewhere beyond the barrier of those corrupted trees lay another dimension, parallel to but removed from their own, and that there lay the object of their search and the source of the blight that had come to Bruhome.

But she didn't want to think of that. Not now, with the image of the forest still so clear in her memory. It opened too many old wounds.

Grimya read her thoughts and said nothing more. But as they hastened on, with the brooding, stifling cloud ramparts spreading across the sky towards them, her memories, too, were awakening. And on a deep level, in ways that delved far beyond a natural mortal instinct, she felt afraid.

They arrived in Bruhome as the afternoon was waning. Turning the weary ponies into the river meadow, they found the Brabazons, together with the other players who still remained in the town, busily making their wagons fast against the elements. Fires had been put out, possessions stowed away; though the broken axle had now been mended, it was clear that no one would be making any attempt to move until the storm was over.

Stead greeted them with a mixture of dismay at the failure of their mission and relief that they were safe. Forth had promised to say nothing of Indigo's revelation that she meant to leave them; but he wasted no time in describing what had happened to them on the road. Stead listened with growing disquiet to the tale, and when he'd heard all there was to tell his brows came together in an unhappy frown.

'So it's true, then? This forest – it isn't just drunkards' stories?' He eyed the rapidly darkening sky as though it presented some personal threat. 'I don't like this. Seems to me that things hereabouts are growing worse too quickly for comfort. They've abandoned the Revels, did you know? Can't say I was surprised, but it shows how worried the townsfolk are now. There've been seven more taken the sickness since you left; two of them here among the players. And more disappearances. Now this storm: they're saying it's likely to be the worst there's been in these parts for a good many years, and folk are starting to fear that it's all one with the other bad events.'

Indigo asked, 'Chari's no better?'

'No better and no worse. She just lies there as though she was sleeping, but nothing will wake her. And there's a smile on her face that turns my blood cold when I look at her.' Stead shuddered. 'They all smile like that, so I've been told. It's uncanny. Horrible.'

'Da,' Forth put in. 'There's nothing more we can do for her until the storm's over. I'd best get the ponies unsaddled and tether them with the others. By the look of that sky, I'd take any wager that it'll be on us within the hour.'

As though in answer to his words, a faint rumble echoed in the distance, the first threatening murmur of thunder far off to the west among the fells. Stead nodded.

'Yes. Get them all together on the lee side, and make sure the stallion can't chew through his rope this time. Then come into the main van. Better if we all stay together tonight.' He hunched his shoulders defensively, as though he already felt the chill bite of rain through his shirt, and added, more to himself than to Indigo and Forth, 'No: I don't like this. I don't like it at all.'

Forth's guess proved right, and the storm broke almost an hour later. The light had changed from sullen brassiness to a tricky, unreal gloom that deepened as the sky's menace intensified. The air felt alive with suppressed energy, and in the caravan's softly lit interior faces were drawn and nervous with anticipation. The first, gargantuan flash caught them all by surprise; the lightning was answered by a rolling bawl of thunder, and seconds later came a rising, swelling hiss as the rain began.

The downpour was torrential, and the lightning continuous. Between the roaring of thunder and the racket of rain battering on the roof, conversation inside the caravan was all but impossible. To distract the younger children, Esty, Rance and Indigo devised a mime game, but as they played, striving to maintain a cheerful facade, Indigo's eyes were frequently drawn to the pallet in a darkened corner of the van, where Chari lay still and silent under a patchwork blanket. The frequent lightning flashes starkly illuminated the girl's face, and the smile which had so unnerved Stead looked chillingly like a corpse's rictus in the glare. Once, to her shock, Indigo thought that Chari's eyes had opened and that she was staring wildly at her; but as the next flash lit the van she realised that it had been no more than a momentary illusion. Nonetheless, she tried not to look at Chari again.

It was impossible to judge how long the storm lasted. It seemed to go on for hours, so that minds and senses became numbed to it, awaiting the lightning and listening to the thunder and rain with a weariness that bordered on indifference. But at last they became aware that the intervals between the elemental explosions were growing longer, until eventually the drumming on the roof lapsed to a gentler pattering, and the flashes diminished and the thunder's voice began to fade as the storm marched away into the east and left Bruhome behind.

When the children, under Esty's direction, had counted to one hundred five times without seeing another flash, Stead got to his feet and picked his way to the caravan door. As he opened the upper half, cool air rushed in, and with it a faint smell of ozone. A sound which previously had been masked by the storm now became audible; the hectic rush of water not too far away: and Forth scrambled up, his eyes alarmed.

'Da, the river – '

'It's all right.' Stead waved him down again, then poked his head out into the night. 'It's in spate, but it hasn't burst its banks. The tents down by the edge are still standing; I can just make 'em out.'

'Thanks be for small miracles,' Forth said fervently.

'Right enough; but all the same we'd best take a look round and see if anything's been damaged.' Stead pulled his head back in. 'Everybody all right, then? Come on, Pi; you can take your face out of Honi's skirt now, the storm's gone.'

Tension eased in talk and laughter as they emerged from the caravan and descended the steps to the sodden ground. The youngest Brabazons reacted to their relief

with a surge of energetic excitement, and were allowed to
help their elders with the checking of the vans and
animals. By a second small miracle there seemed to be no
damage either to the Brabazons' camp or to those of the
other travellers who now emerged from shelter; a swift
count revealed the ponies and oxen all safe and sound,
and Stead finally announced that there was no more to be
done and they could all retire for what was left of the
night.

Indigo was asleep almost as soon as she slipped
beneath her blanket and laid her head on the pillow she
shared with Esty. The day had been long and exhausting
enough to give her a reprieve from dreams, and she rested
undisturbed until a faint presence, a niggling sense of
disquiet, began to intrude on her dormant mind. She
tried to ignore it but it persisted, until she found herself
awake in the dark van with the silhouettes of her
companions around her. For a few moments, still
drowsy, she didn't know what had woken her: then she
saw Grimya's faint outline against the part-open door
and realised that the wolf was trying to communicate.

Grimya? She wanted only to turn over and go back to
sleep, and her mental query was tinged with irritation.
What is it?

I don't know. Grimya's head turned; Indigo saw her
sharply-pricked ears move against the night. *But something is wrong.*

Indigo sighed, and sat up. *What do you mean, wrong?*

I don't know, Grimya said again, unhappily. *But my
instinct is telling me . . .* She paused, then a shiver ran
down the length of her body. *My instinct is telling me that
day has come.*

Grimya, it's still pitch dark!

*Yes. But I feel it should be day. The night has passed. I
feel it.*

Indigo quelled her anger. Grimya, too, must be weary
and still tense in the wake of the storm; little wonder that
her sense of time, usually so reliable, had slipped out of
kilter. She could hardly blame her for her agitation.

Come here, love. She held out a hand, beckoning.
Come and lie down by me. We're both very tired, and your

mind's probably playing tricks with you. Try to sleep until it gets light again. You'll feel better then.

Grimya whined softly, as though unconvinced, but padded over nonetheless and stretched out at Indigo's side. Slipping an arm over her Indigo felt the rapid beat of her heart under the coarse fur, and stroked her head soothingly.

There, now. She yawned hugely. *Better?*

I . . . think so.

Good. Go to sleep, love. The world was already slipping away into soft, dark velvet. *Go to sleep.*

Again, there were no dreams to haunt her. When, refreshed, she woke naturally at last, she turned on to her back, stretched her arms, and opened her eyes.

And as the darkness of sleep gave way to the darkness of reality she realised with a growing sense of horror that Grimya had been right.

Indigo sat up in a flurry of movement. For a bare few seconds her mind tried to tell her that this was a mistake, that she too had succumbed to overtiredness and dawn hadn't yet broken. But she knew the truth. By the same instinct, less acutely honed than Grimya's animal awareness but now refusing to be gainsaid, she knew she'd slept for many hours, and the night should have been over.

Fear, unformed but horribly real, crawled over her skin like cold spiders, and she projected a tentative call. *Grimya?*

Movement in the dark; and the she-wolf slid out of the deeper shadows towards her. *Indigo! At last!*

How long have I slept?

I don't know. I, too, was asleep, and I can't tell how many hours have passed. But it must have been a long time.

And it's still dark . . .

Yes, I tried to tell you before, but –

I'm sorry. I should have trusted your instinct. In all this time, Indigo thought, she should at least have learned that lesson. *Grimya, what time of day does your instinct tell you it should be now?*

Mid-morning, the wolf said.

Mid-morning. In Bruhome the market should be in

full swing; in the lea the encamped travellers should be lighting fires in readiness for their midday meal. Indigo got to her feet and stumbled to the caravan door, peering out. There was movement by some of the other encampments, and the faint sound of voices; but none of the busy activity of daylight.

Some others are awake, Grimya told her. *But they're confused; they don't yet know what has happened.* She glanced at her friend in trepidation. *When they realise the truth, there will be panic.*

Somewhere down by the river a horse whinnied piercingly, and the sound broke Indigo's paralysis. She cast a quick glance over her shoulder at the sleeping Brabazon girls, then eased the lower half of the door open.

Come on, she said. *We'd best go and see what we can find out.*

With Grimya at her heels she went quietly down the caravan steps. As they started across the grass a shadow moved in the first van, then a voice, low-pitched, hissed Indigo's name.

'Stead.' She stopped as he emerged from the van and came towards her.

'Lass, what's the hour?' Stead tried to sound casual, but his expression, and a slight tremor in his voice, gave him away. There was no point in making a pretence, and Indigo said, 'I don't know, Stead; not for certain. But – '

He finished the sentence for her. 'But the sun should have risen by now. Shouldn't it?'

She nodded. 'Yes. I think it should.'

'By the Great Mother, Indigo, what's happening in this forsaken place?' He grasped her arm, hurting her in his agitation. 'What's *happening*?'

She was saved from attempting to reply by a new voice hailing them from the direction of the river. A thin young man, with a woman and two small children doggedly following in his wake, was hastening towards them.

'Steadfast! There's something wrong, terribly wrong!'

'The daylight,' the woman wailed fearfully, and one of the children, moved to copy her, started to howl. 'Where's the *daylight*?'

Others, alerted by the voices, were looking up, starting

towards them. From the boys' caravan came a querulous complaint, then Forth appeared at the top of the steps with Rance behind him. 'Da? What's going on?'

Stead glanced at him. 'Best come out here, lad. Wake the others and send someone to fetch the girls.'

The babble was swelling as more people arrived, drawn by the primitive instinct to congregate together in a time of uncertainty or danger. Some had already realised the truth but were too afraid to admit it; others, still more fearful, rejected it and clamoured for a saner explanation. Voices were becoming more strident, arguments more emphatic, and Indigo knew that before long reason and control would break down and give way, as Grimya had predicted, to panic.

Suddenly one harsh voice cut through the hubbub. Heads turned, and Indigo saw the young man who had approached Stead a few minutes earlier. His wife was clinging to him, her face hidden against his chest, while the two children, both now grizzling loudly, hung on to the hem of his shirt.

'It's all *talk*!' the young man shouted, and Indigo heard the unmistakable timbre of rising hysteria in his voice. 'What good's *talk*? The Mother alone knows what could be creeping up on us while we all stand here clacking like a flock of chickens! We've got to get *out* of this place, get *away*, before something worse happens!'

Everyone stared at him. The young man looked wildly from one face to another.

'We've heard the stories of what's been happening in this town,' he shouted. 'Sickness, blight, people disappearing – and now this! I tell you, Bruhome's cursed! This isn't the Mother's doing; it's *sorcery*! And if we don't make a run for it, we're all going to be caught up in whatever comes next!' Suddenly he grabbed the children's hands, pulling them and his wife back out of the crowd. 'All right – all right, you stay and wait for it if you're too stupid not to! But we're going!' And he turned and pelted away towards his ramshackle wagon.

Murmuring started, swelled to a crescendo. Another man broke away and ran off across the meadow; then two more. A woman with a bandaged ankle – an acrobat who'd taken a fall on the rickety Revels stage – limped up from the river, calling for someone named Kindo to come away, come away *now*. The gathering began to collapse into chaos, and within minutes the first wagon, with the thin young man in the driving seat, lashing the horse with a length of rope, came lumbering towards the meadow gateway, careless of anyone who might be in its path. Children scattered, screaming; the wagon rocked perilously in a rut, collided with the gate, splintering one of its uprights, and rumbled away along the road. Moments later a string of rawboned horses stampeded out of the meadow, barely under the control of the rider who sat the leading animal cursing them volubly. Several families were packing hastily; one small group simply gathered up everything they could carry and left on foot.

'Da.' Forth turned to Stead, grasping his arm and shaking him to bring him out of the paralysis that seemed to have fallen on him. 'What about us? What are we going to do?'

A shudder ran through Stead and his blank look cleared. He glanced about him, saw that all his children had now emerged from the caravans and were waiting, wide-eyed, for his guidance.

'Whatever we do,' he said, 'I'll have no panicking. Is that understood? Sorcery or not, we've got to keep clear heads. Forth, Cour – I want you to saddle two ponies and ride ahead of us. We'll move out, but cautiously. That young sprig might have been a coward and a fool, but he was right in one thing – we don't know what might be out there waiting for us. And we don't know how far the dark extends.'

'Stead.' Indigo alerted him suddenly. 'Over there – look. Lanterns.'

They all turned. Lights were approaching from the direction of the town, bobbing like a string of agitated glow-worms in the darkness. As they drew nearer, metal glinted in their reflected glow, and the silhouettes of some ten or a dozen men became visible.

'It's the town watch.' Relief coloured Stead's voice. 'Maybe they'll have news.'

'Steadfast Brabazon? Stead, is that you?' The voice of

70

Burgher Mischyn called out of the gloom, and Stead stepped forward, raising a hand.

'Mischyn! Over here!'

'By the Mother, I'm thankful to see you safe!' Mischyn was breathless, and in the unsteady lamplight his face looked haggard. 'There's great panic in the town; we didn't know how the encampment fared; we feared – '

'Half of 'em have left already.' Stead nodded over his shoulder.

'*Left?* But – '

'Burgher Mischyn!' Someone else had seen the new arrivals, and frantic voices burst out.

'The watch! It's the watch!'

'Help us!'

'Burgher, what's happening to us?'

The dispersed throng began hastily to gather again, though their numbers were considerably fewer than before. The sight of a known figure of authority, with ten armed men of the watch to back him, boosted their confidence and their courage, and they crowded round Mischyn, shouting questions, demanding answers.

'My friends!' At last Mischyn managed to make himself heard over the commotion, and the crowd gradually subsided as he waved his arms for quiet. 'Please, listen to me! I can't answer your questions, for I *have* no answers. I know only what you know – that the sun, which according to the town's timepiece should have risen six hours ago, has not done so.'

There was a fresh outburst.

'Six *hours?*'

'It must be almost noon – Great Mother, what's *happening?*'

'Sorcery – someone said it's sorcery – '

'QUIET!' Stead bellowed. His voice, like a bullroarer and far more powerful than Mischyn's, brought a stunned silence, and he glared at the assembly. 'Damn you all, let the man speak!'

'Thank you,' Mischyn said pallidly. 'My friends, I've come here to appeal to you for calm. There has been panic in the town, but our militia are doing everything possible to restore order. If we are to face what has come

71

upon us and find a way to deal with it, we *must* keep our reason. There's to be a meeting in the Brewmasters' Hall in one hour's time – I ask you to attend, and to join with us in finding a solution to this grave situation.'

From the back of a crowd came a voice quavering with fear. 'Damn your meeting! What good's that going to do? If you don't know what's afoot, then I'm not staying here a moment longer!'

There were shouts of agreement: Mischyn tried to say something over the sudden uproar, but his voice was inaudible and he turned in appeal to Stead.

'Stead, they don't understand! None of you understands; but it's what I've come here to tell you. You *can't* leave.'

Stead's look darkened, as though he suspected some threat. 'What do you mean?'

'Just what I say – you can't leave Bruhome. No one can. We've tried every direction – the roads, the fell paths, everything. Riders, runners; they've been going out since an hour after the dawn should have broken, and every one's come back with the same report.' And, seeing that Stead still didn't fully comprehend, Mischyn added, his voice close to breaking, 'Stead, it's the forest. The black forest. It's all around us, and we can't get out!'

Chapter VI

The burghers had tried their best, but the meeting was doomed to failure from the start. Entering Bruhome's main square with the Brabazons – all but Honesty and Gentility, who had stayed behind to watch over Chari – Indigo immediately felt the perilous instability that lurked beneath the prevailing tension like an ember under a powder-keg. One touch, one misplaced word or action, and the town could flare into riot.

The square looked eerie. The blackness overhead was intense, the dark reaching down like a shroud, dense and stifling and unnatural. Flamboys burned on every post, lanterns had been strung all over the square and wedged into every available cranny, but their flaring light seemed to give little real illumination and the overwhelming impression, as the frightened crowds milled and jostled, was of a scene from some feverish nightmare.

Indigo slipped an arm round Piety, who was clinging tightly to her waist. For a fleeting moment she wished that they'd listened after all to the dissenter in the meadow, and at least tried to get away from the town; but the impulse died immediately. She'd seen the forest; she knew the truth; perhaps she'd even known it before Burgher Mischyn's revelation. Something demonic had come to Bruhome. The third evil of seven. There could be no doubt of it now, no room for question. But if the third evil was here, what was its nature? The question sent a cold shaft of fear through her, for it seemed that this demonic power had no nucleus, nothing that she could identify and challenge. The blight, the sickness, the disappearances, the forest, even the coming of this malevolent and unnatural night, were but manifestations. There was evil, *great* evil here; but unless the vital key could be found, she and Grimya were trapped as effectively and as helplessly as the townsfolk.

On a balcony that overhung the square from the imposing frontage of the Brewmasters' Hall, someone had begun to speak. Looking up, Indigo saw Burgher Mischyn flanked by two of his fellow officials; he was trying to address the throng, but at sight of him the crowd had surged forward and started to shout, pleading and haranguing by turns. A horn blew deafeningly as the militia tried to establish some form of order, but it was hopeless. The hubbub was rising, fear feeding on fear; a flamboy crashed down as the press of the crowd proved too much for its tall post, and there were screams and howls of pain before a group of men with more presence of mind than most stamped the flames out. Over the racket Indigo could hear the occasional despairing plea of 'My friends – my friends – ' from Mischyn, but the throng were deaf to his entreaties. Two lines of watchmen began to move forward from the hall's main entrance in a valiant attempt to push the jostling horde back, but the gesture, though well-intentioned, only made matters worse. The tide of panic was running out of control.

Suddenly a shriek seared through the darkness, and a small group on the crowd's furthest edge began to shout in earnest. Indigo had time to register the nature of the shouts – horror, shock, disbelief – before more took up the cry, spreading it like a wave through the throng.

'What is it? What's happened?' Esty, at Indigo's elbow, jumped up and down in a vain effort to see over the ocean of bobbing heads.

'I don't know!' Indigo had to shout in her turn to make herself heard. 'Something on the southern side – '

Behind her light spilled on to the cobbles as a door opened. She turned her head reflexively and saw someone emerge from one of three narrow houses wedged between a tavern and a bakery; for a moment, registering nothing untoward, she started to turn back to watch the disturbance again –

Then froze, as her mind caught up with what her eyes had told her.

The woman emerging from the house was barefoot and dressed only in a long nightgown, and her skin was the sickly white of a dead fish. She stared ahead, unseeing, and her mouth was curved in a beatific but mindless smile. Those closest to her drew back in shock; someone choked off an oath – and the woman hesitated only a moment before turning and walking with an awful air of purpose away into one of the side streets.

'Indigo!' Esty hissed, horrified, in her ear. 'Did you – '

'I saw it.' Indigo's heart was pounding; beside her Grimya bristled with alarm and she reached down to grip the she-wolf's ruff.

'Save us, there's another!' Esty cried, pointing. 'Over there: look, *look*!'

A child, naked, with the same ghastly pallor, was moving along the edge of the square, oblivious to everything but his own progress. No one tried to stop him; as with the woman they drew back, too stunned to react. And from the bakery next to the narrow houses came another, an old man incongruous in nightshirt and cap, white-faced, blind-eyed, smiling.

One by one, under the paralysed gazes of the townsfolk, the men, women and children who had fallen prey to Bruhome's mysterious sickness were emerging from their homes. Gradually the uproar in the square sank to a horrified silence as more and more people realised what was afoot, but still no one moved to intercept the sleepwalkers or try to stop them. Shock had rooted them where they stood: their overburdened minds slammed their shutters, unable to accept this new assault, and they stood staring, helpless, incapable of any rational response.

Then suddenly a hoarse voice from the balcony broke the thrall, as Burgher Mischyn cried out: 'Frenni! No! Not my little Frenni!' He spun round, racing back through the balcony's open doors, and as he pelted down the stairs towards the main door, Indigo heard him calling to his son. 'Frenni, *no! Come back!*'

Mischyn's son . . . suddenly a terrible thought slipped into place and she whirled, clutching at Stead's arm.

'Stead! What about Chari?'

Stead looked at her as though he'd never seen her before. His face was empty, uncomprehending, but Forth and Esty had overheard, and took their father by the shoulders, shaking him.

'Da! Da, Indigo's right!'

'Da, the sleepers! They're waking – Chari's in danger!'

Like a man lurching abruptly from a dark dream, intelligence returned to Stead's eyes as their entreaties penetrated his stunned mind. He drew breath with a terrible sound. 'Chari – my Chari . . . oh, by the Mother!' And he swung round, barrelling through the crowd.

'Esty – Indigo – bring the little ones! We've got to get back to the meadow!' Forth was already off in pursuit of his father. Indigo and Esty exchanged one appalled look, then Esty began to shrill out the children's names, calling them to her.

'Hold hands! Quickly, *quickly*! Come *on*!'

In a chaotic scramble they set off, treading on toes, elbowing stomachs, fighting their way through the crush. By the time they reached the edge of the square, Stead and Forth were out of sight and the crowd had eased. In the distance Indigo thought she glimpsed a pale shape in a narrow street, walking . . .

She began to run.

'Honi?'

Honesty looked up at her younger sister. Gentility was sitting crosslegged in a corner, frowning as she obsessively pulled threads from the hem of her own skirt.

'What is it? Stop doing that, Gen; you'll ruin it.'

Gen's eyes were lambent in the dimly-lit van. For a moment her lower lip trembled; then she said,

'Honi, I'm scared.'

Honi sighed. 'We're all scared, kitling. Except maybe Da, and even he – '

'I don't mean that. Not the dark. I mean, yes, I'm scared of that, but . . . ' She cast a nervous glance to the pallet and its silent occupant. 'I think I'm even scareder of Chari. The way she just *lies* there, as if she was . . . ' She stopped, unable to bring herself to say the word *dead*.

76

Honi sympathised. She too had been feeling uneasy since the others departed for the town, leaving the two of them to look after their sister; but from the heights of her thirteen years she was determined not to admit it, least of all to Gen, who was only ten and couldn't possibly understand adult responsibilities.

She said, 'Do you want to go to the other van?'

Gen shook her head. 'Not if it means being on my own. That's even worse.'

'Well . . .' Honi looked out of the half-open door. 'Tell you what, let's go outside for a few minutes. We can take a lantern, and it wouldn't hurt to look at the animals, anyway.'

Gen accepted the idea gratefully, and they padded down the caravan steps. Honi allowed Gen to carry the lantern, and by its lurching glow they checked the ponies and oxen. All seemed well – Honi refilled their water-buckets at the river, but that was all – and at last they turned, neither willing to admit to her reluctance, and retraced their steps back towards the van.

Suddenly, Gen stopped. 'Honi . . .'

Honi's heart skipped. 'What is it? Gen, don't *do* that to me!'

'*Shh!* Listen – I heard a noise, in the van . . .'

Honi started to say irritably, 'Don't be – '

But the words died in her throat as Chari appeared at the top of the steps.

'*Chari!*' Gen's squeal made the ponies whinny in alarm. She backed away, clapping both hands over her mouth, and Honi stared at her sister in disbelief.

'Chari? Chari, are you all right?' Hope and fear mingled in her voice and she started forward. Chari's face bore a strange and awful smile; she stared at Honi, through her, and with a shock Honi realised that whatever she was seeing, it wasn't the night and the meadow and the distant lights of Bruhome. Slowly, and with a peculiar limpness that brought her bare feet down with a heavy thump on each step, Chari descended to the ground, and started to walk purposefully away.

'Chari!' Honi's fear was swamped by a wave of concern, and she ran to intercept her sister, catching her arm and tugging. 'Chari, wake up! It's me, it's Honi! Oh, Gen, help me!'

Gen dropped the lantern and ran towards her, but before she could join her strength to Honi's, Chari turned and looked directly at her sister. Honi recoiled from the unfocused eyes, the rapt rictus of a smile – then Chari's free hand came up and smacked her hard in the face.

Honi stumbled back, lost her balance and fell onto the wet ground as Chari, unconcerned, turned away and continued walking towards the gate. Gen hauled her to her feet and for one confused moment the two of them could only watch helplessly as Chari's figure moved away into the gloom. Then Honi yelled, 'Catch her! Gen, get her, *quickly*!'

They ran after Chari, caught up with her and grabbed an arm each, pulling her back with all their strength. Chari's feet continued to move as though she were an automaton, and her strength was incredible, so that Honi and Gen found themselves being towed along behind her for several yards before they could dig their heels into the soft earth and drag her to a halt. Chari stopped. For a moment she stood rigid, frozen – then, so fast and so ferociously that the other two girls were caught completely unawares, she spun round, wrenching her arms free from their grip. Honi glimpsed her face, and her eyes above the unchanging smile were insane: she screamed, horrified, and Chari lunged at Gen, lifting her off her feet and hurling her away. Gen's thin shriek as she flew through the air cut off in a gasp and a sickening thud, and Chari turned to glare at Honi again as though challenging her to risk similar treatment.

'Chari . . . ?' Honi's voice was a pitiful whimper. 'Chari, what's *happened* to you? Gen; she – oh, by the *Mother*!' And, blinded by bewildered tears, she turned and ran to where Gen lay.

'Gen! Gen, kitling, are you all right?' She dropped to her knees, lifting Gen's hair away from her face. Gen was unconscious and breathing shallowly: she'd hit her head on a half-buried stone as she fell, and blood was trickling darkly from a nasty gash just under the hairline.

She couldn't leave Gen lying out here. She had to get her back to the caravan, then run to the town for Da, or Esty, or Indigo. They'd know what to do. But that would mean leaving Gen alone. There was no one else here to look after her; they'd all gone to the meeting. What if something happened while she was away? What was best? What should she *do*?

Honi raised her head and stared miserably at the empty meadow. Chari had vanished. Chari had hit her, and hurt her little sister, and gone walking off into the dark like all those strange travellers on the road. And she was alone; and frightened, so very frightened.

'Oh, Da . . . ' The words broke from Honi's throat in a gulping sob. 'Da, come back! Please, come back . . . '

When Stead and Forth arrived five minutes later, they found Honi kneeling on the grass in a small circle of lamplight, hugging Gen close to her and still crying. Honi was too distressed to be coherent, and only when Forth ran to the caravan, looked inside and saw Chari's empty pallet did they realise the essentials of what had happened.

'Chari!' Stead shouted into the darkness, his face drawn with terror. 'Chari, where are you? *Chari!*'

'It's no use, Da.' Forth gathered Gen into his arms. She was beginning to stir, thankfully; and he judged that apart from a few bruises and a sore head she'd be well enough. 'Even Honi doesn't know which way she went. She could be anywhere!'

'But where are they all *going*?' Stead pleaded desperately. '*Where?*'

Forth saw lanterns approaching, heard the sound of voices. 'Here's Indigo and the others,' he said. 'Da, perhaps Grimya can track Chari – it might be our only chance to find her!'

Hampered by the slower pace of the smaller children, Indigo, Grimya and the rest of the Brabazons had fallen far behind Stead and Forth, and were only now coming through the meadow gate. Forth ran to meet them. In a few terse words he explained what had happened, and asked Indigo if Grimya could help.

Of course I can, Grimya told Indigo as she overheard him. *But we must waste no time. I think Chari is in great danger!*

And without waiting for a further word, she ran back to the gate and started to sniff around.

Forth stared at her. 'It's as if she understands . . .'

'She does.' Indigo didn't attempt to deny it; this was no time for charades. 'Don't ask me about that, Forth; just follow her. Hurry!'

Grimya had already picked up Chari's track, and was moving carefully away into the darkness. Forth called his father, and the three of them set off after the wolf, Stead shouting over his shoulder for the others to stay close by the vans and not move until their return.

At the road Grimya paused, but only for a moment before turning northward. Following her, Indigo recalled her own journey with Forth on the previous day, and shivered as she wondered how far along that road Charity meant to travel, and what awaited her at its end.

'We should have brought a lantern.' Forth's voice cut into her thoughts as he loped beside her. 'Road's like a ploughed rut. All too easy to turn an ankle.'

'Too late for that now.' They were both breathless, clipping their words; the run from the town and the peculiar, stifling airlessness of the dark had taken a toll of their energy. And the dark was intensifying as Bruhome's lights fell further behind, emphasising Forth's warning. Indigo could barely see Stead's vivid hair before her, and when, experimentally, she held a hand out before her face, its outline was dim and blurred.

Grimya. She projected the thought urgently. *We can hardly see in this blackness. Don't leave us too far behind!*

The she-wolf's silent voice answered her. *I dare not wait! I think there is someone ahead of me in the distance, and it might be Chari.*

Keep in contact with me, then. Keep telling me where you are.

Yes. For now, all you need do is stay on the road. There was a pause, then: *The figure is closer now. I think it's her, but I can't be sure. When I know, I will call out.*

For a while longer – it might have been minutes, it

might have been mere seconds; normal judgement was distorted by the blackness and their own trepidation – the three stumbled on. Then suddenly a spine-chilling sound echoed distantly out of the dark: the full-throated, ululating howl of a wolf.

'Mother preserve us!' Forth started violently.

'It's Grimya!' Indigo caught his arm to steady him as he seemed about to lose his footing on the uneven road surface. 'She's found her!'

Seconds later Grimya came racing out of the gloom.

Indigo! I've found Chari, but there's danger! The black forest lies across the road ahead, and she's walking towards it!

'The *forest*? Oh, no!' Appalled, Indigo spoke aloud before she could control her tongue. Stead looked at her in horror, then gave an inarticulate cry and broke into a run, careless of the pitted track.

'Stead!' Indigo shouted. 'Be careful!' He ignored her, and she swore. 'Forth, hurry! Grimya says the forest lies dead ahead of us – if Stead runs into those thorns, they'll impale him!'

Forth's eyes widened. '*Grimya* says – '

'I can't explain; there isn't time! Come *on*!'

They raced after Stead, who by now was some way ahead of them. Grimya overtook him, leaping at him in an effort to turn him aside, but he ignored her and staggered on like a mad drunkard. And then Indigo saw a greater darkness looming out of the unnatural night; a huge, shapeless mass that blocked the road ahead. She heard the malevolent rustling, the soft scraping of branch against branch, the faint, sinister clashing of the thorns, and she yelled with all the force she could muster.

'Stead! Stead, stop! If you value your life, *stop*!'

Stead was no more than ten yards from the deadly trees. And ahead of him something else moved in the gloom; a slight figure, pale, ghostlike, walking forward as though in a trance.

'*Stead!*' Indigo forced her legs to carry her faster, yet knew that she couldn't hope to catch up with Stead before he reached the thorns. And, now only two paces ahead of her father, Chari stepped up to the edge of the monstrous forest.

The thorns parted. Their clashing rose to a sudden frenzy, and the misshapen branches drew back to form a black tunnel, like a gaping, ravenous mouth, leading into the forest's impenetrable depths. Chari didn't falter but stepped straight into the dark maw – and Stead, howling her name, made a blind, flying rush as he strove to reach her and drag her back.

'NO!' Indigo cried frantically. 'Stead, come back! Grimya – Grimya, *stop him!*'

Grimya flung herself forward. Her teeth snapped together on Stead's sleeve; he wrenched his arm up, trying to shake her off: then suddenly he seemed to lose his balance, teetering forward. His flailing hand caught a handful of Chari's hair; Grimya leaped again, trying to renew her grip –

The thicket snapped together like a trap at their backs, shutting all three behind a solid wall of thorns.

Indigo shrieked, '*Grimya!*' and hurled herself at the black barrier, beating at branches, leaves, thorns, struggling to force a way through. Her voice rose hysterically, screaming Grimya's name again and again, until she was hauled back and wrestled violently to the ground, still screaming, still fighting. A weight crushed down on her, she tried to kick it away, biting, clawing, spitting: then pain flared at the back of her head, breaking through the madness, overtaking it, and suddenly she slumped back as the last of her energy fled.

She was lying on her back in the road, with Forth sitting squarely on her stomach. He gripped hanks of her hair in both hands; in sheer desperation, not knowing how else to overpower her, he'd banged her skull – not fiercely, but hard enough to hurt – against the ground until she stopped screaming and fighting; and now, as panic faded, they stared at each other in mutual, wordless horror.

'Grimya . . .' Indigo said in a small voice. 'Oh, Forth . . .' She shut her eyes and her mouth twisted into an ugly contortion as she strove not to cry.

Forth scrambled upright, fumbling at his belt and

drawing his knife from its sheath. 'Maybe I can cut a way through. They can't have gone far in yet.'

'No.' The pendulum had swung back; in the wake of hysteria came chill rationality. 'It won't work, Forth. No blade could cut through those trees.'

'I can at least *try*!' Forth ran to the thicket, knife raised, and started to hack at the branches. For several minutes he worked, slashing at the black vegetation, his curses growing louder and more furious; then at last he stepped back, breathing heavily and with sweat running down his face.

'I can't do it.' He sounded like a bewildered child. 'It's not even making any *impression*!' And he spun to face the trees again. 'Da! Chari! Da, answer me! *Da!*'

The unnatural trees rustled secretively, but there was no answering cry. Shakily, Indigo got to her feet. As she approached him, Forth turned blindly towards her with a sob, and they hugged each other tightly and silently, trying to ease their shared misery.

Finally Forth drew back. He was trembling, and his cheeks were wet, but there was a determined set to his face despite the fact that he seemed reluctant to meet Indigo's eyes.

'We've got to go back,' he said. 'We've got to tell the others.' A sharp, angry breath. 'We'll come back with torches. Maybe we can burn a way through.'

Indigo said hollowing: 'I don't think so. Whatever those trees are, wherever they came from, I don't think fire can touch them any more than knives.'

He rounded on her. 'Well, we've got to do *something*! Don't you understand? Da and Chari are in there!'

'And Grimya.'

'Yes, and Grimya! And we've got to get them out!'

If it isn't already too late, Indigo thought, and instantly regretted it. Grimya couldn't die: that was a part of her own curse which the she-wolf shared. But she could suffer. And Stead and Chari were another matter . . .

She looked up at the trees again. Their tops were invisible, merging into the dense night. And their rustling sounded to her inflamed senses like mocking, sniggering laughter.

83

Indigo took hold of Forth's hand. 'Come on,' she said quietly. 'Perhaps you're right; perhaps fire will work. It's at least worth trying. Let's get back to the camp, quickly.'

They turned away, back down the road. The trees' laughter seemed to follow them, until even the small, malign echoes of creaking boughs and whispering thorns were swallowed in the brooding silence of the dark.

Chapter VII

'All right.' Forth glared at the circle of faces around the camp fire, his expression daring anyone to argue with him, and his eyes finally focused on Indigo. 'It's a good idea, and it should work. But you're not going alone.'

'Forth – '

'I said, *no*.' Forth thumped the heel of one hand down on the grass for emphasis. 'While Da and Chari are gone I'm head of this family, and what I say stands. Two of us go with you, or you don't go at all. And don't think we can't make you stay if we have to.'

It wasn't true, but Indigo let it pass. Forth needed this show of authority, not only to reassure his brothers and sisters but also to reassure himself, and to restore his self-esteem. On the nightmare journey back to Bruhome she'd heard him sobbing as he ran, and he knew it and was ashamed. She'd tried to tell him that there was nothing unmanly in tears, but he'd rejected her comfort angrily: as with the argument they'd had at the river – so long ago now that seemed – he hated any suspicion, however misplaced, that he might seem like a child in her eyes.

She cast her gaze down. 'Very well.' He had the right, too, she reminded herself: though she was solely responsible for this predicament, it was the lives of his father and sister, not hers, which were at stake. And – conscience aside – she admitted privately that the thought of companionship in what she might have to face was more than a little comforting.

'So,' Esty spoke up, 'who's to go and who's to stay?'

'I go with Indigo.' Again Forth gave them all a challenging look, and no one dissented. 'And I think there should be one other. Three will be better off than two if there's any trouble, or if Chari or Da are hurt. We'll have to decide who'll be the best choice.'

Esty stirred the cooking pot. 'That's easy.' She looked up, and her green eyes met her brother's determinedly. 'Me.'

'Don't be stupid. You're a girl.'

'So's Indigo, and it isn't going to stop her. No, Forth; shut up and listen. None of us knows what might happen here while you're away, and if there's any more trouble we might need physical strength and the ability to fight. That means Cour, Rance and Forti. The other boys are too young to go – ' There was an outburst from the three, and Esty waved a ladle at them. 'Quiet! This isn't a game, it's *serious*. They're too young. Harmi and Honi are both better than me at organising everyone, and they'll make a better job of seeing that the camp runs smoothly. So it's obvious, isn't it? I'm the only one who can come with you.'

Forth looked helplessly at Indigo. He clearly didn't like the idea, but Esty had pre-empted his argument. 'Indigo? What do you think?'

Indigo regarded Esty for a few moments. Of all the Brabazon girls she was the most unpredictable; yet there was a core of strength to her. Esty was shrewd and knew how to look after herself; and her argument was sound. Provided her impulsive excesses could be kept in check – and Forth's too, for that matter – they were the only logical choices.

She said, 'I think Esty's right. She should be the one to come with us.'

Piety, who hadn't fully understood all that was being said but sensed intuitively that the family's troubles were far from over, began to cry; a reaction to the chaos that her life had so bewilderingly become. Harmony, already beginning to slip into the role that Chari had previously held, went to comfort her, and Forth pushed himself back from the fireside.

'Right. Well if that's settled, there's no time to be lost. I'm going to get the things I'll need; Indigo, Esty, you'd better do the same. Then I want to see Cour, Rance and Forti in Da's van.'

86

'Honi'll bring you some food,' Esty said. 'No point us leaving on empty stomachs when we don't know how long it'll be to our next meal.'

The nature of the atmosphere around the fire was changing. There was tension still, but it was leavened by a feeling that the helpless hiatus of recent hours was at last broken. However, Indigo was aware that it would be all too easy, in the enthusiasm of the moment, to overlook one vital matter that, as yet, she hadn't had the chance to discuss with Forth and Esty. Neither of them had any real grasp of what they might be facing if the plan she had devised worked. Brave talk was all very well, but the reality would be different: even the strategy for getting through the thorn barrier might be their undoing if the Brabazons proved more squeamish than they claimed; and beyond that . . . she didn't know what lay beyond that, but intuition and old experience told her that it could be worse than any nightmare. She couldn't let them go into this unprepared: in all conscience, she must tell them what truly lay behind this quest.

The two Brabazons were already heading towards their caravans, and she got to her feet, calling to them. 'Forth! Esty! Before you make your preparations . . .' She hastened towards them and lowered her voice so that the others wouldn't hear. 'There's something I have to tell you, and it's vital that you should know it before we set out.'

Esty sighed impatiently, but Forth's eyes narrowed shrewdly. 'Something to do with what you said to me on the road?'

'Yes. And it has a bearing on our journey.'

'All right. We shouldn't waste more time than we have to, but . . . come into the main van. We can talk there.'

And so, in the privacy of the van, Indigo told them her story: or rather, as much of her story as she felt they needed to know and would believe. She told them of her quest to find and destroy the seven demons, and of her discovery that the third of those demons was the motivating evil behind the blight that afflicted Bruhome. She told them, too, the truth about Grimya. And though she said nothing of her old, lost identity, or of the curse of immortality that was a part of her burden, she told them, hesitantly and painfully, of Fenran, whose life hung in the balance as hostage to her success or failure.

When she had done, there was silence in the van for some while. Then, very slowly, Esty reached out and took hold of her hand.

'Oh, Indigo.' The girl's eyes were bright with emotion. 'We had no idea; none of us.' She glanced quickly at Forth, who was watching Indigo with a taut expression, but he said nothing. 'Such a terrible story. So *sad*. It's like . . . I don't know, like the legends we sing of in our shows, but – '

'Don't be so crass!' Forth interrupted angrily. 'They're just folk tales. This,' he looked at Indigo again, more intently than ever, 'is *real*. It's *happened* to Indigo, and if all you can say is that it's like some stupid children's fable – '

'That wasn't what I meant!' Esty retorted. 'Of course I know there's a difference: what d'you think I am?'

'Then you know that Indigo means exactly what she says when she tells us that rescuing Da and Chari is going to be dangerous, don't you?' Forth's anger was under control now, but it still simmered; and Indigo suspected that there was a little more behind it than simple if misplaced disgust for his sister. 'When Indigo says we'll be facing a demon, she means a *demon*. Not some make-believe figure from your romantic daydreams, but a – '

'I *know* what she means!' Esty fired back. 'I know what a demon is!'

Indigo, who had watched the quarrel with growing disquiet, intervened.

'Forth, Esty: I mean no insult, but I doubt if either of you really understand yet exactly what it is we'll be facing,' she said quietly. They both turned to look at her, but she forestalled any denials, continuing: 'The truth is, none of us knows what to expect. This power, this – demon,' she was reluctant now to use the word, for it had planted too many preconceptions in their minds, 'might take any form, or no form at all. We may not even be able to recognise it if we find it – '

'*When* we find it,' Esty corrected fiercely.

'Very well, when we find it. I told you my story because I want you to understand my reasons for making this attempt, and because it would be a gross injustice to lead you into such danger unless you know the whole truth.' A small, wry smile curved her mouth. 'I wish I could have told you of the demon without having to reveal my own predicament, but that would have left too many un-answered questions. Now, though, you're armed with as much knowledge as I can give you. All we can do is hope that it'll be enough.'

Esty, sobered, cast her gaze down. 'I'm sorry,' she said. 'I didn't mean to sound frivolous, Indigo. And Forth and I shouldn't have quarrelled.' She flashed her brother a defiant look, then returned Indigo's smile a little weakly. 'It's not an encouraging start, is it? You must be asking yourself whether we'll be more trouble than we're worth!'

'Of course I'm not.' It wasn't entirely true, but Indigo knew that it was far too late to reconsider. Forth had meant what he said earlier: she couldn't stop them from going with her. Even if she were to set out alone, they'd follow her, and the consequences of their entering the demon world without her to help them didn't bear thinking about. However much of a liability they might prove to be, she had no option but to take them with her.

She said: 'Let's say no more of it, Esty. We've still got a lot to do before we set out, and Forth's right about not wasting time.' She looked from one to the other of them. 'Peace?'

'Peace,' Esty agreed eagerly. Forth hesitated, then nodded. 'Peace.'

Indigo's plan for penetrating the black forest was simple, if a little macabre. Things had changed in Bruhome during the last few hours; in one way for the better, in another for the worse. The feared riot in the market square had been averted after all: by a bizarre twist of fate the emergence of the sleepers had been the saving factor, for it had acted like ice-cold water on the crowd's rising temperature, focusing attention away from personal terrors to something more shocking and more sobering. The townsfolk had been stunned into helplessness, unable to do anything but watch in blank incomprehension as the victims of the sickness, like moths drawn to some invisible flame, emerged from their beds and their homes and walked away into the night. A few hardier souls had tried to stop some of the walkers and had fared no better than Honi and Gen; with their failure, a kind of apathy had settled on the town, a numb acceptance that this, like so many frightening events before it, was simply another link in the chain, another manifestation of the evil that held Bruhome in the palm of its hand. They couldn't fight it any more: their will was gone, shrivelled with the crops, vanished with the lost loved ones, caged as the unnatural forest now caged the town. All they could do was passively accept the fate that no one seemed able to change, and weep for their own misfortune.

But though Bruhome was now quiet, it seemed that the evil wasn't yet done with its victims. An hour after the last sleepwalker had left the town, two children – twins – slumped down at their family's hearth and couldn't be woken. Another hour later they rose, white-faced, smiling, oblivious to their mother's screams and their father's drunken entreaties, and walked out of the house and away eastward. Shortly afterwards, two men and a woman were seen moving purposefully along the eastern road. And in other parts of the town, in homes, taverns, even in the Brewmasters' Hall where many had gone to share their distress with their neighbours, new sleepers fell and new walkers emerged. It seemed as though whatever beckoned to them, whatever slipped deep into their consciousnesses and called them away, it would not be satisfied until there was no one left.

That news, brought by Cour who had ventured into the town before her return, had shown Indigo how she could defeat the barrier of thorns. She knew, now, where the sleepwalkers were going and why the directions they took were so random. They were being drawn to the forest, and the forest was all around them. As each blind wanderer approached, the thicket would open, admitting

90

a new victim to whatever unholy world lay beyond. And where Stead and Grimya had fallen through into that world when the trees parted for Chari, so Indigo and her companions meant to follow the next sleeper who left Bruhome, and break through in their turn.

They gathered by the fire to make their farewells. Everyone was present, even Gen, who had recovered and showed no sign of her injury but for a light bandage tied rakishly about her head. Esty, self-conscious in a shirt and trousers borrowed from Indigo – she had declared that skirts were impractical for such a venture – hugged everyone in turn, saving a special kiss for little Piety, then made a show of checking the bag of provisions slung over her shoulder so that no one would see her uncertainty. Forth was falsely cheerful, telling the younger ones to be sure to make up a song about their exploits and challenging Cour to learn a complicated pipe tune on his hurdy-gurdy during their absence. Indigo felt she could say nothing, but when Rance and Honi, emotion overcoming shyness, ran to her and hugged her, she held tight to them for as long as she could before stepping back. Then, all too hastily, the last words were said and the last kisses exchanged, and the three left the meadow and the diminishing group of waving figures beside the fire, and set their faces towards the town.

They'd gone no more than twenty yards before a shout halted them. Turning, Indigo saw Cour signalling wildly and pointing back towards the river: Forth drew a sharp breath, and she realised that another figure was moving up behind them.

'Earth Mother!' Forth said softly. 'It's an omen – it *has* to be!'

The travellers who had tried to leave Bruhome in the wake of the storm had all returned, sobered and cowed by what they had encountered outside the town. Most had sought the comfort of the local taverns, but after the abortive meeting in the square some had slunk back to the meadow encampment to wait fearfully for whatever might befall. Now, someone had emerged from a tent close to the river bank, and the moment she saw him Indigo knew that he had fallen prey to the sickness, and was now following the dreadful, inevitable compulsion that had carried off so many before him. She and her companions froze, and the man walked up to them and past them and on to the gate, staring fixedly ahead, unaware of anything around him.

'Follow him.' Forth's voice was an eager, tense whisper. 'Quickly. Don't let him get out of sight!'

Indigo saw fear in Esty's eyes, but said nothing. She looked back at the camp again as the three of them started after the sleepwalker, and signalled a last acknowledgement to Cour, who stood alone and a little apart from the others. She raised a hand in thanks for the warning, and he returned the gesture. But he looked bereft.

The entranced man turned northward from the meadow gate, taking, ironically, the same road that Chari had done. Indigo hoped the direction might be a good omen, though experience had taught her to be sceptical and she wasn't about to place any reliance on the hope. Even if they entered the forest world at precisely the same point where Grimya, Chari and Stead had disappeared, the chances of being able to track them were remote; and if they did find them, what then? She hadn't yet dared to consider that question.

The walker ahead was moving surprisingly fast, and keeping up with him wasn't easy in the darkness despite the lantern Forth carried. Indigo could hear Esty muttering under her breath in time to her own steps; she wasn't sure whether the words were a walking rhyme or a charm against ill luck. There was no one else on the road and an eerie quiet hung over the land, intensified rather than relieved by the quick shuffle of their footfalls. Nothing moved in the rank grass by the side of the track, no other sound disturbed the stillness. Fanciful though the thought might be, Indigo felt that the land was holding its breath, waiting for some unspecified but certain event.

When they caught the first glimpse of the black trees blocking the way ahead of them all three halted instantly. Esty, who hadn't encountered the monstrous forest before, stared at the thicket in awed silence, but

Indigo's chagrin – and Forth's, she saw when she glanced at him – had a different and more alarming cause.

The forest had moved. Even a few hours ago, when they'd tracked Chari along this very road, they had travelled, by Indigo's calculation, at least another half-mile before coming upon the dark wall of trees; and on the day of the storm, when they'd set out on the abortive mission to the next town, the forest had been a good number of miles away. Now though, it was clear that it was encroaching, closing in on Bruhome as a snare might slowly strangle its captive. How long, Indigo asked herself in trepidation, would it be before the supernatural wood reached the town itself, and engulfed it?

Forth, who had had the same thought, said tersely, 'We daren't let ourselves consider it, Indigo. We *have* to go on.'

She nodded, and Esty said sharply, 'He's going up to the trees!'

The sleepwalker had almost reached the thicket, and directly before him the thorns were starting to agitate. Their malevolent clicking sent a chill through Indigo and she turned to her companions.

'Esty, take our hands, quickly!' Their fingers linked, Esty between Indigo and Forth. 'We'll only have a few seconds – now, *run!*'

They raced towards the sleepwalker, who gave no sign that he was aware of their presence, and as the black tunnel in the forest yawned open, Indigo made a grab for his sleeve. At the sight of the gaping darkness, Esty's courage suddenly faltered; she uttered a frightened whimper and tried reflexively to pull back, and for a precarious moment Indigo thought she'd lose her grip on their quarry. But then Forth lunged forward, snatching desperately at a handful of the man's shirt. The lantern swung wildly as he tried to hold on to it and the walker together; the four of them swayed, teetered: then momentum carried them forward – and as the sleepwalker stepped into the tunnel that had opened like a devourer to welcome him, they plunged through the thorns in his wake.

'We're through!' Forth's cry was a hoarse yell of triumph. 'We've done it, we're – '

As though an entire world had opened its mouth and roared, a shattering tumult of noise hit them like a wall. Indigo reeled backwards, losing her contact with Forth and Esty as she jammed the heels of both hands against her ears in a frantic but useless effort to block out the din. Voices – thousands upon thousands of mad, unhuman voices, shrieking, howling, laughing, battering and buffeting her from all directions as she twisted wildly from side to side like a terrified animal in a trap. Her mouth was open but she made no sound; she could only gag and gasp. The titanic din rose to a crescendo and she fell on her knees, on her face, writhing blindly in the blackness.

'*Stop! Oh, make it stop!*' Someone else screeched close by her ear and she felt hands clawing at her. Indigo clung to her invisible companion, neither knowing nor caring who it was, and in the mindlessness of pain and shock she too began to cry out in protest.

The appalling noise started to diminish. At first the change didn't register on Indigo's stunned brain, but suddenly the part of her that still hung frantically on to a vestige of reason realised that the howling din was receding. She could even hear her own voice through the tumult, and her screams broke off in a racking gasp as she struggled to raise herself from the ground. A hand pulled her up and in the darkness she made out the dim oval of Esty's shocked face.

'Esty – ' But she had no chance to say anything more before the vile noise started to swell towards them again, roaring out of the blackness. Suddenly, a spark of angry memory fused with intuition in Indigo's mind, and she realised what was happening. A trick – a warped trick, to stun the unwary, to cow them, to batter their minds – and she clasped Esty's shoulders, shaking her violently.

'*Shout!*' Her voice was only just audible over the howling that rose like a tidal wave around them. 'Esty, *retaliate!* Scream back at it – now, *now!*'

Esty didn't comprehend, but she was too terrified to do anything but obey. They began to yell at the bellowing

94

darkness, shrieking, screeching, hurling words, sounds, anything their lungs and throats could muster, against its terrible onslaught. For a hideous moment Indigo thought she'd been wrong, and that the ploy wouldn't work: but then, perceptibly, the noise began to ebb once more.

'Keep shouting!' She howled the words with all her strength. 'Don't stop; whatever you do, don't stop!'

They screamed like banshees in shrill disharmony. Now Esty too was beginning to understand, and her voice took on a furious edge as indignant anger replaced her fear. Twice the howling tried to swell again, but their cries beat it back: then there was a third voice joining with theirs, as Forth, belatedly realising what was afoot, added his yells to lend them more power. And finally came the moment when Indigo realised that all other sound had ceased.

She held up her hands, and as their cries fell away there was utter silence. It lasted only a moment before Esty succumbed to a fit of coughing and turned aside, thumping a clenched fist against her own breastbone and swearing volubly between the racking spasms.

Indigo rocked back on her heels, shoulders heaving as she regained her breath. When she was recovered enough to speak, she looked up and said, weakly but heartfeltedly, 'Thank you!'

Esty gave one last, convulsive cough, then wiped her mouth and raised her head to meet Indigo's eyes. 'Great Mother!' she said hoarsely. 'I promise I'll never complain of having to sing for too long again!'

The spark of humour was grotesque in the circumstances, but none the less Indigo felt tension ebb a little. 'Lucky for us that we discovered in time how to stop it,' she said.

'Lucky for us that you knew what to do, you mean.' Esty rubbed at her sore throat, then her hand fell away. 'How *did* you know?'

Indigo hunched her shoulders and looked around her. Though the darkness was intense, she thought that she could just make out faint differences in the shades of blackness, the suggestions of tall trees crowding about them. There was grass beneath them, peculiarly dry but grass nonetheless. That much, at least, was physically real and stable. And by good fortune they seemed to have stumbled clear of the thorns . . .

'I didn't know,' she admitted. 'It was simply an intuition. But,' she shivered, 'I've seen something like this world before. It didn't look the same, but it had the same feel, the same atmosphere. It was a world of illusions; and I learned there how dangerous illusions can be. Then, when the noise struck us, I thought, even if this isn't real, it could still drive us insane or worse, and I was too terrified to do anything but scream.'

'And when you screamed, it began to fade,' Forth said thoughtfully.

'Yes. That was what gave me the idea, the hope. I was trying to turn it back on itself – to reply to it, but matching illusion with reality.' Her eyes hardened. '*I* was real. It wasn't. That was what I told myself. *I* was real.'

'And it worked.' Forth let out a soft, hissing breath.

'Yes. This time, it worked.' Another shiver racked her, but she had to say what was in her mind. 'Next time, though, we may not be so fortunate.'

For perhaps half a minute no one said any more. Then, without warning so that Esty started like a nervous animal, Forth stood up.

'Well,' he said, and in the muffling darkness his voice sounded oddly remote. 'One thing's for sure: we've broken through into the forest, but there's nothing to be gained from staying where we are.' He looked down at Indigo and despite his effort at leadership she sensed his uncertainty and the still-lurking fear. 'Do you have any idea which way we should go?'

The question, Indigo thought, might have made her laugh under other circumstances. The darkness was so acute that even with their eyes adjusted to the perpetual night she doubted if they could see any obstacle more than a handsbreadth away. The sleepwalker on whose heels they had been catapulted into this eerie world was gone; oblivious to the dreadful cacophony that had assailed them, or even in some bizarre way commanded by it, he had vanished into the forest's depths, and they wouldn't find him again. They had no clues, no trails to follow, nothing but their wits to guide them.

She rose to her feet, brushing her clothes down. 'Firstly,' she said, 'I think we should look to our belongings and see if anything's been lost. The lantern, for instance –'

Forth smacked the heel of his hand against his forehead. 'Damn my stupidity, the *lantern*!' He turned, feeling in the surrounding grass with one foot. 'I must have dropped it after we came through; I'd forgotten – ah!' Something metallic rattled and he swooped like a hunting hawk. 'Here!' He fumbled with the sliding glass side, feeling for the stump of candle within. 'It's still in one piece. Must have gone out when I dropped it.'

Indigo rummaged in her belt-pouch for flint and tinder. Flint scraped in the blackness; a tiny flame kindled, shifted, and the lantern-candle flared into life, creating a small circle of illumination that brought their faces into sudden, startling relief.

Forth rose, lifting the lantern high, and the light spilled over their immediate surroundings. As Indigo had surmised, they were on the edge of a dense wood, which seemed to be composed of huge, black-trunked trees rising out of thick undergrowth. The leaf canopy overhead was impenetrable and unnaturally still; there were no small movements of birds or animals, no sounds, nothing to disturb the silence. She looked over her shoulder, and shivered as she saw that no more than two paces behind them was a hedge of thorns more than twice her own height, a forest of dark spears glinting evilly in the lamplight. The fact that one or more of them hadn't been impaled during the chaos following their arrival was little short of a miracle, and instinctively she drew back, away from the barrier. Whatever else befell them, they couldn't go that way: which left the wood itself.

'I wonder how far it extends?' She spoke more to herself than to the others, but Forth looked at her keenly. 'The forest? It doesn't really matter, does it? There's no other direction we can take.'

Esty said uneasily, 'We don't know what might be in

97

there. Wild animals could be the least of it.' She fingered the sheathed knife at her belt.

'Well, we won't find out unless we look.' Forth, Indigo suspected, was forcing himself to sound more confident than he felt. 'Maybe we can find a path or some such.' He raised the lantern higher still and took a cautious step towards the trees, then another – and suddenly Esty grabbed Indigo's arm.

'Indigo! The light!'

As Forth stepped forward, the lantern had abruptly dimmed, its glow losing its yellow warmth and fading to a sickly, colourless glimmer. Forth froze, stared at it in horror. Then he took a pace back, and immediately the lantern brightened.

'Forth, come back!' Esty cried.

Forth held up his free hand. 'No,' he said. 'Wait.' Again he moved forward; again the lantern dimmed. He stopped, peered into the wood for a moment, then turned quickly and beckoned to them.

'Indigo – Esty – come here, quickly!'

They hastened to join him, and he pointed into the crowding trees. 'Look. There's light. It's very faint, but I'm sure I'm not imagining it!'

Indigo narrowed her eyes and saw that he was right. A dim and apparently sourceless greyish glow was filtering among the leaves in the distance.

'Take another step forward,' Forth said, 'and watch what happens.'

Puzzled, Indigo obeyed him – and the faraway glow grew fractionally brighter. Forth said: 'Now watch the lantern,' and moved up to join her. She drew in a sharp breath as the candle immediately dulled to a colourless ember, and suddenly she understood.

'We're in some kind of borderland, aren't we?' Forth's voice was tense. 'Half in one world, half in another. We can't truly see into this otherworld until we step completely out of our own. And when we *do* step out . . . well, it's what you were saying about reality. Once we leave our world behind it isn't real any more.'

'And so artefacts from our world become less real, and lose their strength.' The theory made sense, and Indigo was surprised by Forth's insight when he had so little knowledge of dimensions beyond the physical plane of Earth. But before she could say anything more, Esty spoke up.

'Does this mean . . . ' There was a slight tremor in her voice; she looked nervously from one to the other. 'Does this mean that . . . *we're* not real, either?'

Indigo considered this for a moment. She recalled the sleepwalkers, the dying crops, the overwhelming sense that something was feeding upon Bruhome, sucking the life from it like marrow from a bone. Even a demon couldn't sustain itself on nothing.

'No,' she said at last to Esty. 'We're still real enough, and so is every living thing that finds its way into this world.'

But the thought that accompanied her words was far less reassuring. For the demon would surely find them, as it would find the sleepwalkers and their lost companions. And if it fed upon life, then the lives of three souls who had entered its realm of their own volition and by their own will might be a more desirable prospect than most.

Chapter VIII

They set off into the wood in single file, moving slowly and cautiously. Indigo had unslung her crossbow and nocked a bolt; after the incident with the lantern she doubted whether the weapon would be of any use, but the solid feel of it in her hands was reassuring.

The dim glow strengthened as they advanced, until it was possible to see their surroundings as though through a heavy, moon-drenched fog. Still the silence was uncanny; the air didn't stir and not a single leaf moved among the branches. Forth insisted on leading; Indigo had been reluctant but at last gave way, not wanting to waste energy arguing with him and privately reasoning that she could at least keep a watchful eye on her companions if she walked behind them. Once, she looked over her shoulder, and saw that the thorn hedge had vanished, leaving only the crowding trees that seemed to stretch back into infinity. She wasn't entirely surprised; the thorns had been a part of the indistinct border between their own world and this, and now that they had penetrated the no-man's land that straddled the two dimensions, their reality and all it contained was truly lost to them. The thought was discomfiting, for it begged the question of how they would find their way back, and she decided not to draw her companions' attention to what she'd seen, but to continue on in silence.

For some while no one spoke; then Esty, who still jinked at every shadow, looked back at Indigo with an apologetic yet hopeful attempt at a smile.

'It's silly,' she said, 'but I want to sing. Just to hear a voice. Anything.'

Forth glanced back, his expression scathing, but before he could speak Indigo forestalled him.

'Why not?' Their progress through the undergrowth was noisy enough to have alerted anything that might be lurking in the vicinity to their presence; a song would make no difference and might help boost all their spirits. 'If I could handle my harp and crossbow at the same time, I'd accompany you.'

'Forth's got his pipe.' Esty gave her brother a wicked look. 'I saw him packing it.'

Forth flushed. 'That was in case of need, not – '

'Need?' Esty laughed, too loudly. 'What were you going to do with it, Forth? Though mind, your playing's probably enough to scare the demons away!'

Forth stopped and turned, ready to make a furious retort, and Indigo snapped,

'Esty! Forth! For the Mother's sake, will you stop quarrelling over something so trivial?' Then she drew breath, quelling her anger, and continued more quietly. 'If Esty wants to sing, I can see no harm in it; in fact it might cheer all of us. And if you can play while you walk, Forth, so much the better.'

Forth snorted and turned away, but the reprimand had gone home and he said nothing. Esty, unabashed, started to hum a tune which Indigo recognised as one of the younger children's chorus-pieces, lively and lilting. After a few bars, gathering courage, she began to sing the words, and Indigo joined in. Their voices sounded strangely toneless; the wood gave back no echoes and the effect was disconcerting, but better, Indigo thought, than the oppressive silence. As she'd hoped, Forth finally relented, drew his reed-pipe from his pack and put it to his lips.

'Come on, Forth,' Esty said when no trilling whistle joined in with the song. 'We've known this one since we could barely toddle! Play the descant.'

Forth stopped walking and turned to face them. 'I am playing the descant,' he said pallidly. 'Or at least, I'm trying to.'

Indigo stared at him, Esty, not yet comprehending, muttered irritably about blocked reeds, but her brother shook his head.

'There's nothing wrong with the pipe. Nothing at all.'

He held it out, and now anger suffused the unease in his eyes. 'Here. See for yourself if you don't believe me.'

Esty took the pipe and turned it over in her hands, frowning. When she put it to her lips and blew, there was only the sound of her exhaled breath. She tried again, harder, then looked fearfully from Forth to Indigo.

'It won't work . . .'

'Like the lantern.' Forth's voice was grim and he held the lamp up for emphasis. The candle had by this time dimmed to a feeble, bluish pinpoint, no brighter than a glow-worm. 'And your crossbow, Indigo. What would happen, do you think, if you tried to fire it? Or tried to play your harp?'

She acknowledged his meaning with a grave nod, but Esty protested angrily. 'It doesn't make any sense! *Why* won't the pipe play? If we can still sing, then surely –'

'Don't look for sense,' Forth said sourly. 'Not here.'

He was learning fast, Indigo thought. To Esty, she said, 'He's right. The rules of our world don't apply in this place. We're going to have to learn the new rules as we go along.'

'If there are any,' Forth added.

Indigo glanced obliquely at him. 'Oh, I think there will be. But whether or not we'll be able to recognise them might be another matter.' She looked down at the crossbow still poised in her hands, and decided – irrationally? – against shouldering it. 'We'd best go on. And if all we can do is sing, well then, let's sing.'

'Yes!' Esty agreed fiercely, and swung round, glaring up at the trees. 'D'you hear? D'you *hear*? We're not afraid of *you*!'

Indigo laid a restraining hand on her arm. 'No, we're not. But all the same, I think it would be as well not to issue our challenges too loudly as yet.'

They continued on their way, but Esty was no longer in a mood to sing, and so the only sound to sully the quiet was the rustling of their progress through the undergrowth. Time in the forest's unchanging gloom was meaningless, and if hours were passing at all it was impossible to estimate their number; but eventually Indigo began to tire. She hadn't slept since the few

102

snatched hours after the storm, and knew that the others had fared no better: they, too, must be flagging though neither would be first to admit it. And she was hungry. There was no point in trudging doggedly and endlessly on for the sake of it, and she called out to her companions, suggesting that they should look for a suitable spot to make camp and rest for a while. Esty concurred thankfully, but Forth was dubious.

'Camp here, among the trees?' he said. 'I don't know . . . I don't like the idea. I'd rather be somewhere where there's some kind of vantage point.'

'So would I; but we might walk for days without reaching the edge of the forest.' If there was an edge . . . 'We're all weary, Forth, and we can't go on indefinitely.' She smiled thinly. 'I assure you, I'm as reluctant as you are to stop here, but I don't see that we have a choice.'

Forth chewed his lower lip. 'Just a little further, then,' he said, ignoring Esty's groan. 'Maybe there'll be a clearing. We've passed one or two already.' Suddenly he grinned at her. In the cold half-light the grin looked ghastly. 'Or maybe I'll change our luck. Da always says I'm the luckiest one of the family.'

Indigo nodded. 'All right; just a little further. But we'll have to rest soon.'

Forth turned and walked on. He'd gone no more than ten yards when abruptly he stopped again, holding up a hand to halt the others. Esty hissed in a sharp breath and Indigo whispered, 'What is it?'

'Remember what I said about luck?' There was an odd catch in Forth's voice. 'I think I might have been right. Look – look ahead, maybe another twenty paces.'

They looked, and Esty said softly, 'I don't believe it . . .'

'Then you're blind to what your eyes are telling you!' Forth broke into a run, forging ahead of them, then stopped once more, signalling with one arm and shouting back, 'I *was* right! Come and look!'

Indigo and Esty hastened after him, and stumbled to a halt at his side. Even in the tricky twilight there could be no mistake – a mere few paces ahead of them, the forest ended. The trees didn't gradually thin and peter out; they

103

simply stopped, as though some gigantic scythe had swathed a sharp, clean line through the forest. And beyond the last black trunks, dimly visible like a grey and misty ocean, was open ground.

Esty let out a shriek of delighted relief and hugged her brother, while Indigo looked at Forth with renewed interest, wondering if he realised just how significant his wry joke might have been. Lucky . . . perhaps he was. Or perhaps, unconsciously, he had exerted an influence over their surroundings, imposing his will over the will of whatever power governed this bizarre land. The thought that such a thing might be possible both excited and disturbed her, and she judged that it might be wiser to say nothing to Forth of her suspicions. Not yet; not until she could test the ground a little further.

Forth and Esty were running on ahead of her and by the time she caught up with them they had reached the edge of the trees. Esty, leaning against one of the massive trunks, simply stared mutely at the vista before them, while Forth ventured a pace or two beyond the leaf canopy before halting. His head turned slowly as he surveyed the landscape, and at last he said softly,

'It's like the fell country around Bruhome. But . . .'

'Dead.' Esty spoke with quiet emphasis. 'No colour. No life. Nothing.' She shivered and pushed herself away from the tree, hugging her upper arms. 'There isn't even a wind.'

Indigo gazed at the land that spread away from the forest's edge like something from an eerie dream. Dark and brooding under the coldly diffused nightglow, it was, as Forth had tried to say, almost a parody of the Bruhome fells. But the slopes were steeper and the scarps more angular, creating deep hollows that fell away into hard-edged shadows black in sharp contrast to the softer, silvered undulations of the hills.

She shifted her gaze to where, at an unguessable distance that might have been one mile or twenty, the land met the featureless pewter bowl of the sky. The horizon was etched with a thin silver-grey shimmer, like the herald of moonrise, but she knew instinctively that there was no moon here. Overhead the sky was uniform,

104

featureless: there was no sign of the source from which the dim light emanated, no stars, no faint shadow of cloud. *No colour, no life*, Esty had said. Not a sign of movement anywhere in the empty land.

Forth, whose thoughts had been running in a similar direction to her own, said quietly, 'At least here we can see anything that might be abroad.'

'Yes . . . ' Indigo shut her eyes momentarily and shook her head to clear it; the nightscape had an oddly hypnotic effect, and she was glad to refocus her vision on the grass at her feet. Black grass. No colours but black and grey and silver . . . She pushed uneasy thoughts of the significance of silver from her mind, and set down her crossbow, unslinging the pack she carried on her back. 'It's as good a place as we're likely to find. The trees for cover if we should need it; but as you say, we'll see anything that might approach before it sees us.'

'I don't think anything will,' Esty said sombrely. 'I don't think there *is* anything here. Only us.'

Forth flashed her a sharp look. 'And Da, and Chari, and Grimya. And all those others. Don't ever forget that, Esty. Not for a moment.'

She glanced up resentfully. 'That wasn't what I meant, and you know it.'

To Indigo's relief Forth didn't press the point; either he'd taken her earlier admonition to heart, or he was too tired to argue. He dumped his burdens on the ground, and looked about him.

'There's enough dead leaves and debris to make a fire,' he said. 'Do you think it would light? Or will our flints and tinders fail, like the pipe and the lantern?'

'I don't know.' Indigo fingered her belt pouch. 'It's worth trying.'

Forth gathered a double armful of leaves and fallen twigs – leaves did die in this world it seemed; suggesting that there must be seasons of sorts – and heaped them on the grass. Then he struck flint and tinder.

Nothing happened. The flint scraped, overloud in the silence, but there was no answering spark. Forth tried a second and a third time, then sat back on his heels, shaking his head.

'It won't work. I was afraid that might happen.'

'Try again.' Esty urged.

'No.' Indigo held out a hand as Forth made to strike once more. 'Let me.' She met his eyes in the gloom, and smiled faintly. 'Maybe this time I'll be the lucky one.'

Forth shrugged and handed the tinder-box over. Indigo held it before the leaf-pile. *Concentrate*, she told herself silently. *Forth willed the forest to end, and it ended. You can succeed in this. Will it. Make it happen.*

'There's a spark!' Esty said eagerly. Indigo struck again; the second spark caught the dry leaves, and a tiny tongue of flame began to lick at the pile's edge. Esty squealed with delight and hunched over the precious fire, cupping her hands around it and breathing gently, expertly on the flame to encourage it, and Forth stared at Indigo.

'How did you do it?'

She sat back on her heels, only a little less surprised than he was. 'I'm not quite sure,' she said. 'I was remembering how we came upon the edge of the wood – and before that, how we defeated that howling voice – and I wondered if – '

She was interrupted by an exclamation from Esty. The outer leaves of the pile were beginning to crackle and curl, and Esty had straightened, triumphant, as the fire took hold – only to freeze abruptly.

'The flames are the wrong colour!' Elation turned to chagrin as she called out. 'Look at them – they're *blue*!'

Indigo and Forth stared at the fire. The flames appeared to be burning normally, but instead of a cheerful yellow light, all they gave off was a cold, colourless flicker, while the bright tongues at the fire's heart were tinged a sickly blue-green.

For a long, silent moment they all continued to gaze at the flames, and then, cautiously, Esty stretched out one hand. Her face was eerily lit, her spread fingers looked like those of a corpse; she turned her hand this way and that, then looked up at the others.

'It isn't even hot. I can't feel anything, and it should be scorching me by now. See, I can put my hand right into – *aah!*' As she spoke, Esty had reached out to touch the flames, and she leapt back with a yell of pain, jamming her hand under her armpit.

'Esty!' Indigo hastened to her side.

'It b-*burned*.' Esty stammered the words out between clenched teeth. 'I thought – ohh, that *hurts*!'

'Let me see.' Indigo had medicinal herbs and salves in her pouch, relics of the small wisecraft skills she'd learned as a child, and carefully she took Esty's wrist, turning the injured hand to examine it. The skin of the fingertips was red and already blistering; however little light and heat the unnatural fire might be giving off, it cerrtainly burned like any ordinary flame. Indigo started to smear salve from a small phial on to Esty's fingers, then from the corner of her eye saw Forth approach the fire, a hand outstretched.

'Forth, be careful!'

'Don't worry; I shall. But Esty's right. Even a hands-breadth away from the flames, I can't feel any heat.'

Indigo didn't reply, but returned her mind to the conundrum. Esty hadn't expected to be burned, yet the fire had seared her. That made a mockery of the theory she'd begun to formulate and had been about to expound to Forth, and emphasised her earlier comment about the laws of this world being irrational and unpredictable. This incident served as both confirmation and warning; and she resolved to be vigilant in even the smallest matters from now on. Step by careful step. Or the consequences of the next mistake might not be so trivial.

Under the circumstances, Indigo was relieved to find that Esty's accident had put the puzzle of the fire out of Forth's mind. She didn't raise the subject again, but finished salving Esty's hand and, grouped around the strange, flickering light of the fire they ate a spartan meal from their rations. Forth rigged a tripod over the fire and tried to boil a pan of water; but time passed, the water remained cold, and eventually he gave up the attempt and carefully poured the pan's contents back into his water-skin.

Disappointed by the fact that there could be no hot brew to complete the makeshift feast, they considered their next move.

'The trouble is,' Forth said morosely, scraping at the grass with a short length of twig, 'we don't know how far this land extends. Da and Chari could be anywhere.' He looked up. 'How can we ever hope to find them? That's the question I keep asking myself.'

'I know.' Indigo gazed beyond the fire's dull circle to the sweep of grey moorland and fell reaching away into the distance. 'I'd hoped we might be able to track the sleepwalker we followed: if he was being drawn towards some central place, Chari might have followed the same path.'

'Or any other sleepwalker, for that matter.' Forth's eyebrows knitted together. 'I'd have thought we might have seen some sign or another. The Harvest Lady knows there were enough who fell prey to the sickness.'

'Indeed; and I can't answer that conundrum either. But there's one thread of hope. If Grimya hasn't become separated from the others, then there's a chance – just a chance, mind you – that I might be able to make mental contact with her.'

'Have you tried?' Forth's gloom lifted a fraction as he grasped at the thought, then sank again as Indigo nodded.

'Only tentatively, while we were walking, and there was nothing. But I couldn't give it my full concentration. Later, while I'm watching, I'll try again.'

'What about your stone?' Esty asked. 'The one you told us about? Might that give us a clue?'

Indigo drew the lodestone from its pouch and held it towards the fire, the others craning to see. In the chilly glow the golden pinpoint looked dull and uncertain; it was pointing out over the fells, but even as they looked it shivered and darted first to the left and then to the right before settling at the pebble's centre.

Esty said: 'What does that mean?' and Indigo shrugged.

'Either the lodestone can't function in this world, or it's telling us that the demon is all around us.' She slipped the stone back into the leather bag and pushed down the ice spiders that were crawling on her spine. 'Neither prospect is very comforting.'

108

There was thoughtful silence for a while. Then Forth said:

'Well, it looks as though we've no option but to keep searching until we find some clue to where they've gone.'

'If we ever do,' said Esty.

'No.' Indigo laid a hand on the girl's arm, troubled by the fact that her earlier optimism seemed to have slipped away so quickly. 'Don't start to think in that way, Esty, whatever you do. We *have* to believe that we'll find them.'

Forth gave her a probing look, but she didn't respond. This wasn't the moment to return to her idea concerning this world's malleability; it was embryonic at best and she needed more time to think it through – not to mention more evidence – before anything was said. Besides, at this moment sleep was more important than talk. She was feeling soporific in the wake of the food, and had seen both Forth and Esty yawning surreptitiously behind their hands. In the morning – she checked herself, realising that the reflex phrase had no meaning here – in a few hours they'd be fresher and could look at their predicament with clear minds. Until then, there was nothing more to be said.

With no way of measuring the time, they had agreed on a pragmatic solution to the problem of keeping watch. Indigo would sit the first vigil (Forth had argued, wanting to take the responsibility himself, but her will had prevailed) and when she felt she could no longer trust herself to stay awake, she would rouse her relief. So, as Forth and Esty settled down with their heads pillowed on their packs, she fed more leaves to the fire and stared out across the eldritch, silent nightscape.

Grimya? Her thoughts reached out into the dark, and she listened in her mind for an answering flicker of acknowledgement. Only the deep quiet and the ripples of her own uneasy consciousness answered, and she sighed. The hope was so slender, so frail. Even if Grimya could sense her presence she might be unable to answer, though that was a possibility Indigo didn't want to dwell on. And Stead and Chari. Were they still alive? Were they wandering helplessly in this world, or had something come out of the dark, out of the silence, to claim them and to drain their lives, as the crops had been drained of life in Bruhome?

Indigo was overtaken suddenly by a miserable surge of despair as she asked herself how she and her friends could ever find their lost ones in this benighted world. There was nothing here: nothing to aid them, nothing to sustain them, nothing to give them hope. Only the dead land and its darkness, and no road to lead them forward or back. They were as lost as those they'd so foolishly set out to save; lost, like the sleepwalkers, in a nightmare from which there'd be no awaking . . .

A deep-rooted warning bell sounded suddenly in her mind, and with a small shock Indigo saw the trap into which she'd so nearly fallen. Despair. Isolated and lonely, with no one awake to distract her, she'd come close to allowing herself to slip into a dreamlike miasma, seduced by the atmosphere that pervaded this colourless world. The gloom, the empty land, the leaden silence – they were lures working on a tired and unwary mind, drawing her subtly towards the same snare that had caught the sleepwalkers of Bruhome. Despair, and apathy. They were the watchwords of this dimension, the fountainheads of its strength, its greatest weapons. And she had almost succumbed to them.

'*No!*' Indigo hissed the word softly but savagely, and, before reason could get the better of her, thrust her left hand straight at the fire's blue flames. Scorching pain flared in her fingertips and she swore, biting her lip hard and snatching the hand back to slam it down on the grass. It burned agonisingly, but the ploy had worked, breaking the insidious influence. Indigo looked about her quickly, angrily, as though half-expecting to see some disappointed shade slinking away, and groped in her pouch for the salve she'd earlier used on Esty's fingers.

Then paused.

Will. The thought came to her abruptly, perhaps goaded by her angry reaction to the demon world's effort to ensnare her mind. Because of what had happened to Esty, she'd believed that her hand would be burned. Yet the unnatural flames had no true heat; water had refused to boil, and it was only when Esty had touched the fire

110

itself that she had felt pain. Indigo frowned and, trying not to wince, raised her injured hand to examine it. The skin was blistering, the nerves still sent agonised messages to her brain. But – she gathered mental strength, telling herself fiercely that it must be so – she was not burned. She was *not*. It was an illusion.

For a moment, in the cold firelight, it seemed that the blisters on her hand wavered and almost vanished altogether. Indigo concentrated harder. No burn, no pain. *Go*, she told the wound with silent determination.

And flexed an unmarked hand as the sting of agony faded and vanished.

Very softly, and with intense satisfaction, Indigo exhaled a long, slow breath. This was corroboration of her tentative theory, and she believed she was beginning to understand the bizarre nature of this dimension. Not fully as yet, and certainly not well enough to allow for complacency; but a few skeins of the mystery were unravelling, and, as she'd suspected, strength of will was the key. She glanced at Esty, who lay curled with her back to the fire, her scorched hand unconsciously hooked and resting on her other wrist to protect it from contact with the ground. With a little help Esty should be able to negate her own injury, and once the seeds of belief and confidence were sown in both her and Forth's minds they would have a valuable weapon to aid them.

Indigo flexed her hand with stern satisfaction, shifting her position and stretching her legs out before her to ease stiffness. She didn't feel tired now; that had vanished along with the creeping apathy, and she knew she'd stay awake for a good few hours yet, perhaps even until Forth or Esty woke naturally. A pity she didn't possess a spy-glass. Even in this dim light she would have liked to scan the landscape and study the finer detail that at this distance was invisible to the unaided eye.

Then, as she stared out at the dark fells, she heard a sound that made her stomach clench with the shock of familiarity. Far away, carrying with eerie clarity in the still air, a throaty yipping; rising, repeating, finally translating into the long, ululating howl of a wolf.

'*Grimya!*' Indigo sprang upright, almost overbalancing as one foot caught in the strap of her pack. Beside the fire there was a flurry of movement, and Esty sat up. 'Wha– ?'

The howl had died and vanished, bringing back silence, and Indigo swung to face Esty. 'Did you hear it?' she pleaded hoarsely.

Esty blinked. 'Great Mother, but you frightened me!' she said, then: 'Did I hear what?'

Indigo's heart pounded painfully beneath her ribs and her mouth felt very dry. 'A wolf.'

'A wolf? You mean, *Grimya*?' Esty scrambled to her feet and came to stand beside Indigo, peering across the tricky, silvered vista. 'Are you sure?'

Indigo nodded. For a few moments there was quiet as they both listened intently, but the distant cry didn't come again. Indigo had begun to shiver with reaction, and Esty took her arm, squeezing it soothingly.

'Sit down, Indigo. No point standing here like a pair of lallygaggers.'

Indigo obeyed, but distractedly. Then she gathered her wits and said, 'I'm sorry, Esty. I didn't mean to wake you.'

'Oh, it doesn't matter. I couldn't sleep properly anyway.' Esty glanced to where Forth still lay undisturbed. 'Not like him. Once he's away, you could put him inside a drum and start thumping it and he wouldn't stir. But . . . ' Her green eyes were abruptly serious. 'Are you *sure* you heard Grimya?'

Indigo looked quickly, defensively at her. 'I wasn't dreaming.'

'No, no; that's not what I meant. I meant, are you sure it was Grimya, and not – well, something else?'

The thought hadn't occurred to Indigo, and dismay showed in her face as she realised how foolish she'd been. She had jumped to the conclusion that the far-off, howling wolf could only be Grimya, but even her small knowledge and experience of this world should have warned her that such an assumption couldn't be trusted. It might just as easily have been an illusion. Or it might have been something more tangible. A wolf perhaps – that cry had been unmistakable – but a wolf which owed

112

its existence to this world, and not to the natural Earth.

Her shoulders sagged and she stared down at the black grass, feeling shamed. Esty patted her shoulder, then turned to rummage in her pack.

'I know what we both need.' She produced a small metal flask and shook it conspiratorially. 'Forth doesn't know I brought this. It's grain spirit. Good for the human spirit, too. And then I'll take over the watch, and you can have some sleep.'

Despite herself, Indigo smiled. 'You're very kind, Esty, but I'm not tired. And I couldn't sleep now.'

'Neither could I.' Esty uncorked the flask and sniffed it appreciatively. 'Well, then: at least I can keep you company.' She took a mouthful of the flask's contents and held it out. Indigo shook her head, and the girl re-corked the flask and settled down companionably beside her.

'D'you know,' she said after a pause, 'If it wasn't for the colour of the fire, I could almost believe that we were sitting round a proper camp, with the vans behind us and Chari cooking a good meal . . . ' Then she realised what she'd said and the forced cheerfulness evaporated. 'Oh, Indigo . . . '

'How does your hand feel now?' Indigo spoke up quickly. Mention of the fire had abruptly reminded her of her discovery, and she was anxious both to distract Esty and to test her theory.

'Ohh . . . it's all right, I suppose. Still hurts. But the salve helped.'

Indigo leaned forward. 'Esty, listen. While you were asleep, I – ' And she stopped as something rustled in the trees behind them.

Esty's head whipped round. '*What was that?*'

What Indigo had been about to say collapsed in the face of a tension which became palpable while they both stared hard at the dark wall of the forest. Indigo's hand had reached instinctively for her crossbow, Esty's for her knife. But whatever had disturbed the leaves was not, it seemed, about to show itself.

'I *did* hear it.' Esty's gaze slid furtively to Indigo's face. 'Didn't you?'

'Yes. But – '

'*There!*' Esty pointed as a low bough of one of the trees just beyond the forest perimeter dipped down and sprang back, as though something had forced it aside. There was a shadow, Indigo thought; a shadow that hadn't been there moments before.

'Wake Forth,' she said quietly. 'Hurry!'

Esty crawled away to shake her brother's shoulder, still looking fearfully back at the trees. 'Forth! Forth, wake up! There's – ' The hoarse whisper died in a gag of terror.

'Esty?' Indigo swung round, startled, and saw Esty crouched like a frozen statue. Her mouth was working spasmodically, but no sound came out. And her eyes were staring, bulging with inarticulate horror.

Suddenly, Esty screamed at the top of her voice. The scream was wild, insane, tearing from her throat in blind and insensate terror, and it brought Forth shouting from his sleep. Her mind buffeted between shock and her own fear of whatever Esty had seen, Indigo lurched towards the girl, then swung back in confusion, her stunned eyes focusing on the forest as something crashed among the leaves –

'Ahh, *no!*' The image smashed against her brain even as she heard the whistling exhalation that through a hundred childhood nightmares had heralded the malignant, dismal hooting of one of the most appalling horrors in Southern Isles mythology. Framed among the black trees she saw the one eye glaring from the huge, misshapen head, the single, distorted leg with its splayed foot thumping through the undergrowth, the gnarled arm reaching towards her to rend and rip, the mouth in the thing's fleshless chest puckering, working, drooling. She flung herself back, almost falling into the fire, and turned blindly, hands and feet scrabbling for purchase. Esty's screams dinned in her ears; then suddenly there was a sound like fabric tearing, a rush of displaced air, and Esty plunged past her, running like a deer before hounds away into the dark.

'Stop her!' It was Forth, Indigo realised through her own roiling terror, and his yell spun her back from the

114

whirlwind of panic. Footsteps thudded in the grass; hands grabbed her, dragging her to her feet –

And there was nothing in the forest. No reaching claw no drooling mouth, no hooting. Just the trees, silent and still.

Sanity came back in a dizzying rush and Indigo felt as though her legs were about to buckle under her. But Forth was oblivious to her state; he was already starting after Esty, dragging Indigo with him. Indigo stumbled in his wake, tripped, somehow stayed upright: then suddenly the fear of being left behind, alone, sent a surge of adrenalin through her and with it new energy, and she was racing desperately at Forth's side, following Esty's fleeing figure and shouting her name like a charm against evil.

Chapter IX

'I won't go back there!' Esty said savagely, through clenched teeth. 'I don't care if we leave everything to rot – I won't go!'

Forth released his grip on his sister's wrists and looked helplessly at Indigo. 'It's no use. She won't see reason.'

They had caught up with Esty on the slope of a gentle escarpment, had succeeded eventually in calming her, and sat now on the scarp edge, unwilling to look over the brink into the well of intense shadow below. Their camp fire was faintly visible in the distance – and with it were all their belongings.

Esty pulled her arms away from Forth's hold and sniffed, wiping her eyes on her remaining sleeve. Forth crumpled the other, which he'd torn away as he tried to stop her flight, and dropped it on the grass.

'Well, someone has to go back,' he said firmly.

'No, Forth!' Esty protested. 'You didn't *see* it – '

'Then I haven't got so much to fear, have I?'

'But it was the *Jachanine*! The hair, the teeth – and those *eyes*!'

'Wait.' Indigo spoke sharply, catching Forth's arm. '*What* did she say she saw?'

'The Jachanine,' Forth told her tersely. 'It's a troll that haunts pinewoods in our homeland. Our Mam used to tell us stories about it when we were little.' He repressed a shiver.

'What does it look like?'

Forth frowned. 'You saw it for yourself, didn't you?'

'I saw something. But I gave it another name.' She leaned forward so that Esty was less likely to hear her. 'We have tales in the Southern Isles of a demon called the Brown Walker. It's immensely tall and thin, and it has

116

one arm, one leg and one eye. Its mouth is in its stomach, and it hoots.' She tasted bile in the back of her throat as the image resurged in her mind, and forced it back. 'That was what I saw. Does it describe the Jachanine?'

'No.' Forth's eyes narrowed. 'So you and Esty didn't see the same thing, did you? She believed it was the Jachanine; you believed it was a Southern Isles demon. And I saw nothing at all. It wasn't real, then. It was another illusion.'

'Yes.' Indigo stared speculatively back towards their camp and the menacing wall of trees beyond. 'But what manner of illusion? That's what troubles me, Forth. Did we create it ourselves, out of our own imaginations? Or did some outside power see into our minds, and conjure the images to reflect our childhood fears?'

Forth uttered a soft imprecation and looked back at the forest, his eyes furtive with unease. 'By the Mother, that doesn't bear thinking about. It'd mean that this demon knows we're here, and it's watching us.' He glanced at her obliquely. 'Playing with us, perhaps.'

He echoed Indigo's own suspicions, and she said, 'I think we should go. There can be no question of returning to the campsite for any longer than it takes to retrieve our belongings: even if Esty was willing I don't think it would be wise. I believe we should move on, and quickly. If you and I fetch our things – '

Forth shook his head. 'I agree; but Esty won't wait here alone. One of us will have to stay with her. Better if I do the fetching.' In the dark his smile was a pallid but determined attempt at humour. 'I'm the fastest runner among us.'

Esty crept close to Indigo, gripping her hand tightly, and together they watched in some trepidation as Forth loped away over the turf towards the fire's fading light. As he bent to gather their possessions the forest canopy rustled suddenly and ominously. Indigo's pulse missed a painful beat, and Forth looked up quickly; but the trees quieted once more and he resumed his task, working rapidly and not stopping to stamp out the dying fire. When he returned, Esty hugged him wordlessly; then they all turned to look out at the shimmering, night-

117

drenched land that stretched away towards the distant horizon.

'There's a track, of sorts.' Indigo, whose night vision was sharper than average, pointed to where a ridge ran diagonally between two steep-sided vales. Along the crest, faintly and patchily phosphorescent in the deep gloom, was what might have been a narrow, uneven path.

'No way of telling where it leads,' Forth said dubiously.

'Away from the forest.' Esty cut in. 'That's good enough for me.'

In the distance, on the forest's edge, the dim blue flames of the fire still glowed. As they shouldered their packs, Indigo looked back and wondered whether that small, chilly light would eventually fade and die. The natural laws here were so unpredictable that the fire might well endure even with no fuel to sustain it: at least until the decay that seemed strangely and unpleasantly endemic in this bizarre world finally overcame it. She continued to gaze at the fire until she heard her name called, a tentative, puzzled query, and it broke the thrall of her musing. Forth and Esty were watching her, and Forth asked,

'Indigo? What's on your mind?'

She turned towards them, back to the dark sweep of the unknown land ahead. 'Nothing that won't keep for a while,' she told him, and made herself smile. 'Shall we go?'

Time and distance had no meaning as they walked through the silent night. The thin, phantasmic twilight didn't change, the fells and scarps and moors reached endlessly in all directions, and no landmarks were distinguishable from the surrounding barrenness. Tiredness had given way to an odd, dreamlike sense of inevitability, and even Indigo, who hadn't slept at all, felt that she could have trudged on under the featureless sky forever.

Esty had put the worst of her terrors behind her, but her courage had suffered a blow and she had been uncharacteristically subdued since they left the scarp. Indigo and Forth had explained the nature of the apparition in the woods, but it made little difference. What had happened once, Esty argued, could happen again. And there were far worse childhood nightmares than the Jachanine lying buried in her mind. What might the next phantom be? Another troll? A voracious pack of the Wichtlenen? Or even the Oaken Worm itself? Sharply, Forth told her to hold her tongue and stop being so foolish: did she want to invite further trouble? Though the names Esty had conjured meant nothing to her, Indigo could see that even Forth's determined bravado was shaken by them, and she intervened, anxious to change the subject before the fear became too contagious. Hoping to lift the prevailing mood, she told them of her experiment with the fire, and of how she had banished a burn on her own hand by believing that it couldn't exist. Esty was excited by the idea, and studied her scorched fingers with new interest.

'You mean that if I say I don't believe in it, it'll go away?'

'It's not quite that simple,' Indigo warned her. 'You can't merely say you don't believe: you must be *convinced* of it.'

Esty frowned, flexing her hand. 'But it still hurts. I don't see how I can stop believing it doesn't when it still does.'

'Try,' Indigo urged. 'Esty, this could be vital to us! If we can learn to manipulate the forces that are at work here – '

'Like the voice?' Esty's eyes lit.

'Exactly like the voice.' Indigo glanced at Forth, who nodded understanding. 'Try, Esty – please.'

But nothing happened. She had, perhaps, been expecting too much of Esty, Indigo told herself. Self-will was a subtle weapon even for the most skilled mind, and she had few illusions that she herself was anything but a poor practitioner: for the Brabazons this was new and untried territory, and wouldn't be easily conquered.

'Don't fret,' she told the frustrated girl. 'It will come, in time. You must be patient.'

119

They walked on. Esty still stared at her hand with determined concentration, and Forth too was preoccupied, so that for some while no one had anything to say. The ground was beginning to rise perceptibly, though the landscape was still an uneven patchwork of ridges and valleys: peering into the gloomy distance Indigo thought that a mile or so ahead – perspective was impossible to judge accurately – it changed to become high, flat moorland, which would make for easier going and also, possibly, give them a broader vista from where to plan their direction. Privately she admitted that she would be glad of the change, for the vales that yawned on either side of the ridge were beginning to unnerve her. Deep, silent and utterly lightless, they were more like pits than true valleys: they might reach down for ten feet or ten miles, and it was all too easy to imagine nameless horrors shifting down there in the blackness, sensing their presence and slithering up from the abyss in blind, mindless hunger. She thought of the Bruhome sleepwalkers, wondering with an unpleasant inward shudder how many of them might have stumbled, in the throes of their enchantment, into one of these gaping pits. The fact that thus far they had seen no trace of any of the forest's hapless victims added an extra dimension to her disquiet, but she kept her speculations to herself, not wanting to sow new seeds of fear in Forth's and Esty's minds.

The ground was still rising, becoming noticeably steeper now, and when they paused to rest for a moment on the gradient it was possible at last to see that Indigo's surmise had been right. A short way on, the land levelled out on to open moor; and where the ridge joined the moorland, a lone, gnarled tree stood, leaning at a drunken angle as though battered by prevailing gales.

The gradient increased abruptly, and they were forced to use their hands to scramble the final slope to the top. Reaching the top of the rise they straightened, breathless, and stared in awe at the new landscape stretching away before them.

The moor was vast and almost entirely featureless. A smooth black sward, patched only by the occasional tussock of rougher grass, reached away into immeasurable and unbroken distance. Far off was a will-o'-the-wisp gleam of phosphorescence; water or mist or something less natural, it was impossible to tell. There were no hills to speak of, no valleys, no trees. And, as before, not one sign of life.

'Great Mother,' Forth said with feeling.

Indigo made no comment, but she guessed what he was thinking. For all they could tell, it might be possible to walk forever across that bleak, unchanging plain without finding anything to guide or lead them towards their goal. Even with careful rationing their supplies of food and water were strictly limited, and though the unnatural laws of this dimension might enable them to survive without sustenance, she wouldn't care to put such a theory to the test.

The lone tree stood a few paces away to her left, and she went to examine it more closely. It was, she saw now, little more than a stunted bush, leafless and covered with small, sharp prickles, like a withered hawthorn. The scoured and leaning boughs seemed to point like a petrified finger, and when she sighted along them she saw that their direction aligned perfectly with the phosphorescent glimmer in the far distance. A hint? Or merely a misleading coincidence? Weighing the thought in her mind she idly fingered one of the black branches, then glanced down as a twig snapped off in her hand. The twig felt dry, brittle; for a moment only it retained its shape, then even as she looked at it, it crumbled to flakes of bark and dust.

Dead . . . Indigo raised her head and stared again at the faraway glimmer. Forth, who had moved to stand beside her, said, 'That way?'

'It's as good as any other,' Indigo replied. 'And that light may be significant.'

Forth shrugged. 'Whatever it signifies, it can't be any worse than what we've already passed. Those valleys . . . *ugh*.'

'You felt that, too?'

'Yes. I couldn't stop asking myself what would happen to anyone who missed their footing and fell from the track. It didn't make for pleasant thinking.'

'Well, we've only the moor to trouble us now. Let's hope it doesn't hide any deadly secrets.'

Forth nodded, then, quickly and a little surreptitiously, gripped her hand and squeezed it. 'So long as we're all together, eh?'

His face was faintly flushed and he was suddenly unwilling to meet her gaze directly. Indigo's heart sank. Not this, she thought; not Forth. They had sufficient problems; surely he must realise that there was no room for further complication? Gently but firmly she withdrew her hand and stepped away from him, putting a clear distance between them and hoping that her message would be conveyed without offence. 'Come on,' she said, not unkindly. 'We should be on our way.'

She glimpsed his face only briefly as she turned aside. He wore a peculiar expression in which embarrassment, hope, resolve and resentment all vied for precedence, and part of her wanted to stop, face him and say: *Forth, don't be foolish; put these notions out of your mind and don't even consider them again.* But she couldn't. The painful pride of Forth's nineteen years would neither understand nor accept such a rebuke; he was too young – and the fact that he believed her to be only a few years his senior added its own hollow irony to the dilemma. Forth would have to learn that the reality of their relationship couldn't mesh with what he saw in his imagination. But she could not be the one to teach him that lesson.

The way across the moor proved a good deal easier than the uneven and precarious track along the ridge. Though the path itself – real or imagined, Indigo still couldn't reach a conclusion – had vanished at the edge of the plateau, there were no pitfalls to make the way hazardous. Esty was trying to compensate for her earlier sombreness by being determinedly if artificially cheerful, at first launching into a flow of brittle, inconsequential chatter, then when neither Forth nor Indigo responded, singing a riddle-song to herself. Though she was reluctant to spoil Esty's mood, Indigo found that the singing jarred on her already taut nerves, and constantly had to crush an urge to look back over her shoulder lest anything might be following them. Everything was too quiet, too empty. Where *were* the sleepwalkers? They should surely have found some trace of them by now. Where could they possibly have gone?

They walked on. Esty still sang, though now the tune had changed to a bawdy ditty that Stead had long ago banned from the Brabazon Fairplayers' official repertoire. The peculiar glimmer seemed perceptibly closer now, no more than half a mile away, Indigo surmised; and she tried to listen to the acute silence that gripped the land in the moments between Esty's crude verses. Perhaps it was imagination, but she thought she could feel a growing tension in the moor's atmosphere. It was a little like the airless hush before a storm, but closer, more confined. A sense of *waiting*.

'Esty!' She had to listen to the atmosphere; needed to. 'Esty, I'm sorry, but could you – '

She didn't get any further. For out of the blackness beyond vision, far away across the moor, came the chilling, shivering howl of a wolf.

'By the Mother!' Forth stopped with a visible jolt and looked wildly about. 'What was *that*?'

Esty had cut off in mid-song, and stared at Indigo with wide eyes. 'Was it . . . ?' she began nervously.

The dying echoes of the howl were shivering away across the moor. 'I don't know,' Indigo whispered. 'But . . . ' *No*, something inside her said emphatically. *I know Grimya's voice, and that wasn't her. That was no flesh and blood wolf*. She wetted her lips. 'No. It wasn't Grimya.'

'Then there *are* other wolves out here.'

Other wolves. Indigo recalled the first time she'd heard that cry, while keeping vigil by the camp fire. They'd covered many miles of ground since then: and that made her suspect that this pack, whatever its form, whatever its nature, was following them; keeping a distance but tracking them none the less.

She looked quickly across the moor to where the thin patch of light glowed, now no more than five hundred yards away.

'It might be another illusion,' she said tensely, 'Another image drawn from our minds . . . '

'I wouldn't lay a wager on it,' Forth said. 'You were the one who warned us about the rules, remember? I think we should move from here, and fast!'

'Make for the light!' Esty pleaded. 'Even if there's no shelter there, I'll at least *feel* safer.'

It made sense. They were vulnerable in this semi-darkness; it would be all too easy for some silent denizen to creep up on them unseen. Light would give them an advantage, however small.

The unnatural night was silent again. There was no repetition of the howling as, wasting no words, they set off at a fast walk through the grass. The peculiar, ethereal glow drew closer, closer – then at last it was only a few yards ahead of them, and all at once the light's source was revealed.

All thoughts of wolves fled from Indigo's mind as she and her companions slowed, stopped and stared. Before them, cut into the moorland turf, was a still and perfectly circular pool. It was some twenty feet in diameter, and far too symmetrical to be natural – and the chill, eerie light seemed to be emanating from below the water's smooth surface, filtering up from a depth impossible to guess at and spilling out into the surrounding air. Around the pool's edge for a distance of some three paces – again, disturbingly symmetrical – the grass gave way to what looked like greyish-white shingle, as smooth and level as though some proud tender had recently raked it.

Esty was the first to move. Cautiously at first, then with growing confidence, she stepped to the edge of the shingle and tested it with a foot to see if it would bear her weight. It seemed to be only two layers deep, and the ground beneath was solid.

'Just shingle,' Esty said wonderingly. 'But why? What possible purpose could it serve?'

Even if her question had an answer, it would probably make no sense to them, Indigo thought. She crouched and picked up one of the pebbles that formed the shingle circle. It was smooth, surprisingly light, almost like pumice; and it felt neither warm nor cold. A neutral thing, lifeless. On an impulse she tossed it at the pool. It struck the surface with a small splash, and sank like any normal stone in normal water.

Forth, who had been watching her, said speculatively, 'I wonder if it's drinkable?'

'I wouldn't risk it,' Indigo cautioned. 'Even if it's not poisonous, it might affect us in ways we couldn't predict.'

'Yes . . . all the same, though,' Forth reached into his pack and pulled out a small boiling-can that, before the fiasco with the fire, had been intended as a cooking utensil. 'I'd like to look at it more closely.' Crossing the shingle, he crouched down by the pool's edge and, taking care not to touch the water with his bare hand, dipped the can in.

'It's so clear, the reflection's just like looking in a mirror,' he called back. 'If it wasn't for the ripples, you'd never believe it was water and not – Earth's blood, what's this?'

Startled by the sudden oath, Indigo and Esty looked up quickly, and Indigo said, 'What's wrong?'

'I don't think I believe it . . . come and look!'

They went to join him and peered at the can he held. It was empty – and the surface was quite dry.

'I dipped it in the water,' Forth insisted. 'Damn it, I saw the ripples, I saw the thrice-blasted thing *filling*!' He thrust the can at her. 'Try for yourself, and you'll see.'

Indigo leaned out over the pool and plunged the can under the surface. Ripples, as Forth had said; and water flowed over the lip. But when she lifted the can again, it was as though she drew it out from a mirage: it was dry, and empty.

Forth, on his knees now, reached towards the pool surface and, very tentatively, touched it. 'It *feels* like water,' he said uncertainly, and let his whole hand slip under to the first finger-joint. 'Wet, and cool.' He flipped the hand, and there was a splash, like a small fish jumping. Then he withdrew his fingers and, without comment, showed them to Indigo and Esty.

His hand was dry.

'Water,' he said, 'and yet not water. What do you make of it?'

Indigo gazed thoughtfully at the pool. This new discovery made her feel inexplicably resentful; as though someone or something had laid this pretty but useless image in their path as an unkind joke. Aloud, she said: 'I wonder how many travellers in this world have been lured here by a promise of water, only to find that whoever set the lure had an unpleasant sense of humour?'

Forth looked surprised. 'You think it was deliberately placed?'

She sighed. 'I'm beginning to think that everything in this world is far more deliberately and carefully contrived than we realise. I feel . . . ' She hesitated, rising to her feet and pacing as she searched for the right word. '*Manipulated*. That's the only term I can give it. As though since we broke through the thorn barrier, we've been like puppets dancing on strings.'

'But without knowing who the puppet master is?'

'Oh, no. I know the answer to that question; at least in essence.' Indigo hugged herself, staring up at the remote, featureless sky. 'But it's so elusive. I'd anticipated a tangible enemy, something I could see and assess and challenge. This, though,' she indicated the pool, the moor beyond, with a sweep of one arm, 'is like . . . '

'Looking for one special flea on an old dog,' Esty put in.

Despite her mood, Indigo couldn't help but laugh. 'One flea among many,' she said. 'I wonder how our unseen host would react to such a comparison? But seriously, I do feel that we're being toyed with. The illusions, the images, the peculiar phenomena – it's as if they're all gewgaws set to divert us from the path we should be following. We may have got into this demon-world, but it's like a temple to the Goddess, where the outer courtyards and public rooms tell only half the story. We haven't yet penetrated the veil that hangs before the sanctum. Do you understand what I mean?'

'Yes,' Forth said. 'But in a temple – at least, in the ones I've seen – only the Goddess's own servants are allowed to go through the veil.'

Indigo had continued to pace as they talked, but now she paused and looked keenly at Forth. Unwittingly, he had made a remark that might be significant; for if the parallel he drew held true, then perhaps only the servants of the demon entity which had created this world might be able to pass beyond the outer shell of illusion and trickery to the real core beyond.

Or if not its servants, then its victims . . .

Suddenly, she felt a quick, unlooked-for stab of prescience, as though some sardonic intelligence had read her thoughts even as they took form. And seconds later, carried from a great distance on the still air, the voice of a hunting wolf cut through the night in a long-drawn, ululating howl.

Esty jumped like a shot rabbit and the short hairs on Indigo's scalp and neck prickled. Forth, also shaken but trying not to show it, stared out beyond the reach of the pool's strange radiance, trying to penetrate into the nether darkness.

'They're still out there.' He sounded awed, angry and frightened together.

Esty shivered. 'And they sound as though they're waiting for us.' She glanced at her brother, then at Indigo. 'What are we going to do? If we move on, they may ambush us; but if we stay here they might close in!'

Indigo considered for a few moments. Whatever they decided to do, sheer necessity would oblige them to strike camp again before too long, as it seemed that, despite her hope, they couldn't go without food or sleep. She herself hadn't slept at their last camp, and was beginning to feel the effects of that deprivation. It would surely be safer to stay by the pool, where at least the light would give them some protection against any surprise attack. Fully refreshed, they'd be far better prepared for whatever might await them on the open moor.

Forth and Esty agreed immediately with her suggestion when she put it to them; though Esty was honest enough to admit that it was, as she wryly put it, like being asked to choose between death by fire and death by water. They chose a site and after a hasty meal – there seemed no point in attempting the ritual of lighting a fire – Indigo and Esty settled to rest while Forth took the first watch. Indigo had feared that sleep might not come

127

easily; but, to her relief, only minutes after closing her eyes she felt consciousness beginning to drift away. She dreamed strange, fragmented dreams of dark woods where a voice she knew and loved, but to which she couldn't give a name, called to her from a distance, urging to follow, its sound swelling and fading as she searched vainly for the source. When she woke at last, a leaden weight of sadness had lodged somewhere deep in her. It fled as she shook off the last dregs of sleep, but the memory of it was acute and disturbing.

Forth was sitting with his back to the pool, staring out at the moor, and Indigo was surprised to see Esty beside him. She'd slept for a while, Esty explained, but had woken suddenly and, unable to settle again, had elected to keep Forth company during the remainder of his watch. Nothing had disturbed their vigil – the wolves, it seemed, had either chosen to stay silent or had slunk away to new territory – and now Forth, trying to disguise his yawns, went gratefully to the makeshift couch and curled up to sleep.

Indigo settled beside Esty, and smiled at her. 'Are you sure you don't want to rest?' she asked. 'I'll be content enough with my own company.'

Esty returned the smile and shook her head. 'No. I'm wide awake: I won't sleep again now.'

She seemed, Indigo thought, oddly keyed up. Her green eyes were faintly feverish and her manner a little self-conscious, as though she was trying to hide some emotion about which she felt either embarrassed or ashamed; and Indigo said tentatively, 'Esty, is anything wrong.'

'Wrong? Why, no!' Then a hesitation as Esty realised that the denial had been too quick, too glib. She laughed. It sounded contrived. 'Well . . . I had some strange dreams while I slept. And when I woke, I felt so *sad*.'

Indigo looked at her with new interest. 'What were the dreams about?'

Esty's face flushed. 'I'd rather not talk about them.' A quick, almost furtive smile. 'You might laugh at me.'

'I promise you, I'll do no such thing.'

'All the same . . . ' Esty looked away, and tossed her

hair back. 'Ohh . . . I feel so *grimy*. I wish I could bathe in that pool!'

'Don't attempt it,' Indigo cautioned, though her mind was still distracted, pondering Esty's peculiar evasiveness.

'I wouldn't, of course. Though I did try to wash my hands earlier.' She spread her fingers and contemplated them. 'It was strange. It *felt* as though my hands were under water, though when I took them out they were still dry, like Forth said, and the dirt wouldn't rinse off.'

'Whatever that pool contains, it certainly isn't water,' Indigo agreed. 'Yet another form of illusion, I suspect. And that worries me, Esty, because it means that there may be no water anywhere in this dimension. And if that's true, then when our own supplies run out we'll be in a great deal of trouble.'

Esty said vaguely, 'Yes, I suppose we will,' and Indigo realised that she hadn't been paying attention, but instead was staring towards the pool with a thoughtful frown on her face.

'Esty?' She reached out to touch the girl's arm.

'What? Oh – I'm sorry. I was looking at the pool.' Esty blinked, and the frown turned into an odd little smile. 'Do you know, Indigo, that if you sit and look into the water, you can sometimes see the strangest reflections; almost like pictures of another world.'

Something in her tone, redolent of her earlier fey mood, alerted an uneasy instinct within Indigo. 'What do you mean?' she asked cautiously.

'Come and see for yourself.' Esty got up and walked to the pool's edge, where she crouched down in the shingle and peered over. 'We'll see nothing but our own faces at first. But after a while, something seems to change. It's quite beautiful.'

Warily, Indigo knelt beside her and looked into the pool. Against the blank, charcoal-dark reflection of the sky, their images gazed back at them; her own face angular and bony, Esty's finer, more feline and youthful. But some quality in the pool had sapped colour from the reflections, giving their skins – which in reality were both tanned from the summer – a sickly, parchment look, and

129

dulling Esty's vivid red hair to the shade of neglected brass.

Esty leaned forward a little further, and blew on the pool's surface so that the two mirror images fragmented in a scatter of ripples. As the ripples died away, the picture reformed – and just before it swam back into focus Indigo glimpsed – or thought she glimpsed, for it appeared and vanished in a single instant – what looked like a strange and lovely garden behind their own reflections. A lawn, starred with flowers, led away to a gate set in an old and mellow wall, shaded by slender trees whose branches swept down almost to the ground. And, framed by the garden's eerie beauty, a disembodied face, ghostly and barely formed, hovered between herself and Esty.

'There!' Esty hissed in an exultant whisper, pointing. 'Did you see?'

Indigo looked sidelong at the excited girl. 'I saw a garden. And someone's face. Or I thought I did, but – '

'Yes. Oh, *yes*.' Esty was staring into the pool more intently than ever, as though silently and furiously willing the phantom to reappear. 'It was *him* again; just as I saw him before.'

'Him?' Indigo queried uneasily. Her heart had missed painfully with the shock of the momentary vision; now it seemed to slow to a crawling, suffocating beat. 'Esty – who is he?'

Esty shook her head. 'I don't know. But he looks so beautiful, and so *sad*.' She leaned at a perilous angle, then gave another soft cry. 'There! He's there again – look.'

This time there was no sign of the unearthly garden; but the face had reformed, blurred a little by the water but still clearly visible. It was a young man's countenance, but thin and narrow and deadly white, with eyes that seemed to be no more than vivid but colourless pinpoints in deep and hollow sockets. Its expression combined savage intensity with a chilling, unhuman longing, and Indigo's momentary fascination was overtaken suddenly by a surge of revulsion. She reached out, meaning to pull Esty away, but Esty misinterpreted the movement and took her fingers in a tight grip, as though acknowledging some deep, shared secret. Then she raised her other hand in a gesture that warned Indigo to silence, and slowly, carefully, turned to look behind them. Pulse quickening again, Indigo, too, turned – but there was no one there, only their own thin and insubstantial shadows cast by the pool's light, and the darkly shimmering moor beyond.

Esty swung back to face the water, hunching so that the heavy mass of her hair obscured her face. But Indigo had already seen her expression: the extraordinary flare of avid pleasure, followed by frustration and disappointment as hope was thwarted. Swiftly Indigo, too, looked at the pool again; but the disembodied face had vanished and the surface reflected only their own bleached figures.

'Ahh . . . ' Esty's sigh was soft, and something about it made Indigo's flesh creep. 'I'd thought perhaps he might . . . ' She broke off and shook her head.

Indigo watched her in silent, clenching horror. For a moment, when the apparition had appeared for the second time, its eyes had seemed to drive like hot nails into her own and through to the skull beyond, locking her mind and body with the burning intensity of their stare. And like Esty, she had felt the upsurge of an emotion that was part pity and part longing and part desire. An agonising *needing*, an unhuman lure.

But the spell hadn't had the power to hold her. Indigo knew the nature of demons only too well, and in the instant when she pulled back from the lure of the vision she had sensed its mocking acknowledgement and dismissal. She wasn't a ready victim; therefore she was of no interest. Esty, though, was another matter.

'Esty.' She turned towards the girl and took hold of both her hands, taking care not to let her voice betray the alarm she felt. 'Esty, there was no one there. What we saw wasn't real. It was another illusion; like the wolves, and the Jachanine.'

Esty gave her a long look. Then: 'Yes,' she said quietly. 'You're right, Indigo; that's what it must have been.'

She averted her gaze as she spoke, casting her lashes down so that her eyes weren't visible. Indigo hesitated, unsure if the girl had truly taken in what she'd said, then added gently, cajolingly. 'You understand what I mean, don't you? And you do believe it?'

Esty looked up again and smiled at her with an odd brilliance. 'Of course I do.'

But the agreement was too glib, the capitulation too easy. Esty's expression had just the smallest hint of slyness; something which Indigo had never seen in her before. She was hiding behind a bland pretence, recalling again the phantom face and the power of its sighing, yearning lure. The unpleasant possibility occurred to Indigo that perhaps there had been more to the apparition than mere illusion. She had looked into its eyes, and had seen a little of what lurked there. It was enough – more than enough – to entrap an unwary and impressionable soul as a spider might prey on a fly.

She opened her mouth to appeal to Esty again, but the words died on her tongue. There was nothing she could say. Her reasoning didn't accord with what Esty wanted to hear, and no amount of persuasion would sway matters. Esty would simply continue to pay lip-serve to whatever arguments were voiced, whilst keeping her true feelings a close secret.

Once more, Indigo glanced back at the pool. The surface was an innocent mirror now, reflecting only the featureless pewter sheen of the sky overhead. She couldn't talk to Esty; and she felt that, as yet, it would be wiser to say nothing to Forth. She had, after all, no more than an unproven suspicion to confide; and besides, she didn't want to alert Esty and make her more secretive still. But from now on, she would need to watch the girl very carefully. And, she thought, wolves or no wolves, she would be thankful when this rest was over and they could move on; for if her growing fear had any foundation, then the hungry, unhuman thing that haunted the pool might prove far more dangerous than anything they had yet encountered.

To Indigo's intense relief, the remainder of the watch was uneventful. Esty, despite her earlier protestations, fell asleep after a while, curled like a cat at the edge of the shingle. Now and then Indigo glanced at her, and tried to ignore the chilly frisson that shivered through her when she saw the strange, small smile on Esty's unguarded lips.

There were no more phantoms, no distant wolf-cries. Perhaps if she'd looked into the pool again Indigo might have caught another glimpse of the eerie garden and its occupant; but she was keenly aware of the pitfalls of such a temptation, and instead simply sat staring out at the black moor, until at last Forth stirred and awoke.

Forth, refreshed from his sleep, was restless and anxious to be taking action. He agreed instantly to Indigo's suggestion that they should forego the third watch – which would have been Esty's – and move on without any further delay; and when Esty herself was roused, she too seemed eager to be away. Indigo was surprised and a little troubled by her easy acquiescence, but tried to put the worry from her mind as they packed up their belongings and made ready to go.

The only bone of contention between them was the route they should take. Forth was for heading on in the same direction from which they'd approached the pool: there was no reason for the feeling, he said, it just seemed logical if they were to avoid the risk of mistakenly circling back to their starting point. But Esty had other ideas. They should strike out to the left of that line, she said, and as she spoke Indigo saw again the faint slyness creep into her eyes. Like Forth, she had no real reason for the suggestion; it was simply a feeling.

Forth shrugged and looked at Indigo. 'If Esty has an instinct, I'm willing to gamble on it,' he said carelessly. 'She does this now and then: her intuition, Da calls it. And she's right more often than not.' He smiled. 'After all, we've nothing to lose, have we?'

His words were unwittingly ironic, but Indigo couldn't argue without revealing her suspicions. 'Very well,' she said. 'Let Esty lead us.'

Was there a flicker of triumph in Esty's eyes? Hard to be sure; and easy to let imagination run away with her. Nonetheless, as they completed their preparations she had the distinct feeling that Esty was taking care to keep a distance between them – until, as they scoured the ground for anything that might inadvertently have been left behind, Indigo heard the shingle crunch behind her, and Esty moved to stand at her elbow.

'You know, don't you,' Esty said in a strange, taut voice, 'that Forth's in love with you?'

Indigo tensed; then, unsure of her ground, dissembled. 'What do you mean?'

Esty smiled. Again, it was a peculiar smile. 'Oh, don't think I mislike the idea. Not at all. It's wonderful. But then, love is, isn't it? We should never deny love, Indigo. That would be a terrible thing to do, don't you agree?'

Before Indigo could respond, Esty turned and, flinging back her coppery hair as though it had been newly released from confinement, walked away to where Forth was waiting for them.

Chapter X

'Esty!' Forth's voice jarred with irritation. 'Stop mithering and come *on*! There's nothing here – you're simply wasting time.'

Esty's shoulders hunched defensively, but she returned, picking her way through the black grass. She said nothing, only shot her brother a contemptuous glare, then turned her back and strode on.

Forth stared at the rough tussock she'd been investigating, wondering exasperatedly what had caught her eye – or rather, her imagination – this time. He saw nothing unremarkable, and looked helplessly at Indigo as they set off after Esty's retreating figure.

'I don't know what's got into her,' he said in an aggrieved undertone. 'If I didn't know better, I'd think she'd been at the applejack.'

It was yet another disquieting sign, Indigo thought. They'd been walking for what seemed like a good many hours; the pool had fallen far behind and even its nacreous aura was now out of sight; yet if anything, Esty's peculiar mood had intensified rather than lessened. At first she had set a rapid pace across the moor, as though she were hastening to some vital tryst; then, just as Forth had been ready to protest that there was no need for such haste, she had instead begun to dawdle, pausing, or so it seemed, every few paces to stray from the path in pursuit of some imagined find, or simply to gaze up at the sky. She answered when spoken to, but either vaguely or with waspish irritation; and now Forth, who was impatient at the best of times, was almost at the end of his tether.

'I'm damned if I know what's got into her,' he persisted. 'Anyone'd think she was performing the Chalila fiasco all over again!'

'Chalila?' Indigo was baffled.

'Oh, that was before you joined us.' Forth scowled again at Esty flouncing ahead of them. 'You've never seen the play we used to do called "Chalila and the Demon", have you?'

A cold worm moved in Indigo at the word *demon*. 'No,' she said cautiously.

'Ah. It's funny; in the far west it's one of the most popular things in our repertoire; always has been. But further east we've never performed it. Da says,' pain showed momentarily on his face as he recalled suddenly what had brought them to this world; something which, since the illusions and phantoms began to haunt them, had been all too easy to forget, 'Da says it's too complex for the simpler folk; they get bored and start shouting for drinking songs. But anyway . . . it's a story about a girl who's spirited away by a demon lover and discovers that he's really a prince under a curse. It's always been Esty's favourite, but Da'd never let her play Chalila. She's supposed to be demure, innocent – you know the sort of thing. Da said Esty couldn't be demure if her life depended on it, so Chari always took the part. But there was one time when Chari got a bronchus and lost her voice. Esty knew the role by heart, so Da had to let her do it.' Suddenly his mood shifted and he flashed Indigo a quick, gleeful grin. 'She was *awful*. But before the show began, she was in such a state you'd have thought she really was waiting for some story-book lover to stride into the van and carry her off. She drove us all half out of our wits with her goings-on; just the way she's behaving now.'

The cold worm writhed a second time, and Indigo thought she understood. For a long time Esty had harboured a secret romance in which she saw herself as Chalila. Now Chalila's demon lover had come, a phantom in the mirror of an unreal pool, to show her his face and to call her to his deadly garden. Vulnerable, impressionable, Esty had been no match for the warped intelligence that lurked behind the phantom, and she had fallen in love with a horror that was preying on her deep-rooted longings and slowly but surely turning her to its own purpose. Indigo had dared to hope that by leaving the pool behind they would free Esty from the spell. She should have known better; should have realised the whole truth when Esty had insisted that they follow the course they were now set on. The demon was leading her, and, blindly, innocently, lovingly, Esty was following. It was a beautiful, lethal trap.

Yet how lethal? An earlier thought began to gnaw at Indigo; something that had slid into her mind at the pool only to be forgotten in the turmoil of later events. The puppet-master and his willing victims. And the uneasy suspicion that perhaps only those who *were* willing might penetrate the veil to the demon's inner sanctum. The creature that had come out of the dark to touch Esty's mind with its poison was stronger and more tangible than the phantoms they'd encountered before; which suggested that this particular manifestation of the demon entity was closer to the heart of its progenitor. And if the precarious balance between Esty's safety and the demon's lure could be maintained, then to follow where it led might be their only chance of breaking through this world's illusions to the reality beneath.

Forcefully pushing down an attack of conscience, Indigo said, 'I don't think we should worry overmuch, Forth.' She smiled at him, ingenuous and hating herself for it. 'The atmosphere of this land's enough to set anyone's imagination off on a peculiar tack.'

'You mean, she's playing Chalila all over again?' The significance of this observation seemed to have escaped Forth; he laughed, causing Esty to flick him a venomous look over her shoulder. 'I wouldn't be surprised at that. Well enough, then; just so long as her daydreaming doesn't cause us any problems. Though I don't mind admitting that I wish she'd snap out of it. All this dithering and dawdling – she seems to forget that we've better things to do.'

Indigo found herself unable to meet his gaze directly. 'Yes,' she said as her conscience assailed her again. 'We have.'

*

Forth's wish that Esty would 'snap out of it' was – at least as far as he was concerned – granted as their trek continued; for shortly afterwards the girl seemed to undergo another unpredicted shift of mood and her dreamy, distracted meanderings were abruptly transformed into a new sense of purpose and direction. Forth was too thankful for the change to wonder at his sister's suddenly reawakened determination, and Indigo, keeping her thoughts to herself, said nothing but only watched Esty more keenly than ever.

The moor flowed on unchanging. It was impossible to judge whether they had been walking for days, hours or merely minutes; the dark land spreading away in all directions seemed to defy such considerations and make them meaningless. For a while Indigo and Forth attempted to find some light subject for conversation, but there was nothing to say that wasn't too redolent of buried fears and hidden disquiet, and eventually they lapsed into silence. Esty seemed calmer and more sure of herself and was no longer swinging unpredictably between haste and lethargy. In fact if anything she was now setting a sterner pace than ever across the black turf: she seemed tireless, and every so often she would look back over her shoulder to where the others laboured behind her, and urge them on with a gesture or an eager word. Indigo was growing more and more certain that, consciously or not, Esty was indeed leading them towards some unknown goal.

But where, she asked herself, could that goal possibly lie? There was nothing on the moor as far as the eye could see, and they must by now have walked countless miles without any sign of an end to the barren, unchanging nightscape. Food and water would soon be in seriously short supply; and when their rations ran out, what then? The unpleasant thought occurred to her that perhaps that was precisely what the demon intended: to lead them on a fruitless, endless chase that would achieve nothing, until finally they succumbed to hunger and weakness and despair. Again she thought of the Bruhome sleepwalkers, and shuddered. *Why* had they encountered none of those benighted souls since they had entered this world? What had become of them? And were she and Forth and Esty blindly following a dead hope and a path that could lead them nowhere?

She tried not to dwell on the subject as they walked on. The silence was growing oppressive; Forth, lagging a little and pausing every now and again to scan the empty moor behind them with unquiet, speculative eyes, was clearly restless, and only Esty seemed untroubled by the deepening atmosphere of doubt.

At last, Forth couldn't keep silent any longer. He said suddenly, sharply, 'Indigo – Esty. Stop a moment.'

Indigo halted and looked back. Forth's face was a pinched oval in the thinly silvered twilight; the gloom made dark, indistinct slashes of his features, like something unhuman.

She said: 'What is it?'

Esty, too, had stopped, but reluctantly, and her stance was tense. Standing between the brother and sister, Indigo felt suddenly like a reluctant mediator caught in the midst of something potentially dangerous. For a few moments Forth stared past her, focusing on Esty's face. Then he said,

'Where are we going?'

Indigo didn't answer him: the question hadn't been intended for her. Esty only continued to stare back at Forth, and he repeated, 'I said, where are we *going*? Because it seems to me that we've been walking for hour upon hour – the Goddess alone knows, it might even be *days* – and for what?' One arm swung in an arc, indicating the bleak moorland. 'Just this, with no end in sight. Damn it, we haven't seen one living creature, let alone any sign of Da and Chari!'

Esty shrugged, and half turned away. 'That isn't my fault.'

'I'm not saying it is. But since we left that cursed pool with its non-existent water, you've been leading us, Esty, and that makes me think that you must know something we don't.'

Esty turned her back completely. 'Don't be stupid.' Her voice was muffled; Indigo thought she'd raised one hand to her face and was biting her knuckles. 'How could I?'

'Right.' Forth exhaled a long breath; it was what he'd expected to hear and he had come to a decision. 'Well, I'll say what I have to say and be done with it. I think we're fools. We got into this world without any idea of what to expect, and without any plan of action; and since we arrived we've just walked as blindly as any of the Bruhome sleepers, with a sheep-headed notion that sooner or later we'd get somewhere. But we haven't got anywhere, have we? The way things are, we might as well have stayed in the forest for all this trek's achieved. Where's Da? Where's Chari, and Grimya?'

Esty was beginning to look rebellious, and Indigo intervened. Gently, she asked, 'What are you saying, Forth?'

He glanced at her, and she saw his shoulders stiffen as he sensed patronage in her question. Then, curtly, he replied, 'I'm saying that I'm not prepared to go another step until we've worked out a proper plan. Until we've sat down, right here, and *talked*.'

'No!' Esty snapped.

Startled, they both looked at her. Forth said, 'What d'you mean, no?'

Esty's face froze. 'I – don't . . . that is, I – can't see why we need – ' She floundered, fell silent.

'Oh, come on, Esty!' Forth was nonplussed. 'We're simply walking on and on, without any idea of where we're going! How can we possibly hope to find Da and Chari this way?'

'We *will* find them,' Esty protested, but without real conviction. 'If we just have faith, and trust.' Her gaze moved quickly, furtively from Forth's face to Indigo's; she saw Indigo's expression and hastily looked away again.

'Trust in what?' Forth was growing exasperated. 'Your unerring sense of direction? Damn it, girl, you – '

'*Don't talk to me like that!*' Esty cut across him so savagely that he recoiled, startled. 'Who do you think you are?' Her vivid eyes blazed, then suddenly she shrugged her pack from her shoulders, flung it to the ground and flopped down beside it. 'All *right*. Sit and have your council, if that's what makes you happy. I

140

don't care!' She turned away.

'Right.' Forth, too, sat on the grass, and looked up at Indigo. There was a hint of challenge in his eyes, and when he spoke again his voice was scathing.

'I suggest, Indigo, that we ignore that child until such time as she decides to stop behaving like a spoilt brat. In the meantime, maybe you and I can discuss more important matters.'

Indigo hesitated. She wanted to urge them both to stop squabbling but at the same time she knew that this latest rift had been triggered by something far less innocent than sibling rivalry. She had to mediate: but at the same time she needed to walk the tricky tightrope between pacifying them both and avoiding arousal of any suspicion about her own motives.

She said, 'Listen, both of you. I don't know how long we've been walking, but it must be near on time for another rest.' She forced a wry smile that didn't convince her but, she hoped, would fool them. 'I'm tired, I'm hungry, and I don't doubt you are too. Let's make camp here. And then we can all discuss what's to be done, and satisfy both needs.'

Forth said, 'Yes. I agree.'

'Esty?'

The girl shrugged, still keeping her back turned. 'If that's what you want. I don't care.'

'Very well.' Indigo slipped off her pack, flexing her shoulders gratefully as the dead weight fell away. She *was* weary; and as she sat down Forth, sensing it, said, 'I'll take first watch.' He smiled at her, and the smile conveyed a hint of apology. 'We'll talk later, yes? When you've slept for a while. You look as though you need it. And don't worry about Esty. We'll patch it up; we always do.'

Indigo hesitated, then realised he was right. The quarrel would pass. For now, at least, there was little to fear, and she returned Forth's smile before settling down to make herself as comfortable as she could on the uneven ground.

Perversely, sleep refused to claim her at first, despite her tiredness. For some while she lay awake, aware of

141

Forth gazing meditatively out at the bleak, silent night-scape and of Esty's occasional restive movement. After a time Esty gave in and lay down, curled up with her head pillowed on her pack: shortly afterwards Indigo heard murmured words that she couldn't quite catch and which at first she thought were addressed to Forth. But Forth didn't respond, and she realised that Esty must be asleep and dreaming.

At last Indigo's consciousness began to slide away. On the brink, just before the quiet inner dark closed in, she had the sense of someone watching her, and tried to rouse herself to warn her companions that they weren't entirely alone. But reality was slipping from her, shifting into the first images of a dream, and she relaxed. A dream. That was all it was. Just a dream.

Indigo slept. Her sleep was sound – so the shock of waking, when it came, was all the worse.

'Indigo!' The voice intruded on the disjointed image of a desert of blinding yellow sand, and as she stirred Indigo heard herself speak a name she'd all but forgotten, and ask a question in a familiar but neglected tongue of the eastern continent. Then the fog of sleep whirled away like a dust-devil, and she found herself looking up at Forth.

'Indigo!' His hand was gripping her shoulder with bruising ferocity as he crouched over her, and there was terror in his eyes. 'Esty's gone!'

Forth's sorry tale was a brief one. He'd been more tired than he had realised and once Indigo and Esty were both asleep he'd found himself fighting a losing battle with his own weariness. Rather than wake either of his companions, he'd determined – foolishly, as it now seemed – to sit the watch out. But the effort had failed, and he'd stirred to find his head slumped on his knees, his back aching fiercely, and Esty missing.

His immediate assumption was that something had crept to the camp and snatched Esty away, and he was torn between ranting self-recrimination and frantic declarations that she must be found and rescued. Indigo, though, knew exactly what had become of Esty, and cursed herself for not having foreseen it. The quarrel should have alerted her: Esty, obsessively pursuing the delusion that had her mind in its thrall, hadn't been prepared to let anything stand in her way, and had snatched the first opportunity to shake off those who, to her distorted reasoning, were frustrating her desires. It was the worst possible confirmation of Indigo's suspicions; and now she couldn't keep those suspicions to herself any longer.

She persuaded Forth to calm down for long enough to listen, and told him what she already knew; of the garden and its deathly white denizen reflected in the pool, of the disturbing sensation of the phantom's power, and of Esty's peculiar slyness and secrecy which had sounded the first alarm in her own mind. Then, frankly and without embellishment, she confessed to the plan she'd formulated of allowing Esty to lead them to whatever was calling her, which had now so appallingly misfired.

Forth heard her out and when she stopped speaking there was silence for a few moments. Then, in a voice pitched unnaturally low by his efforts to control it, Forth said, 'So Esty's run off in pursuit of this – this demon, this *thing*. And you knew about it all along. You knew something like this might happen, and yet you let her run that risk – '

'Forth, I'm sorry! The Mother knows, if I'd thought for one moment that she'd – '

'If you knew Esty, you *would* have thought! *I'd* have known – damn it, she's my sister, she's as transparent as water to me, and I could have predicted exactly what she'd do! Why didn't you *tell* me?'

Indigo shook her head despairingly. 'I should have done. I see that now. But I didn't want to do anything that might arouse Esty's suspicions, or let the demon realise what was afoot.' It sounded feeble, she knew; but it was the truth.

Forth said coldly, 'I see. You didn't think I could be trusted not to give the game away, is that it?' Twin spots of hectic colour flared on his cheeks, and abruptly his voice grew passionate. 'You think I'm a child – you, in all your wisdom and superiority, you think you always know what's best! Well, I hope it comforts you to know that your wisdom and superiority might just have killed my sister!'

'Forth – '

'*No!*' Forth swung round and began to gather up his pack. '*Damn* you, Indigo; I'm not going to listen any more! I'm going after Esty, and I'm going to get her out of the hands of that monstrosity – and you can do as you please!'

He heaved the pack on to his shoulder and would have strode away, but Indigo called after him. 'Forth! We don't even know which way she went!'

Forth hesitated, then turned to look back at her. For a moment she thought he might be too angry even to take in what she'd said, but after a moment he uttered a vicious oath, then flung the pack down as his rage abruptly drained away. 'Oh, Great Mother . . . ' He put a hand to his face in despair.

'I don't want to quarrel with you, Forth,' Indigo said quietly. She felt as though she were walking on fragile glass, but she had to try to mend the rift if she could. 'And I'm ready to admit that I was wrong – terribly wrong. I can't change that mistake, but I want to make amends.' She paused. Forth stood motionless, his face a rigid mask, but he was at least listening. 'If we're to have any hope of finding Esty we've got to do what you yourself suggested earlier: look for clues, and make a plan. It's our only chance.'

Silence for a while. Then, slowly, Forth nodded.

'Very well. In that at least, you're right.' He looked up, and met her gaze with a residue of resentful venom still in his eyes. 'But this time it'll be on my terms.' A finger jabbed at his own chest. '*Mine.*'

He couldn't do worse than she'd already done, Indigo thought bitterly. 'Yes,' she said with the contrition that she felt. 'Yours.'

The clue, when they found it, was so blatant that neither of them could believe for a moment that it was an accident. Ten yards from where they'd slept they saw a glint of unwonted colour on the turf and discovered a

144

bracelet made of small, cheap glass beads lying in the black grass.

'Esty's lucky bracelet.' Forth stared at it. 'And it isn't even broken. She must have dropped it deliberately. She wanted us to know which way she went – or whatever controls her did.'

'Either that, or it was placed to mislead us,' Indigo said.

He glanced sidelong at her. The atmosphere between them wasn't easy yet, and the smallest hint – even imagined – of criticism put him instantly on edge. Then he crushed the bracelet in a clenched fist. 'I don't care. We've wasted too much time already, and whether or not this takes us on a ninny's dance, I'm going to follow it.' A pause. 'Are you coming?'

Indigo didn't argue with him. The bracelet's clue might lead them on a real or a false trail; but they had no choice other than to trust it. She pointed ahead. 'The ground rises a little for the next mile or so. We should be able to get a wider view from the top of the incline.'

'Right. Then let's move, and quickly.'

They set a regime of running and walking alternately for fifty paces at a stretch, taking turns to carry the third pack that Esty had left behind. The rhythm enabled them to keep up a good pace whilst preserving their stamina and when they finally reached the top of the distant rise they were both breathing only a little more sharply than normal.

But the view was a disappointment. Though the sky's peculiar, silvered sheen enabled them to see for a vast distance in every direction, there was nothing but the empty, endless moor stretching on, it seemed, to infinity.

Forth swore under his breath as the hope he'd been harbouring died. 'There must be *something*,' he muttered. 'It can't go on for ever. It *can't*.'

'I don't believe it does.' Indigo narrowed her eyes in an effort to focus on the nightscape's furthest reaches. She was thinking again of the theory, forgotten in the light of more urgent events, that the power of will might be capable of controlling the balance between illusion

145

and reality in this world. Could it be that, beneath the mask of this unending and unchanging moor, the true contours of the demon's dimension and all it contained lay waiting, if only they could summon the will to see it?

She sighed, and let the idea slide away. Whether or not it was true, neither she nor Forth knew how to turn the vital key; and without that knowledge speculation was useless. Just one hint, she thought. Just one sign. Surely, as Forth had said, there must be *something*.

Disheartened as much by her own reverie as by the vista's barrenness, she bent to pick up Esty's pack, ready to move on. But as she shouldered it, Forth suddenly gripped her arm, staring out across the moor.

'There's something moving.' He pointed, his voice rising with excitement. 'There, in the distance – look!'

Indigo turned. Far off, conspicuous against the land's sullen backdrop, she saw a pale and indistinct shape. Distance gave it a flickering, ghostlike quality, but it was indeed moving, though slowly and erratically, across the night.

Indigo heard her own sharp, eager intake of breath even as Forth spoke again. 'Human?' He was looking at her, his eyes fervid.

She bit her lip. 'It's impossible to be sure from here. But . . . I think so.'

'And it's heading in the same direction as we are. It's Esty – it *has* to be!' He grabbed the spare pack from her, slinging it over his shoulder together with his own belongings, and set off across the turf. 'Come on!'

They broke into a scrambling run. The ground, perversely, was rougher on this side of the rise, hazardous with dips and tussocks that could turn an unwary ankle; and the heavy packs made their balance uncertain and progress erratic. Indigo feared that Esty might see them pursuing her; unburdened as she was, they'd have little chance of catching her if she chose to elude them. But she was apparently unaware of their approach, for she only continued to walk at the same steady pace.

They gained rapidly on their quarry, and were only a short way behind her when they both realised to their chagrin that, though the figure ahead of them was human, and female, it certainly wasn't Esty.

'Mother of Life!' Forth slid to a breathless halt and his voice cracked with dismay. 'It's one of the sleepwalkers!'

The woman was dressed only in a woollen night-shift, and her long hair, which by an ironic coincidence was almost the same shade as Esty's own, hung down her back in a dishevelled single braid. Now they were at closer quarters, Indigo and Forth could see that she had no control over herself or her progress across the moor; blind to hollows and hummocks alike, she stumbled on a mindlessly determined straight course like some helpless beast that knew nothing beyond the call of instinct. And with a sense of horror that crawled up from the pits of their stomachs, they saw that her bare arms were as thin as if the flesh and blood had been sucked from them, leaving only her bones stark and angular beneath their emaciated covering of skin.

Shock and pity warred with disappointment in Indigo's mind; but underlying them was a rekindling of excitement.

'Forth.' Indigo stared at the woman, who continued to walk on, unaware of them. 'She's the first we've seen of them. The very first of the Bruhome walkers. So they *are* still alive!'

'Yes.' Forth's eyes were miserable. 'But what use is that to us now? She won't lead us to Esty.'

'She might! Remember that awful sense of purpose they all had when they left the town; as though they had a goal that they must reach at any cost? The entity that lured Esty away may also be drawing them towards itself – her goal and theirs could be one and the same.'

Forth's eyes widened. 'Of course!' Then the feverish eagerness faded abruptly. 'But she's moving slowly; too slowly. If we follow her, then the Mother alone knows what might become of Esty before we can catch up with her. I'm not willing to take that risk.'

'We don't have to.' Indigo gestured towards the walking woman. 'Look at her. Her course never wavers, no matter what obstacles the land puts in her path. I'd be prepared to wager that she's been walking in a straight line from the point at which she first broke through the thorns into the forest.'

'So, if we follow that same course . . . yes! It has to work!' Suddenly the rift between them was forgotten altogether, and Forth took hold of Indigo's hand, starting forward. 'Hurry! Esty can't be that far ahead!'

'Forth, wait.' Indigo stumbled after him. 'When we catch up with that woman, we *must* stop. I know she's still entranced, but there's a chance we may be able to make her respond to us. And anything she can tell us might be invaluable.'

He was dubious, but finally nodded. 'All right; we'll try. But I'm not going to waste too much time.'

Breaking into a run, they caught up with the sleep-walker, and their paths divided to flank her on either side. They still hadn't glimpsed the woman's face, for she'd looked neither right nor left as she trudged on; but as they drew level and then a little ahead of her, Indigo bit back an oath as she saw her features clearly at last.

She looked like a corpse. Long ago, when an old retainer at Carn Caille had died, Indigo – no more than eight years old – had crept surreptitiously into the anteroom where the coffin was set out in readiness for the funeral pyre; eaten by curiosity about the sight which her parents, conscious of her tender years, had forbidden her to see. She'd been appalled by the changes that death had wrought upon the old servant, whom she'd childishly adored; he looked like an effigy in wax and parchment, shrunken, alien. Life and soul had gone, and left nothing behind but an abandoned shell. The image, her first direct encounter with human mortality, had stayed with Indigo all her life, and now as she looked at the woman from Bruhome, the old memory came flooding back with a vengeance. Wax and parchment: the flesh of her face had fallen away. She was a white, cadaverous husk: only her eyes – pale, and slightly protuberant before the dark, inner obsession had sunk them deep into their sockets – retaining any animation.

Indigo heard Forth say softly, 'Goddess preserve us . . .', then he swallowed back revulsion and stepped into the woman's path, reaching out to take her by the arms

148

and halt her. Her steps slowed, faltered; then, grotesquely, she stood where she was but her feet continued to move, up and down, up and down, still walking though they could make no progress.

'It's like touching carrion,' Forth said, and his voice was shaking. 'She's cold, and her skin feels . . . ' He shuddered, and his fingers twitched involuntarily, wanting to withdraw.

Indigo stood beside him and looked into the woman's eyes. Unblinking, the woman stared back, seeing nothing.

'Lady. Lady, can you hear me? Can you understand?'

No response. Still the feet kept fruitlessly moving.

'Lady, we want to help you if we can. Please – if you understand, try to show us some sign.'

Suddenly the woman stopped treading. For one eternal moment she stood utterly motionless – then her eyes brightened with intelligence, and her lips parted in a sweet, childlike and rapturous smile that on the cadaverous face was gruesome. Forth jumped back, releasing her, and she raised one twig-thin arm, pointing out across the moor.

'Look!' she said in the earthy accent of Bruhome. 'Oh, look – so beautiful!'

Indigo and Forth swung round quickly, but there was nothing to be seen except the empty nightscape. Baffled, they turned again to face the woman. She still smiled her dreadful smile, but the light of intelligence in her eyes had died, leaving them void of any expression.

Then, before their horrified gazes, her body broke into fragments, and the fragments crumbled to dust.

Chapter XI

Forth straightened up, wiping his mouth with the back of one hand. His face was the colour of clay and his eyes haunted as, unsteadily, he returned to where Indigo stood a few paces away.

'I'm sorry.' He spoke gruffly, embarrassed and angry with himself for the lapse. Indigo sympathised, though she knew he wouldn't appreciate her saying so: she had seen far worse sights than the woman's disintegrating corpse, but for Forth the shock had been more than his stomach could bear.

She looked at the small, pitiful heap of pale dust which was all that remained of the Bruhome victim. The spark of life sucked from her as the physical flesh and blood and sinew had been drained away. Devoured: gone. The ugly connotation with the withering crops was final confirmation of Indigo's belief about the demon's nature. It was a vampire. In the real world, such legends were rife; creatures of the night, drinking blood, sucking out the lives of others to sustain their own unnatural existence. But this vampiric force drank far more than blood; it took everything. Sap, flesh, even will, until there was nothing more left for it to feed on.

Forth said suddenly, 'Did you hear what she said?'

'What?' Indigo had been wrapped in her ugly thoughts, and didn't fully take in his words.

Forth hunched his shoulders and forced himself to look down at the dust. 'Just before she . . . ' he swallowed, 'before it happened, she saw something; a vision of some kind. And she said "So beautiful, and so sad".' He looked up at Indigo. 'The day Chari took the sickness, Cour told me the last thing she said before she fell to it. You were there: do you remember?'

150

So sad. Memory slid into place, and Indigo recalled the wonder and pity in Chari's voice as she'd uttered those words. And at the pool, Esty's soft exclamation as she'd gazed into the reflected face of the denizen of the garden. *So beautiful, and so sad.* A heartrending sorrow that wrung pity from all who encountered it. Was that the key to the demon's hold over its victims – was that the lure that drew them so willingly to the sacrifice?

Quickly, she looked to where the dead woman had pointed. Whatever the poor creature had seen, it had been revealed to her only at the moment of death, a lifting of the veil and a promise of paradise beyond. For a final instant she had believed in that paradise, and because of that belief the vision had been real, for her will had made it so.

Her will. Indigo raised her own left hand and studied it. There was no trace of any scar where the fire had burned her: she had willed it away, refused to believe that she was burned, and – perhaps because the pain gave her extra incentive – belief had become reality.

'Indigo?' Forth said, his voice a little querulous. 'What are you thinking? You haven't answered me.'

She pointed, as the dead woman had done, across the moor. 'What do you see, Forth?'

'Exactly what you see: the dark, and the open land.' He sounded puzzled, and wary.

'And how far do you think that open land extends?'

'The Mother only knows. For all I can tell, it could go on for ever. Indigo, we can't afford to waste time – '

She interrupted him, unslinging her pack and hefting the hide bag in which her harp was kept. 'Please, Forth. I want to try an experiment. It may not work, but if it does, it could lead us not just to Esty but to the others as well.' She saw him about to argue, and added fervently, '*Please* – bear with me, and help me if you can.'

As she spoke she had slipped the harp from its covering, and sat down crosslegged in the grass with it balanced in her lap. She didn't dare touch the strings, not yet; only when her mind was prepared would she stand any chance of success. She settled the harp more comfortably, then looked at Forth again.

151

'Forth, do you believe in music?'

He stared at her as though she'd gone mad. 'Of course I do! What kind of a question's that? Indigo, I don't know what you're doing, but – '

'Take out your reed-pipe. Don't try to play it; just prepare it.'

Forth swore exasperatedly. 'I will *not*! Not unless you tell me what on the sweet Earth you think you're doing!'

'Very well; I'll tell you.' A quiver of excitement was starting to move in Indigo as awakening intuition told her that this seemingly insane scheme was right. She glanced over her shoulder at the dead woman's remains. 'In my home country, when someone dies, a bard must play their elegy to speed their soul to the Earth Mother. It's something instilled deep in my people's traditions; to fail to do it would be unthinkable. So I mean to play this woman's elegy for her simply because it must be done.'

Forth's eyes narrowed, and the first glint of understanding began to show in them. 'The harp should fail . . . ' he said speculatively.

'Yes. By the apparent laws of this world the harp should fail, as your pipe and the lantern failed, and as fire won't boil water.'

'But if we truly *will* a thing to happen . . . '

Indigo smiled thinly and displayed her left hand; a slow answering smile began to form on Forth's face.

'That's the key,' Indigo said. 'I *must* play the elegy; it's ingrained in me. And that may be enough to overcome the illusion that our music can't exist!'

She knew when he began to reach into his own pack that she'd won. Forth might harbour grave doubts, but he was at least willing to try. He pulled out the pipe and fingered it tentatively. 'What do you want me to play?' Now his smile was faintly sheepish.

'For the moment, nothing,' Indigo told him. 'I'll try first; I'll play one of our traditional requiem songs. Watch my fingers, and *will* the sound to come.'

The harp was probably badly out of tune, but she made no attempt to adjust it, knowing that the effort would be futile and she'd hear nothing. Only when the feel of the elegy filled her might the harp, silenced by this unnatural dimension, be persuaded to speak.

Indigo took a deep breath, closed her eyes, and began to play. For a few moments the experience was bizarre, for where her unconscious mind anticipated the sudden flow of music, there was only silence but for the faint slither of her fingers on the strings. Fiercely she fought the jarring confusion, disciplining herself to forget the physical silence and concentrate on the music in her mind. The melody was an ancient one, known as *Cregan's Farewell*; it had no words, for a Southern Isles elegy must be given with music alone and not with song. Long, long ago, Cushmagar, the great bard of Carn Caille, had taught her to play the piece, and through his inspiration she had come to feel its deeper significance; the sorrow ingrained within it, the loss, the yearning for that which had once been, but now was gone and could never be again. Images flooded her mind; of a blood-red sun hanging above the winter ice; of a great gull, its outline etched with silver, sailing in solitary splendour over an empty plain; of the sea, beating and beating against the ramparts of huge, impassive cliffs, inexorably wearing their might to shingle and finally to sand. Her fingers moved unconsciously on the strings, her body swayed to the rhythm of the music inside her head. And now before her inner eye a face was forming, an old, seamed face, the cataracted eyes silver-grey and blank, the mouth parting in a gentle smile as her old friend and mentor Cushmagar, long dead now, nodded approval of his favourite pupil.

'*Ah, my little singer of songs. The Mother has touched you with Her gift.*' The well-remembered voice, strong despite his years and his failing health, echoed ghostly in Indigo's mind. '*Were you not royal and destined for greater things, what a bard you might have been. Play for me, my singer, my princess. Play for Cushmagar, that he might see again the beauty and the grief of our beloved islands, through your hands.*'

Tears crept between Indigo's closed eyelids and began to trickle down her cheeks. Her heart seemed to swell, as though it might burst; she felt a choking in her throat, felt her lips form the old man's name . . .

Forth's soft exclamation and the sound came together, as a cascade of music rippled from the harp and rang out across the bleak moorland. Indigo's teeth sank hard into her lower lip, and a sound like a sob escaped her as the melody in her mind meshed and merged with the music of her harp. The image of Cushmagar smiled and nodded once more, and an ancient, gnarled hand came up in a quiet gesture that urged and encouraged her.

'*The harp and the pipe, my little singer. Now the harp and the pipe together.*' The voice whispered down the corridors of her mind, and even as Cushmagar's shade stopped speaking, the thin, eldritch thread of a reed-pipe blended with the harp's melody. Shocked, Indigo opened her eyes, and saw Forth with the pipe raised to his lips, eyes tight shut, oblivious to everything but the music.

Cushmagar! Her thoughts rioted. *You* –

'*I am here, my princess. While you remember me, I will always be with you. Play on, dear one. Play on.*'

Stunned beyond hope of understanding, Indigo clung desperately to the music's thrall. They had breached the barrier; they had broken the spell of the demon world and imposed their own reality. They must not let it slip from them now!

Then, through eyes blurred by the tears that she couldn't control, she saw that the nightscape around them was changing.

Where there had been nothing but the black, barren moor, a new land was beginning to take form. She glimpsed trees, their leaves quivering as though in a capricious breeze, ghostly as yet but growing stronger and more tangible. She saw the glint of rushing water, and beyond it a vista of tall, aloof crags, black against the sky's pewter and cloaked with bushes and rocky out-crops. She saw a path, winding up through the crags, glowing faintly as though its phosphorescence was a guide for the traveller . . .

Very slowly, still playing with the harp tucked in the crook of her arm, Indigo rose to her feet. As she did so, a breath of cool air blew against her face, and her nostrils flared as they caught a sweet-sour smell like decaying flowers. Forth, alerted by her movement, opened his eyes; the sharp stiffening of his shoulders confirmed that he too had seen the transformation, but he had the presence of mind to continue piping.

Decaying flowers . . . the smell assailed Indigo again; she thought of rank, neglected gardens, old gates rusting and forgotten, and hard on the heels of that image came recollection of the face reflected in the glowing pool. The garden in which that face had appeared had been a thing of beauty; but instinct told Indigo that the loveliness had been only a mask, and that beneath the mask lay corruption.

Dead flowers, and the sea pounding, eroding the rock, imposing its will . . . she *would* break through. She *would*.

'Ahh!' Triumph and vindication formed the exclamation, as Indigo saw at last what lay at the end of the path leading up into the crags. A gate of iron scrollwork, tall and narrow, set between two rock faces; beyond the gate the unfocused shifting of leaves in the twilight. And the moorland was fading, the new vista becoming more solid and more real with every moment.

Forth paused in his playing and said softly, 'Mother of All Life . . . '

'Don't stop,' Indigo warned him. 'We must hold on to it.' She began to walk forward. The harp made her movements awkward, but she dared not trust this new reality, not yet; if they lost the hold their music had imposed, it might slip away. All around them the changes were intensifying; she could hear the night wind in the trees now, see their dark trunks taking form in a graceful avenue to either side of them. They were on a smooth sward, no longer entirely black but tinged here and there with green, and leading down to the water she had glimpsed, which had now resolved into a bright, fast-running river.

'There's a bridge.' She nodded, unable to point, to where a narrow, rustic span arched over the water to meet the path on the far side.

Forth took his lips from the pipe briefly. 'Our packs – ' he said.

'Gather what you can; but don't stop playing for

longer than you have to. And bring my crossbow – we may need it.' She watched as swiftly he swung one of the three packs over his shoulder together with the two extra water-skins and crossbow and bolts. The doubt in his eyes was being rapidly overtaken by an excitement that matched her own, and, acting on intuition, she began to change the melancholy strains of *Cregan's Farewell* to the quicker, harder lilt of *Annemora*, a walking-song from her homeland's north-western hills. Forth listened alertly for a moment then followed suit, piping with new confidence as he recognised the tune, which had become a favourite with the Brabazon Fairplayers. Unconsciously falling into step with the tune's rhythm, they quickened their pace over the sward, and – if she'd paused to consider, Indigo thought later, her blood would have desiccated at the idea of such recklessness – stepped together on to the bridge.

The span wasn't a phantasm. Instead, they felt the solid assurance of wood beneath their feet, and heard the tramp of their footfalls vying with the river's rush as they crossed over the torrent and, light-headed with their triumph, scrambled from the bridge on to the path beyond.

The barrier was broken. In crossing the bridge they had cracked the outer shell of illusion, and passed through into a deeper level of the demon world. There might be more such barriers to overcome, more shells to break; but whatever happened now, Indigo knew in her bones that this new landscape wouldn't shiver and fade and vanish. The moor and its emptiness were gone for good.

Tentatively, she began to damp the sound of the harp, slowing her fingers, softening the notes with the heels of her hands. As the sound faded she watched her surroundings, holding her breath tautly in case her intuition should be wrong; but the river and the crags and the path remained, and at last Indigo allowed the harp to fall silent. For a few moments the notes of Forth's pipe rose reedy and eldritch above the river's bright noise; then he, too, ceased playing, and in the comparative silence they looked at each other.

156

A snort of laughter from Forth abruptly released them both from the thrall.

'Goddess preserve us – we've done it! Indigo, we've *done* it!' Careless of her harp's safety he covered the ground between them in one stride and flung his arms around her, crushing her in a bear-hug. Indigo laughed too, and hugged him in return as best she could; he kissed her cheek, then in a rush of emotion tried to find her mouth with his lips. Quickly she turned her head aside, and they broke apart in a confusion of exclamation and further laughter. Yet although the embrace was innocent enough, and she had been able to draw back without causing offence or hurt, Indigo knew that it would have taken only the smallest encouragement to tip the balance, in Forth's mind, between comradeship and something far more complex.

You know, don't you, that Forth's in love with you? Esty's sharp, sly words at the poolside came back to her. She did know it: she'd known it for a long time, long before the shadow of Bruhome fell across her happy hiatus. Amid the cheerful chaos of the Brabazons' communal life it had been easy to evade the issue and any tensions it might otherwise have created; but here the situation was altogether different. So far she had had no need to keep Forth at arms' length; she only hoped that, without Esty's presence to stand between them, Forth's attitude would not begin to change.

She pushed the thought hastily away: for the moment there were other and more immediate matters to concern them both. They stood at the foot of a winding track that zig-zagged its way up the clifflike crags, through the stands of scrubby bushes and stunted trees which clung to the rock faces, on and up to the distant gate, which from here was invisible amid the overhanging tangle.

Forth was eyeing the path. 'It looks an easy enough climb,' he said. 'More of a walk, really.' His gaze roamed to the rock faces on either side of the track. 'Funny: it reminds me of somewhere, though I can't quite place it . . . oh, but I can!' He snapped his fingers as memory came. 'Do you remember that abandoned quarry on the edge of the fells, before we reached Bruhome? Where the stone had been cut away like steps, and the shrub had grown back and greened the cliffs over?'

'Yes.' Now Indigo, too, saw the peculiar resemblance. The quarry rocks had been pale where these were black, and the trees a spectacular blend of green and autumnal gold instead of the dour black and lovat of the foliage clothing these cliffs. But otherwise, they might have been gazing at the same landscape.

Except, she reminded herself, for the path, and the wrought-iron gate that waited mysteriously at the path's end.

She returned her harp to its bag and took the crossbow and the two spare waterskins from Forth, settling them on her back. Forth was staring at the path again, and as they readied themselves to begin the climb, he said, 'What do you think we'll find up there?'

Indigo shook her head. 'I don't want to speculate.' She smiled at him, but a little grimly. 'We both know the power of illusion, after all. I'm going to think only of finding Esty – and, I pray, the others.'

Forth didn't comment. They were both haunted by memory of the sleepwalking woman's grotesque end, and dreaded that, entranced and helpless as she was, Chari might suffer the same fate, with Stead and Grimya – if, indeed, the three of them were still together – powerless to prevent it. But, perhaps superstitiously, neither wanted to voice the fears they shared, and the subject was carefully avoided as, sobered now after the first flush of their success, they set off up the twisting, uneven track.

As Forth had predicted, the climb wasn't arduous. Indeed, the meandering progress of the path meant that the incline was relatively gentle, and as they ascended Indigo was struck by the wealth of minute detail which seemed to exist here, in acute contrast with the unnatural barrenness of the moor. Small stones and twigs and dust littered the path; random clumps of seeding grasses and even the occasional wild flower grew wherever a gap in the bushes granted them room. And, for the first time since leaving the real world, the night air was stirred by natural breezes that chilled her skin. This level of the demon dimension might be as illusory as the last, but here it seemed that the illusions at least bore a closer resemblance to reality. Only one incongruity struck a discordant note: there were no creatures abroad, no small, busy rustlings in the undergrowth; nothing to suggest the presence of any sentient life other than their own.

They continued to ascend, not talking but simply peering about them with a mixture of fascination and wary caution. Looking back briefly, Indigo was surprised to see that they'd already climbed a considerable way; the river was a pale and phosphorescent ribbon far below them, inaudible now, and the trees and the sward beyond had merged into a blur of darkness. The effect was eerie and oddly captivating, and she stood gazing down, until Forth, who had gone on ahead and vanished round a sharp bend in the path, gave a sudden shout that made her start and turn.

'Indigo! Up here!' He sounded excited, and Indigo hurried after him. Scrambling round the curve and almost missing her footing in her haste, she pulled up sharply as she saw what awaited them less than twenty yards ahead.

Set into a stone wall that blended almost perfectly with the more natural rock around it was the iron gate. And beyond the gate, like a strange oasis in a desert, lay the garden, with its graceful, sweeping trees and immaculately tended lawns, that she had seen reflected in the pool on the moor.

Forth murmured softly under his breath; it might have been a prayer or an imprecation. 'Look at it,' he said, awed. 'It's hardly credible.' He started to walk the last few paces to the gate, and Indigo followed. Closer to, the scrub cleared to reveal that the path did not in fact end at the wall, but divided, forking away left and right along a broad ledge, finally to disappear round the curve of the cliff. The gate stood precisely at the fork, and Forth, approaching, reached out to touch it with a tentative hand. When nothing untoward happened – the gate didn't vanish, and didn't burn him – he took a firmer hold and shook the iron framework gently.

'It won't open.' He bent to examine the gate more

closely. 'There must be a lock of some kind, though I can't see it. Only a latch, but the latch won't move.'

Indigo, too, moved forward to study the gate. It shone with the faint patina of newly-forged metal, as though it had been made and set into place only that day. Another facet of the illusion? She recalled the whiff of decayed flowers that had come to her on the breeze as the moorland faded to reveal this new vista, and gazed more acutely through the gate's bars at the garden. Tiny flowers glimmered on the smooth lawn, leaves trembled and reflected rippling patterns of light as the trees stirred; it looked a lovely and peaceful place. But she reminded herself again that perhaps this surface beauty was like a clean dressing that hid a festering wound; purity laid deceptively over utter corruption.

'I might be able to climb it.' Forth's voice broke in on her thoughts, and she saw that he had stepped back a pace to look critically at the top of the gate. 'There aren't many footholds, but if you made a back for me I think I could do it. Then I could pull you up after me.'

Indigo shook her head. 'I don't like the idea, Forth. We don't know what's in there; and if we need to climb back in a hurry . . . '

'Yes, yes; I take your point. But have you got a better suggestion?'

She bent to peer at the latch. 'Did you bring the lantern?'

'Yes. It's attached to my pack.'

'Let's try to kindle it. If we have some light we can see if there's a way of opening the gate.'

Forth started to say, 'But the lantern won't – ' then stopped. 'Ah. Of course. This time, it might.'

'Exactly.' Indigo brought the tinderbox from her belt-pouch, and they crouched over the lantern. *Concentrate*, she thought, and saw an equally fierce determination in Forth's eyes. *We can do it. We created music: we can create light*.

Forth yelped with delight as the candle-wick caught and flickered into life. Hastily he closed the lantern, and they watched in tense but eager silence as slowly, and reluctantly the tiny flame grew larger, brighter, and light began to spill through the glass.

'The flame's still blue, though,' Indigo said after a few moments.

'No, it isn't.' Forth shook his head in emphatic denial; the new lamplight made his eyes glint. 'It's whatever we want it to be. And I say we want it to be as yellow as any natural candle.' As he spoke, the flame flickered. To Indigo's surprise and delight the cold, steel-blue glimmer was replaced by a warmer gold.

'You see?' Forth grinned at her over the lantern. 'We're learning fast. And I'm beginning to wonder just what else we might achieve if we put our minds to it.' He straightened and turned back to the gate. 'Like this, for example. I think we both *expected* it to be locked; it's what anyone might anticipate. But the hinges aren't rusted. Others have gone through before us, or so we believe. So if it opened for them – ' He reached out: but before he could touch the gate, Indigo gave a sharp hiss.

'Forth, wait! *Listen!*'

'What is it?'

'*Ssh!*' She raised a hand quickly, and stepped closer to him. Her voice was a barely audible whisper as she added, 'There's something moving on the path.'

Forth tensed and peered into the gloom, listening alertly. For a few moments he heard nothing, and was about to say so when suddenly there came the unmistakable rustle of disturbed leaves. Instantly he reached for his knife; and closing his hand round the hilt he heard the slide of metal on metal as Indigo slid a bolt into her crossbow.

Silence. Their gazes met briefly, tense, fearful. Indigo mentally cursed the lantern, which had suddenly become an enemy rather than a friend; its light intensified the outer darkness, hindering their eyes and blinding them to what might otherwise be visible.

The bushes rustled again, closer this time, and Indigo realised with an unpleasant shock that more than one creature was approaching, and from more than one direction.

And then in the dark there were eyes.

Forth hissed an oath, and caught hold of her arm,

drawing her back against the gate. Looking wildly from right to left, Indigo saw what he had already seen: they were all but encircled. Eyes glowed on the path's forks, on the track they had climbed, among the scrub – there must have been twenty or more of the unknown creatures staring at them, unblinking and feral.

'The gate!' Forth's breath was hot against her ear. 'It's our only way of escape. We've got to will it to open!'

A guttural voice spoke out of the darkness.

'No. The gate w. . .ill not open. You cannot enter the garden.'

Every muscle in Indigo's body locked rigid with shock, and her consciousness seemed to slow to a crawl.

'N. . .' she said, and struggled with herself, forcing the word to come. 'No . . . '

Shadows flowed from the bushes, from the rocks, and she saw the lean, lithe shapes of the wolves as they padded, slinking, towards her. They were blacker than pitch, their coats glowing with a ghostly nacre; their eyes and their open mouths were red, like sullen embers. They were phantoms, she knew, hungry yet mindless . . . but in their midst was one pair of eyes that glowed not crimson but amber, and in those eyes was terrible, twisted intelligence.

The creature moved. Indigo scented musk; saw the brindled fur ripple. And then, white-fanged and growling softly deep in its throat, it stepped into full view on the path before her, and Indigo's voice broke from her lips in a stark wail of horror and despair.

'*Grimya!*'

Chapter XII

They stared at each other, the human and the wolf, and Indigo felt as though her stomach had dropped away into a void as she realised that Grimya did not know her.

'Grimya . . .' Her voice was thin, shaking as she tried to formulate the plea and the helpless question. 'Grimya, it's me. It's Indigo. *Indigo!*'

She could hear the she-wolf breathing; a steady, purposeful sound. Then Grimya said,

'I know no Grimya. I know no In-digo. We are *wolf*.'

The final word was a savage snarl, and a chorus of panting swelled briefly then died away, as if Grimya's ghoulish companions had voiced their agreement.

'Grimya . . .' Forth, stunned beyond speech, was trying to restrain her but Indigo fought him and moved a cautious pace forward before dropping to a crouch. 'Grimya, you *do* know me. I am your oldest friend. Indigo, Grimya. *Indigo*. Oh, love – something terible has happened to you! Try to remember me. Try, *please*.' She extended a hand – then jerked back with a cry of shock as Grimya lunged at her, teeth snapping together an inch from her fingertips.

The she-wolf advanced another pace. Her body trembled now with eagerness; her tail twitched, and her lambent eyes were mad.

'We are *wolf*,' she said, and Forth had never heard such menace in a voice before. 'And we are *hungry*. And we shall *eat*.'

'No . . .' Tears streamed down Indigo's face, grief mingling with terror. 'No, Grimya, *listen* to me! You *must* –'

Grimya raised her muzzle to the sky and howled, shattering Indigo's plea. Taking their cue from her, the entire ghostly wolf-pack lifted their heads in a dreadful banshee chorus, flinging the challenge of their bloodlust to the night – and then, as the dreadful sounds died away, they began to close in.

For one appalling moment Forth was mesmerised; then sanity came back and he spun round, flinging himself at the gate – before freezing again as he realised that Indigo wasn't about to move.

'Indigo!' Panic gave his voice a razor edge. 'Indigo, get up!'

'She doesn't know me . . .' Indigo only continued to stare into Grimya's feral eyes. The ghost-wolves took another step forward, tightening the net. Forth could hear them panting, slavering.

'*Indigo!*' Wildly, he looked about him for a weapon. The knife was all but useless; he couldn't hope to survive with it for more than a few moments if the pack attacked. But there was nothing else.

'Indigo!' He shouted her name again, trying frantically to break through the thrall that held her, and in desperation snatched up the lantern and waved it at the encroaching nightmares.

Light flared across jet-black muzzles and rabid eyes, and a cluster of wolves shrank back, snarling. Indigo too flinched from the light, and with his free hand Forth grabbed her arm and jerked her back, so that she sprawled hard up against the gate. He didn't wait to help her as, dazed and shaking her head in confusion, she started to struggle up, but flailed his arms, feinting with the lantern as he writhed out of his jacket. *Fire* – phantoms they might be, but these horrors feared fire like any real animal. *Fire* – he finally shook the jacket off and fumbled with the lantern-glass, thrusting one of the garment's sleeves into the cage and over the candle stump. *Fire* –

'Catch, you whore's whelp! *Catch!*'

It shouldn't have been possible; the candle flame was too small, the jacket's fabric too heavy; but suddenly a tongue of bright orange fire licked at the sleeve – and as Forth jerked it clear of the lantern, the garment burst into flames.

Forth yelled exultantly, and swung the burning coat around his head like a bolas. A spectacular wheel of sparks scattered from it, singeing his arm and hair, and the flames blazed up as, yelping, the wolves fell back under the onslaught of brilliance and heat.

'*Forth!*' It was Indigo's voice; Forth snatched a moment to look over his shoulder and saw her frantically priming the crossbow. 'To your right!'

There was no time to give thanks for her return to reason; he swung about, and saw four of the wolves, bellies low to the ground and about to spring. He yelled, and brought the burning jacket down in a twisting figure-of-eight that sent them snarling and tumbling back; then Indigo shouted again. Two more, from the left. The crossbow sang fiercely; Forth saw the bolt flash in the flamelight, saw it hit its target –

And pass straight through the black wolf, to crash harmlessly into the scrub.

'Indigo, the gate!' He chanced another swift glance back, saw her face a wide-eyed mask of shock. 'You've got to open the gate somehow – it's our only hope!'

Flaming pieces of fabric were whirling from the jacket now as it threatened to disintegrate; he couldn't hold on to it for more than a few more seconds, and there was no time to tear off his shirt and ignite that too. Just one chance, Forth told himself grimly; just one –

He dropped to a crouch and swung the burning coat in an arc before him, across the tops of the bushes, willing them with all his strength to catch light. Sparks danced madly; a leaf smouldered, a tongue of flame licked – and three ragged patches of fire burst into life.

The wolf-pack were hurled into confusion as panic broke out in their ranks. Howling, scrabbling, they fought each other to get out of the way of the flames, and Forth whirled the disintegrating coat one last time before flinging it from him. It arced up and over in a brilliant fireball, lighting feral faces and snarling jaws, and Forth added his own yelling voice to the wolves' clamour, cursing them, screaming at them, mocking their fear – until the crazed, triumphant spell was shattered by hands that dragged him backwards, spinning him around and pulling him pell-mell from his victory. He ran without knowing what he was doing, zigzagging like a drunkard: dark walls loomed, unyielding iron smacked painfully against his shoulder as he staggered and almost lost his balance; then he was toppling, still propelled forward by his own momentum, and sprawled full-length on a soft sward.

Indigo, who had only just saved herself from falling with him, swung round and ran back to the gate. How she had done it, she didn't know; terror and the blind instinct to survive had somehow combined into a variation on Forth's momentary madness, and she had turned on the gate in a fury, to see it all but burst from its hinges as it smashed open. The pack, the harp, the lantern had all gone through as she flung them, and lastly she had bodily hauled Forth to sanctuary in her wake. Now the gate had slammed shut again – she knew it, she had *willed* it – and it wouldn't open again, for she had willed that too.

But Grimya –

Her hands clamped round the iron bars, and she stared out on to utter darkness and silence.

There were no wolves. No evil eyes in the dark, and no burning bushes. The pack had vanished like blown smoke, and the whole crazed encounter might have been nothing more than another illusion.

But somehow, Indigo knew it was not. And as she turned away, shaking suddenly with the delayed reaction of shock, she heard a voice that seemed to speak in her mind. A painfully familiar voice, though now it spoke in blind hunger rather than in love. Grimya's voice.

We shall follow. We shall find you again.

Forth was sitting up when she returned to him. His eyes were dazed, and reaction had drained all feeling from his face; though he was staring at his surroundings, little seemed to register. But at Indigo's approach he looked up, and when he saw her expression the life began to return to his look and he reached out as though to catch her hand.

She veered aside, avoiding him, and crossed to where

their belongings lay in a tumbled heap on the grass. She didn't speak, but dropped her crossbow beside the pack – the clatter it made jarred against the silence – and then began to sort systematically through the pile. The harp, set carefully upright; beside it the waterskins, then the lantern, the bow, her remaining bolts; all ranged in a rigidly neat line one beside another. Forth watched her for a while, then, determined not to be intimidated although he was aware that he might make matters worse rather than better, said quietly:

'You'll have to talk about it sometime. You can't keep it to yourself forever, or it'll fester like a wound.'

Indigo's hands paused in mid-movement. For a few moments she remained motionless, then she raised her head and looked at him.

She wasn't crying, as he'd half expected. Instead, she looked calm, and utterly wise – and old. 'Yes,' she said levelly. 'I'm aware of that. But at this moment, I'm more concerned with deeds than with words.'

Forth was chagrined by her reaction; and, irrationally, disappointed. He'd expected her to need him, to need his strength as any of his sisters would have done, and he'd been more than ready to give it. The adrenalin of the encounter with the phantom wolves was still running high in his veins, and he wanted to embrace Indigo within his triumph and lend her comfort and reassurance. But she didn't want them. She needed nothing from him, and under her steady gaze he felt reduced from a hero to a superfluous child.

Fury surged; then Forth bit it back as he looked at Indigo's face again and realised that his anger was a poor candle compared to the smouldering furnace of rage within her. It shamed him, and he got to his feet, crossing the short, smooth grass to where she crouched over her careful inventory. She didn't look at him again, but only said, 'Everything's here.'

'Indigo, what do you mean to do?'

Now she did glance up once more. 'What do you think?' Her voice was sharp, then she turned to stare at the dark garden. 'I'm going to find it. And I'm going to *destroy* it.'

'The demon?'

'What else?' She stood up; then abruptly the rigid anger crystallised and she put both hands to her face, pushing back her dishevelled hair with a violent gesture. 'Forth, you *saw* her! She wasn't Grimya any more – she was a thing possessed! She didn't even recognise me. And those monsters with her – '

'They were phantoms,' Forth said. 'I saw what happened when you tried to shoot one of them. Indigo, could it be that Grimya is – '

She interrupted him, knowing what he was about to say; she'd asked herself the same question, but fleetingly, for she was aware of the truth.

'No. Grimya isn't one of them, not in that way. She's alive, and she's real. But something's been done to her; her mind's been twisted.' She drew in a long, harsh breath. 'We talked, do you remember, about images being drawn from our memories and used against us? That's what it's done. It knows what Grimya is to me, and it's captured her and warped her, and now she's become a weapon in its hands.' Another breath, and her head jerked up, hair flicking back and almost catching Forth across the eyes. 'I'll release her. Somehow – because I'm stronger than any illusion this world can conjure.'

Forth put out a hand and laid it on her arm. '*We're* stronger.'

She looked at him, then gave a short, humourless laugh and nodded once. 'Yes; of course. *We're* stronger.'

He risked a grin, though it was forced. 'We don't know the half yet of what we might be capable of achieving, do we? First music, then fire, then the gate. As I said before, we're learning fast.'

It was true; but as the last of her fury dissipated Indigo acknowledged that they had more lessons yet to come. Sobered, she looked back on her outburst and realised how hollow it had been. She and Forth might indeed be stronger than anything this phantom world could set against them, but the key that would unlock the full measure of that strength was as yet beyond their reach. Esty still eluded them. They were no nearer to finding any trace of Stead and Chari, and she hadn't the power to release Grimya from the spell that had trapped her in madness.

A soft, sly rustling impinged on her thoughts. She looked up and, for the first time since their headlong rush through the gate, took in their new surroundings. The garden. Dark trees, smooth black grass starred with flowers, bushes that shifted in the breeze. So alluring, so tranquil. And she felt as though the leaves, moving as the air stirred them, were laughing at her.

She bent to where she'd laid out the stark little line of their belongings, and when she spoke her voice was harsh. 'We're wasting time. I don't want to stay here. I want to get away from this place.'

Forth put his hands on his hips and stared into the gloom. 'Away to where? It looks to me as though there's nothing but the garden.'

'Yes. And that's precisely what the demon wants us to believe.' Indigo swung sharply about, digging a heel into the turf beneath her, wanting to scar and ruin its immaculate surface. From the gate the garden stretched away between two high stone walls. She could see more of the graceful trees, and the walls were clad with climbing plants, roses in full bloom glimmering pale and limpid through the twilight. The far end was invisible; there was only a gradual blurring and merging into the dark. Another endless vista, like the moor? Or would they find themselves faced with more stone walls, this time with no gate that they could pass through?

She looked at the trees again. The breeze had died, and the stillness gave an unpleasant impression that the garden was holding its breath, waiting. Indigo picked up the hide bag that contained her harp and stroked its surface gently. The instrument inside gave off a discord, muffled by the covering, and her ebbing spirits rose a little.

'I think,' she said, 'that we should walk on and see what awaits us at the end of the sward. And I think that as we walk, we should consider what it is that we want to find there.'

Forth glanced keenly at her. 'Esty,' he said immediately and with emphasis. 'That's what I want to find. Esty, unharmed and waiting for us.' He started to gather up the pack, then paused. 'The lantern's out. Should we re-light it, do you think?'

Indigo shook her head. 'The candle won't last forever. Best save it.'

'But the wolves – '

'They can't get in. They can't follow us; not even Grimya can.' She shivered. 'I must keep believing that. I mustn't think of her. Just of Esty.'

They began to walk down the long lawn. The atmosphere felt more eerie than ever; the breeze hadn't sprung up again and the silence was claustrophobic. Their feet left no prints on the spotless sward, and when she trod on one of the tiny flowers Indigo noticed that it bore no sign of crushing. She tried to concentrate on thoughts of Esty, but it wasn't easy; her banked-down anger had begun to reassert itself, and the memory of Grimya's glaring, ensorcelled eyes hovered dangerously close to the edge of her inner vision. Suddenly a bush rustled for no apparent reason, and something close to panic shot through her.

'Forth.' She stopped walking. 'Forth, it's no use. I can't clear my mind. The Mother alone knows what might be conjured if I don't get a hold on my thoughts.'

Forth peered ahead into the gloom for a moment, then looked back. The gate was invisible now, but the sward still stretched on before them with no sign of ending. He licked his lips.

'Talk to Esty,' he said, and pointed into the darkness. 'Talk to her, as though she was here and we were hailing her and walking towards her.'

'Yes . . . ' It was worth trying; it might focus awareness and crush down the unconscious thoughts. Feeling a little foolish, Indigo raised her voice.

'Esty.' *Picture her coming towards you. She's unharmed, unenchanted: just Esty as you know her.* 'Esty!'

'Esty!' Forth's voice echoed hers. 'Where in the name of the Mother have you been? We've been frantic – why did you run off?'

He was smiling broadly, calling on all his acting skills, throwing himself into the role. Spurred by his example,

Indigo thought of the Brabazon Fairplayers and told herself determinedly that this was simply another show, on a rickety wooden stage, under the flare of flamboys, before a crowd waiting to be entertained.

'Don't be angry with her, Forth,' she said, entering into the game and dredging up new confidence. 'No harm's been done, and we're all together again.'

'True. But Esty, if you ever give us another fright like that, I'll – ' And the words jammed in his throat.

It happened so quickly that Indigo had walked several steps ahead of Forth before shock halted her with a jolt. In one moment there had been nothing but the unending lawn rolling on ahead of them: the next instant, the lawn had vanished and a stone wall barred the way. An arch had been cut into the wall, and under the keystone stood a red-haired woman.

Shock gave way to relief, and Indigo cried delightedly, 'Esty!'

But Forth didn't call a greeting. Instead he dropped the pack he was carrying and stood arrested, as though some massive force had suddenly and violently paralysed him. Only his eyes remained animated, and they were filled with horror.

Not comprehending, Indigo looked at the woman again, and then saw that, though her hair was the same vibrant colour as Esty's, and her nose had the same coquettish tilt, she was many years older, her face seamed with the character lines that told of both age and long experience.

Understanding hit her like a physical blow. She turned to Forth, saw the confirmation in his stricken eyes, and heard him say in a weak, strangled voice, 'Mam . . . ?'

'Forth, no.' Indigo held out a hand to bar his path, though he'd shown no sign of moving. 'It's a phantom!'

Forth's throat muscles worked, and he swallowed. 'I . . . know.'

The woman was smiling, fondly and just a little admonishingly, as though her indulgence were being tried. Forth stared fixedly back at her, then his throat spasmed again.

'My mother's dead. That isn't her, it can't be her.' A

great shudder ran through him, breaking the paralysis. 'Make it disappear, Indigo. Please – *banish* it!'

Indigo shook her head. 'I . . . don't think I can.' She glanced at him in trepidation. 'It's been drawn from your mind, just as the Brown Walker was drawn from mine. I can't will it away.'

The phantom figure tilted her head to one side, and her lips made a moue of mock consternation. Indigo's flesh chilled as instinct told her that the apparition – and therefore its creator – had heard their exchange. Then, the figure raised her arms and held them out.

'Eh now, Forth. Come to your Mam. Come and be comforted.'

'*No!*' Forth's scream ripped through the stifling gloom, and with one hand he flung off Indigo's restraining arm, while the other snatched his knife from its sheath at his belt. The blade flashed murderously – and Forth took off like a hare, running at the arch and the smiling phantasm with the knife raised to kill.

'Forth, come back!' Indigo staggered, flailed, regained her balance and ran after him as he careered towards the gap in the wall. The apparition uttered a screech of unhuman laughter, spun about with dervish speed and flicked away into the darkness, and Forth, still yelling, charged through the arch in pursuit.

'*Forth!*' Premonition struck, and Indigo shrieked a desperate warning. Forth paid no heed; he was a blur in the dimness and she willed her muscles to a last, frantic effort to reach him before –

She slammed with tremendous impact face-first into the solid cliff of a blank stone wall.

Chapter XIII

Indigo swore softly but heartfeltedly, pressing her face against the wall's rough surface and shutting her eyes for a few moments while her pounding heart slowed to something akin to its normal rate. Her calves and biceps felt as though they were on fire; she was out of condition, out of practice, and the burden of the pack, harp and crossbow on her back made matters worse. But the grim effort was almost over: looking up, she saw the sky's pewter grey above the denser charcoal of stone, and knew she was close to the top of the wall.

She'd come to, spreadeagled in the grass at the foot of the wall and, putting her hand up to her stinging face and feeling the grazes on her nose and forehead, she'd reflected bitterly that though the rough stonework might be as illusory as anything else in this world, her collision with it had been all too real. But there seemed to be no other damage; no concussion and no bruising.

At last, shakily, Indigo stood up, and began to consider her new and urgent dilemma.

The arch had vanished. Where it had been there was only a blank stone face, and she knew immediately that to search for any trace of a gap would be futile. The wall's fabric had shifted at the same instant that Forth ran under the keystone, and now they were separated by a solid barrier.

Later, when she had shouted his name until her throat was sore and rasping, she realised that the effort had been futile from the start: there could be no answer; for whatever lay beyond the wall was also beyond her reach. The show-master had changed the nature of his performance without warning, and his puppets were suddenly dancing to a new tune. She and Forth were separated by more than stone and mortar: they were a world apart.

Calm, she had told herself then. *Calm. Think.* But the willpower that might have crumbled the barrier wasn't there; she was too angry, and the bile and adrenalin of her anger bound her to mundane means. The demon had skilfully and systematically prised her from her allies one by one, finally to leave her alone and vulnerable. Very well. Very *well*. What she couldn't achieve with the strength of her mind, she would achieve with the strength of her body.

And so the climb had begun. As she set her toe into a tight crevice, inserted her fingers into a niche between stone and mortar and hauled herself up the first vital armslength, Indigo had heard the trees and bushes in the garden behind her begin to agitate, and smiled thinly. *Yes*, she said silently in her mind. *Warn your master, if it pleases you. It will do him no good!*

And, because she had willed it, the footholds and the handholds had been there, tiny and strenuous, precarious and unstable but enough nonetheless to take her like a slow and awkward human parody of a crawling insect up the face of the wall. Now, she had only another few feet to go.

Indigo clenched her teeth against the burning of her muscles and thrust her protesting body up to the next hold. She poised, feeling her tendons strain: then another push, another wrenching effort, and with a gasped, ferocious oath she scissored herself in a convulsive movement to sit astride the top of the wall.

For a few moments breathlessness and relief combined to lock her, both physically and mentally, into a world of throbbing red exhaustion. At last the sensation began to fade, and she exhaled a long gust of pent air. She'd done it. Unfit though she might be, the old skills had come back to her and she'd achieved her goal. Now, somewhere on the far side of the height she'd scaled, was not only Forth but Esty too; and the key – she felt it, she was *certain* of it – to the fate of Stead and Chari.

She opened her eyes and looked down at what lay beyond the wall.

174

And saw nothing but darkness.

'Forth?' She called his name tentatively, and listened for any answering sound from the black well below her. Her voice fell peculiarly flat, as though she'd spoken into a vacuum, and no reply came back from the dark.

'Forth! Forth, where are you?'

Nothing. Indigo looked speculatively at the wall's surface. It was rough enough to provide reasonable purchase: but she could see no more than a few feet down before the darkness encroached like a black lake, and was loath to take the risk of lowering herself into the unknown.

Shifting to improve her straddled balance, she untied the lantern from where she'd lashed it to the pack, and took out her tinderbox. The knack of defeating this world's resistance to fire was familiar to her now, and she was gratified when the candle stub caught and flared at the first attempt, splashing yellow light in a ragged circle.

Indigo leaned as far as she dared from the wall and held the lantern at arms' length. Its light bit into the blackness, illuminating perhaps another five feet of the stonework, but that was all; it told her nothing of any value. Muttering a curse, she fished in the pack for a length of rope, tied the lantern to it and began to pay it out, lowering the lamp down the side of the wall. The circle of brilliance danced crazily as the lantern bumped against the stone, and Indigo counted the rope by the armslength: ten, twelve, fifteen – then she jerked the lantern to a halt as the light glimmered on grass below.

Grim satisfaction filled her, and visions of bottomless pits vanished. Quickly she lashed the pack and harp to the rope's free end and lowered them after the lantern: when the rope went slack she slipped one arm through the remaining loop and, with nothing but the crossbow on her back to encumber her, swung her legs over the wall's edge.

It was a perilous and nerve-wracking descent, harder even than the upward climb. But at last her feet touched the ground and, relieved, Indigo straightened and looked around her.

The illumination from the lantern didn't extend very

far, but it was enough to show her that she was in another garden. Here, though, the grass and the shrubs were neglected and overgrown; rank weeds pushed up through the lawn, and on the brink of the circle of light she could see a sullen tangle of vegetation encroaching on the long grass. Picking up the lantern and holding it high, she glimpsed the shadowy bulk of trees, black trunks encircled by heavily-leafed boughs that arched almost to the ground. It confirmed a suspicion already taking shape in her mind: that this was a distorted mirror-image of the garden on the other side of the wall. Twilight deepened to pitch darkness, rankness and ruin where before there had been peaceful if gloomy order – another veil had parted, and she was closer to the heart of the demon's web.

Indigo lowered the lantern, and turned her back to the wall. If the mirror-image held true, then somewhere ahead of her there would be another gate, reflecting the one by which she and Forth had entered this garden's twin. And beyond that? Better, perhaps, not to speculate as yet, but to walk on and see what awaited her.

She bent to heave the heavy pack on to her shoulders once more – then stopped, nerves crawling, as something moved in the overgrown shrubbery close by.

For a rackingly long moment there was total stillness and silence as Indigo stared into the dark. She hadn't imagined it: the sound of dead leaves rustling under an incautious foot was too familiar for her to mistake. But there was no telltale swaying of a branch or untoward shifting of foliage. Whoever – or whatever – lurked unseen among the bushes knew that she'd heard its approach, and had frozen, waiting to see what she would do.

Very slowly she reached for the lantern again, and as her hand touched it, a twig snapped just beyond the circle of light.

Indigo's heart lurched so violently that she felt it might punch up from her breast into her throat, and – it was madness, but the reaction was instinctive and she couldn't stop it – she snapped out, 'Who is it? Who's there?'

A whole section of a tall bush dipped and parted, and a tremulous voice said, 'Indigo . . . ?'

'*Esty!*' The pendulum swung back from terror to amazed relief, and it was all Indigo could do not to give way to hysterical laughter. Caught in the lamplight, Esty's face as she emerged from the shrubbery was a study in wide-eyed astonishment; with leaves in her hair and a long smear of dirt down one cheek she looked incongruous and comical amid the garden's dereliction.

'Oh, Indigo!' Esty scrambled clear of the entangling vegetation and for a moment stood motionless, trembling, as though she dared not believe what she saw. Then suddenly she launched herself forward, ran to Indigo and flung her arms tightly around her, hugging her with all the strength she possessed. 'Oh, Indigo, you don't know how thankful I am to have found you!'

'I've been so stupid.' Esty wiped her eyes and nose on her sleeve and sniffed loudly. 'I'll never be able to forgive myself for what I did. *Never!*'

Her story was brief and unpleasant. It seemed she remembered little of what had happened when she slipped away from the camp; she'd been aware only of a powerful and imperative longing that blotted out all reason. Like Chalila, whose role she had once played, the demon lover had been calling her and she had run blindly in pursuit – but unlike Chalila, Esty's tale hadn't had a happy ending. She had found herself, without knowing how she arrived there, outside the wrought-iron gate, which had swung open to admit her to the garden. And in the garden, the white-faced man with the dark and sorrowful eyes had been waiting for her.

'He looked so beautiful,' she told Indigo. 'I knew he was lonely, and that only I could comfort him. He held out his arms to me: and I ran towards him, and . . . ' She covered her face with her hands as the memory brought a fresh flood of shame. 'And then suddenly I heard a dreadful laugh, and everything changed, and he was *gone*, and I was here, alone in the dark only everything had changed, and I couldn't find my way back to the other garden . . . Oh, Indigo, it's been so *awful*! I thought I was going to go completely mad!'

Esty didn't know how long she had wandered, alone and frightened with the spell on her shattered, through the rank, silent garden. The first appearance of Indigo's light at the top of the wall had terrified her, and she had hidden among the bushes, certain that some new horror was about to be unleashed on her. Even when the lantern illuminated Indigo's figure, Esty had feared that she might be yet another phantom, and only when Indigo, equally afraid, had called out her challenge did the girl realise that she was flesh and blood, and not an image sent to delude her.

Indigo's relief at having found Esty unharmed was greater than she could express; but it was tempered by deepening concern for Forth. She'd told Esty of what had befallen them and how they had become separated, and tried to convince the girl that she couldn't hold herself to blame. Any one of them might as easily have fallen prey to the deception; Esty had simply been unlucky in that she was the chosen victim. Esty was only a little comforted by her words; whatever the rights and wrongs, she said, she was responsible for their predicament. And if anything should now happen to Forth, she added fiercely, it would be her fault, and she would kill herself.

Indigo hid a smile behind her hand at this, thankful to see that Esty's flamboyant spirit – not to mention her sense of melodrama – hadn't been affected by her ordeal.

'That would be a great loss to us all,' she said, struggling to keep the amusement from her voice. 'But seriously, Esty; we're faced with a great problem. Forth could be anywhere – I don't even know what lies beyond this spot, let alone where to start searching.'

'Ah, but I do.' Esty's eyes gleamed eagerly. 'You see, just before I saw your lantern, I was trying to find another way out, and I found a gate.'

'A gate?'

'Yes. Exactly like the one that led me into the other garden, except that it was set into an arch in a wall.'

A gate within an arch . . . it must be a signpost, Indigo

178

thought. And if Forth, too, had come upon it, he would surely have gone through.

Eagerly, she asked, 'Can you find it again?'

'I'm sure of it.'

'Then let's not delay any longer!' She gathered up her harp, bow and the waterskins; Esty took the pack and pointed into the dark.

'If we walk along the line of the bushes, we'll come to a clump of trees. It's very overgrown, but there's a way through, and the gate's just a short way beyond.' Her hand reached out and squeezed Indigo's fingers, seeking reassurance. 'Do you think we'll find him . . . ?'

'Yes,' Indigo told her firmly, and silenced a small, inner voice that asked: *and what else . . . ?*

As soon as she saw the barred gate under its stone arch, Indigo knew that her surmise had been right. The resemblance both to the original gate and to the arch through which Forth had vanished was blatantly obvious: a clear gauntlet thrown down before them.

Esty said: 'I don't know what's in there. I looked, but I couldn't see a thing, and I was too scared to open the gate.'

Indigo held up the lantern and peered through. As far as she could judge, the vista beyond the gate was much the same as this; a lightless and unpleasant tangle of weed and grass and shrub. She lowered the lamp again, and tried the latch. It lifted, and the gate swung back on silent hinges.

They looked at each other. 'You first,' Esty said uneasily.

Indigo walked slowly under the arch. She heard the latch clank faintly behind them as Esty followed her and closed the gate; then hesitated as she felt a change in the ground underfoot, and looked down.

She was standing on a carpet of sodden, mouldering leaves. Scabrous patches of fungi, moisture glimmering among them, thrust through the slimy litter, and a smell of decay made her nostrils wrinkle. Somewhere, she thought she could hear the sound of water dripping sluggishly.

'Esty, come and look at this.' She moved the lantern from side to side, then stopped again as her eye lit on what looked like the small, nodding bells of a fritillary growing up through the mould. The lovely and familiar bloom seemed grotesquely out of place, and she bent to pluck one of the flower-stems. It trembled in her hand and she wondered fleetingly whether this was some cryptic sign, to what its true nature might be –

The flower collapsed, and Indigo found herself holding a decayed stem of something unrecognisable, so rotten that it was all but liquefied.

Revolted, she swore aloud and flung the black mess away. It fell soundlessly among the sodden undergrowth, and she shook her hand fastidiously. 'Did you see what happened?' she said to Esty. 'It was – Esty?'

Silence greeted her. Esty wasn't there.

'Oh, by the Goddess . . . ' Indigo's pulse quickened to an erratic lurch. 'Esty! Where are you?

There was no answer, and unease began to swell into deep fear. 'Esty!' Indigo called again. 'In the Mother's name, answer me! *Where are you?*'

A voice behind her, sepulchral, redolent with decay, said: 'Esty isn't here, Indigo. But we are.'

And a white, leprous hand reached out of the dark to clamp her wrist.

Indigo shrieked, and the lantern went flying, arcing to fall with a rustling thud among the leaves. The candle instantly went out and Indigo jerked her arm free, stumbling wildly as she tried to turn and face her unknown assailant. Blackness assailed her like a solid wall; accustomed to the lamplight, she could see nothing, and for a terrible moment felt as though the entire dimension were folding in to crush her.

Then, from no more than two paces in front of her, someone laughed.

It was one of the most evil and yet most dismal sounds Indigo had ever heard; a hollow parody of mirth, without meaning and without reason. Her teeth began to chatter; she staggered back a step, and forced her voice to life.

'Wh. . . who are you?'

A chorus of soft laughter broke out, seeming to echo

from all around her. It died away into a long, dolorous sigh. Then:

'Don't you know us, Indigo? Have you already forgotten us?'

She knew that voice. It was changed, as though it came from beyond the grave, but she knew it. And now as her vision gradually adjusted she could see a dim form shifting in the blackness, moving towards her. The mouldering leaves made a soft, wet sound as feet – many feet, encircling her she realised in horror – shuffled them aside – and then out of the murk, deathly white, his eyes as blank and mindless as the eyes of a dead fish, his skin melting and sagging and decaying on his bones, loomed the face of Steadfast Brabazon.

Indigo made a choking sound and stumbled backwards, only to flail to a halt again as she recalled the shuffling feet, behind as well as before her. Breathing hoarsely, raggedly, as though there was no air to sustain her, she tried to croak a denial. 'No . . . oh, *no* . . . '

'We've been searching for you, Indigo.' Stead's mouth widened in a doleful smile that revealed crumbling, blackened teeth. 'We knew you'd come after us, Chari and me, we knew you'd come, because you're a good, brave girl, and you wouldn't abandon your friends in their trouble. So we searched and we searched, and we've found you, and now we're all together again.'

Indigo fought frantically against the panic that threatened to unhinge her. *This wasn't real!* It was another game, another illusion – she had to keep believing that, *had* to –

'Indigo.' Stead's image spoke again in that dead, dreadful monotone. 'You tried, girl. You did your best. But we should have known better, eh? There's no point in fighting any more, because you can't hope to win. None of us can. We know that now.' The smile became wider still, like the rictus of a naked skull. 'We're all here, Indigo. It went back, you see; it went back to Bruhome, and it called the others, and they all came to be with their Da again.'

From all round Indigo came an eerie, muted mumbling; the sound of many voices in wordless agreement.

181

Her stomach heaved convulsively; she dragged breath into her straining lungs and looked wildly to either side.

'No . . . You're not Stead. You're *not*!'

'But I was.'

'*No!* You're phantoms! You, and all the filthy legion crawling around you – you're all *phantoms*!'

The figure of Stead laughed sorrowfully and, she thought, almost pityingly. Then he flung his head back and in a voice chillingly like that of the Stead she had known, the showman, the entertainer, he roared:

'*Light!*'

There was a ferocious, sputtering hiss. And along the hitherto invisible walls of the garden, two rows of glaring, ghostly blue flamboys blazed into life. As if a stage curtain had gone up, the scene lifted out of blackness into cold brilliance – and there, poised dramatically before the iron gate, laughing, stood Esty.

Understanding exploded into Indigo's mind. She whirled round – then cried out in appalled revulsion as she saw for the first time the visions that surrounded her.

Chari, Cour, Rance, Harmony, Honi – the entire Brabazon family stood in the glare of the torches. Their dead eyes glittered silver, their rotting hands were linked to form a chain, their decayed faces smiled a hideous welcome. And slowly, slowly, they all began to move in an awful travesty of a circle dance. The dance became faster and faster around Indigo, while behind them Esty's laughing figure warped and changed and started to take on the form of a tall, gaunt man with jet black hair, sickly white skin and eyes that burned in their hollow sockets like dull, lethal furnaces.

Indigo was trying to scream, but her voice wouldn't obey her. Like a puppet jerking on a string out of control she twisted wildly about, stumbling, struggling to break the dancers' mad circle. Faces bobbed and loomed at her, driving her back: Stead with his smashed teeth, Chari, smiling sweetly, Piety, mad-eyed and giggling, her scalp showing leprous where clumps of her hair had fallen or been torn out. They wouldn't let her go; they were tightening the ring about her. The orchestrator of their gruesome revels, the dark, demonic avatar who had masqueraded as Esty with such appalling conviction, was stalking towards the circle, one arm outstretched, palm turned up in a mockery of greeting and his terrible gaze fixed hungrily on Indigo's face.

The dancing ring parted, wavered for a single instant and then closed again. The demon had slipped into the circle like a shadow, and as she looked into his eyes Indigo felt a numbing paralysis begin to creep from the soles of her feet, through her legs and into her body. She tried to resist, but it was as if her whole being were petrifying, thrusting down roots that held her pinned and helpless.

A thin, white hand with long nails that shone like pearl came to rest on her shoulder, and the demon gazed down. Around them the Brabazons continued their crazed, silent dance. Indigo knew that her grip on reality was crumbling: she could no longer distinguish between truth and illusion; she was starting to believe this insanity, and with the breaking down of her defences came despair.

The demon's hand slid from her shoulder to the soft hollow of her neck, and it bent its head. Indigo saw the lips part, saw the mouth red, like a wolf's maw; saw the fangs, twin white daggers poised above her throat.

The demon is a vampire . . . She had guessed it, she had believed it – and her belief was coming home to claim her. *But it wasn't the truth!*

Ice gave sudden and violent way to red heat, and Indigo shrieked, flinging up her arms in a fighter's movement that took the demon unawares. She yelled again, at the top of her voice, screaming defiance and fury both at the vampire and at the monstrous shades of the Brabazons, and then, with speed and energy born of desperation, spun on her heel and charged at the bobbing, dancing circle.

She heard a thin wail, saw the small, vulnerable figure of Piety bowled over to fall under trampling feet, and in confusion almost made the deadly mistake of halting. Pi was only six; she'd be hurt –

It isn't Piety! her mind screamed. And she was through, bursting the linked hands apart and hurling herself clear of the ring. Cries of dismay rose up behind her, and an animal snarl that snatched her back to memory of Grimya and the phantom wolf-pack. She flung a desperate glance over her shoulder, and as she did so the ghostly flamboys went out, plunging the world into darkness. Indigo yelled with renewed shock, then ran blindly, praying that nothing stood in her path. The gruesome shades were coming after her, she could hear their cries – then her foot turned on a root buried under the rotting leaves, she lost her balance, skidded, and sprawled full-length on the ground.

There was no time to recover her wits; no time to regain the breath that the fall had punched from her. Her feet and hands were already scrabbling, forcing her upright – but suddenly she paused and then froze as she realised that everything around her had fallen utterly silent.

Like a deer unsure of the hunter Indigo crouched motionless, straining to detect the smallest hint of a disturbance in the acute quiet. Had the phantoms, no longer of use to their creator, dissolved and vanished? Or were they waiting, invisible now that there was no light to betray them, listening as she did for a sound in the dark?

Cautiously she rose to her feet, giving mute thanks for the fact that the leaves underfoot were wet and therefore less likely to rustle and betray her position. Reaching behind her, she gripped the crossbow, still slung on her back, and carefully brought it round so that she could heft it. A bolt . . . the Mother alone knew it would be of little use against these horrors, but she wanted and needed the feel of a primed and powerful weapon in her hands. She began to move backwards, feeling each step, staring into the blackness and willing her eyes to penetrate its intensity.

'Indigo . . .'

The voice was a hoarse whisper, and it came from behind her. Indigo swung round, bringing the crossbow up, and saw a white-faced, red-haired figure lurching at her out of the dark. Her mind registered the image of Forth; she shouted in revulsion, slammed a bolt into the bow, wrenched back the string and fired wildly.

The bolt struck the phantom's shoulder, and Forth's

184

image howled with pain, spinning around and clutching his upper arm as he dropped to his knees. For a moment Indigo didn't comprehend: she'd shot at an illusion, and illusions couldn't bleed –

'Oh, no!' Understanding came like a hammerblow. '*Forth!*'

She could hear him swearing as she ran to him and threw herself down at his side.

'Forth, what have I done? I thought you were one of them, one of the phantasms! Oh, by the Mother, are you badly hurt?'

The flow of invective ceased on a gagging note, and Forth grated, 'My *shoulder* . . . '

The bolt had grazed the point where the shoulder and his left arm met, and had torn through the upper layer of flesh. The gash was bloody, but when she bent to examine him Indigo saw that despite its gory appearance it was no more than a minor wound.

'Oh, Forth.' She pulled out her knife and cut one sleeve from her own shirt, ripping it into a makeshift bandage which she started to bind around his arm. 'Forth, I'm so sorry! Here; sit up if you can . . . be careful; I'll steady you. There, now.' She knotted the bandage. 'It'll slow the flow of blood at least. I've some herbs in my pouch; they may help to ease the pain . . . '

Forth met her gaze with blank incomprehension. 'What in perdition did you think you were *doing*?'

She shook her head. Ludicrously, she wanted to laugh: the sheer relief of having found him, despite the circumstances, was all but overwhelming her. She pushed the laughter down, and said soberly, 'I thought you were another of the illusions. First there was Esty, and then – '

'*Esty?*' Forth made an incautious movement and winced with pain. 'You've found her?'

'No. I thought I had, but I was wrong.' Indigo related her story, though playing down her description of the rotting images of the Brabazon family.

'When you appeared out of the darkness,' she finished, 'I was convinced you were one of the phantoms, hunting for me, and I panicked. I didn't stop to think; I simply fired.'

185

Forth nodded and managed a weak smile. 'In your place I reckon I'd have done the same. I'll just count myself lucky that your aim was wild.' He fell silent, staring at the wet ground, then suddenly said: 'It might be true, mightn't it?' He raised his head again, and his eyes were haunted. 'What the phantom told you – for all we know, the others might have fallen prey to the sleeping sickness, and by now they might all be here.'

He was thinking, she knew, of the sleepwalker they'd encountered on the black moor, and remembering her hideous dissolution. Indigo didn't know what to say: reassurance would be hollow, for neither of them could give a sure answer to his question.

'Forth,' she ventured at last, feeling that frankness was the only wise course, 'you might be right. We can't know. But whether or not it's true, it doesn't change anything. We still have to find our way to the heart of this world and we can't afford to brood on what might or might not have happened to your family. That's exactly what the demon wants us to do, because it makes us vulnerable to despair, and despair is one of its most powerful weapons.'

Anger kindled faintly in Forth's look. 'Do you think I don't know that?'

'Of course I don't think it! But knowing something doesn't necessarily stop you falling prey to it.' She glanced over her shoulder, and shivered. 'I found that out for myself a short while ago.'

Forth acknowledged the point with a placatory gesture, and Indigo stood up. 'How does your arm feel now?' she asked him. 'Because if you've the strength, I think we should be on our way.'

There was a pause; then, to her surprise, Forth laughed. 'On our way,' he repeated with irony. 'Ah. Yes. That's something I haven't had the chance to tell you yet.'

'What do you mean?'

He looked up at her. In the gloom she could see that there was a smile on his face, but it wasn't matched by his eyes.

'There isn't anywhere else to go, Indigo. You see, I've

combed this place – you'd be surprised how easy it was to do, and the Mother knows I've had time enough. There isn't a way out. No gates, no arches. Nothing. It's a dead end. If there *is* a heart to this world, a centre of the maze if you like, then I don't know what we're going to do now, because it seems that we've reached it.'

Chapter XIV

'No,' Indigo said. 'It's *impossible*. I don't believe it!'

Forth watched her as she ran her hands over the featureless surface of the wall. At her insistence they had tramped full circle around the garden's enclosing boundary, which was considerably smaller than she'd expected, and the result had been precisely as Forth had said. There was no gate, no way out. And, unlike the wall up which Indigo had climbed, these stone blocks were featureless and sheer, devoid of even the smallest foothold.

At last Indigo stepped back. For a moment she stared at the stone face, then with a furious movement whipped out her knife and stabbed savagely at the wall, venting her frustration.

'You'll damage the blade,' Forth told her. 'And it won't do any good. I know; I tried.'

She threw him an angry look, then sheathed the knife and, arms folded, stood staring at the wall while she got a grip on her boiling emotions. At last, calmer but still with a livid edge in her voice, she said, 'This stone's so smooth, I'd defy a spider to climb it, let alone a human being! There are too many things that don't make sense.'

Forth shrugged. 'Gates can vanish. Look what happened before. And the wall – '

Indigo turned quickly to face him. 'I'm not talking about the gate and the wall. They're nothing, not the half of it – I'm talking about one glaringly obvious fact that we've both been too stupid even to see before now!'

Forth stared back at her, his expression blank, and she began to pace, still hugging herself.

'*Think*, Forth. Remember what happened to me when

I came in here; the scene I described to you. You were in this garden too: you should have been as caught up in that horror as I was – damn it, you couldn't have *missed* such a thing! So why didn't you even see what was happening?'

Forth was stunned. That didn't once occur to me!'

'Nor to me, until a few moments ago. You were here, I was here. But it seems we occupied different dimensions, though they were both contained in the same physical space.' Indigo stopped and turned full circle, staring challengingly into the dark. 'Now we've been thrown back together, which suggests that the game has changed again, and this is yet a third dimension. It looks the same as before; but we know how deceptive appearances can be.' She frowned. 'Nothing quite like this has happened before, Forth. We've seen landscapes alter, but this is different: it's as if *time* has been shifted, rather than space.'

'The game has changed.' Forth repeated her words thoughtfully. 'Is that what this is, Indigo? A game?'

'A game. A play.' Indigo smiled humourlessly. 'You should recognise that better than I do, in your line of country.' She began to walk again. 'Since we entered this world the demon has been toying with us. We've learned a little; we've made mistakes, but they've taught us some valuable lessons. And so now I think that whoever created this little show has decided to change more than the scenery.' She was thinking as she paced, and her mind was moving swiftly as it groped towards its goal. 'I think – no; I *believe* – that the key we've been looking for has been placed in our hands, if only we have the wit to see it.' A pause. 'Have you ever lost something, in pitch darkness, and driven yourself near-crazed with searching before discovering it again right under your nose?'

Forth grunted. 'Often.'

'Then apply that principle now. Look around you. And remember what you said to me about the centre of the maze.'

He understood. 'This place?'

'The demon's stronghold. Yes. I believe it is.' Indigo turned, and looked up at the black invisible sky. 'I *believe*

189

it!' she repeated, raising her voice to a shout that echoed back from the encircling wall. 'Do you hear me? *I know where you are!*'

There was a soft, imploding concussion, and a violent sensation of air being displaced. Forth swore, jamming his fingers against his ears as pressure swelled in his head. For one shocking moment all sensation vanished, as if the world had suddenly ceased to exist – and then awareness erupted back.

And the world had changed.

They stood in a huge, dim and empty hall, without windows but with many arched doors, all closed, leading off the flagged floor. The thin, blue-grey light that filtered through the chamber had, again, no visible source; silent shadows were gathered in the corners, and the ceiling was lost in gloom.

Forth turned slowly, staring at the grim place, and at last found his voice. 'Mother of All Life . . . you were right, Indigo. We've found the heart of it!'

Indigo didn't answer him; for she didn't share his conviction. Something about their surroundings wasn't right. From an oblique angle the pillars and flagstones and doors looked solid enough, but whenever she tried to focus directly on any one spot, the outlines seemed faintly blurred, and lacking in fine detail. They might be close to the centre of the maze, she thought; but this wasn't the exact heart. Not quite . . .

'I've never seen anything like it.' Forth, unaware of her doubts, had begun to pace across the floor. His initial shock was giving way to awed fascination, which for the moment at least had driven all other thoughts from his mind. 'It's like some great temple that hasn't been used in centuries. Do you think it could – '

And he stopped as they both heard a sound from the far side of the chamber.

Indigo whirled, snatching reflexively at her crossbow. In the shadows of a pillared corner, something moved close to the floor; there was a slithering, then a weak, muffled oath.

Forth's eyes widened. 'That's *Esty*!'

'Forth, no!' Indigo shouted in alarm as he started to

190

run across the floor. She saw a glint of red hair, then, horribly redolent of the way the earlier phantom had appeared to her from the bushes in the garden, Esty emerged, on hands and knees, from the shadows. She gave a cry of anguished relief as she saw Forth, tried to struggle to her feet, then collapsed.

'Esty! Es, come on, it's all right now; it's all right!' Forth reached out and started to pull her to her feet, but Indigo's voice cut harshly across his comforting words.

'I said, *no!* Get back – stand away from her!'

Astonished, he jerked his head round, and saw Indigo standing with the loaded crossbow levelled at his sister's heart.

'Indigo, what are you doing?' Forth protested. 'It's *Esty!*'

'How do you know that?'

Forth's expression changed to one of horror. He'd forgotten Indigo's own experience, and the colour leached from his face.

'Blind my eyes . . . you don't think . . . ' He released Esty as though she were a poisonous snake and backed away.

'Forth!' Esty wailed. 'Indigo! What's the *matter* with you? I don't understand – Forth, she's going to *kill* me!'

'I'm not going to fire,' Indigo said evenly, 'unless you give me reason. Come towards me. Come here.'

Confused and terrified, Esty looked in appeal to her brother. '*Forth* – '

'Do what she says, Esty.' Forth's eyes were mistrustful. 'If you are what you seem, she won't hurt you.'

'But – '

'Don't argue. Just do it.'

Shaking, Esty began to walk very slowly towards Indigo. As she approached, Indigo lowered the bow – if this was a phantom, it would be of no use anyway – and unsheathed her knife. When the shivering girl stopped in front of her, she said, 'Hold out your hand. The hand that was scorched.'

Esty obeyed. The blisters were still visible, surrounded by puckered skin. But it wasn't sufficient evidence, and before Esty could protest or pull away,

191

Indigo dropped the crossbow and caught her wrist in a tight grip.

'I'm sorry,' she said, 'but there's no other way to be sure.' And she pressed the tip of the knife against the girl's thumb.

Esty yowled like a scalded cat, more from anger than from pain, and leaped back, wrenching her hand free. She stared uncomprehendingly at the vivid bead of blood that appeared on her thumb, then her head came up and her eyes blazed with fury.

'You – you *bitch*!'

'Esty!' Forth intervened as she lunged forward at Indigo, nails raking at her face. Esty cursed and tried to throw him off, but he pinned her arms back, shouting, 'She had to do it! We thought you were an illusion – it's happened before!'

Esty's face froze and she stopped fighting. 'You thought *I* was an illusion?' Her expression began to crumble. 'Oh, that's funny! After all I've been through, that's such a sick, horrible *joke*!' And she burst into tears.

'I'm sorry,' Indigo said with genuine contrition. She tried to touch the girl, but Esty shrank quickly away, turning to Forth for comfort. Over her bowed head Forth glanced at Indigo and raised helpless eyebrows, and Indigo moved back, feeling shamed and guilty and wondering how she would ever convince Esty that she hadn't wanted to hurt or frighten her. She didn't know what manner of ordeals the girl had already undergone, but her own experiences allowed her to make an informed guess. Yet there'd been no other way to be sure. She'd *had* to put Esty to the test.

Perhaps, she thought, there would be a chance to redeem herself later. For the moment, the wisest thing she could do would be to leave Forth alone with his sister. She began to pace across the hall, staring up towards the shrouded ceiling and trying not to listen to Esty's gulping, halting whispers as Forth coaxed her to tell her story. Amid the furore of the last few minutes, the implications of their arrival in this bizarre hall had flown from her mind; now though, she began to consider them afresh, and to consider, too, what might lie at the root of

192

her immediate suspicion that this was not quite the heart of their journey.

The doors. She stopped, and looked at the nearest of them. Apart from the fact that its outlines still refused to swim into perfect focus, it looked ordinary enough, the peak of the arch just level with the top of her own head. How many were there? She started to number them; lost count, tried again, failed a second time. That peculiar visual shift . . . it was as though the doors were slyly refusing to be counted: she thought there were twelve, or thirteen or perhaps even fourteen, but she couldn't be certain.

Esty and Forth were still talking. Esty seemed to have stopped crying now and was calmer. Indigo watched them for a moment, then turned to the door once more. It had a simple latch, and she reached out, wondering if she could touch it or if it would prove ephemeral. Her fingers closed round chilly metal: she hesitated a bare moment, then lifted the latch and, cautiously, pushed.

The door swung open. Beyond it, a black garden overgrown with mouldering shrubbery met her gaze. Leaves moved sluggishly; and somewhere she thought she could hear water dripping . . .

Indigo closed the door once more and stood thoughtfully gazing at it for a few moments. The third garden. She cast another quick glance at Forth and Esty, saw they were oblivious to her, and moved on to the next door.

Again, the latch lifted easily. This time, Indigo found herself gazing out on a dense and impenetrable forest of black, unnervingly still trees . . .

She moved on. And from the third door, she saw the moor, bleak, barren, the far horizon etched by a thin line of silver, as though an unnatural moon were about to rise.

Nightscapes of this spectral world, echoes of their own experiences . . . this hall could indeed be compared to the centre of a web, from which all avenues radiated outwards. But would these scenes hidden behind their doors all be drawn from experiences of the past, or would some hold visions yet to come?

Indigo walked towards the fourth door. It opened, like the others, on soundless hinges. And beyond the threshold, in darkness so intense that it was almost physical, a vast, dim and shapeless bulk moved.

Indigo's heart lurched and she wrenched the door shut, turning away and taking a deep breath to calm herself. She'd seen nothing clearly, but her imagination had fired into life, and images of the Brown Walker and countless other, unnameable horrors surged in her mind. Sternly she told herself that, as with everything else here, they were harmless images, reflections, and reached out, determined to conquer her fear and open the door again. But before she could touch the latch for the second time, a voice spoke behind her.

'Indigo . . .'

Every nerve was pitched taut, and Indigo started violently. 'Forth! By the Mother, you startled me!'

Forth smiled a pallid apology. 'Esty has something to say to you.'

Esty was standing a few feet behind him, Indigo saw now. She wore a hunted, embarrassed expression, and she was twisting her hands together. Indigo moved towards her, and suddenly the girl flushed crimson, and said in a rush,

'Indigo, I'm sorry! If it hadn't been for me, none of this would have happened, and we wouldn't have been separated in the first place, and Forth's told me everything and I understand why you had to test me, and, oh, *damn* it!' Her fists clenched. 'I've *never* been able to apologise properly!'

'Neither have I.' Indigo smiled at her, feeling a calming and deeply welcome wash of relief. 'But I'm sorry, too, Esty.' She took the girl's hand, felt the answering squeeze. 'Friends?'

Esty nodded. 'The trouble was,' she said wryly, 'It all seemed so *real*. And then when everything went wrong, and I came back to my senses . . . well, Forth'll tell you about that. I don't think I could say it all a second time; it makes me feel such a fool.'

Indigo glanced at Forth and saw confirmation of her surmise in his face. 'I don't think either of you need explain anything,' she told Esty. 'The image of you that was sent to dupe me was a very thorough simulacrum – it even told the truth.'

'It was uncanny,' Forth put in. 'The same story that you said the false Esty told you, in almost the same words.'

Indigo nodded. 'I'm beginning to suspect that our demon friend has a sense of humour, albeit warped.' She turned, and gestured towards the wall. 'And I think that now we may have another example of its jests to contend with. I've seen for myself what lies beyond some of those doors, and I believe it's playing a new game.'

Forth and Esty listened with increasing interest as she described the scenes that the doors had revealed. They opened the first two doors again, staring through at the dank, decaying garden and the still forest, and as Forth closed the second door, Esty said, 'What of the others? How many are there?'

'I'm not sure,' Indigo admitted. 'I tried to count them, but each time I failed.'

'And each one appears to lead into a different part of this dimension.' Forth looked about him, surveying the entire hall. 'What would happen, I wonder, if we tried to go through one of them?'

Indigo laughed drily. 'I haven't put that to the test.'

'No. No; that wouldn't be wise, would it? At least, not until we know what lies behind each one.'

Esty was moving towards another of the doors, one that Indigo hadn't yet explored, and Indigo called after her. 'Be careful, Esty! I don't think they're all as innocent as they might seem.'

Esty hesitated, looking back at them. 'We won't know that unless we try, will we?' Then her eyes widened eagerly. 'What if – what if Da and Chari are behind one of them?'

Or Grimya, Indigo thought involuntarily, and the thought was followed by a pang of anguish. So much had happened since that dreadful encounter with the wolf-pack that she'd barely given Grimya a thought. But might she be there, she and her ghostly followers, beyond one of the doors? Spellbound, and waiting, and hungry?

195

She said nothing as Esty opened the next door, but when the girl gave a sharp cry of shock, her heart missed painfully and the hairs rose at her nape. Esty, though, was staring through the door in stunned fascination rather than fear, and at last Indigo ventured to look for herself.

There were no wolves; nor the Brown Walker or the Jachanine, nor any shapeless monstrosity shambling in darkness. Instead, the scene beyond the door fell away into a thousand miles of nothing, under a sky ablaze with cold stars. At a mind-numbing distance below, an ominous landscape turned slowly like a titanic wheel under veils of cloud, lit for brief, explosive instants by lightning that forked silently and ferociously across its seared hills.

Vertigo assailed Indigo's stomach and her sense of balance together, and Forth called urgently, 'Esty! Shut it again, for all our sakes!' The door slammed, the dizzying vista vanished, and Esty shuddered.

'Ugh!' She shook her head as though to clear it. 'One step through that door, and . . . ' She made a sharply expressive downward motion with one hand.

Indigo said sombrely, 'We have a conundrum. There's clearly nothing to be gained by staying here – but which exit should we take?'

Forth shrugged, scanning the chamber again. 'There's only one way to decide, surely? We'll have to open every single door and see what lies beyond. Until we've done that, I don't see how we can make a decision.'

He was right, and she pushed down her irrational unwillingness to agree. 'Very well. Let's start with the one after Esty's, and work our way round.'

They began to move round the hall's perimeter, opening one door after another. Some of the sights that greeted them behind each portal were reflections of scenes they'd already seen in the demon world: the moor, the crags above the river, the deserted gardens; but others were chilling, sometimes horrifying. One gave on to a forest; not the still and silent forest that they had seen before, but a black, lush, wild place of huge, shivering leaves, snaking tendrils and stabbing thorns, bristling

196

with a feral and primeval life of its own. From its furiously agitating depths came appalling sounds, as though a thousand misshapen beasts were fighting to the death among the trees. Another door opened to reveal swirling, choking mists, and a ghastly singing sound, as of a dismal choir. Yet another swung back, and they were confronted with nothing – a void so complete that they stepped quickly back with a sick feeling of shock, and shut the portal without more than a moment's glance. A fourth showed them a breathtakingly beautiful landscape, woods and hills and streams under a mellow sun, yet redolent with an aura of complete and implacable evil.

The search went on and on, scene after scene, each one different yet none offering them any clue or any hope – until, as Indigo was about to lift the latch of yet another door, Forth spoke up.

'Wait a moment. How many have we opened?'

'Fifteen,' Esty said immediately. 'I've been counting.'

Indigo frowned. 'I've tallied sixteen. Or seventeen . . . I'm not sure.'

'No; and I make it thirteen, which differs again.' Forth moved back a pace and glared at the rows of doors. 'Earlier, you tried to count them and you failed. I think this is another damned game! We might go round for ever, opening door after door and finding a different scene behind each one.'

Indigo and Esty were silent for a few moments. Esty began to count the doors, then gave up the attempt with a frustrated shake of her head. 'I think Forth's right, Indigo. We could continue like this until our heads are spinning. So,' she looked quizzically at her brother. 'What are we to do?'

'I've an idea,' Forth said, 'though I don't know if it'll achieve anything worthwhile. Open all the doors again, and leave them open. See what that reveals. If something *is* playing games with us, that might force it into a new move.'

Indigo nodded. 'It's worth trying.' She walked towards the nearest door, lifted the latch, flung it open. Taking their cue from her, Forth and Esty began to move from portal to portal. As the doors were opened, a cacophony of clashing sounds began to fill the hall; the grisly choir singing, the monstrous beasts quarrelling in the primeval forest, sighs, moans, the distant, echoing shrieks of a gale. Indigo's jaw clenched tight as the discordant noises swelled, assaulting her senses; her palms were clammy with sweat and she wanted to scream for the din to stop; but she forced herself to move steadily on, lifting another latch, and another, and another.

And then they had reached the last of the doors – and as Forth pushed it open, all sound instantly ceased.

'What – ?' Esty's startled, truncated question was loud in the sudden silence. Indigo looked at the door they had just opened and saw that the scene behind it – a flock of birds winging across a stormy night sky – was motionless, as though time had been frozen. Quickly she looked at the other open doors, and saw the same. All sound and movement had been arrested; and suddenly she felt a sense of impending change.

'Look!' Esty's shrill exclamation made her swing round.

At the far end of the hall, between two of the open doors, a third and larger portal had appeared. Its surface was black, all but petrified with age; and it had no latch, and no visible hinges.

'Ah!' Forth's eyes lit eagerly. 'I *thought* something like this might happen!' He started towards the door, Indigo and Esty following, and the three stopped before it.

'There's no means of opening it,' Esty said tensely.

'Push it,' Indigo urged.

Forth reached out. But before he could touch the door, it quivered, and they all jumped back as the portal began to open of its own accord. It swung back slowly, revealing darkness beyond, and Forth took a cautious step forward.

'I can't see anything . . . I think there's a chamber there, but – ' And his words cut off abruptly as blue-white light flared from the darkness.

Something stood within the light. It had human shape – and as the glare faded it stepped forward, resolving into the figure of a child, barefoot and dressed in a simple tabard, with silver eyes and a nimbus of silver hair crowning its head. It looked at each of them in turn, then its alien gaze fastened on Indigo.

The blood had drained from Indigo's face, turning it the colour of clay. Bile choked at the back of her throat, and she stared in shock and loathing at the creature before her.

The being smiled, showing sharp, feral cats' teeth. And Nemesis, Indigo's deadliest enemy, the child created from the dark pits of her own soul, said:

'Welcome, sister. I have been waiting for you.'

Chapter XV

It wasn't Nemesis's voice. The figure of the child was the same, and the evil smile, and the cold aura that glimmered around its slender frame – but the voice belonged to another. From the corner of her eye Indigo saw Forth's and Esty's stunned faces as they swung round to look at her, but she couldn't speak to them, couldn't even attempt to communicate or explain.

Then Nemesis vanished, and another figure stood in its stead. What replaced it caused her companions to start violently, but for Indigo the second shock was far greater than the first, and she gave a choked cry. Dressed in a cloak that shimmered with the colours of spring leaves, its face framed by russet hair, its milky golden eyes filled with sorrow and sternness and subtle strength, the emissary of the Earth Mother Herself, who so many years ago had set Indigo upon her long and lonely road, smiled at her, and spoke.

'Welcome, sister. I have been waiting for you.'

Nemesis's words – but, as Nemesis had done, the bright being spoke with the voice of another.

Her own voice.

'No,' Indigo whispered hoarsely. 'Not you . . . not *you*!' She was starting to panic, felt it rising like an unstoppable tidal wave in her head, and backed away, colliding with Forth as he moved to intercept her.

'Indigo, what is it?' he demanded urgently. 'What *is* that creature?'

She shook her head violently, unable to answer him. Then Esty gave a squeal of fright, and they both looked back towards the door.

The emissary had gone. In its place stood a young woman dressed in the formal court attire of the Southern

Isles. Gems sparkled on her fingers, a belt of silver links encircled her waist; she wore a silver torque set with agates, and a circlet adorned with the same stones. Her hair, long and unbound, fell in a rich auburn cascade over her shoulders, and her eyes were a vivid blue-violet. Stunned, speechless, Indigo confronted herself – not as she was now, but as she had been in that other, lost life, when she was not Indigo but Anghara, princess of the Southern Isles.

Forth and Esty were rigid, staring at the apparition and not comprehending what they saw. The image smiled, quite gently but with sweet, supercilious malice.

'What, Indigo – do you fear me?' The sound of her own voice emanating from this phantom travesty made Indigo start to quiver, but anger was fast replacing fear as she began to understand. The image laughed.

'Surely you know by now that I reflect only what I see within the minds of those who enter my domain? What is there, I wonder, in what I have drawn from your secret thoughts that makes you so afraid?'

Very slowly, Indigo exhaled the air that shock had trapped in her lungs, and with its release the burgeoning anger bloomed. Confusion and fright evaporated to a hot ember of contempt: she knew that, at last, she was facing the demon she had come to find. She had, indeed, been right – this was a vampire. But a vampire that must not only feed on the lives of its victims but must also create its form from among the wealth of memories and dreams it found within their minds; for it had no form of its own.

'You,' she said scornfully, and saw Esty and Forth glance quickly at her, surprised by the sudden authority in her tone. 'Now I know what you are, and why you cloak yourself in the images of others. You haven't the courage, have you, to show yourself as you really are? Because you are *nothing*!'

'Indigo!' The truth, she saw, was beginning to dawn on Forth, and he reached quickly for the hilt of his knife. 'If this is the demon – '

'It is.' She put a hand out to stay him. 'But you can't kill a shade; not that way.' Her gaze shifted to her phantom self again and she felt an unwonted surge of loathing, and of outrage that such a being should presume to taunt her with her own semblance. 'You can't use a blade against a thing that has no substance, and which can take only the forms which it usurps from their rightful owners.' She took a step forward; was gratified to see the demon move a prudent pace back in response. 'Isn't that true, my shadowy friend? You can't show us your true shape, for you have none.' She smiled cruelly, taking cold pleasure from her hatred. 'What a pitiful thing you are!'

The image lifted its shoulders fractionally, and inclined its head in an all too familiar gesture. 'Oh, yes,' it said softly. 'I am pitiful. But I live. And I will continue to live, and to thrive in my own fashion – unless you can complete the task you have come here to perform, and kill me.' The violet eyes looked up, challenging. 'Do you think you can do that, Indigo? Or will you and your friends succumb to me in the end, as so many others have done?'

Indigo's eyes narrowed. 'You cannot kill me.'

'True. But I can hold you. There is no exit from this world, unless I should choose to create one. And while you may not die, your companions are another matter.' It looked speculatively first at Esty, then at Forth. 'The substance of those who fight me takes longer to absorb than that of those who give themselves willingly; but the sustenance they offer is the greater for that. I will consume your friends, eventually. I *must* consume them, as I must consume all that is within my reach.'

'*Must?*' Indigo repeated with harsh disgust. 'I see no *must* in the draining of Bruhome's crops and land and in the devouring of innocent souls!'

'They are life,' the demon replied. 'And I must consume life, if I myself am to live.' It sighed heavily. 'I wish it were otherwise, but I cannot change the inevitable.'

Disgusted by this sham of regret, Indigo opened her mouth to fire back a furious retort, but before she could speak, Forth stepped towards her. He had one arm protectively about Esty's shoulders; now he slipped the other around Indigo and glared hotly at the demon.

'You won't cow us!' he declared venomously. 'And you won't have our lives, however invincible you claim to be! We came here to destroy you – and we'll do it!'

'Ah.' The demon regarded him sorrowfully. 'Would that you could, little human. Would that it were possible; for in death there might be freedom from the hunger that drives me.' The violet gaze slid now to Esty's face, and the demon's expression grew poignant. 'Esty knows of my loneliness and my suffering. Do you remember, sweet Esty? Do you recall how you shared the grief of my burden, and how you pitied me?' And suddenly what faced them was not Indigo but the sad, beautiful young man of the moorland pool, his face pale and fragile about the swathe of his black cloak, his deep-set eyes haunted with longing.

Esty made a dreadful sound and Forth swung her round, forcing her to avert her gaze.

'Enough!' he said ferociously. 'You don't deceive us, and we have no pity for the likes of you. We want only one thing from you before we kill you – we want our family and friends restored to us.' He released the two women and stepped menacingly forward, touching his knife again. 'We *demand* it!'

'Forthright.' The demon smiled again, thinly. 'You were aptly named, were you not? But I'm afraid I must disappoint you. I could not release your kin, even if I wished to. They are mine now; and I must use all that is mine to sustain me.' The smile widened a little, and became predatory. 'My hunger is unending, and it can never be sated. When all the husks of Bruhome are drained and have nothing left to give me, then I must find more. I must take all there is, no matter how insignificant. I must *feed*.'

'Vampire!' Esty spat. 'Hell-spawned *leech*!'

The being nodded. 'That, yes; but also far more than that, as Indigo knows.' The hollow, glittering eyes turned to regard Indigo once more. 'Can you name me, Indigo? Can you name one who has the power to contain everything, and yet contains nothing? Can you reach into the darkest corners of your mind, and tell me, from the

203

depths of your own experience, what I am?'

Indigo didn't reply. Her lips had whitened and were pressed tightly together, and memories roiled in her mind. Nemesis, laughing. Slaughter and carnage and destruction, as the Tower of Regrets fell. Her family dying. Her lover, Fenran, tortured and imprisoned between dimensions. And the Earth Mother's emissary, whose pity was tempered with implacable will . . .

The demon chuckled softly. 'Yes,' it said. 'You know me, Indigo. I am *Despair*. And despair never sleeps, and always hungers for a release which it cannot achieve.'

The intense gaze was hypnotic, and as the demon spoke Indigo felt her mind respond with a kindred surge of misery. She understood the bleakness of its existence, the hopelessness, the futility of eternally living, eternally hungering, without even the cold comfort granted by the promise of eventual death.

'It is a poignant paradox, is it not?' the demon said more gently. 'To live forever, without hope of death. I want nothing more than to die, Indigo, for my future is an empty one with nothing to cheer me. But I cannot be killed. Not by you; not by any living being. And so I must continue in my dismal sojourn, and hunger, and feed, and suffer, for all time.'

A constricting pain assailed Indigo's lungs as empathy swelled within her. Surely this creature's plight had terrible parallels with her own? She *knew* its despair, and knowing it, she could feel for the demon, almost pity it.

'No!' With a great effort she threw off the thoughts, and as she banished them the hate came back, redoubled by realisation that, again, the demon had lured her into perilous waters, almost seducing her into its own miasm of hopeless misery. She stared again into the mesmeric eyes, but this time her own eyes were hard and ablaze with anger.

'I *shall* kill you,' she said savagely. 'There will be a way, and I'll find it!'

The demon sighed, and it seemed that shadows began to gather in on them from the corners of the hall, intensifying the gloom. Esty looked nervously about her, and moved closer to Forth.

'Try, and with my blessing,' the demon said. 'I would welcome death. But you will fail.'

The shadows deepened, and at the periphery of her vision Indigo glimpsed indistinct shapes stirring within them.

'I won't fail.' Now her voice was contemptuous, though the growing darkness and the suddenly claustrophobic atmosphere were making her pulse quicken uneasily.

'Ah, but you will.' The demon's tone became sibilant. 'For how can any of you fight a power that draws its inspiration from your own dark selves?' It raised one hand in a graceful gesture, then pointed towards her. 'Remember your own words, Indigo. All that I am, and all that my world contains, can take only the forms which I usurp from their rightful owners. To prevail against me, you must first prevail against yourself. Solve that conundrum, if you can!'

Behind them, something snarled. Esty cried out, and Indigo spun round to see a wall of churning darkness boiling across the hall. Tendrils of the dark reached out to become hands, clawing in desperation: among the hands thorns clashed murderously; and twisting and turning in the midst of the blackness was a mayhem of silently screaming human faces, and misshapen horrors, and crimson-eyed, slavering wolves.

'*Your* darkness, Indigo!' the demon called mockingly. '*Yours!*'

Hooting, monstrous, filling the hall with its shadowy presence, the Brown Walker stalked through the gloom. With it came a vast, bloated, winged worm with the head of an owl, and behind the worm lurched a huge and grotesque troll that Indigo knew could only be the Jachanine. Horrors from her homeland's mythology and from the legends of Forth and Esty's people, dragged from the depths of their minds and memories and conjured to a hideous semblance of reality as the truth of the demon's taunt slammed home.

Esty began to wail on a high, hysterical note and the sound fired Indigo's own straining nerve almost to breaking point. She shut her eyes, feeling terror swelling in her like a rising storm-wave, and tried desperately to control the wild surge, channel its energy, impose the strength of her will over the power of the demon –

A hoarse shout rang through the hall and Indigo's eyes snapped open again in time to see Forth launch himself at the black wall as his own fear and fury erupted. He had snatched his knife from its sheath, and he stabbed and hacked like a madman at the roiling darkness.

'*Kill* them!' he yelled frenziedly. 'Slay them, tear them apart – they don't exist! Nothing exists in this hell but us – we're real, but they're only phantoms!'

Black fingers writhed from the fog to snatch and snare him, and he tore at them with his free hand, ripping them apart and casting the smoking shreds to the floor. The maelstrom heaved and twisted upon itself like some massive but mindless beast dimly sensing threat, and Forth's yells took on a manic, triumphant timbre.

'Help me! Help me, and we can *slaughter* it!'

Indigo's pent paralysis snapped at the goad of his voice, and she and Esty screamed a challenge together, drawing their own knives as they, too, ran at the churning horror, slashing furiously at the blackness. The wall heaved again, and then began to collapse. The warped forms, both human and monster, melted into a chaos of shrieking faces and writhing arms; from the heart of the darkness a howling rose, a myriad voices in ghastly discord. Indigo howled back, venting all the loathing and defiance and savagery that until that moment had been locked within her, and the mad scene leaped and flickered as, for stunning instants, she seemed to see it through other eyes than her own. Silver eyes, glittering vengefully: eyes of milky gold, remote and detached: the hunting, amber eyes of a wolf –

Suddenly, thunder bellowed through the hall, drowning all other sound under its roar. The flagstones beneath Indigo's feet heaved, humped upward, and the scene erupted in a single blast of light as she was thrown sideways to land with terrific force on the floor. Her ears rang with the thunder's echoing ricochet; the black wall above her seemed to coalesce into a whirling, tornado-like column –

206

Then she was flailing, struggling to regain her feet as grim and total silence took the hall in an iron hand.

Close beside her, someone said, in a voice too strained to be recognisable, '*Goddess preserve us . . .*'

Miasma cleared, and Indigo opened her eyes.

The black cloud was gone. The hall was empty, silent, completely still. The doors and the demon had vanished, and in their place were rotting walls that gaped to the blind stare of a cold, indifferent sky. Ancient stone shone with the cold nacre of decay, and great fissures had split the walls' fabric, letting through the rampant, grasping arms of gnarled trees that coiled and clung. Hollow in the silence, she heard the steady, relentless drip of water on flint, and beneath her the ground shifted sluggishly, sodden with old and stagnant moisture.

Hands clasped her upper arms, pulling her up, breaking the thrall that held her. She sensed Forth's closeness, heard Esty murmuring a heartfelt imprecation, and saw their eyes like the fearful eyes of a hunter's prey, shocked and uncertain in the silent gloom.

From a dank, crumbling distance, a thin voice spoke.

'Your courage does you credit. But it is futile. It will all be one, in the end.'

At the end of the hall one door remained, sagging on rusted hinges. Before the door, a vague shadow sat in a rotting chair of petrified wood that was all but obscured by moss and mould. Though the shadow had no face, they could sense that the demon was smiling.

'One round in the game, my friends. Or, as the Brabazon Fairplayers might prefer it, one scene in the play; and you have acted your parts commendably. What entertainment can be devised next, I wonder?'

Forth tensed angrily. 'Damn your entertainments! Release my father and sister!'

'Ah, yes; of course.' The shadow quivered, as though with silent laughter. 'As I have said before, I will not, and I cannot. But you have awakened my interest, Forthright Brabazon; you and your fellow performers. Isn't that what you wish of your audience when you step out on to the stage? I am amused by you. I am entertained by you. And perhaps it will give me some small respite from my

207

eternal misery to continue with this play for a while yet.'
The nebulous form rose from the chair. 'You think you
can destroy me. You are wrong; but perhaps, while you
persist in your fond delusion, I might arrange some
diversion that will lead our drama towards a satisfying
final act.' One dark, nebulous hand rose, and gestured
towards the decayed door. 'Beyond that portal lies a
road which will lead you to your friends. *All* your
friends.' The emphasis was clear, and Indigo sensed with
a chill frisson that the demon was looking intently at her
alone as it spoke. 'It is a dangerous road, but no doubt
you are well prepared for danger. And while you face
what lies ahead, and learn or suffer from what you find,
the modest entertainment of following your progress will
hearten me a little in my unhappy sojourn.'

Indigo retorted furiously, 'We are not your puppets!'

'Oh, but you are. For I shall set the scene as I please,
and you shall be my fairplayers, with survival instead of
coin as your fee. He whose purse is deepest is master of
the revels: isn't that the keystone of your trade? And my
purse is deeper than that of any master you have ever
known.'

Esty clenched her fists until her fingernails dug deep
into her palms. 'We *won't* be your playthings! You monstrosity, you serpent's spawn – we *won't*!' She spat, like
an angry cat, towards the chair, but the spittle fell short.

'That choice is yours,' the demon said indifferently.
'You may follow the road I offer, or you may stay here
until you become as decayed as the stone walls around
you. Whichever you choose, we will encounter one
another again before long. And now, I shall leave you to
debate your decision.' It paused. 'One last word of
caution. The wolves have teeth.' Its spectral form shimmered as though, again, it laughed soundlessly. 'I bid
you goodbye, for the present.'

The rotting chair vanished. For a moment the dark
shadow stood gaunt and alone; then, like smoke blowing
away on a gentle wind, it shivered, its form dissolved,
and it was gone.

There was a long, tense silence. Finally, Forth broke it
with an explosive and crude oath.

208

'Well,' Esty said ferociously as the tight atmosphere relaxed a fraction. 'What are we to do?'

Indigo was staring silently at the crumbling door, and it was Forth who answered.

'I think we have to go,' he said. 'If it wasn't lying to us, and there *is* a chance of finding Da and Chari, we must try. The Mother knows it goes against the grain, knowing that we'll be dancing to its filthy tune, but I can't see any other choice.'

Esty, her earlier defiance sobered, nodded and looked uneasily at Indigo. 'Indigo? What do you think?'

All your friends, the demon had said. And: *the wolves have teeth . . .* Indigo forced back her dark thoughts, and met Esty's gaze.

'I agree,' she said. 'There's no other choice we can make.'

In subdued silence they gathered the few meagre belongings that were left to them, and finally, though none of them was anxious to face it, turned towards the door.

Forth reached out and touched it. The hinges groaned – then abruptly the whole structure gave way, the wood splitting, crumbling, collapsing to splinters and dust, to reveal the new land beyond.

A pale dust road led away from the door, under the same starless, featureless, dimly lit sky that had hung over the moor and the gardens. To one side of the road, dark hills humped with a still air of menace; to the other lowlands swept away towards an indistinct horizon, patched here and there with darker areas which might have been tracts of woodland.

Esty said softly, 'The fell road . . . '

It was a perfect replica of the main drovers' way into Bruhome; the very road along which the Brabazon Fairplayers' caravans had rolled to their ill-fated attendance at the Autumn Revels. Indigo could imagine the demon's amusement at such an ironic jest; but she preferred not to consider what might lie beyond these black hills and vales where, in the true world, Bruhome itself should be.

She said nothing, but shouldered her harp more

209

comfortably and, trying to ignore the feeling of fore-boding that crept through her like the threat of some dire fever, stepped over the shattered door and through the arch. Forth and Esty followed, unspeaking; as their feet touched the dust and gravel of the track there was a sound like a softly inhaled breath, and they looked back.

The arched doorway and the rotting hall beyond it were gone. Behind them, the road stretched away under the empty sky, pale and faintly shining until it curved around a fold in the dark fells and was lost to sight.

Still no one spoke, but in the quiet gloom Esty reached out and took Forth's hand, squeezing his fingers. Whether it was to reassure herself or him, Forth didn't know; but he returned the gentle pressure before, side by side, they set off along the track in Indigo's wake.

Chapter XVI

Esty said, in an undertone: 'She's crying.'

'I know.' Forth didn't want to look across the short stretch of turf to where Indigo sat with her back to them. He'd seen the quivering of her shoulders, though she was trying to hide it, and was both embarrassed and disconcerted. This wasn't like the Indigo he'd thought he knew so well, and he didn't know how best to react.

'Forth, *one* of us has got to talk to her,' Esty persisted. 'After what happened in the hall, what we saw – '

'Damn it, I *know* that!' He kept his voice to a furious whisper, then saw his sister's face distort. 'For the Goddess's sake, don't you start too! One's bad enough!'

'I'm not crying,' Esty retorted fiercely. 'I'm just worried. Worried sick, if you really want to know. She's hardly said a word all the time we've been walking, and now, when we stop for a rest, she behaves as if we weren't here.' Her worried green eyes focused on Indigo's back once more. 'I think she must know what happened to her, and that we witnessed it; and now she doesn't know what to do. We've got to reassure her; but at the same time we've got to find out what's going on.'

Forth shifted uncomfortably. 'Well, then, you ask her, seeing as you're so keen.'

'No. I think it should be you. And you know why.'

He flashed her a quick, resentful glance. 'Don't be stupid! You don't know what you're talking about.'

'Oh, yes I do. You're just too embarrassed to admit it.' Esty paused, eyeing him shrewdly. 'If I was in love with someone, and I saw they were in distress, *I* wouldn't sit on my rump like a dumb ox and do nothing.'

Forth opened his mouth to retort, but then closed it again. In truth, he couldn't gainsay his sister: but his reluctance stemmed from the fact that he felt hopelessly out of his depth. During the long walk, which had led them through the fells without, as yet, any sign of an end ahead, he and Esty had been too intent on watching for any sign of danger to have much opportunity for talking. But the occasional exchanged glance had been enough to tell them both that their thoughts were dwelling on the same subject; and now they knew that it couldn't be avoided for much longer.

In the decayed hall, when the demon had conjured the black cloud of illusions to bear down on them, Indigo had *changed*. The transformations had been swift, brief and too shocking for them to take in more than the barest impression, but they had both recognised the silver-eyed child who had stepped through the final door to mockingly greet them, and the strange and unnervingly beautiful being with the milky golden eyes. Both of those creatures, they recalled, had named Indigo *sister*, and the recollection chilled them. But, last and worst of all, there had been a third metamorphosis: for one horrifying moment, as the black cloud boiled towards them, Indigo had become a wolf.

It might have been the demon's work, a further trick to disconcert them; but somehow neither Forth nor Esty believed that. The truth lay elsewhere, and its implications, which as yet were beyond their understanding, unnerved them. Forth's own feelings for Indigo complicated the matter still further, and now as she saw his discomfiture Esty understood why he was so reluctant to face Indigo and broach their worries.

She sat back on her heels, and sighed contritely. 'I'm sorry. That wasn't very tactful of me.'

Forth shredded a stem of grass. 'You're right, though. Someone should talk to her, and it should be me.'

'If you love her, yes.' A pause. 'Do you?'

He shrugged awkwardly and his face reddened. 'That's not the point, is it?' Quickly, before she could see his expression, he got to his feet. 'All right. I'll ask her.'

Esty watched as, trying to appear careless, Forth strolled towards the spot where Indigo sat. She felt sorry for her brother, for despite the fact that he was two years

212

her senior, she knew that he was more naive, and therefore more vulnerable, when it came to affairs of the heart. Esty might be equally inexperienced, but a firm core of pragmatism – hard-heartedness, her sisters teased – lay beneath her romantic inclinations and she'd vowed long ago that she would never do anything so foolish or painful as to pursue a hopeless love. Forth, though, had no such inbuilt defence and Indigo was the first woman for whom he had felt more than a passing fancy. Rationally, he knew that his hopes were futile; Indigo loved another, and even if that love was forever lost to her, she didn't return Forth's feelings and never would. But Forth still dreamed, and there was no place for reason in dreaming.

Forth was now sitting beside Indigo, and they were talking. Esty sighed sadly and turned her back to them, looking away across the dark fells. She couldn't hear what was being said, and didn't want to eavesdrop; better to keep her own counsel and let Forth resolve this as he saw fit. She tried to find some point of interest among the hills' black folds, but there was nothing; not even the occasional outcrop scoured by the elements into some fantastic shape, as there might have been in the true world. Not a sheep, not a hare, not a bird. The land was utterly quiet and empty, and in the wake of the demon's mocking warning about the dangers of the road, Esty mistrusted the emptiness. It was, she thought, a little too reminiscent of the calm before the storm.

A sound behind her made her start, and she looked quickly round to see Forth walking back towards her – with Indigo a few paces behind him.

'Esty.' Forth dropped to a crouch beside his sister. His eyes, she noted with surprise, were alight with suppressed excitement, and Esty stole a glance at Indigo. Her expression was more solemn, but the same eager flicker showed for a moment as their gazes met.

'I told her.' Forth didn't trouble with any preamble. 'I told her what we saw back there in the hall, and – well, I'd best let Indigo speak for herself.'

'I didn't know.' Indigo sat down on the grass. The tears were gone now, though her eyes had a telltale trace

213

of red at their corners. 'I remember being suddenly disorientated – it happened several times, as though for a moment I was seeing through someone else's eyes. But the transformations . . . I wasn't aware of them; I had no idea!'

Forth couldn't contain his excitement. 'Esty, don't you see what this means? It wasn't the demon's doing, it was Indigo's – even though she didn't know it at the time, she *willed* the changes to happen! If she can do that – if she can even cause *us* to see her in another form – then think what that says about this world, and how we might manipulate it!'

Esty's eyes widened as she began to comprehend more fully. 'Your hand!' she said to Indigo. 'The burn that healed. And the music – the way you willed the pipe and the harp to work – '

'And so much else!' Forth interrupted. 'We've always suspected that it was possible to influence things here, if only we could will it in the right way. But this – ' He shook his head in wonderment. 'I believe we could do anything! Create artefacts, creatures, even people!'

'Create *illusions*,' Indigo corrected him. 'Don't forget that, Forth. We can't summon Chari or your father, even though we might call up their images. But,' she continued, addressing Esty now, 'in this world, everything is an illusion. So, can a phantom sword kill a phantom attacker? I think it can.'

'And phantom fire can burn if we want it to, and an illusory horse can be ridden!' Forth put in. 'All we have to do is make it happen!'

Esty stared from one to the other. The excitement was infecting her, too; but at the core of her mind was a small, nagging worry. It was an insignificant thing, but it troubled her, and she felt she must voice it.

'I understand what you're telling me,' she said, and saw Forth frown at the cautious note in her voice, 'but . . . Indigo, when the demon first appeared to us, it took two forms. That awful child with the silver eyes, and the other figure, like a tree spirit. And when you were transformed, you took those same shapes. What *are* they?'

214

Before Indigo could answer, Forth cut in. 'Isn't it obvious, Esty? The demon drew those images from Indigo's mind – they're something from Southern Isles legend, probably, but that doesn't matter; what they are isn't important. It simply found them and used them. That made Indigo remember them, and so when she willed herself to change, she was unconsciously trying to throw the demon's own trick back in its face.'

It made sense. Esty nodded slowly. 'And the wolf,' she said. 'Grimya; of course.' She looked sympathetically at Indigo. 'You were thinking of poor Grimya.'

Indigo stared down at the ground between her crossed ankles, and said nothing.

'It even tried to mock her, by giving itself her face,' Forth went on. 'Thinking it could throw her off balance by showing her her own self but dressed as something she isn't – ach, it's *pathetic*!'

Indigo looked up. 'Don't underestimate the demon, Forth,' she said quietly. 'It may have failed to thwart us thus far, and it may have inadvertantly shown us the way to a vital weapon. But the play isn't done yet.'

'True.' Forth smiled at her. 'But we know who the heroes are, don't we? And the heroes always win. That's the first rule of the Brabazon Fairplayers' repertoire.' He looked up at the blank, pewter darkness of the sky, and raised his voice to a shout. 'Do you hear me? The heroes always win!'

They made ready to move on. As burdens were shouldered, Esty moved quietly to Indigo's side and, softly so that Forth wouldn't overhear, said, 'Indigo . . . why *were* you crying? Was it for Grimya?'

Indigo looked at her, at the innocent but genuine concern in her green eyes. There was so much that Esty and Forth didn't know; so much she had kept hidden from them because to reveal it would try their credibility too far and make them mistrustful. In truth, she had wept because in reminding her of both Nemesis and the Earth Mother's emissary, and in showing her herself as she had once been, the demon had held up a mirror that reflected a dreadful truth. Little wonder that, in a moment of crisis, those images had surged again from her mind and transformed her in her friends' eyes. And little wonder that, subconsciously struggling to escape from what they represented, she had sought refuge, as she had done before, in the form of a wolf.

Esty and Forth knew nothing of that: nothing of the deep-buried and unpredictable natural talent, unwittingly uncovered by Grimya one night many years ago, that allowed Indigo to shift both her physical form and her consciousness into those of a she-wolf. A long time had passed since she had needed to call on that power; but she'd always known it was there, dormant but waiting, and the demon's games had finally brought it howling from her unconscious to reality.

She couldn't explain to her friends. She couldn't tell them of the crowding, ugly emotions, or of the true meaning behind the game the demon had played with her. It went too deep, was too frightening. They wouldn't understand; and it wasn't fair to ask such understanding of them. Better that she should leave them to draw their own conclusions, and that their innocence, which she so envied, should remain unsullied.

'Yes,' she said at last, in response to Esty's question. 'I was crying for Grimya.'

The thought had been in all their minds for some time, but it was Forth who eventually broke the silence to voice it. They had walked some considerable way since their rest, each preoccupied, each aware, as Esty had been earlier, that their journey had so far proved suspiciously uneventful in the light of the demon's warning. The quiet and the seeming lack of danger had led them, separately but by parallel routes, to the conclusion that their peril lay not here in the empty fells, but ahead of them, at the road's end.

When Forth spoke their names, both Indigo and Esty looked up, surprised out of their private reveries by the unexpected call. Forth said: 'You do know, don't you, that if this road really is the same as in the real world, Bruhome's less than a quarter of a mile ahead of us?'

Esty slowed her steps, her face tensing. 'Are you sure?'

'Certain.' Forth nodded towards a rock buttress that intruded on to the road ahead, forcing it to curve out to avoid the obstruction. 'That's the Ram's Nose. Once we round the edge of it, the river bridge is dead ahead.' He paused. 'Does anyone want to make a guess as to what we might find?'

Esty looked away from the buttress with a shiver, and Indigo said, 'I'd take a wager on trouble.'

'So would I.' Forth scanned the fells quickly. 'It's been far too quiet for comfort, hasn't it? I keep asking myself, what's being stored up for us? It doesn't make for pleasant thoughts.'

'Doubtless that's what the demon intends,' Indigo said. 'The longer we're left to anticipate some new evil, the more nervous we'll become.'

Esty spoke up. 'I don't think anything will happen to us until we reach Bruhome, or where Bruhome should be. But I keep asking myself, what are we going to find when we get there? And I'm not sure that I want to know the answer.'

Indigo gave her a sympathetic look. 'I know how you feel. But we can't turn back now.'

'Oh, I know that. I'd just wish to be . . . better prepared, maybe.' Esty clasped her hands together and swung them from side to side, as though wielding an imaginary club. 'Mam used to have that old blackthorn stave, d'you remember, Forth? She always said that breaking heads was better than stabbing innards if it came to a fight. I wish I had that stave now.'

'You could create it,' Forth told her.

'No, I can't. I've been trying, but nothing has happened.' Esty smiled ruefully. 'Knowing it can be done's one thing; but actually doing it's quite another, it seems.'

Forth exchanged a look with Indigo, and the glance was enough to tell them both that Esty wasn't alone in her failure. There seemed no point, Indigo thought, in asking Forth what he'd tried to conjure from this world of illusions, and no point in cataloguing her own futile efforts.

She said gently, 'Perhaps we're all trying *too* hard –

too consciously.' Her shoulders hunched slightly. 'I suspect that it might need more than a simple wish.'

'The goad of fear?' Forth suggested.

'That, or pain, or something similar. At least until we've learned a little more than we know now. It's the difference, isn't it, between wanting and *willing*.'

Forth, she thought, understood; though Esty was dubious. 'I can't see that there *is* any difference,' the red-haired girl said. 'If you want something to happen, you want it to happen and that's all there is to it. No; I think it's me.' She held up her hand, displaying it. 'After all, Indigo, your burn healed; mine's still . . .' And her voice tailed off.

Forth stared at her unblemished fingers. '*When did you do that?*'

'I . . . I didn't . . .' Esty looked up at them, her eyes wide. 'But – '

'But you did.' Indigo cut in. 'Tell me, Esty: while we've been walking, were you aware of your hand hurting you?'

'Yes. It was sore, the way burns are while they're healing, and it was nagging at me – '

'And you wanted to be rid of it?'

Esty nodded.

'The goad of pain,' Forth said softly.

Esty started to protest, 'But I didn't try – '

'No. But you *willed*,' Indigo said. 'That's what makes the difference between success and failure. Forth's right; it takes a goad.'

Forth looked over his shoulder at the Ram's Nose, and at the road curving round it to their unknown destination. 'We might have goad enough when we turn that point and find out what's in store for us.'

'Don't say that,' Esty protested quickly. 'If I know I might have to do it again, I'll never be able to!'

'Well there's no point in anticipating a fall before it happens.' As she spoke Indigo unslung her harp, looking speculatively at the road ahead. 'Let's strike up some music to take us into Bruhome. We're part of the Brabazon Fairplayers, after all – and we'll show the demon what we think of its attempts to intimidate us.'

Privately, she doubted if the demon, or anything else

218

that might be lurking in wait for them, would be swayed by a show of bravado; but it was a calculated attempt to steer them all towards a bolder and more positive mood, and Indigo was relieved to see Esty's eyes light with fervour.

'*The Spavined Old Mare*,' Esty declared. 'And I'll dance it!'

Forth grinned. 'Da's favourite.' Then his expression changed and he looked uneasily at Indigo. 'Do you think . . . Da and Chari – if there *is* an illusion of Bruhome ahead of us, do you think they might be there?'

'If they are, then they'll hear us arriving!' Esty said eagerly. 'Come *on*, Forth! Play!'

Indigo held Forth's gaze, knowing that he was remembering the sleepwalker. She, too, dreaded what they might find, but if there was to be such a discovery it couldn't be put off forever. She shook her head faintly, warning him to say nothing to Esty, and at last he lifted his shoulders in a small shrug.

'Right, then.' He took out his pipe. 'Ready when you are.'

Esty skipped three or four paces down the road and began to clap her hands in a marching, dancing rhythm. Indigo's fingers poised above the harp and she let the tune, with its skittering hop to imitate the mare's spavin-legged walk, form in her mind. A stop and a stutter, and one, two, *three* on the down beat and –

Harp and pipe burst into life together, and Esty uttered a yelp of triumph as she sprang light-footed into the air, came down on her heels and launched into the lurchingly comic dance. Spinning and jumping with the music that rang out across the fells like a vivid challenge, she skipped on towards the edge of the buttress now looming before them. She looked, Indigo thought in a sudden flight of fancy, like a moorland sprite conjured from legend, and it would be easy to imagine an entire host of mythical celebrants swarming about her and dancing in her wake –

'*Ah!*' Shock made her strike a discord, and Forth looked up in alarm, taking the pipe from his lips to call out, 'What– ?'

'It's all right! Keep playing!' Indigo snatched back her self-control and bent to the harp again. The glimpse had been fleeting, vanishing in an instant – but for one extraordinary moment she had *seen* them dancing at Esty's heels. People, animals, creatures that were part of both, laughing and revelling to the lively melody. For one moment, imagination had become reality . . .

Esty was ahead of them now. She had reached the turn in the road, and Indigo and Forth were forced to jog to catch up with her. They, too, rounded the buttress – and almost collided with Esty, who had stopped, rigid, on the track.

The Spavined Old Mare faltered to a chaotic halt, and all three stared at the scene that lay before them.

It was, indeed, Bruhome. There was the old stone bridge with its weathered parapets, spanning the river. There was the dust road turning to neat cobbles as it became one with the town's main street. There were the houses and the shops and the market-stalls, with the distinctively ornate gables of the Brewmasters' Hall dominating the jumble of rooftops.

Stillness and silence, like a death pall, held the scene in a cold grasp.

'It's so . . . *still*.' Esty was shivering, staring at the image of the town as though transfixed. 'There's no one about, nothing moving . . . '

Neither Indigo nor Forth could muster a reply. To see Bruhome – even a false Bruhome – reduced to a shadowed and empty ghost was unnerving enough to Indigo: for the Brabazons, who had known its bright and vibrant bustle since their birth, this vision must be more grotesque than she could ever begin to comprehend.

There was no question of resuming the music and the dance. Forth was already putting the reed-pipe away, all thought of merriment forgotten. His face was haggard and he seemed mesmerised by the silent town, while Esty had transferred her attention to the ground, scraping at it with one heel and seeming to stare unhappily into another world.

'We have to go in,' Indigo said at last, softly.

Forth nodded. 'I know. Best get it over with then.'

In silence that felt doubly discomforting after the music's cheerful lilt, they walked towards the bridge. The truly unnerving thing, Indigo thought as they began to cross, was that the scene looked so *normal*. Every familiar detail was there, undistorted; the river's quiet splash and gurgle, the ruts on the bridge where countless wagons had rolled across, the buildings on the far side. This might have been any peaceful autumnal night in the Bruhome they all knew.

But for the dreadful sense of emptiness . . . .

They reached the end of the bridge, and stopped as they felt the uneven contours of cobbles under their feet. 'Perhaps we should go to the Brewmasters' Hall,' Forth said uncertainly. 'If there's anyone . . . or anything . . . abroad, that's the most likely place to find some sign of life.'

Esty gave him a nervous, almost furtive look. 'What about the meadow?' she whispered.

He did his best to turn a shudder into a shrug. 'Afterwards, we'll look.'

'I'm not sure that I want to.'

Forth didn't answer, but started to walk on into the town.

All the way to the main square, the story was the same. Bruhome was like a ghost town. Everything was neat and well-kept but devoid of any sign of a living creature. No candles glowed in the windows, no faces peered from behind half-open doors. And when they reached the square itself, they walked into a place of chill and silent desolation. The buildings, some shuttered, others with their windows gaping like blind eyes, stared out across the square's clean and empty space. No flamboys burned on the tall poles which stood gaunt sentinel. There were no market-stalls, no banners, no makeshift Revels stage. And not even the smallest scrap of litter blowing randomly across the paving.

'It's *horrible*.' Esty still spoke in a whisper, awed and unnerved by the scene. 'It's as if everyone who ever lived here has just been . . . spirited away.'

Neither Indigo nor Forth said anything in response,

221

but to Indigo at least Esty's words went sharply home. Could this, she wondered, be a *true* reflection of what Bruhome was now? Was that the crux of the demon's jest on them – that they were too late, and in the real world the town was now drained of life, its inhabitants all snared and gone to feed a new and ever-hungry master?

No: she mustn't think it, mustn't consider it even for a moment. She turned her face from the empty windows of the Brewmasters' Hall and, only pausing to check that Forth and Esty were following, headed across the square towards the street that led westward to the riverside meadow.

Their footfalls echoed between the house walls to either side, serving to emphasise the stillness. Esty constantly looked back over her shoulder as though she feared that some shadow might be stalking in their wake, but again there was no untoward movement, no sign of life. And when they reached the lea, and stood by the open gate, they found the meadow deserted, dark and empty under the featureless sky, with only the river flowing smooth and slow and black like a quiet mirror beyond.

Forth stared at the desolate scene for a few moments. Then he said, '*Why* is there nothing here? What game could the demon be playing now?'

'I can only surmise,' Indigo replied quietly, 'that whatever it has in store for us isn't to take place in the meadow.' She glanced at him. In the uneasy twilight he looked tense, and far older than his years. 'Perhaps this is too obvious a setting.'

A chill breath of air blew from the river, and Esty began to shiver. 'Let's go back to the square,' she said. 'At least there are houses to shelter in.' A quick, self-deprecating smile. 'Even if they're as unreal as the rest of this place, I'll feel safer.'

'The Brewmasters' Hall might be our best choice,' Forth suggested. 'It's the tallest building in the town, and its balcony would make a useful vantage-point. We can at least camp there while we decide what's best to do.' He could have added: *or while we wait for whatever's to be*

222

sent against us, but thought better of it. Esty and Indigo concurred, and so they retraced their steps to the square. The main door of the Brewmasters' Hall stood open; beyond the door, the hall and the imposing staircase were sunk in shadow.

'I wish we still had the lantern.' Esty took care not to look at the carved gargoyles that adorned the building's frontage as she stepped under the lintel at Forth's heels. 'It's like walking into a tomb . . . '

'Be careful what you say.' Indigo made an attempt at ironic humour, but regretted it when she saw the rapid change in Esty's expression. She paused on the threshold, allowing her eyes time to adjust to the deeper darkness. 'We may be able to create light for ourselves; but let's wait until we're settled upstairs before we try.'

Forth, who was standing at the foot of the stairs and listening intently, let out a breath. 'There's no sound from up there. I think it's as deserted as everywhere else seems to be.' He set foot on the first step and was about to start the climb when suddenly, from the door, Indigo said sharply, '*Wait!*'

Esty jumped nervously and both she and Forth looked back to see Indigo, one hand still on the lintel post, staring out across the square. Everything about her radiated tension – and fear.

'Indigo?' Forth covered the distance between them in three strides. 'What is it?'

'On the far side of the square.' Her voice was low-pitched, not quite steady. 'I thought I saw something move . . . '

'Human?'

'N. . .no. Not human.'

They peered across the dark expanse to the further houses and side-streets, straining to make out anything that might be more substantial than shadows. After a while Forth whispered, 'I can't see anything. Whatever it was, it's gone.'

'Perhaps I imagined it.' But Indigo clearly wasn't convinced. 'The gloom plays tricks; it's easy to – *oh, Goddess!*'

The fine hairs at the nape of Forth's neck rose and ice

223

locked his spine as, somewhere beyond the square, from one of the black and narrow alleys that ran between the houses, came the rising, shivering cry of a wolf. And instantaneously, like a hellish chorus, the cry was answered by a choir of eerie, phantasmic howls.

'No . . .' Indigo tried to back away, but tangled with Forth, who was in her path. She spun round to face him, and her face was bleached and haggard.

'That's what the demon meant!' Appalled revelation burned in her eyes and she clutched at Forth's arm. '*All* our friends – that's the trap it's set for us, don't you see? The wolf-pack – Grimya's still leading them! And they've found us again, as she said they would! *They mean to tear us apart!*'

For a few seconds Forth stood frozen, staring at her – then the howling rose anew, and he glimpsed something darker than the twilight forming at a street's gaping mouth . . .

'Upstairs!' Practicality resurged like an ice-cold slap and he pushed Indigo from him, grasping the heavy door and throwing his full weight against it. It grated shut with a terrible noise, and Forth scrabbled to set the heavy bar, desperately telling himself that a phantom door would keep out phantom wolves, trying not to think of whether it would hold back Grimya. Feet clattered on the staircase as Indigo, regaining some measure of self-control, started up the flight, pulling Esty with her; the bar fell into place – it felt substantial enough, and Forth prayed that the illusion, at least, would hold – and he ran after the two women as they gained the landing above. For a moment all three halted, not knowing which direction to take, and the gloom was filled with a sudden, crawling silence. Shadows crowded in on them from the walls and rafters, tight and stifling. Forth looked down into the well of the hall below, saw the dim outline of the barred door, listened with a pounding heart to the unearthly quiet, then looked again at Indigo's face. She was dead-white, but self-control had returned, and with it an iron calm.

'The balcony,' she said in a peculiarly level voice. 'I must find the balcony.' A pause, while her knuckles whitened on the rail. 'This is the test. I have to face it. There's no other way.'

And before Forth or Esty could respond, she swung round and walked away from them, into the darkness of the upper floor.

Chapter XVII

They came like the insinuating trickle of a river slowly but lethally overflowing its banks; gathering first in the deeper dark and then spreading gradually, cautiously into the square. From where she stood in the tall casement that opened on to the balcony of the Brewmasters' Hall, Indigo could see the crimson flickering of their eyes, unnatural embers in the night. Behind her, she knew, Forth and Esty were crouched on the floor, frantically concentrating as they tried to conjure the illusion of light, but she gave them barely a thought, and couldn't help them. Every part of her consciousness was focused on the gathering wolves, and on her agonising, futile efforts to reach the bewitched mind of Grimya.

There had been no more howling; nothing that might have enabled her to separate Grimya's real, physical voice from the eldritch echoes of her phantom pack. The silence was intense and nerve-racking; and as yet she had glimpsed no brindled grey among the black outlines that slunk and lurked between the buildings. But Grimya was there; Indigo knew it with cold certainty; a plaything in the demon's hands, a toy and a weapon, she was there and she was waiting.

Movement behind her. Someone approached, soft-footed, across the floor and she heard Esty's quick, nervous breathing.

'We can't do it.' The sky's dim glow reflected on Esty's hair like starlight on copper as she eased forward to look out of the window. 'We're not strong enough.' She hesitated. 'What are they doing . . . ?'

Indigo shook her head slowly. 'Nothing, as yet. They seem reluctant to venture into the open. I think . . . ' Her voice caught and she swallowed. 'I think that for the moment they're content simply to intimidate us.'

Esty looked at the crossbow, which Indigo held loosely in one hand. The weapon was loaded, though the string and trigger hadn't been set.

'You're not going to . . . '

'No.' No power would induce her to shoot at Grimya; that was something Indigo had decided long ago. The bow was a crutch to her courage, nothing more.

Esty fell silent, scanning the square. Then, abruptly, she clutched at Indigo's arm. 'Indigo – what's that, over there?'

Indigo's heart had missed a painful beat at the unexpected touch. 'What?' she demanded, more sharply than she'd intended.

'There.' Esty pointed to a cluster of buildings on the square's south-eastern side. 'The attic window, at the top of that steep-gabled house – there's a light!'

She was right. Faint, unsteady, but unmistakable, a candle was glowing on the house's topmost floor. And, unlike others around it, it looked as though the window was half open.

'Forth!' Indigo swung round, her pulse quickening afresh, and beckoned. 'Come here, quickly!'

He joined them at the window, and Esty pointed again across the square. 'Look at that.'

'Goddess blind me . . . ' Forth's eyes widened, then narrowed to slits. 'That's the Apple-Barrel, isn't it? Look; you can just make out the inn sign over the door.'

Esty turned to stare at him, stunned, as the same wild thought occurred to them all at the same moment. 'You don't think – '

'No,' Forth interrupted harshly. 'It's a deception. It must be.'

'But Da knows the Apple-Barrel so well. It would be the first place he'd think of!'

Forth shook his head, though Indigo saw from his expression that he desperately wanted to be contradicted. 'It can't be them, Esty. It *can't*!'

Indigo said, with quiet tension: 'There's one way to be sure.'

They both looked at her, hope and fear vying for precedence in their faces.

'Whistle,' she said. 'Call out, in the fellmen's code. If it's Stead, he'll answer.'

Forth uttered a muted oath. 'It'll carry all right . . . '

'Try, Forth!' Esty's eyes were fervid. 'Please!'

The muscles of Forth's throat worked convulsively as he stepped out on to the balcony. He didn't look down, keeping his gaze averted from the silent, shifting forms that lapped on the fringes of the darkness below. 'I . . . don't know if I can do it. My mouth's so dry . . . '

Esty cursed and ran to fetch a waterskin. '*Try!*' she pleaded again. 'I'd do it myself, but I don't know the codes!'

'All right.' He pushed the skin away, put his fingers to his lips, then drew breath, and five clear notes shrilled piercingly across the square.

Instantly, a howling clamour rose from the streets below them. Esty gasped and shrank back into the room; then, as the wolves' cries died away, took a grip on herself.

'Wh-what did you call?' She forced the words out between clamped teeth.

'I said: *family here – answer and identify.*' Forth was trying not to show his own discomfiture at the wolves' spine-chilling challenge, though sweat had broken out on his forehead.

'Maybe they didn't hear. Maybe those – those *creatures* drowned it out.'

Forth said nothing. They waited, and Indigo's hope began to fade. Then, distant but clear, two notes echoed back across the square, repeating once before the wolves' renewed cries swamped them.

'Oh, Forth!' Esty clutched the window's frame, almost dancing with fearful excitement. 'What was it?'

'They said, *repeat who.*' Forth wetted his lips. 'If there was anything else, I didn't catch it. *Curse* those monstrosities down there! Wait; I'll send the same call, and add the code that'll give our position. If we stand at the balcony rail, perhaps they'll see us.'

Esty looked dubious. 'We'll draw the wolves' attention

228

as well as theirs.'

'That's a risk we'll have to take. Come on.' He held a hand out to her and, reluctantly, she let herself be drawn out on to the balcony. 'Just pray it *is* Da, and we're not walking into a trap.'

Esty bit her lip, and stood close to Indigo as, again, Forth whistled the shrill sequence of notes, adding an extra cadence at the end. Despite the wolves' clamour, the sound rose clear on the still air, and he repeated the sequence twice for good measure.

'There's a shadow at the window!' Indigo pointed suddenly. 'Look – it's opening wider – '

The faint light had dipped and flickered, as though something had come between it and the casement. The window dimmed as the shape leaned out.

'I can't see properly!' Esty wailed. 'It's too dark!'

Even Indigo's sharp eyes couldn't make sense of the silhouette that now all but obscured the faint light from the attic room. But the answering whistle came loud and clear, and Forth's eyes lit with excitement.

'It's Da!' He stretched up, waving his arms wildly. 'It *is* Da!'

'He can't see us.' Frustration filled Indigo as she saw that the silhouetted figure wasn't responding to Forth's frantic gesturing. 'There's no light behind us; to him we're one with the darkness.' She turned to Forth. 'Forth, we must let him know what's afoot. And Chari – ' She didn't need to elaborate; her eyes expressed her thoughts all too eloquently.

But Forth shook his head. 'I can't,' he said unhappily. 'The whistle-code's too simple; it's impossible to send such a detailed message.'

Indigo stared down into the square. So close, and yet so distant . . . they *had* to find a way to communicate more directly with Stead. And she could think of only one ploy that stood a chance of success.

She looked at her companions again, and her face was tense. 'Very well,' she said. 'Then we – or rather I – must go to the Apple-Barrel.'

For a long moment Forth and Esty stared at her as though she'd lost her mind. At last, in a small, bemused voice, Esty said, 'But that's *impossible*. You *know* it is.'

'It isn't.' Indigo's mind had been moving rapidly, calculating her chances against the odds that would await her outside. 'With a little luck on my side, I think I can do it; but – '

Forth interrupted. 'If it can be done, then I'll go. I'm not going to let you risk yourself!'

'No, Forth.' Indigo smiled at him. 'I appreciate your gesture, but I'm the only one who stands a chance of getting across the square unscathed.'

He frowned, uncertain. 'Because of Grimya, you mean? Indigo, you know what happened last time we encountered her. She doesn't know you any more – she'll kill you, if she can!'

Indigo shook her head. 'I don't think so. And I have another advantage. I can't explain it to you now; there isn't time. All I can ask is that you trust me.'

Forth made a last effort to dissuade her. 'Indigo, listen to me! No human can outrun those monsters out there; it'd be madness to try!'

'I don't intend to outrun them.' *At least*, she thought, *not in the way you mean*. To forestall any further protest, she put out a hand and laid it on his arm. 'Forth, we have to reach your father somehow.'

He couldn't argue with what she said but he still had doubts. 'If – ' he began.

'No.' Indigo's voice was emphatic. 'Forth, I'm going and nothing you can say will sway me, so you'd best save your breath. Come down to the entrance hall with me, bolt the door at my back, then look after Esty.' She glanced across the square at the inn with its one lit window. 'And if you can use the whistle-code to tell Stead that I'm coming, so much the better, I don't relish the idea of being thwarted by a locked door when I may only have seconds to spare.'

His arguments rebuffed, his objections thrust aside, Forth's shoulders sagged in defeat. 'All right,' he said, but with taut misery underlying the resignation in his tone. 'But be careful!'

'I shall.'

He accompanied her down the dark staircase. Esty, who throughout the discussion had sensed that Indigo couldn't be swayed and had therefore said nothing, watched them go, then shut her eyes tightly, her lips moving in silent prayer as she heard their footsteps diminish. Below, in the entrance hall, Indigo and Forth reached the bottom of the flight, and stopped before the main door. Indigo couldn't see Forth's face clearly in the gloom, but she felt his tension, and when he started to say 'Indigo – ' she let him get no further.

'Unbar the door, Forth.' Her voice was quiet and steady.

He moved to obey, then paused and, turning, caught her in a tight embrace, kissing her face in a sudden rush of emotion.

'The Goddess go with you, Indigo! And I – I – ' But he hadn't the courage to say what he felt.

The bar slipped from its place, and she lifted the latch. Outside, the square was silent. Did the wolves have wind of her approach? she wondered. Had some demon-inspired sense already warned them of what she meant to do? She tried to take comfort from the knowledge that, whatever else might happen, they couldn't kill her, but it was small reassurance. And if she should come face to face with Grimya, what then? Would she be able to face the encounter, or would her nerve – and therefore her ability to do what must be done – fail her?

She thrust the doubts down, knowing how dangerous they were. The door swung back, just enough to allow her to slip through, and a whisper of colder air touched her face. She didn't look at Forth, but took a slow, steady breath, and eased herself cautiously through the door. It tapped shut behind her; she heard the bar slide home again.

A hundred yards, no more. She couldn't see the ghostly pack, but they were there; they were there. A hundred yards. Indigo gathered her courage, gathered her will, and shifted her mind into a new pattern, groping tentatively for the spark, the certainty. *Wolf.* The word formed in her head, and with it the image. *Wolf.* She felt the flow of it, the surge of a new strength which was unfamiliar yet not alien. *Wolf*. The square was changing, the cloying darkness ebbing as her vision intensified; she saw it now from a very different perspective. And she breathed, rapidly, roughly, wanting to snarl but holding the impulse back.

Wolf . . . Slowly, lithely, her amber eyes alert for any movement and her lips drawn back to expose the white gleam of fangs, Indigo padded out into the square.

Forth found Esty crouched in the middle of the upstairs room, her back to the window and her head bowed. At the sound of his approach she looked up. Her eyes were fearful and hunted.

'I can't go and look,' she said. 'I just *can't*.'

Forth glanced towards the window. Still there was no sound from outside, and he didn't know whether that boded well or ill.

'I'm going to signal Da.' He brushed past his sister, had to force himself to step out through the casement. The light in the distant attic window still gleamed, but the silhouetted figure had disappeared. Forth sucked at his tongue in an effort to induce enough saliva to whistle, then put his fingers to his lips and shrilled the code for *someone coming – be ready*. Three long notes; four quicker, sharper ones. He repeated them again – then realised that this time the wolves gathered below in the square hadn't set up their howling clamour in response, as though suddenly they had something more urgent to occupy them . . .

It took all the willpower he could muster, but Forth forced himself to look down.

Nothing moved. He could see no wolves and no sign of Indigo. His heart quickened to a painfully erratic thump. Where was she? And the pack – they must be lying in ambush – Forth's fear for Indigo, and shame at his own weakness in being persuaded to let her go alone, surged abruptly into something close to panic, and he swung round, not pausing to think coherently but acting on a blind impulse to go after her. But before he could duck back inside the room, a piercing whistle rang across the square from the direction of the beleaguered tavern. It was a simple acknowledgement of his own message, but it startled him, arresting him so that he turned again –

And saw the huge, tawny and grey wolf which had emerged from the Brewmasters' Hall and was walking with slow, controlled deliberation towards the centre of the square.

She was afraid, but fear was tempered with a hot flame of excitement that came from the animal adrenalin running in her veins. She knew her own power and her own strength. The silence that greeted her as she padded, with only the faintest clicking of claws on stone, into full view of the phantom pack told her that, thus far at least, her transformation had had the effect she'd hoped for. The wolves – and doubtless their unhuman master – hadn't expected this, and were unsure of themselves. For a few moments Indigo had the advantage: but she knew that it wouldn't last. She must time everything perfectly, or the plan would end in disaster.

More years than she cared to remember had passed since she had consciously used her shape-shifting power, and she'd feared that she might be unable to conjure it at will, or – worse – that in taking on a wolf's aspect she might lose control of her human self. But with the first giddy rush of the change, she had known that all was well. She was wolf-Indigo again; and the agility, the speed, the cunning, had all returned to her. Now, she must face the greater test.

Shadows were gathering more intensely at the dark openings that led into the side streets. She was perhaps a third of the way across the square; still the pack had made no move, though with her heightened senses she could feel a sharp change in the atmosphere, from uncertainty to a new, tense anticipation.

Another pace. Another, and another. Now Indigo could make out the more definite silhouettes of individual wolves, though she hadn't yet glimpsed Grimya's distinctive form among them. *Still* the pack did nothing. Surely, she thought, by now they must –

The thought collapsed into chaos as from the corner of her eye she saw two black shapes explode silently from an

233

alley mouth and streak like bolts from a crossbow towards her. Instinct made her spring round to meet them; she braced her legs, snarling as they sprang for her throat – and the snarl became a yelp as the first wolf's teeth tore at the soft flesh of her shoulder. Shocked by pain and the revelation that these horrors could bite as fiercely as any living animal, Indigo rolled, squirming to escape the attack and snapped savagely at her assailant. Amid the blur of its threshing black body she saw its mad eyes flash like evil red stars – and then the second wolf was on her. She twisted desperately about, lunged at its face with bared fangs as the three of them rolled together over the cobbles.

Suddenly a single, sharp bark rang out. Indigo's attackers sprang back as though at an order, and for a moment she stood alone, shaking, feeling blood trickling down her shoulder and matting her fur. Then an ululating cry echoed from somewhere behind her. Indigo whipped round – and as the cry coalesced into a chorus of yelps and snarls, Grimya emerged from the darkness, her eyes glaring, her hackles bristling, to stand confronting her not twenty paces away.

Indigo felt the surge of insensate hunger from the she-wolf's mind and the small hope she had nurtured of being able to break through her friend's bewitchment shattered. This creature might have Grimya's flesh and Grimya's blood; but the consciousness that stared out through those insane and brutal eyes was that of an alien monster. A whimper rose in her throat, caught, died. Grimya continued to stare, and mingling with the insatiable hunger she felt hatred; the blind hatred of anything that lived, anything that was not born of this nightmare of illusions. Grimya's lips drew back, and the black wolves' yelping grew louder and more urgent, rising towards a crescendo – then the she-wolf raised her head to howl a challenge and a command, and like a bursting wave the entire pack erupted from their hiding place and surged towards Indigo.

Terror and instinct slammed together into Indigo's wolf-brain, hurling all reason aside. Her hind legs powered her away and she ran, streaking across the

234

square, dodging and weaving as black shapes came howling out of the dark at her. *The tavern – must get to the tavern –* but the part of her mind that screamed the imperative was swamped and bowled away; she could only flee, not knowing her direction, driven by the blind desperation to escape.

A black wall reared out of the gloom ahead and Indigo yelped, contorting her body and bringing herself thrashing to a halt a split second before she would have cannoned into the building's solid facade. No door to give her sanctuary, no side street to gape for her – she spun about, her claws scrabbling for purchase, and saw the dark wave flooding towards her with Grimya a starkly paler phantom in its midst. She was trapped against the wall: they were closing in to tear her and rend her, and immortality was no proof against the agony they would inflict. Indigo opened her mouth to howl – whether in fear or in misery or in a last, frantic appeal for help she didn't know –

The howl was drowned by a titanic roar that ripped through the wolves' triumphant clamour and thundered deafeningly across the square.

As though a massive cross-current had hit their tidal wave full on, the pack's rush disintegrated into a boiling mass of bodies, yelping in panic-stricken confusion. For a moment Indigo was too stunned to understand; then she felt a vast shadow rearing above her, smelled the sulphurous wind of a huge, exhaled breath, and with a snarl she twisted about, looking up.

The monster towering over her was a pulsing apparition at least twenty feet tall. Its four treelike legs, ending in eagle's talons, were braced to either side of her, and the vast bulk of its reptilian body seemed to have erupted from the wall at her back. Rumbling air buffeted her as the creature lashed a forked tail as thick as three men's torsos, and the giant lion's head, with its mane a flying corona of fire, raised its muzzle to the sky and roared anew.

Chimera! Recognition smashed into Indigo's consciousness as the bellowing noise ricocheted back from all sides of the square. Driven to the brink of despair, on the edge of its mad chasm, her panic-stricken mind had blindly summoned the most fearsome image it could create, and, fuelled by the raw power of terror, the illusion had exploded into existence. The wolf-pack were falling back in disarray; one creature, slower to react than its fellows, was even now scrambling to join the retreat. The chimera raised a taloned foot; the talon whistled through the air like a gigantic sword, and the hapless wolf howled in maniacal agony as, split from head to tail, it dissolved in a flurry of black smoke.

Illusion can kill illusion – adrenalin powered through Indigo's veins and a shudder ran the length of her body. She could do it! She had the power, she had the weapon! Her teeth bared, and above her the chimera tossed its blazing head as though daring the cowering wolves to attack again. Indigo could see the Apple-Barrel now; could see the attic light still feebly burning. Carefully, alert for any untoward reaction, she took a pace forward and excitement surged afresh as the chimera's great bulk moved, matching her step for step. Still in its shadow, she eyed her goal again. Thirty yards, no more. She could run the gauntlet in seconds; before the pack had time to recover its wits. And the chimera would take care of any that tried to come after her . . .

She braced her hind legs, knowing that her thoughts were also the thoughts of the phantom creature she had created. Her muscles tensed, she felt energy build, ready to run –

The tawny-grey wolf shot from under the chimera's shelter, taking the phantom pack by surprise as she raced for the door of the tavern. Behind her she heard furious cries, a third awesome roar, shrieks of pain. Something burst from deep shadows, bearing down across her path; her will screamed silently, and she was all but thrown off her feet by a gale of displaced air as talons plummeted from above to impale and splinter a howling black form. The door was only yards away now; she would do it, she would reach it – with that knowledge perspective lurched and shuddered, and the square seemed to topple towards her at a drunken angle, one image superimposed on another. The door rose up before her; it was opening, swinging back – she howled in triumph and relief, and what came from her throat was a human scream –

Big, rough hands wrenched the door back on its hinges, and with a cry that shattered into a choking gasp, Indigo flung herself through and collapsed with her hands clutching at Steadfast Brabazon's legs.

CHAPTER XVIII

'Lass, I'm so thankful! So *thankful*!'

Stead wouldn't let go of Indigo's hand; he had gripped it tightly as she told him that Forth and Esty were safe. He shook his head, repeating the words over and over.

Indigo was still shaking from the aftermath of her experience, but gradually her calm was returning. Outside, the square was still and silent. The chimera, its work done, had dissolved from the world, and the wolf-pack had slunk away into the dark, deprived of their quarry. She believed they were still there, waiting for her next move, but, for the time being at least, they presented no threat. And with rigid determination, she was forcing herself not to consider Grimya.

The fire which Stead had made from a broken chair had burnt down to embers now and the attic room was sunk in heavy gloom. It seemed Stead had had no trouble in finding materials for building and lighting a fire in the tavern, and no trouble in persuading the flames to kindle. Indigo suspected that his own ignorance had come to his rescue; he knew nothing of the demon world's nature, and that innocence had protected him from much of its perversity.

Hastily, she and Stead exchanged the barest bones of their adventures; for the moment Indigo had more urgent matters to concern her. But certainly Stead had run the gauntlet of many nightmarish illusions before finding his way here. He refused to detail the horrors that had been sent to plague him, but from her own experience she could piece together a clear enough picture. One thing alone had given him the determination to press on, Stead said. He looked towards the corner of the room where, on a pile of mats and cushions plundered from the Apple

Barrel's lower floors, Chari lay in seemingly peaceful but profound sleep.

Indigo's relief at seeing her was greater than she could express. With memories of the other sleepwalker painfully sharp in her mind she had feared the worst; but it seemed either that the demon had not yet chosen to fasten its hungering attention on Chari, or that in some subtle way her father's presence had acted as a buffer against its influence. From what Stead had told her, it hadn't been easy. Chari had fought like a wild animal when he tried to sway her from her mindless path; Stead was on the verge of tears as he described the brute force he had been driven to use to subdue her, and livid bruises on Chari's arms and jaw were testimony to his desperate measures. But finally, and very suddenly, the force that held Chari enthralled had given way, and she had slumped at his feet; unwakeable still but at least no longer fighting him. Since then he had carried her until, finding himself on a familiar road, he had followed it and arrived here.

He had, though, been unable to tell her anything of how Grimya had come to her present pass. After breaking through the thorns they had become separated almost immediately, and in his concern for Chari, Stead had forgotten the she-wolf until, much later, he had heard a howl echoing out of the distant dark. He had called out, trying to locate the source of the cry; but as soon as he shouted Grimya's name a chorus of eerie wailings had answered him, and he was too afraid to draw further attention to himself by calling to the wolf again. He had discovered the truth only when, with Chari in his arms, he had finally tramped footsore and weary into this phantom town, to find the wolf-pack waiting for him with Grimya at their head. In that moment, Stead admitted sombrely, he'd thought that he was about to breathe his last. But the wolves hadn't attacked. Instead they'd let him pass by with his burden, merely watching until the door of the Apple-Barrel slammed shut behind him before slinking away. But he'd seen Grimya clearly enough.

Stead whistled a message to Forth, telling him that all

was well and that Indigo had arrived safely. Forth acknowledged, adding two cadences that signified *must join together* and *urgency*. But how, Indigo asked herself, was she to get Forth and Esty across the gauntlet of the square? For Stead to cross to the Brewmasters' Hall was out of the question; the burden of Chari would hamper him too greatly if the wolves chose to attack. Indigo must return alone, and find a way to bring the others back with her. The prospect wasn't pleasant, but she believed she could do it, for the chimera had taught her a valuable lesson. If she could only pass that lesson on to Forth and Esty, then at least there might be hope.

Stead was reluctant to let her go again, but finally acknowledged that there was no other choice. He hadn't witnessed what had taken place during Indigo's first crossing of the square, for as soon as Forth had signalled the *be ready* code, he had run down to the tavern's main door and waited in readiness for her arrival. Privately, Indigo was thankful for that. She hadn't attempted to explain to Stead the nature of this world's illusions and how they might be controlled, and didn't intend to, for she had a strong intuition that the less Stead understood, the more valuable his own as yet untapped abilities might prove to be.

She persuaded him to whistle *coming to you – be ready* across the divide to Forth and, heart thumping, went down the stairs of the inn. This time, she had resolved not to make any attempt to face out the wolf-pack, but simply to change shape and run with all the speed she could muster straight to the Brewmasters' Hall.

The phantom wolves seemed to have gathered on this side of the square, which gave her a slight advantage; for there would be none to cut across her path or head to meet her. With luck, and the element of surprise, she believed she could outrun them without the need to call on the chimera, or any other powers.

Again, she felt the thundering of her pulse, the suffocating tension as she eased the door open. The image of the tawny-grey wolf formed in her mind – it came faster this time, as though it had been waiting for her summons

240

– and her muzzle went up to sniff the air, her hindquarters braced –

Indigo burst from the doorway at full speed, head down, legs powering her forward. She heard the clamour go up, and her heightened instinct recognised fury in the rallying cry. Grim pleasure at the wolves' confusion gave her an extra edge, and even as the pack came howling after her she knew that this time she had been too fleet for them. Ahead, the door of the Brewmasters' Hall was opening; she glimpsed the blurred white oval of someone's face. The wolves were closing, but not fast enough; with a last, tremendous effort she flung herself towards the portal and went careering through, cannoning into a human figure which yelled out as they crashed to the floor together in a tangle of fur and limbs and –

She was lying, gasping, winded by the bottom stair which had broken her fall, and clutching at the banister rail as wolf-Indigo fled and humanity returned. She heard someone scrambling to slam the door, and the thud of the bar returning, then hands helped her to turn and sit, and she saw Forth and Esty staring at her wide-eyed.

Esty made a religious sign, but couldn't find her tongue. Forth, though, was looking at her in open admiration.

'You controlled it!' He sounded awed. 'Indigo, you *controlled* it! And that – that creature – ' He gestured helplessly, unable to describe the chimera in words.

'You saw it?' Indigo struggled to regain her breath.

He nodded. 'Esty wouldn't look, but I . . . ' his voice tailed off and the nod transmuted into a shake of the head. 'Great Goddess . . . '

Indigo hauled herself to her feet. She had breath enough to climb the stairs now, she thought; and so much to say.

'Let's return to the upstairs room. We must let your father know that I'm back safely. And then we have plans to make.'

From the balcony Forth sent a new message shrilling across the square, which Stead acknowledged. Indigo suspected that Stead hadn't witnessed her transformation, and was relieved: though how he'd react to what – if her idea worked – would return across the square to the inn, she didn't dare to imagine.

She was glad that Forth, at least, had seen both her wolf-form and the chimera, for it would strengthen his own will and resolve. In his young pride she surmised that Forth would be fiercely determined to match her in every way. What Indigo had learned from her own experience had given her the key that would unlock Forth and Esty's powers, as hers had been unlocked.

And so she explained her plan. Forth and Esty listened with growing excitement, but that excitement was tempered with trepidation, and Esty voiced the doubt that was in both their eyes.

'Indigo, it's a splendid idea. But how are we to achieve it? You have the ability – we've seen that with our own eyes. But what about Forth and me? We've only achieved the most trivial changes so far. How can we hope to do what this will demand of us?'

'There's a simple answer to that,' Indigo said. 'It's what you said earlier, Forth. The goad of fear triggered my ability to conjure the chimera. I was cornered, trapped; I had to save myself, and there was no time to think clearly. So I just reacted.'

'And the chimera appeared.' Forth's eyes were sharply speculative. 'Yes. I understand. So if Esty and I are in the same straits . . . '

'It's dangerous,' Indigo admitted. 'But I can't think of another way for the three of us to reach Stead and Chari. And if it works – '

'*If*,' Esty interjected.

'Esty, I'm not underrating the risk. But it's our only chance, and *if* it works, then it'll break the final barrier.' Indigo hesitated. She'd been undecided whether to attempt this, but decided that it had to be done if she was to convince her companions. She only prayed that she was right about her own skills: but, as Stead would doubtless have said, half measures wouldn't sway a hostile audience. Give it all, or get off the stage.

'Look over there,' she said, pointing to the far corner of the room.

They turned their heads, and Indigo summoned her will. For a moment nothing happened; she concentrated harder, then felt the quick spark of adrenalin –

Esty uttered a high-pitched cry, and Forth gasped. In the corner, a tree had appeared; a birch sapling with mottled silver-grey bark and young leaves a vivid spring green. It seemed to grow out of the floor, and its slim boughs quivered as though in a breeze.

Elated, Indigo focused her mind once more. This wasn't the dead shade of Bruhome, but a woodland glade in her own homeland. She could see it, feel it, smell it . . .

Grass began to spread out from the tree's foot like an encroaching wave. Small flowers patched the green carpet: they looked so real that she felt she could have reached out and plucked one, and her nostrils flared at a new, warm-hay scent that suddenly seemed to fill the chamber.

'It's *incredible* . . . ' Esty's voice was awed.

Forth shut his eyes, pinched the bridge of his nose then looked again, as though he expected the vision to vanish. But Indigo knew it wouldn't vanish; not until and unless she willed it. Illusion laid over illusion: she had imposed her will on this unreal world. It was the final test, and it had succeeded.

Very quietly but with great emphasis, she said, 'Fear unlocked the door for me. And I think it can do the same for you.' Another pause, 'I may be wrong, and I can't make the final decision – '

Forth looked keenly at her. 'But you believe we can do it?'

She nodded. 'Yes.'

There was a long silence. Then Forth said: 'Well, then. That's good enough for me.' He looked up, glanced a little uncertainly at the tree and then turned to his sister. 'We've got to reach Da and Chari somehow, Es. And I reckon we could sit here forever and not find a safer way. So I say we try it.'

Esty hesitated, then: 'Yes.' She blinked, tossed her hair back with a self-consciously confident gesture. 'It's the only way.'

Indigo gave silent thanks, at the same time pushing

243

down a worm of guilt. She had to trust her judgement, and believe that she wouldn't be leading her friends into disaster. Otherwise, what hope did they have?

'And when we've done it,' Forth said. 'If our own abilities are unlocked – what then? Because it seems to me that if this *does* break down the barriers, it's going to change the nature of the play. What d'you think our demon friend will make of that?'

'I've an idea about it,' Indigo told him, 'but I haven't had the chance to think it through.'

'Tell us.'

She hesitated. 'I'd prefer not to say too much until we have your father with us, for if this is to work, we'll need him perhaps above all. But . . . well, you used the analogy just now, Forth. The play. That's how the demon sees us: as puppets dancing on its stage and to its tune.' She smiled, and there was something lupine in the smile that sharply recalled wolf-Indigo. 'I've been thinking that perhaps we should give the demon precisely what it wants – but not necessarily in the way that it anticipates.'

'A *play*?' Esty was baffled.

'Yes, and no.' Indigo glanced at the tree which still rustled gently in the corner of the room, then at the square of the balcony window. 'I'd rather not say anything about it yet. Wait until we're with Stead; then we can all talk more fully. For now, I think it would be better to concentrate on the more immediate problem. After all, if we don't solve that successfully, there'll be little point in discussing any further plans.'

Reluctantly Forth and Esty agreed, and they began to make ready. The possessions that they'd brought with them into the demon world were now whittled down to a few sorry remnants, and they divded them evenly, ensuring that everyone would have as little as possible to carry. Their water supplies were dangerously low and food almost non-existent; and Esty said wryly that it was a pity they couldn't conjure something to eat and drink that was more substantial than an illusion.

At this, Forth froze. 'Water . . .' he said. 'Great Mother, how has Da survived without water?'

Indigo stared at him. It hadn't once occurred to her

that Stead had entered the demon world without so much as a thimbleful of water in his possession: yet he'd shown no sign of thirst, and hadn't even asked her if she had water with her. She recalled the fire he'd built with materials from the illusory tavern. The tinder-box which had worked; the broken chair which had fuelled the flames . . . could Stead's innocence have extended even to finding water simply because he believed it must be there? If that was so, then Indigo had gravely underestimated the potential value of his abilities, and she felt the hot, shivering clutch of inner excitement as she thought of how such an asset might aid them in the final phase of her plan.

Aloud, she said, 'When we reach the Apple Barrel we'll get to the root of the mystery. And the sooner we can do that, the better.' She looked at them both in turn. 'Have you decided on the images you mean to fix in your minds?'

'Bears,' Esty said firmly. 'That's what I think wolves are frightened of. Bears, and those great hunting cats that live in the northern lands.' She glanced at Indigo. 'I've never seen such a cat, but I've seen pictures of them; and if I was a wolf they'd terrify me!'

Forth grinned. 'Anything that comes into my head will do. I doubt if I'll have a chance to be that fussy!'

Indigo returned his smile drily. 'You're probably right. And whatever comes most strongly will have the most power.'

'And what of you?' Forth asked. 'Will it be the chimera again?'

She'd considered one particular illusion she might conjure, and the thought of it sent a sensation like a cold spike through her stomach. But she didn't want to reveal it; not yet.

'No,' she said. 'It won't be the chimera. It'll be something very different.'

And so for the third time the breathless waiting, the tight-shut eyes and the silent prayers for good fortune. This time, though, Forth's square, roughened palm was closed over Indigo's right hand, while Esty's smaller, softer fingers gripped her left. And for a moment of sheer fancy, in her mind Indigo was again a part of the Brabazon Fairplayers, standing ready with her good friends and co-performers in the last keyed-up moment before they stepped on to the stage.

That was it. Hold to that; keep the image, don't let it go. Suddenly she recalled a piece of doggerel that had become a long-standing private jest among the family when a hostile or apathetic audience awaited them, and on impulse she spoke the first two lines of it aloud.

'We'll take the stage and we'll take a bow,
And if they don't like us, this we vow –'

Forth smothered a laugh – taut and high-pitched, but a laugh none the less – and he and Esty joined in to complete the rhyme.

'We'll take their money, and when we're done,
Then we'll take to our heels and run!'

Fired by a rush of reckless confidence, Esty gave a high, yodelling cry as Forth wrenched the door back, and together, still holding hands, they rushed out into the square. For a dizzying moment Indigo almost believed that they were indeed running out on to a stage, under the glare of flamboys, with a sea of eager faces and applauding hands waiting to greet them. For a moment she felt the spring of wooden boards beneath her feet, glimpsed Esty in her dancing costume, tambourine raised; heard a ghostly snatch of the fiddle and the hurdy-gurdy –

Then the howling went up from a hundred phantom throats and the images whirled away, too tenuous to hold, and she heard her own voice shouting a warning.

'They're coming! Drive them back! *Drive them back!*'

Black shapes erupted from the shadows across the dark square, crimson eyes blazing, drooling, fang-filled mouths gaping wide in anticipation of the prey. Esty's momentary defiance collapsed into a scream of fear and her fingers splayed rigid so that Indigo almost lost her grip on them. They were running, but the wolves were faster, surging towards them, cutting off retreat, spreading like an evil tide, a wave to swamp and overpower and drown them. Forth yelled as the first of the horrors swerved across his path and leaped to snatch for his unprotected right arm. He stumbled, evading the clashing teeth by a hairsbreadth, then lost his balance and his hold on Indigo's hand and went staggering away, his own momentum spinning him helplessly around.

'Forth!' Indigo cried desperately. But he couldn't heed her, and she had no chance to shout again, for another wolf came snarling at her and she was forced to spring to one side to evade it. There was no time for reason: her free arm swung in a wild, reflexive attempt to beat the monster off – and suddenly there was a sword in her hand, glittering with an evil sheen, and she felt the jarring of her arm, *felt* it as the blade smashed into flesh and through bone, and the wolf, shrieking agony, bowled and bounced across the cobbles with black blood spraying from its severed throat.

Esty cried out and flung herself against Indigo, trying to hide her face in Indigo's hair. In the chaos of darkness and milling, leaping forms Forth was invisible, but Indigo could hear him shouting in a fury of terror and desperation. And Esty was screaming, her legs giving way, threatening to drag Indigo with her down on to the cobbles.

'No, Esty! The bear – call the bear!' Indigo was frantic; her sword had flickered and vanished, and she couldn't rally her wits while the girl still clung to her. Everything was going wrong; she couldn't control it – her friends would be hurled down, torn apart –

Suddenly a maniacal shriek split the air, a shrill, impossibly high-pitched screech that came from behind and above them. The wolves yelped, falling back momentarily, and Indigo whirled.

From the balcony of the Brewmasters' Hall, a living river of squat, ungainly creatures was swarming down towards the ground. More shrieks echoed in the wake of the first, and, hopping and jumping with a horrifyingly bizarre gait, the creatures sprang to the cobbles and flung themselves into the fray.

Indigo's heart missed so painfully that for a moment she thought she'd lose all control and vomit with a mingling of revulsion and relief. She'd succeeded – the

247

image she'd striven to implant in her thoughts had taken root, and out of the night, out of nightmare, out of her imagination, the Scatterers, grotesque, cat-like horrors from Southern Isles mythology, had come, yammering their ravenous greed, to aid her. She heard the first panic-stricken howl as six of them set upon a single wolf; glimpsed the flurry of blood and viscera as the phantom was disembowelled, saw, only moments later, shattered splinters of bone flying in all directions as the creatures hurled the stripped bones of their victim to the four winds. Their countless hundreds of teeth chattered and clattered with an awful sound that seemed to fill the square; and more were squirming like maggots from the very fabric of the buildings, streaming down the walls, leaping at their quarry in mad, insensate hunger.

But the wolves were beginning to fight back. Three Scatterers went down under an onslaught of snapping jaws and were bitten in two before they could retaliate; and others, outnumbered, were ripped limb from limb. The pack was rallying, and, urging them on, calling them to turn on their attackers, the howling cry of one single animal rose above the din.

Grimya! But Indigo couldn't see her, couldn't reach her mind. And now the Scatterers were falling back under the wolves' renewed onslaught. They couldn't hold their ground, the illusions were shattering, breaking apart –

Suddenly a throaty roar sounded to her left. Two wolves, clear of the bloody mêlée, were turning to come at her, and in striving frantically to recreate her sword she had no chance to turn her head and look. The wolves crouched, snarling – the sword materialised but it was unstable, flickering wildly – then a huge, dark bulk barrelled across her line of vision, and a massive, ghostly bear, jaws wide and bellowing in fury, charged at the wolves. It hit them like a battering-ram and they spun away, howling and disintegrating into tatters of smoke as the bear lumbered on across the square. Indigo heard Esty cry out again, but this time it was a scream of triumph: and the next instant the square seemed to erupt, as though the very Earth had opened, and from every

248

side, every street, every house, a horde of phantoms came screaming and roaring and howling. Beasts, birds, chimerae – giant cats with the wings and beaks of eagles, horse-headed serpents, titanic, web-footed hounds – disgorged into the demon world and falling on the wolf-pack in a nightmare tide.

Esty was on her knees, still clinging to Indigo's arm. They were in the heart of the fray, and with no ceremony Indigo dragged the girl across the cobbles at a run, ducking as a white owl with a twenty-foot wingspan hurtled past a handsbreadth away and swooped down on a cluster of fighting, boiling monsters. The wolves were in chaos, their quarry forgotten in the desperate fight against this new attack, and Indigo gained the shelter of a wall, slamming her back against the stonework and dragging breath into her lungs. Esty's eyes had rolled up in their sockets and her breath was coming in great, agonised gasps; one rapid scan of the square told Indigo that they were perhaps twenty yards from the Apple-Barrel, and she searched wildly about her for Forth, yelling his name.

A shape broke from the roiling darkness, swerved as a tumbling tangle of three wolves, a bear and two Scatterers bowled across his path, and Forth came racing towards them. He slid to a halt, his eyes alight with a fever of excitement.

'It worked! It worked!' He tried to hug Indigo but she pushed him back, knowing that they dared not delay even for a moment. 'Get to the inn!' she shouted above the din of battle. 'And help me with Esty, she's – '

'I'm all right!' Esty's face was scarlet and slick with sweat, but she was recovering her wits and her strength. 'Come on!'

They ran for the tavern door, and burst through it together, the force of their bodies almost snapping it from its hinges.

'Go upstairs!' Indigo propelled her companions before her as the door slammed at their backs. She heard the stampede of their feet as they obeyed, and Esty's voice calling, 'Da! Da!'; but instead of following them immediately she paused for a few seconds at the foot of the staircase, shutting her eyes and trying to gather her senses.

They'd succeeded. The barrier was broken not only for her, but for Forth and Esty too. She'd gambled and won, and the relief of that knowledge was shattering. Now, they must . . .

And the thought died as, through the pounding of her own pulse in her ears, Indigo realised that the terrible noises from the square outside were fading. She could still hear the howls, the shrieks, the shattering roars, but they seemed to be draining away like a stream going underground, fainter and fainter and –

Silence. It was so acute that for a few moments it seemed to swell and beat in Indigo's head as loudly as the din that had gone before. She turned her head, listening to it, wondering. Had the wolf-pack fled, with their own creations in pursuit? Were they all destroyed? Or had the battle somehow been transferred into some other dimension? Curious, she half-made to move towards the door – then stopped as, from the square, a single, dismal howl rang out.

A prickling shiver shot through Indigo's torso and arms. She knew what the sound was. What it could only be. Slowly, she reached out and raised the door-latch, pulling the door open a few inches, and looked out.

All traces of the fight had vanished. The square was dark, silent. But not quite empty. Alone in the centre, her brindled muzzle raised to the featureless sky and her flanks still quivering from the cry she had uttered, stood Grimya.

'Grimya!' Indigo felt a constricting rush of emotion and, careless of any danger, stepped out into the square. Grimya tensed instantly; her head swung round and Indigo saw the twin reflections of her eyes, like points of yellow fire in the gloom.

'Grimya . . . ' Indigo tried to link her own mind with the she-wolf's, entreating her, wanting to give her love and comfort –

Grimya snarled. With no phantom pack to support her the snarl was uncertain and born more of fear than aggression; but still Indigo felt the wave of red hatred that surged from Grimya's mind in answer to her own plea. The she-wolf backed away, tail between her legs, still staring with that dreadful, insensate fixity. Then she howled again, a cry of utter defeat and misery, and turned, loping away into the shadows to vanish like a whipped cur.

And left Indigo staring helplessly after her, with tears streaming down her cheeks.

Chapter XIX

'Well, then.' Stead put his hands on his hips and stared about him as though challenging anyone to argue with what he was about to say. 'We go after it, and we kill it. That's all there is to be said.' The frown that had made his face thunderous deepened, and he began to pace. '*Demons*, by the Harvest Mother's eyes! I never thought I'd live to see such filth come to plague the lives of decent folk!'

Forth glanced at Indigo, who sat on the windowledge a little apart from the rest of the group. Throughout the Brabazons' noisy and emotional reunion she had stayed in the background, saying little while Stead and Forth and Esty had talked themselves to a standstill. That was understandable enough, she must feel that she had little personal part to play in the family's celebration; but Forth suspected that something more lay behind her silence. She was brooding; but he didn't know what the cause of her mood could be, and didn't know how to broach the subject with her.

Besides, he had other demands on his attention. A great deal had happened since he and Indigo and Esty had burst through the door of the Apple-Barrel and been reunited with Stead. At first everyone had been talking and laughing and crying at once, and for some time it had been impossible to make much sense of anything. But at last the atmosphere had sobered, and gradually they were able to piece together the salient facts of their position.

That discussion had taken place over the first square meal that the new arrivals had had since leaving the real Bruhome behind. Indigo's theory concerning Stead's innocence had been startlingly vindicated; when asked how he had survived during his travail he'd looked at them in surprise and said that he'd done what anyone short of a halfwit would do; drunk water from streams and pools along the way. True, there had been no food available on the black fells, but once he reached this empty town, naturally he'd found food and water aplenty in the tavern's store-rooms, and since then he'd shifted very well. And when the store proved, indeed, to be well stocked with supplies that were both visible and edible to everyone, Forth had begun to realise just how potent a force his father's unquestioning mind could be in this dimension. Without a moment's doubt or hesitation, Stead had imposed his own reality on the unreal world; and the potential of that ability was awesome.

But after the meal and the first wave of stories and revelations were done, they were faced with the last and hardest task of all. Stead staunchly believed that he was still in the real world and that the black forest into which he and Chari and Grimya had stumbled, together with all its horrors and illusions, was some sorcerous creation which had been conjured out of the dark to surround Bruhome. He couldn't – or wouldn't – accept that this silent, empty town wasn't Bruhome itself, still trapped in the unnatural night between the forest's boundaries, and when Forth and Indigo tried to explain the truth to him, he argued vehemently with them. His theory, and he wasn't about to be disabused of it, was that all the town's inhabitants had finally been lured away by the evil influence which held the district in its grip. By a combination of good luck and grim determination, he and Indigo, Forth and Esty had found their way back; but the others – including the rest of his children – were still lost and wandering somewhere in the depths of that vile forest.

They had tried to reason with him, tried to make him comprehend the real truth, but Stead was obdurate. Theory had become firm fact in his mind and he refused even to consider the logical flaws that contradicted his belief. Indigo had abruptly withdrawn from the argument and Forth, too, eventually gave in when he realised that nothing of any value would be achieved.

But there was one fact that Stead was ready and willing to accept; for, like any native of the south-western lands, Stead didn't doubt the existence of demons. When – choosing his words carefully – Forth told him of their encounter with the being that held Bruhome in thrall and of the challenge it had issued to them, the spark of indignation that had helped Stead to overcome his fear for so long suddenly kindled and blazed into furious anger. Stead had only one reaction to such anger: to seek out the cause, and eradicate it.

So, pacing the narrow room like a pent boarhound, he warmed to his theme. The demon would *die*. He would find it, and he would take it apart, with his bare hands if necessary. As his father ranted, Forth looked again at Indigo. She was watching Stead, but obliquely, as though barely listening. Forth wondered why she hadn't yet spoken up about her plan, and wished that he could have been privy to her thoughts.

Suddenly Stead stopped again. They could hear him breathing, sounding like a sweating horse in the confined space. Then he swung round.

'Well? What are we all waiting for?' His gaze raked them, then settled on Chari's still, silent form on her makeshift bed in the corner. 'If we're to save my Chari, we've got to destroy that thing before matters get any worse! We'll set out back across the fells, find that thrice-accursed stronghold you told me of – '

'No,' Indigo said quietly.

Stead halted in mid-sentence. 'What?' He looked taken aback, as though he'd forgotten she was there, but collected himself quickly. 'What d'you mean, no?'

Indigo slid off the ledge, flexing her legs to ease a twinge of cramp. 'Stead, there's no point in our searching for the demon's stronghold. We won't find it; not unless the demon wants us to, and I don't believe it does. We could comb those fells for eternity while it leads us a dance. I think we'd be better off staying exactly where we are.'

'Where we are?' Stead echoed, incredulous. 'Where's the good in that?'

Forth was trying to catch Indigo's attention, but she

254

either didn't notice or didn't want to acknowledge his surreptitious gestures. 'I want to see the demon destroyed just as much as you do,' she said, 'but we won't succeed in destroying it by simply marching out like soldiers to a battle. We'll need to be far more subtle than that.'

Stead's brows knitted. 'How so?'

'We won't go in search of the demon. We'll lure it here, in search of us. I've been thinking about it, and I believe it's the surest way to achieve our ends.' Now her eyes did acknowledge Forth, but very briefly and with a warning not to interject. 'I have an idea for a trap, Stead, and I'm confident that it will work.'

Stead began at last to look interested. 'What manner of trap?'

A pause. Then Indigo said: 'A full performance by the Brabazon Fairplayers.'

The second pause was far longer than the first. Then Stead said: 'Damn me, woman. What are you talking about?'

Indigo caught Forth's eye again, and this time the warning was emphasised by a quick, negating gesture of one hand. 'Stead,' she said, 'I don't mean to sound arrogant, but I have a better idea of what we're up against than you. I know the nature of our adversary, and I think – I *think* – that I also know how we might defeat it. What I'm going to say may sound mad to you; but I have to ask you to trust me.'

'Lass, I trust you; you know I do.' Stead was perplexed. 'But this . . . I don't understand. What could one of our shows possibly have to do with this sorcery?'

'Potentially, everything.' Indigo returned his intimidating gaze steadily. 'In our shows, we aim to give our audience an illusion, and impose it over the reality of our lives. What I have in mind is to do exactly the opposite – to impose reality on a world of illusion.'

Sharp intakes of breath from Forth and Esty told her that they understood. Well and good: but Stead's frown had deepened. 'Illusion?' he said tetchily. 'Reality? What sort of high-flown nonsense is that?'

Indigo shook her head gently. 'It isn't nonsense, Stead: at least, I pray to the Goddess that it isn't. During our

255

travels, Forth and Esty and I have learned a good deal about this world. Forgive me, but we've learned far more than you, and – '

Forth could keep silent no longer, and cut in. 'It's true, Da! We *know* – everything in this world's an illusion; it isn't real – '

Stead rounded on him. He was confused, and confusion gave rise to fear, and fear in turn gave rise to belligerence. 'Be quiet, boy!' he growled. 'What do you know about anything? Illusions, indeed! I've never heard the like of it!'

Stung and insulted by such a cavalier dismissal Forth opened his mouth to retaliate, but Indigo intervened quickly, forestalling him.

'Stead, I understand your feelings,' she said. Something in her voice made both Stead and Forth pause. 'And I'm not going to even try to explain what I mean in words.' She hesitated. 'You said a few minutes ago that you trust me. I ask you, then, not to question, but at least to give me the chance to prove my theory.'

'Da, please listen to her!' Esty urged, jumping up and clutching at Stead's arm. 'There's nothing you can lose.'

Stead began to waver; but he wasn't quite ready to capitulate. 'I don't *understand*,' he said, half-aggressive and half-pleading. 'I don't see how it can possibly help!' He turned, indicating the makeshift bed with one hand. 'How can it help my Chari? How can it bring my other children back to me?'

Indigo wetted her lips. 'I can't promise you anything, Stead. But I believe that if we follow my plan, we'll break the demon's power over her – and over everyone in Bruhome. Forth shares my belief, and so does Esty,' she glanced quickly at them; they both nodded emphatic confirmation. 'And we need you with us, Stead. You're the core of the Fairplayers; your role is vital. I want you – *need* you – to devise a show that will be the most spectacular that Bruhome's ever seen!'

Silence fell. Stead stared at Indigo, struggling to comprehend, to gain even a glimmer of what this bizarre request was all about: but understanding was beyond him. He looked in appeal to his son and daughter. They, too, were watching Indigo, but instead of sharing his bafflement, their faces reflected eager confidence: and abruptly Stead's shoulders sagged in defeat.

'All right.' He scrubbed at his chin with the fingers of one hand. 'All right, lass; I'm not going to argue with you. Any of you.' His brows knitted briefly and he glared woundedly at Forth and Esty. 'If that's what you want me to do, I suppose I'll have to agree. Otherwise you'll do it without me, won't you?' He saw confirmation in their eyes. 'Yes, I thought as much. And the Harvest Mother alone knows what manner of shambles you'd make of it. All right. I'm outnumbered, so I give in. But shrivel me if I don't think you've all gone staring mad!'

Indigo let out her breath in relief. Stead's capitulation was unwilling, his agreement precarious; but she'd gained his promise to co-operate and for now that was sufficient.

'Thank you,' she said warmly, and Esty concurred, leaning over to kiss her father's cheek. Forth didn't speak – he was still smarting with resentment from Stead's earlier tongue-lashing – but he nodded his head grudgingly.

'Well, then.' Stead folded his arms and looked bullishly at them each in turn. 'No one can say Stead Brabazon does anything by halves.' Now his gaze settled on Indigo. 'What sort of a show d'you want?'

'The best we've ever done,' Indigo replied immediately.

'With only four of us to perform it? That's asking a lot. And how, might I ask, are we supposed to get back to the vans for our props and costumes, with those – ' he indicated the square beyond the window with a sweep of one hand, 'those *things* out there?'

'We won't need to. Everything we'll need is here in this room with us. Including as many performers as we want.'

Stead's expression changed. '*What?* Now look, woman – '

Indigo interrupted him before his temper could explode. 'Come to the window.' She'd hoped to avoid this gamble, at least for a while longer; but she saw now that the hope had been futile. Stead's patience and willingness to be manipulated only extended so far. They'd effectively blackmailed him into going along with their scheme up to a point; but beyond that point his credibility was stretched too far and he dug in his heels. She dared not extend the velvet glove any longer or the ground she'd gained so far would be lost. Stead had to see the truth for himself.

'Please, Stead. Do as I ask.' Her voice was steely. 'Just this one last time.'

For a tense moment Stead continued to glower at her. Then, slowly, he stepped forward. Indigo summoned all the willpower she could muster, praying silently that she hadn't miscalculated, that it would work . . .

'First, we need lights,' she said, and turned to the window.

Below them in the square, six patches of flickering, pale orange illumination sprang into being. They were faint, unstable as yet; she concentrated harder, and suddenly the hazy glimmers became flames, leaping skyward from the tops of the flamboy-posts.

Stead made an incoherent noise and jerked back. Indigo smiled reassuringly at him. 'So, we have lights,' she said. 'And now, a stage.'

It was a perfect replica of the stage on which, an age ago it seemed, the Brabazon Fairplayers had performed at the Autumn Revels. The torchlight danced across the empty boards, casting shadows on the closed curtains; and more tiny torches burned in a line along the front of the platform.

'And,' Indigo said, 'we have all the costumes we need.'

Eyes bulging with disbelief, Stead had turned to gape at her, struggling to give voice to the questions that tumbled through his stunned mind. She smiled at him again – and he found himself staring into the milky-gold eyes of a creature clad in all the greens of spring, with hair the colour of warm earth and a face more beautiful than anything human –

'*Ah!*' Stead stumbled back, putting an arm up over his face as though to protect himself. Esty caught his other arm, steadying him – and an icy shock ran through Indigo as she realised what she'd done.

She hadn't meant to take on that form! It had come unbidden and completely without her willing it – she'd meant only to show Stead an illusion of herself in one of the familiar fairplaying costumes. But something else had come powering through her, swamping her consciousness, turning her, instead, into the image of the Earth Mother's emissary.

'I – ' But she couldn't articulate it. *How could it have happened?* Control snatched out of her hands; she hadn't wanted that; not that image of all things –

'Indigo, are you all right?' It was Forth, who'd seen her sway back against the wall and hastened to her side.

'Y-yes . . . I . . . I'm . . . ' With a great effort Indigo took hold of herself. 'I'm quite all right.'

'You startled us all; not just Da.' Forth glanced across the room to where Stead had sat heavily down with Esty beside him. 'The image was so *real*.'

Indigo took several quick, deep breaths. She didn't want anyone else to know of the shock she'd had. She just wished she could get away, be alone for a few minutes to recover her wits and her composure.

She forced down a desire to run from the room and, trying to maintain at least a pretence of normality, said to Forth, 'I'm sorry I had to do that. But it was the only way I could think of to convince him.'

'Oh, he'll be well enough.' Forth smiled faintly. 'Give him a few minutes to get over the surprise, and we'll explain it all to him. It had to be done, Indigo.'

'Yes. But now he knows the truth, how will that affect him?'

Forth grinned. 'It won't affect him in the least; not if I know Da. He's a very practical man. Once he's seen something with his own eyes, he believes in it. We won't have any more problems with him now; and once he knows how it's done, he'll probably outvie us for creating illusions of his own. You wait and see.' He looked speculatively at the window. The torches and the stage had vanished; in her moment of mental furore Indigo had lost her hold on those images and they'd flickered away, but Forth neither knew nor cared about the reasons for their disappearance. They'd be easy enough to recreate when the moment came.

'Reality imposed on illusion,' he said. 'We can do it, Indigo. We truly can turn this accursed world on its head! And when the demon comes running to our lure – it dies!' He snapped his fingers.

Indigo smiled thinly. Forth's description was simplistic, but close enough to the truth. The demon had claimed it couldn't die; yet she believed that it couldn't continue to live in a world that was real. That was the core of her hope. The demon had no true life of its own, but existed only through the illusions it created. Tear down the fabric of those illusions, scatter them and replace them with the reality of flesh-and-blood life, and there would be nothing to sustain its vampiric hunger.

They could do it. They had the power – perhaps she thought uneasily, in the wake of the image she'd inadvertantly created, more power than they yet realised. Now, all that remained was to use it, and use it well.

She said: 'We'd best talk to your father.' Her gaze met Forth's and she smiled at him. 'This is the final act of the play. Let's make sure it's the best performance the Brabazon Fairplayers have ever given!'

Esty had dubbed it the Council of War, and no one was inclined to disagree with her. Stead, as Forth had predicted, threw himself headlong into the discussion – Indigo's gamble had paid off handsomely, and Stead's attitude had changed from scepticism and bafflement to wholehearted enthusiasm. If they'd only *told* him what this was all about from the start, he said in some pique, then a good deal of pointless wrangling could have been avoided. At this Esty had been forced to cover her mouth to suppress a snort of laughter, and Indigo and Forth exchanged a wry grin.

But as the council became more serious, the atmosphere rapidly sobered. The conversation had a bizarre and uncomfortable edge to it; on the surface they might have been discussing plans for any normal Brabazon entertainment; but underlying the familiar arguing about the practicalities was the unspoken but emphatic knowledge that this show would be a very far cry indeed from anything that had ever gone before. But at length the fragmented ideas began to shape into a coherent picture; and at last Stead, who by now had stepped back into his customary role of troupe leader, called a halt.

'We've said all we can say.' He thumped the heels of his hands together; a gesture that they all knew, from long experience, meant that he'd accept no further dissent. 'Esty's near asleep where she's sitting – oh, yes you are, my girl,' as Esty tried to protest and swallow a yawn at the same time, 'and I don't doubt that the rest of us could do with a few hours' sleep. No more talk now. We know what we're going to do, so we rest, and then we begin.' He scanned the faces around him. 'Any quarrel with that?'

No one argued. What Stead proposed made sound sense; they were all weary, and it would be foolhardy to face what lay ahead of them unrefreshed. The Apple Barrel's linen cupboards yielded a plentiful supply of blankets, and so an armful was brought to the attic and they settled themselves to sleep.

And, sleeping, Indigo dreamed of Grimya.

In the dream, the she-wolf was calling to her and she was running over an endless black moor in pursuit. Sometimes she glimpsed Grimya's racing form in the gloom ahead of her; but each time she tried to galvanise herself to greater effort to catch up, she would stumble and fall. And as she ran, two figures ran alongside her, reaching out as though to take her hands but never quite touching. To her right, the Earth Mother's emissary glided spectrally across the grass, hair and robe flying as though in a wind. To her left, fleet-footed and agile, Nemesis showed its cats' teeth and laughed shrilly at her distress. And she was sobbing, because Grimya was in pain, Grimya needed her, and no matter how she strove she could never, never catch up with her.

Indigo woke sharply from the dream, and knew instantly that she wouldn't be able to sleep again. In the dim room her companions were motionless bulks on their rough beds; Stead was snoring. Quietly, not wanting to wake them, Indigo rose, tiptoed out of the room and descended the stairs to the tavern's middle floor. She felt restless, disturbed by the dream; and deep within her was an aching desire to run down to the ground level, fling open the bolted door and rush into the square to call Grimya's name. It was foolish, of course: Grimya wouldn't come; or if she did, she would come as an enemy and not a friend. But the nightmare had awoken feelings that were too tangled, too deep and too personal to rationalise even to herself.

She had been wandering aimlessly along the first-floor landing, peering into the empty rooms but without any interest. One room, larger than its neighbours, boasted two windows that overlooked the square, and Indigo walked in and across the floor to lean morosely on one of the window ledges and gaze out. Nothing to see in the square; nothing moving. And no trace of Grimya . . .

It was strange, but after her brief burst of grief when she'd confronted Grimya in the square, she'd been utterly dry-eyed. Even if she'd wanted to weep now, tears weren't in her. Instead, she felt a cold, hard core of misery that was made all the more acute by guilt as she realised clearly, perhaps for the first time, just how little effort she'd made so far to save her friend. She despised herself for that; though she knew that Grimya – the old Grimya – would have argued the point vehemently. Well, for once Grimya would have been wrong. The dream, with its images of Nemesis's mockery and the emissary's cool, dispassionate judgement, had brought the truth home to her, and in the wake of it she had made a resolution. Before anything else, and above all other goals, she had to find Grimya and win her mind back from the demon's thrall. It wasn't simply a matter of loyalty, though that in itself would have been reason enough. It was a matter of responsibility, and of love.

Preoccupied with her unhappy thoughts, she didn't hear the uncertain footsteps on the stairs and in the passage outside, nor the soft sounds of doors being opened and closed. Only when a floorboard behind her creaked did she start out of her reverie, and look round.

Forth stood on the threshold of the room. There was concern in his eyes.

'Indigo? I – wondered where you were. Is – is everything all right?'

Indigo pushed down a twinge of irritaton at the intrusion into her privacy. Forth wasn't to know; she couldn't in fairness be angry with him.

'I'm fine, Forth. I just didn't want to sleep any longer.'

Encouraged, he came into the room and shut the door behind him. 'Da and Esty are still dead to the world.' A pause. 'I suppose there isn't any sign of her? Of Grimya, I mean?'

Indigo had turned back to the window; she didn't look at him. 'No. No sign.'

Forth sighed. 'That's what's troubling you, isn't it? Indigo, I understand! I know Grimya's as dear to you as – as Chari is to Da.' That wasn't the comparison that he'd intended to make, but at the last moment his courage had failed. He came forward and took her left hand. Indigo didn't draw it away, but neither did she respond; her fingers only lay limp in his.

'We'll save her,' Forth continued urgently. 'Somehow, Indigo, I know we will!'

He was trying to help, but his concern only made matters worse. Indigo gently pulled her hand free. 'Forth, I don't want to talk about it. Not now.'

'But I think you should. You're hurting yourself, damming up your feelings this way. Indigo, I'm going to find her for you, and I'm going to free her! Whatever it needs, whatever the cost – '

'*Please.*' She spoke more sharply than she'd meant to, and instantly regretted her tone. Forth's earnest hazel eyes were chagrined, and she saw how eager he was to be of value to her, how much her approbation would mean to him. She saw how much he loved her, and had to look away again. Poor Forth: there was so much he didn't know; so much that would, were he to discover it, shatter his ideal of her. He was a sad and precarious blend of man and child, his untainted experience almost as far removed from her own as it was possible to be. She could see his dreams as clearly as if he'd gone down on one knee and declared them to her: they were the dreams of youth, of optimism and of unquestioning belief in his own

263

invincibility. Poor, dear, loving Forth. He was like a young animal, a young brother. To tell him that she loved him in that way would be to destroy his fondest hopes: for whatever else he might be, Forth was not Fenran. And no one, least of all this eager, would-be suitor who strove so hard to be strong and courageous in her eyes, could ever take Fenran's place.

She said: 'Forth, I'm deeply grateful for your kindness. But in this, there's nothing you can do. If the enchantment on Grimya can be broken, I'm the only one who can break it.'

'You can't be sure of that.'

'I can.' She smiled pityingly. 'Please, Forth. I *do* appreciate how much you want to help, but – '

'But you don't want the help I can give.'

'It isn't that.'

'Oh, but it is, isn't it?' Suddenly Forth's eyes were filled with angry pain. 'You talk as if I'm a child; as if I haven't the strength or the wisdom to do anything. But I'm not a child – I'm a *man!*' Suddenly he moved, taking hold of her upper arms. She tried to evade him, but the window was at her back and she was cornered.

'Indigo.' Forth's tone had changed. The quick flash of anger was gone, but the urgency that had replaced it was no less intense. 'Indigo, you're not blind. You must know how I feel about you. Goddess help me, I *love* you!'

She looked steadily back at him, trying not to let the sympathy she felt show in her eyes. 'Please don't say that.'

'Why shouldn't I say it? It's true!'

She shook her head. 'You don't know me. You may think you do, but you're wrong.' Then, seeing that he wasn't going to accept that, wasn't going to listen, she added, 'And haven't you considered *my* feelings in the matter?'

'Of course I have! I've barely thought of anything else – I want to *help* you; I want to make you *happy* – '

'*Happy?*' She, too, was growing angry now; angry at his presumption. She tried to shake his hands off but he tightened his grip, and her anger increased. Naïvety and youthful love, however deeply felt, didn't excuse this behaviour.

'Forth, let go of me.'

'Indigo – '

'I said, *let go!* What *right* do you think you have to behave like this?' Indigo's face was white with fury, and suddenly she didn't care if she hurt him; indeed she *wanted* to hurt him, pay him back for intruding so selfishly on her, and for awakening an old, ingrained grief. Her blue-violet eyes narrowed to painful slits, and she said savagely: 'I don't love you, Forth, and I never could. I love Fenran. And Fenran is a *man* – not a half-grown, foolish boy!'

Colour blazed into life in Forth's cheeks – and without warning his tight-strung emotions boiled over.

'Fenran is dead!' He shook her, with a violence that shocked her. 'He's *dead*! But I'm alive, and I'm here, and I'm *real*!' And before Indigo could react, he pulled her forcibly towards him and his mouth locked hungrily on hers, tongue probing, forcing between her teeth.

Indigo uttered a muffled, inarticulate sound and tried to writhe free. But Forth pushed her back and her spine jarred against the window ledge, pinning her.

'I love you!' He broke away for long enough to gasp out the passionate words, kissing her chin, her cheeks, any part of her face he could find in his excitement. 'And you can love me – I *know* you can, I *know* it! Please, Indigo. Oh, *please* . . .'

His lips sought hers again; he was panting, gasping, his angular young body pressing hard against her. And suddenly Indigo's anger flowered into violent rage. She wrenched her head aside, drawing a huge, gulping breath – then with a strength fuelled by her fury she twisted free and hit him across the face. Despite the fact that she had little room to manoeuvre, a good deal of her weight was behind the blow, and Forth reeled back, almost losing his balance as he staggered into the corner. He put a hand up to his burning cheek and stared at her, unable to speak but with mingled emotions brimming in his eyes. Shame, misery – and anger. Above all, anger.

Indigo didn't move. For a time that seemed endless yet

was probably no more than a few seconds they looked at each other, aware of the frozen stalemate between them. Then Forth pushed himself away from the wall and stumbled across the room, groping for the door, jerking it open. It smashed back on its hinges behind him, and Indigo heard his feet clattering on the boards as he ran away down the landing.

Chapter XX

They were ready. And in the gloomy, shadowed market square of the phantom Bruhome, the stage was, literally, set for the most bizarre and yet most important performance of the Brabazon Fairplayers' lives.

Indigo had conjured the platform into being once more, but this time in a form that was solid and substantial. As the four of them stood gazing at it in the darkness she had, ironically, felt a sudden and disorientating sense of utter unreality: the stage looked grotesquely out of place in the square's emptiness, like something from a feverish dream, and the deep silence that surrounded them made it all the more bizarre.

Nothing had threatened them when, cautiously, they walked out of the tavern and into the square. There were no wolves waiting to ambush and attack: Indigo wondered whether the entire pack had been destroyed by the illusions she and Forth and Esty had created and, if so, what had then become of the illusions themselves; the bears and the chimerae and the Scatterers. And Grimya. Where was Grimya, now that her ghastly followers had vanished? And would the events that were about to begin in the square lure her back?

She refused to allow herself to dwell on that thought, forcing her mind to concentrate instead on the task ahead. The show that they were about to perform would be in two parts. The first part was intended to draw the attention of the demon, throwing down the gauntlet of defiance and challenging it to face them; while the second part – and by far the more perilous – would, if they could achieve it, bring about the demon's final downfall.

If they could achieve it. That was the crucial question, and one to which Indigo had no answer. As she stepped up onto the stage behind Forth and Esty the sense of unreality swamped her for the second time, and with it came a wave of doubt and fear. Was she asking too much, both of herself and of the Brabazons? Or was the whole scheme one of utter and hopeless insanity?

Surreptitiously, she glanced at Forth a few feet away. He hadn't spoken a word to her since the dismal fracas in the tavern, and his face was tense and grimly set. Esty, she knew, was aware of the rift between them and had guessed at its nature, if not the details. But Indigo had avoided giving her any chance to ask private questions, and Forth just went about his preparations in mechanical, stony silence. Part of Indigo wanted to approach him and try to patch up the quarrel; but another, greater part counselled against it. It would be all too easy to make matters worse; and she still felt a residue of her earlier anger that made her unwilling to unbend in any way. She only hoped that Forth was wise enough not to jeopardise their plan through some twisted desire to strike back at her. She didn't think he'd be such a fool; but the fear was there none the less.

So many pitfalls; so many risks. *Earth Mother*, Indigo prayed in fervent silence, *help me. If you can, please help and guide me now!*

But it was too late for second thoughts. Stead had taken up his position at the front of the stage, and despite her mood, despite the disconcerting emptiness of the square, the tense anticipation that always preceded the start of a performance was beginning to prickle like ice-cold needles in her veins. She could hear Esty's rapid, exciting breathing, and Forth's feet shuffling in nervous restlessness. Stead turned to face them, a bearlike silhouette in the gloom; they felt, almost palpably, that he was taking the reins, exerting his control. The atmosphere tensed; Indigo gathered her will, readied herself –

Stead spread his hands in a dramatic gesture, and roared: 'LIGHT!'

Mental energy surged from three minds together, and all around the square, the dark flamboy-poles flared into sputtering life. Illumination was hurled across the stage as the entire scene lifted from gloom to startling brilliance, and Esty caught Indigo's hand in a quick, tight clasp that wordlessly communicated their shared triumph. Then Stead turned, and called out across the square.

'Greetings, my friends! Greetings to you, and welcome to this revel! Tonight we bring you music and song, and laughter and tears – tonight, we, the Brabazon Fairplayers, will make your dreams come true!'

He was magnificent. Undaunted by the bizarre setting, the emptiness and silence that gaped before him where his audience should be, he had stepped instantly and powerfully into his place as the consummate showman. He might not have learned the skills that would enable him to conjure illusions from the fabric of this world; but suddenly Steadfast Brabazon was the undisputed revel-master around whom all else must revolve. Now he spun on his heel, holding out one arm, and Esty ran forward. Glimpsing her face, Indigo saw taut fear in her expression, but she took her father's hand and dropped a sweeping curtsy to the imaginary crowd; then her voice rang loud and clear over the square.

'Good people all, we bring you greeting, and welcome you to this night's meeting!' It was the traditional opening chant usually performed by little Piety, and Indigo wetted dry lips, glancing sidelong at Forth. He didn't look at her, but he was holding his pipe, flexing his fingers in preparation.

'Gather round, all grief forsaking,' Esty chanted, 'and join us in our merrymaking!'

Stead made a quick gesture, and Indigo and – to her intense relief – Forth, added their voices to the chorus.

'For we can dance and we can sing, And so to you our gifts we bring, With mirth and music, jest and play, To wish you joy this Revel day!'

For one breathtaking moment, as her lips formed the words, Indigo heard the swell of new voices, children's voices, raised with theirs like ghosts from another world. Her heart skipped with an erratic thump that made her gasp – and then there was no time for further thought, for Stead was stamping the beat, *one, two*, and harp and pipe swung into the lively skip of the first dance.

Indigo's fingers flew across the harp strings, and her mind whirled with a new, eager surge as Esty leaped and whirled to the music. This *was* Bruhome – this was the Autumn Revels, and the Brabazon Fairplayers were on stage, to give the performance of their lives! And at any moment the other players would come in, and the music would swell to its full, joyful volume – *hear it*! she exhorted herself, *make it happen, will it to happen!*

Suddenly there was a second pipe playing, threading a vivid harmony with Forth's tune. Indigo's face broke into a triumphant grin as the pipe was echoed by the ghostly strains of a fiddle, a hurdy-gurdy, the thump and rattle of tambourines. *Yes!* It was coming, it was beginning, gathering power and momentum. Her eyes snapped open again and she saw that Esty now had a tambourine in each hand, and her begrimed shirt and trousers had been transformed into an embroidered costume, the skirt flying about her thighs as she danced. Stead was clapping, calling the figures for a strip-the-willow as though his invisible audience were joining in the dance; and Indigo imagined the empty square filled with upturned faces, people shouting, singing, while others bobbed through the crowd in a weaving figure-of-eight. For an instant the torchlit square seemed to lurch and flicker, and she thought she glimpsed – no, she *saw* them, like ghosts in a distorting mirror; the throng, the revellers –

Suddenly Esty gave an ecstatic yell and leapt from the stage, vaulting over the row of footlights to land lightly on the ground. Spinning like some impish sprite, she whirled across the square, then held out her hands as though to an imaginary partner. And suddenly a masked man, dressed in leaves and with a tall, antlered head-dress, was dancing with her, the crossed arms linked as they stamped and jumped together.

Forth's eyes widened and he shouted to Stead a word Indigo didn't know but which sounded like '*Kirnoen!*' Other forms were materialising around the dancing couple; Indigo glimpsed tiny, humanlike figures with foxes' heads, a beautiful woman with the eyes and wings of a hawk, another brown-faced horned man –

Stead swung round and, cutting across the music,

began to clap out a new beat. 'Change tune!' he bellowed. '*Hunters To The Harvest* – NOW!'

The pipe's shrilling note veered sharply, then swung into a new and more urgent melody. Indigo swiftly followed, the harp thrumming out the rhythm of a galloping horse as she recognised the song; and seconds later the ghost-instruments, the fiddle, the hurdy-gurdy, the drum, added their emphatic support. The antlered figure caught Esty about the waist, lifting her high into the air, and suddenly the square seemed to be filled with dancing figures – masked men and women, small, eagerly jumping dogs, and a myriad of creatures whose forms celebrated both the human and the animal. A cry went up from massed throats, a mingling of human shouts and animal barks, shrieks and yelpings, and Forth, his face afire with wild excitement, yelled over and over again, like a war-chant, '*Kirnoen! Kirnoen!*'

Suddenly Indigo remembered. *Kirnoen* – it was the south-westerners' name for the wild huntsmen, the supernatural servants of the Earth Mother who rode out under the blood-red orb of the Harvest Moon to cleanse the land after the last days of gleaning and prepare it for its winter sleep. They had such mythic figures, too, in the Southern Isles, though they rode under a different name; and they were celebrated at the great hunting feasts when the first frosts came and the great winds began to blow out of the south . . .

A cry quivered on her tongue, demanding to be given voice. Images surged into her mind: of Carn Caille, her long-lost home; of the tundra, and the great forests, and the winding horns echoing their litany to the sun that blazed on the horizon like the Goddess's pulsing, life-bringing heart. She could hear the baying of the great hounds, the snort and thunder of the horses as they breasted through the bracken like ships cleaving the sea, the twang and thwack of bows, the joyous shouts of the hunters – and the cry burst from her lips, a cry of release and fierce triumph. The harp fell from her hands, its protesting discord lost as the leaping, whirling celebrants answered her, and she felt the change coming, felt herself growing taller, her hair cascading like a stream in spate,

271

her rough garments stripped away to leave her clad in leaves and in light and in the warm, rippling colours of earth. Her eyes turned to gold, and the cry went on and on, pouring in a torrent from her throat as new forms erupted from the square's blazing night to join in the wild dance. Huge brown and chestnut horses reared and pranced; lean grey deerhounds bayed a deep, melodious chorus, and the vivid, shouting laughter of the Southern Isles hunters, brown-skinned from sun and salt winds, rang like bells to echo from the empty houses and shake the square.

'Indigo! *Indigo!*' Someone was calling her name, and though from another time, another world, she knew the voice, Stead's stunned face and corona of red hair meant nothing to her as she turned her golden eyes on him. She felt the power within her rise anew, and Stead fell back as though buffeted by a gale. Part of her mind tried to reach out to him, but another part, by far the stronger, was beyond such considerations; beyond even her own control. She didn't know what he'd seen; all she knew was the glorious energy that was rising in her as the music swelled and the dancers leapt and whirled in the square. Faster and yet faster – and suddenly the joyous noise was punctuated by shrieks, whistles, screams, roars, as out of the alleys and the side streets, from doors and windows, a new throng of celebrants came racing and tumbling. Indigo's heart rose as she recognised their own illusions, the creatures which had driven off the phantom wolves. Massive bears, brown as the forests or white as the icebound polar wastes; giant owls; chimerae – even the Scatterers were there, whirling like dervishes and screeching their maniacal delight. Her vision seemed to burn into spectra beyond human limits, and in the middle of the mad dance she saw Esty, partnered now by a giant shadow that changed with stunning speed from man to horse to cat to sprite to hound. The girl seemed to blaze with a rainbow aura, an earthbound star of real and physical life among the illusions; she was laughing, her head thrown back, and from her upraised hands streamers of light flew across the square to explode like celebration flares among the flamboys.

And then, in the heart of the bobbing, leaping throng, Indigo saw another star, another blaze of life. It was moving, threading its way towards the stage, but erratically, as though torn between fear and desire. A wild, irrational hope clutched at her – whatever this might be, it was no illusion. It *lived*: her heightened vision could see the life pulsing within it; her heightened senses could *feel* the beating heart, the roiling consciousness – and suddenly she knew, knew without a thread of doubt, who came towards her.

She turned, and a rush of wind flung itself across the stage, swirling her cloak of leaves, whipping her hair. Stead – but he was gone into the dance, carried away like a twig on a tumbling current. Forth – but there was only his reed-pipe, abandoned on the boards. She was alone. When she looked back, the pulsing light was poised at the foot of the stage – and within the coruscating spectrum that betrayed the living, breathing flesh stood Grimya.

Mad eyes stared into her own. Grimya did not know her; yet the she-wolf recognised the golden-eyed creature that Indigo had become, and her hatred was distorted by fear and by another emotion, as yet unrealised but struggling for existence. She drew back her lips, exposing fangs that drooled hungrily. And then she sprang up on to the stage.

They stood two paces apart, facing each other, neither moving. Indigo felt the red surge of Grimya's mind probing her. Hating. Ravening. Yearning to feed, and yearning to avenge her vanished pack. And yet somewhere beyond the demented glare, beyond the warped consciousness, something else was pleading to be heard; something that cried out in pain and misery; *heal me!*

Grimya . . . Indigo projected the wolf's name with all the strength she could muster; all her love, all her protectiveness. Suddenly the boards of the stage dissolved away; there was grass beneath her bare feet, and a tree towered at her back, its leaves molten gold in the torchlight. The wolf began to tremble, and a snarl died stillborn in her throat.

'Grimya.' This time she spoke aloud, and with the gentle authority of utter confidence. The voice that came

273

from her lips wasn't her own, but she knew it well. She had the power; she knew it now. She *was* the power. The power to take control. The power to heal.

'*Ah, my little sister of the forests.*' She dropped to one knee, and a golden-brown hand, her own hand and yet not her own, stretched out towards the shuddering wolf. '*Know me, beloved one, and come to me. Be healed. Be whole again.*'

Grimya whimpered. As the being who was Indigo reached out, she bared her teeth again and tried to snap at the outstretched fingers – but paused. Her shivering redoubled, and for a moment Grimya's sane, anguished mind stared out in desperation from the manic lupine eyes.

P...please... The weak mental cry struggled across a vast gulf. *P...please help me*...

The golden-brown hand touched her head, and a massive shudder shook the wolf from jaw to tail. Indigo felt a violent crimson pulsing, and a black core beneath the crimson; vampiric, malignant. Disgust and contempt filled her, and for an instant she seemed to be looking down from a great height at the tableau of herself and Grimya, seeing them through other eyes, another mind. A rod of blinding light flared within her; her fingers flexed once, and Grimya howled like a banshee as the black core, the evil fragment of the demon's influence, disintegrated. As it shattered out of existence, the scene about Indigo seemed to twist and collapse in on itself. Impossible colours erupted across her line of sight; the world splintered to fragments, reformed –

And she was kneeling on the bare boards, sobbing as she hugged Grimya with all her strength, while the wolf licked her face, whining –

Shock made her skin crawl as she realised that Grimya's frightened whimpers were a lone sound against a backdrop of total silence. Quickly, pulse pounding, Indigo looked up.

The square was empty. The flamboys still burned on their tall poles but the dancing revellers had vanished. There was no music; there were no shouts and cries and yammerings. Only the isolated figures of Stead, Esty and

274

Forth, standing helplessly on the cobbles, staring about them in bemusement.

Very slowly, Indigo rose to her feet. Grimya pressed hard against her thigh, still too shocked to speak or even project any mental message. *What had happened?* Surely Esty and Forth hadn't banished their illusions? Or –

The thought collapsed as from the darkness of the street that led to the river-bridge came echoing, measured footsteps.

'Stead!' Indigo's voice cracked across the square as premonition rapidly shifted towards certainty. 'Bring the others! Get back to the stage – quickly!'

The three Brabazons heard her and came running. Forth jumped up onto the boards then turned to help Stead, while Indigo hauled Esty hastily over the foot-lights.

'What's amiss?' Esty was breathless and flushed. 'Everything just vanished! And – ' She stopped, her eyes widening as she saw Grimya for the first time. 'Indigo – ' she cried fearfully.

'It's all right.' Indigo cast a swift glance at the she-wolf. 'There's no time to explain now, Esty, but Grimya's safe.' Esty obviously hadn't seen what had taken place on the stage; but as Stead scrambled up, Forth caught Indigo's eye for a brief instant, and she knew immediately that he had witnessed the scene. The look he gave her was angry, but the anger was tinged with uncertainty and a measure of fear.

Stead, however, was oblivious to the momentary silent exchange. He clambered upright, and turned to stare at the street's dark maw. 'If that's what I think it might be . . . ' he began grimly.

Indigo was still suffering from the aftermath of her experience with Grimya: her senses felt distorted and her mind sluggish and unclear. She had to pull her wits together. 'I suspect it is,' she said, breaking through her confusion with an effort. 'And it's sooner than I anticipated.'

Esty had quietly crossed the stage – carefully avoiding Grimya – to take Forth's hand. Stead treated them all to a fierce glare.

275

'Well, then. Time for the second part of the show to begin.'

'Not yet.' Indigo gazed at the street entrance. The footfalls were louder now, though they had slowed. And she could feel eyes, an almost tangible sensation, regarding them from the darkness.

A shadow moved out from the street's maw. It approached the first of the flamboy-poles, and as it passed by, the torch guttered and went out. It passed the second flare; that, too, died. Esty made a small, nervous sound, and Grimya whimpered.

By the light of the remaining flamboys Indigo could see now that the shadow was human in shape, but without feature or substance. It was a silhouette, devoid of detail. But still she could feel the cruel intensity of its gaze.

A third torch flickered and died, then a fourth. The demon approached the stage, and the tiny footlights began to gutter.

'No!' Indigo said sharply. She saw Forth and Esty shut their eyes, concentrating, willing; and the row of lights brightened once more. The demon halted.

Then the thin, abysmal voice that she remembered so well from the rotting hall said, with sweet and pitying contempt:

'I applaud you all, and I thank you for the entertainment. But oh, you are all such *fools*.'

Chapter XXI

'Fools, is it?' Stead's voice exploded into the deathly silence that had descended. His face was reddening, and a vein in his neck pulsed with suppressed rage. 'We'll see about that, you aborted whore's-get! We'll see who's the fool!'

'Da!' Esty tugged at his sleeve, horrified by his complete lack of caution. 'Don't provoke it!'

Stead shook her off and strode to the front of the stage, staring down at the shadow with fists clenched on hips. *'Give me back my daughter!'* he roared. 'Or, by all the good harvests the Mother sends, I'll see your fragments scattered on those cobbles and fed to your own squalling followers!'

Soft laughter issued from the shadow's invisible mouth. 'Steadfast Brabazon, you are truly a revel-master,' it said. 'You will nourish me well when I feed on you. Better than the feeble souls of Bruhome. Better than their crops, and their animals, and their children.' It glided to one side, until it stood directly opposite Indigo. The silhouetted head tilted fractionally downwards, and Indigo felt Grimya shift behind her. A thin, fearful snarl bubbled in the she-wolf's throat, and again the demon chuckled.

'Your companions found, and your friend freed from my little spell. I congratulate you, Indigo; you have achieved a great deal, and learned much about yourself in the process, I think. How sad that it has all been to no purpose.'

'Oh, there's a purpose,' Indigo said icily. 'And our show isn't done yet.'

'More entertainment? How gratifying. It will cheer me further in my unhappy sojourn. And might I enquire' –

now the featureless head lifted again, and Indigo felt the near-physical intensity of its stare – 'what form this new diversion is to take?'

Indigo couldn't be certain, but she thought she detected something more than laconic mockery in the question. The thin, inflectionless voice gave nothing away, but she suspected that the vampiric entity was a little more concerned for her answer than it cared to admit. She smiled.

'Such curious interest, when your sorrowful burden denies you even life's most modest pleasures? You surprise me, demon.'

The shadow-shoulders lifted in a weary gesture. 'Even the saddest of us are sometimes prone to whim.'

'Or to fear.' Stead was watching her keenly, and Indigo hoped fervently that he wouldn't attempt to intervene; she needed this hiatus to continue a little longer, for something the demon had let slip was burning in her mind. *You have learned much about yourself.* It sensed some change, some quickening of her abilities, and she recalled the dizzying sensation that had overtaken her as she strove to bring Grimya out of her enchantment. She had had the power then; she *was* the power . . .

Her heart started to thump erratically with excitement. She should have realised it before, long before, when the demon first greeted them in the decaying hall and flung in her face the two images which named her *sister*. For where could it have drawn those images, but from her own mind? Not, as she'd believed then, from her memory; but from another, far deeper part of her. From her soul.

Oh, yes. She could do what needed to be done. She had achieved it once; it could be so again. All it took was the understanding that would trigger her will, and now that understanding had come to her.

She knew, without needing to turn her head, that the Brabazons were waiting in trepidation. She was aware of their confusion, but there was no time to stop and warn them of what she meant to do. The demon had inadvertantly placed a weapon in her hands – she must use it.

She returned her full attention to the hovering shadow.

It might have been easy to pity it; this pathetic, unreal thing that was neither truly alive nor truly dead. But to pity was to feed the illusion and give it strength. In its own right the demon had no strength; so, surely, it had no true power? Only the power which its victims unwittingly granted it by believing in the force of the illusions it created – and thus believing in the demon itself.

Indigo smiled again, and said: 'We have one last entertainment for you, my ever-hungry friend. A dance. We call it *Bruhome's Return*.'

The shadow flickered, as though some emotion had moved it. 'An amusing title,' the insubstantial voice said, and this time there was no mistaking the uneasy edge. 'Your ability to jest at such a time does you credit.'

'I'm glad you think so. For the jest will be at your expense.' She took a pace back. 'Will you step up on the stage and dance with us, demon?'

Behind her, Stead hissed, '*Indigo, what in the Mother's name are you doing?*' but she waved one hand in a quick, negative gesture. The shadow was motionless. Indigo's smile became less pleasant. 'Or shall I find you a more apt dancing partner?'

She could feel the energy building in her, as it had done with Grimya. The distance was so much greater; she didn't know if she could succeed, if she could summon the will – *no, don't think that! You have the power! You are the power!*

Blinding light erupted from beneath the stage – and in the heart of the light, where an instant before Indigo had been, stood the tall, graceful figure of the Emissary. The being raised one arm in a commanding movement, and out of the night, from somewhere beyond the square's confines, the thin strains of a hurdy-gurdy shimmered on the air.

Esty uttered a cry of anguished longing. 'Cour! It's Cour's tune!'

Yes, Indigo thought wildly, *hold to that, call them all – Cour and Rance and Honi and Pi – all of them, all of them!* Lost within the churning chaos of her own mind, swamped by the image she'd created, she focused the burning core of her will into her invocation.

Flute and pipe and tambour joined in with the hurdy-gurdy, and the tune coalesced into a lively march. The sound swelled, drawing nearer, nearer, and now it seemed to be all around them, as though an entire army of musicians were dancing through the unlit streets and alleys, converging inexorably on the square and the stage. Forth, his eyes wild with excitement, snatched up his own pipe, and Esty, a tambourine in her hand, cried out to Stead, 'Da, play the fiddle! You can, you *can*, if you'll only will it!'

The shadow had fallen back as the light and the Emissary's form blasted into being, but now, recovering, it surged towards the stage, elongating, stretching out its phantom hands as though to snatch the shimmering vision and shatter it. But a golden arm rose again, and pointed towards the door of the Apple-Barrel inn.

'Dance, demon! Dance with the Brabazon Fairplayers! Dance with the living folk of Bruhome!'

Two flamboys burst into life in the sconces that overhung the tavern door, and the door itself crashed open. On the threshold stood a solitary figure, and the flaring torches lit a crown of shining auburn hair –

Esty shrieked at the top of her voice, '*Chari!*'

Stead whipped round, and the hectic colour drained from his skin. The demon, too, turned, hissing furiously, and the black shadow's outline distorted as it saw what was afoot.

'Your spell is broken!' The awesome form of the Emissary flashed out of existence and there was Indigo, dishevelled, screaming in hatred and triumph at the vampire. 'You have no power over us – we are masters of the revels now!' She whirled. 'Stead, bring Chari! Bring her to us!'

Howling his daughter's name, Stead leaped from the boards and raced away over the cobbles. Chari had seen him and was stumbling from the doorway, reaching for him; they met, and Stead swung her up into his arms, kissing her face and her hair as he turned and ran back towards the stage. The demon watched his progress, then suddenly turned to face Indigo once more. She felt the venom in its mind, the gathering strength, the mounting rage – and then a hideous, fiery mouth opened in the silhouetted head, as though the door of a furnace had been flung wide, and she rocked back on her heels as a single, terrible note emanated from the mouth, a malevolent booming that drowned the swelling music and shook the stage. The torch flames leaped high in protest: then every light in the square went out, and silence crashed down as the appalling note swallowed all other sound, and ceased.

Stead skidded to a halt, and Forth and Esty, who had been scrambling to the edge of the platform to help him, froze in mid-movement. The shadow had changed. Now a thunderous purple aura, shot through with tongues of flickering silver, pulsed about it like the slow beating of some malignant heart. It exhaled a slow, harsh breath that seemed to go on and on and on, and Indigo felt her skin prickle as the air turned ice-cold. In a voice that carried all the bleak, deadly fury of an arctic storm, the demon said:

'Ah, Indigo. Now you have made me *angry*.'

The platform began to shake. Forth lost his balance and fell, while Esty clutched at the curtain, almost bringing it down on herself, and Grimya, still dazed from shock, backed whimpering into a corner. But Indigo felt the flexing boards beneath her feet, heard the protesting creak of wood, and smiled.

'No, demon. You can't destroy what we have created. What we have created is real, and reality is beyond your power to control.'

The entity laughed softly. 'Reality, perhaps. But not illusion. And I believe you still have a lesson to learn.'

The platform stopped shaking. For a moment there was total silence; and then a sound that went beyond sound thundered through the square. The pewter sky turned pitch-black, and constellations sprang from the blackness to glare coldly down on the scene. The shattering noise died away, and a wind began to rise, an arctic blast that moaned over the rooftops and hurled a flurry of snow against Indigo's face. And then out of the dark, out of the polar night, she heard the first titanic footfall of something approaching.

A terror bred into her through centuries of legend sank diamond claws into Indigo's stomach. *The Nameless* – stalking out of the titanic ice ramparts and driving the huge winter gales before it – she felt herself beginning to shake as the blindness of panic swelled in her; and her eyes were being drawn up, up to the black heavens, where among the constellations she knew she would see the twin stars that were not stars but the remote and glittering eyes of the formless harbinger that heralded the falling of the sky –

Illusion! The howling cry burst on her mind like fire, and something hurled itself against her, throwing her down. She struck the hard reality of the stage, shouting out as the thundering tread of the Nameless dinned in her ears.

Illusion, Indigo! Illusion! Grimya's teeth were locked on the shoulder of her shirt and the she-wolf writhed with the effort of trying to drag her to her feet. Indigo rolled, sprawled, screaming as the ghastly footfalls sounded again, again, closer –

'H-elp me!' Grimya twisted about, releasing her hold on Indigo and barking the desperate words at the stunned Brabazons. Esty was transfixed, too shocked to move – but Forth reacted. He snatched up his pipe again, and a cascade of notes – anything, any melody, it didn't matter – shrilled out across the stage, slicing through the dire noise of the Nameless's approach. The music acted on Esty like a physical blow: she reeled, and intelligence snapped back into her eyes as she realised what Forth was trying to do.

'Da!' She shouted to Stead who was hunched against the platform's edge with Chari clutched tight in his arms. 'Da, play! Play – Forth can't do it alone!' She stretched out, trying to wrest Chari from him and pull her up on to the stage. '*Help us!*'

Chari sprawled on the boards, Stead scrambling behind her. Grimya had dragged Indigo into a sitting position, and she was shaking her head dazedly. Music – Forth was playing, he was driving the Nameless away, and the Nameless was only a myth, a phantom, an illusion – but the snow still stung her cheeks, and the wind was howling like a thousand lost souls –

'Chari, dance with me!' Esty shrieked at her sister over the gale's moaning, and shook her as though she was a rag doll. Chari's head rolled on her shoulders; she gasped, clutched Esty's arms. 'Dance!' Esty shouted again. 'We're in Bruhome! The Revels, Chari, the Autumn Revels! *Dance with me!*'

Forth, hearing her frantic exhortation, struck up an eight-hand reel called *Merry Maidens*, in which traditionally Chari and Esty always led their audience. His foot stamped the beat ferociously, and Chari blinked her glazed eyes. 'Ohh . . .'

'*Dance!*' Esty screeched, and yanked on her sister's arms, spinning her around and forcing her to skip to keep her balance. Suddenly Chari's body, if not her mind, seemed to comprehend, and next moment she and Esty were whirling into the dance-figures. Stead, who thus far had been too bemused to do anything but gape, shook his head violently and clapped both hands to his skull as though struggling to blot out the scream of the wind and the pounding of the Nameless's footfalls. The demon was laughing at him, *laughing* – he would not be laughed at! He would not be mocked! And Indigo needed his help. Indigo had saved Chari, and now she needed him!

He flexed his broad hands, and without conscious control his fingers curled into a familiar pattern before his face. Wood and resin; and the bow in his hand, and the strings vibrating under his fingers –

Stead yelled aloud in shocked triumph as the fiddle, his own fiddle, battered and pocked and precious, materialised in his hands and he heard its voice soar and mingle with Forth's pipe.

'*Louder!*' Carried away with his own success, he roared to Forth. 'Come on, boy, where's your breath? Louder, and faster! Dance, my lasses – dance that whorespawn to dust!'

Light blazed out suddenly as the two flamboys nearest the stage, galvanised by Forth and Esty, leaped into life again, hurling brilliant illumination across Indigo's face. Fire battled with ice for a single instant, and then the snow, the illusion, flicked out of existence, and awareness came jolting back. *The Nameless* – but no, it was gone, it had never existed –

Indigo, get up! Get up! We must help Stead! Grimya was bounding around her in a tight circle, ears flat and fangs bared in agitation. Half blinded by the torchlight Indigo groped for balance, pushed herself upright, swayed.

The music – Stead and Forth, their fingers flying over their instruments while Esty and Chari whirled with manic, dervish-like energy. And the demon –

The demon was a black whirlwind, a towering column of rage rising before the stage. For a frozen instant Indigo stared at it, and then without warning her vision slipped into another dimension, another spectrum, and she saw into it, through the smoke and the shadow to its heart. There was nothing there. Nothing but a vacuum, a vortex, an empty space without life or meaning.

'DAMN YOU!' Her voice shrieked above the wild dance and the stamping, tramping of the Brabazons' feet. 'YOU DON'T EXIST!'

Grimya yelped and fell back as, like a tree bursting into flames, Indigo's form lit with a blinding rainbow radiance. Silver hair streamed over her shoulders, golden eyes glared from her skull, and she was demon-child and goddess-figure and virgin and mother and hag, and flawed, embattled human.

The demon shrieked. Over the rooftops of Bruhome's market square came twenty huge, skeletal reptiles, hopping and shrieking and flapping their membranous wings as they scrabbled and slithered down the tiles. Indigo's burning eyes turned on them, and they exploded in flames. As the blazing shards fell to the cobblestones and dissolved, the chimneys of five houses began to smoke . . .

The demon howled again. In an alleyway, a vast shadow moved. The Brown Walker, hooting, swinging his great club, loomed out of the dark with a hundred Scatterers screeching and yammering around his single monstrous foot.

Indigo said: 'NO.' And where the Brown Walker had been, lanterns glowed in four upper windows, and a ghostly snatch of cheerful laughter echoed from a distant tavern as the Scatterers vanished into nothing.

The whirlwind that the demon-shadow had become began to spin faster, elongating and darkening to a black so intense that it seemed to suck in all light around it. Now it was wailing, a high, thin, lethal note that seared through the music, trying to sever and shatter it. Indigo turned, and the voice of the Emissary sang out, drowning the devilish shrieking.

'Cour! Rance!'

Stead heard his sons' names cried above the demon's din, and a wild, uncontrollable excitement took hold of him. 'Cour!' he bawled. 'Rance! Where are you, you idle braggarts? Play! If you value your hides, PLAY!'

Shadowy forms leaped at the edge of the stage, and a second pipe and a hurdy-gurdy added their eldritch voices to the dance. Cour, freckled and grinning, was crouched over his instrument, Rance, tossing sweat-soaked hair from his face, had his eyes tight-shut as he piped. They were solidifying; they were *real* – and as they took form, Indigo saw through eyes that were blue-violet and gold and silver all at once, saw the demon writhing, heard its scream of fury, of frustration, of burgeoning and horrified fear.

She swung round, and her shimmering stare focused on the Apple-Barrel tavern. Light leaped in the ground floor windows, and from the gaping door came the sound of talk and laughter, while shadows – human, mortal shadows – moved across the glass. She turned again: and over the balcony of the Brewmasters' Hall three Bruhome guild banners appeared: a scythe crossed with a sheep-herder's crook, a pyramid of casks wreathed in hop-garlands, a scarlet apple emblazoned on a green field. She looked up: and the sky, which had returned to featureless pewter night, was suddenly ablaze with stars; the familiar, kindly constellations of the south-west.

In the distance, a dog barked enthusiastically for the sheer joy of its own existence.

'BRUHOME!' It was Indigo's voice and yet a hundred, a thousand voices together. 'BRUHOME!'

'Bruhome!' The Brabazons took up the cry and Esty

285

yodelled her shrill, triumphant exuberance. She and Chari broke apart, and suddenly there was Honi, and there was Gen, and there was Piety, joining with them, skirts and hair flying. Indigo flung her head back, laughing, and a golden hand pointed.

The sisters shrieked, and, hands clasped, sprang from the stage and onto the cobbles of the square. They formed a ring around the whirling black column, jumping, dancing, mocking the demon as it strove to break through their ranks. And all around them, faint as phantoms but growing stronger with every moment, a crowd was growing out of the night as more and more flamboys flared to light the scene. Drinkers and dancers and lovers and gawpers – the boiling tides of living, revelling humanity. New lights were appearing all over the square, in windows and over doorways decked out with garlands. Flowers and bunting sprang out of emptiness to bob and swing in the torchlight; doors were flung open, laughing figures more substantial than ghosts emerged from their homes to join in the celebration –

Bruhome was returning. Not the cruel mockery of a town of phantom memories, but the thriving and bustling reality, celebrating their harvest, celebrating their Goddess, celebrating life itself. And Stead, Forth, Cour and Rance were playing, and Esty and Chari and Honi and Gen and Pi whirled faster and still faster, their hair a wheel of fire, their skirts a glorious kaleidoscope of colour as they circled the screaming, panicking shadow: as colour and solidity and reality came powering into the demon world to tear its illusory fabric apart and cast it away into the limbo whence it came.

A huge, shuddering sensation powered up through Indigo, as though she were a tree with its roots buried deep in the life-giving Earth. *The demon was dying!* The sensation swamped her, filling her body, her mind, her soul, and she flung her arms skyward, her voice rising in a singing, shattering cry of joy and triumph. *One last great willing. One, the final one –*

Her hands came together like a diver soaring from a cliff, and her eyes burned molten as her arms came down, down, bringing down the sun and the moon, the power screaming through her, *life, life –*

The black column that twisted and writhed in the circle of dancing sisters uttered a howl that blasted to the stars. There was unbearable agony in the howl, and defeat, and misery, and at the very last a shrieking, dying spear of futile hatred, as, smashed by reality, hurled to utter oblivion, the last shreds of the demon's being scattered and fled from the world.

Fled from the world . . .

Fled . . .

There was silence, and there was stillness. She was held rigid, mind and body locked by a force she couldn't comprehend and couldn't control. The golden-eyed Emissary was gone. She was Indigo; only Indigo. And the demon was dead, and she –

She raised her head, and it felt as though her body belonged not to her but to someone – something – alien, unknown. The stage: she was on her knees on the stage, in Bruhome, at the Autumn Revels. Behind her were Stead and Forth and Cour and Rance; but their instruments were silent; they watched her, uncomprehending. *Waiting.* And down below the stage, among the motionless crowd; the girls, their dance arrested. Watching her . . .

She had done it. She had killed the cancer, the vampire, the soul-eater. She, and the Brabazons. And Grimya. Grimya was beside her; but silent, silent as the others.

And on the far side of the stage . . .

Forth saw Indigo's body freeze, and saw the expression of disbelief and terror and another emotion far beyond his experience that crept slowly over her face. In an instant all his anger and resentment were forgotten, and he dropped his reed-pipe, starting forward, reaching out to her –

And stopped.

The man was black-haired, dark-eyed, dressed in the sober garb of one who knew and loved the life of a wide and varied world. His face was brown and scarred, as though he'd known the scourges of wind and fire and salt

287

seas and other torments better left unspoken. And as he looked at the man's eyes, and then at Indigo's face, Forth knew who he must be. And in that moment he understood at last what love – *real* love, and not youthful passion – truly was.

Fenran smiled and the smile made Forth look away in shame. He couldn't watch as, silently, the dark-haired figure stepped towards Indigo and reached down to take her hand; couldn't witness the twining of their fingers, the kiss that Fenran, leaning down, planted lightly and yet so poignantly on Indigo's upturned lips as she raised her pleading, longing eyes to his. A board creaked under Fenran's foot, old wood protesting. And when Forth looked again there was only Indigo, kneeling on the Revels stage and weeping silently as sounds of life and activity began to swell slowly about them, and the first rays of the true sun began to slant across the rooftops of Bruhome.

Bruhome

Grimya said: *So we can stay? For a little while?*

'Yes.' Indigo smiled gently, and reached out to stroke the she-wolf's brindled head. 'At least for a little while.'

Outside the caravan she could hear the crackle of the fire, and the first rich aromas of the meal Chari was preparing drifted on the light early-evening breeze, mingling with the cooler scents of the river. In a few minutes they would eat, and then it would be time to make their way to the square for the evening's performance. Nine days of the Autumn Revels. Nine days of celebrating the harvest, and of thanksgiving to the Earth Mother for Bruhome's deliverance.

The sickness was gone. There had been no new victims, and in the light of the dawn that had finally broken after the long, supernatural night, most of the sleepers had been found safe in their beds, waking with nothing but memories of a feverish dream. Deliverance had come too late for some, whose souls had already gone to feed the vampiric hunger of the demon; but the numbers of the dead were few, and though they mourned the lost ones, the living still had much to celebrate. Even some who had disappeared in the early days of the blight had returned, dazed and weak but fundamentally unharmed. And though the hop harvest had fallen prey to the blight, the grapes were recovering and the apples would yield a rich bounty.

Now, Bruhome wanted music and song and laughter, to heal the last wounds and help the district to forget the horrors of recent days. Already, with their customary pragmatism, the townsfolk had devised their own myth to explain the ills that had assailed them. The myth was not the truth, but it was more comfortable to rational minds, and in time it would become enshrined as the harsher truths faded into the past.

But for Indigo and Grimya, the memories wouldn't fade and the truth would not become obscured by time. The secret that they shared with the elder Brabazons – and in particular with Forth and Esty – was one which, by instinctive agreement, would rarely be spoken of even in their most private moments. Perhaps, in years to come, the Fairplayers would create a new allegorical tale for their repertoire; but the true secret would be kept forever.

Indigo's hand closed over the lodestone, which she had taken from its pouch and held in her hand for a while. The stone felt warm, and the golden pinpoint was now quiet at its centre. She had watched the tiny light tremble, shifting towards the stone's edge to point northward; but at sight of it something had risen in her; a sense of strength, a sense of certainty. She would not be commanded. The lodestone had been her master, and she had danced to its tune. But now, that would change. The lodestone would be a master no longer, but a servant; and as a servant, it would also be a friend. She would follow where it led; but in her own way and her own time. And that time was not yet. She would stay a while, for here she had found friends, and had learned again what it was to be happy.

Silently in her mind, Indigo said: *No*. The golden pinpoint quivered, and obeyed.

She had the power. Strange that it had taken an entity whose watchword was illusion to reveal such a truth to her; but the lesson had been profound. She was beginning to understand a little of what she truly was – and perhaps a little of what really lay behind her enduring quest. And as time went on, as she embarked upon new journeys, she would continue to learn.

An image slipped fleetingly past her inner eye. Fenran. One brief moment, one precious touch. Her strength had brought him to her. *Her* strength, alone. Then in the wake of that knowledge a new image formed, and she smiled as she slid the lodestone back into its pouch. Golden eyes and silver eyes; and between them, her own young-old, blue-violet gaze. Three disparate entities. Or were they? she thought. Or were they?

Footsteps sounded on the van steps, and a shadow fell across the half-open door. Indigo looked up, and saw Forth.

'Behind the moon?' He smiled at her, still a little tentative although, slowly, the diffidence was fading.

Indigo smiled back. 'Just daydreaming, Forth.'

'Food's ready. And then we'd best be getting along to the square, or our public will get restive! And –' he hesitated.

'And?'

Forth's smile broadened into a faintly sheepish grin. 'There's to be dancing in the square after the show's over. I was wondering if you might partner me in the first reel?'

She looked into his eyes and felt a blend of sadness and thankfulness. Forth loved her; but he understood now that she would never be for him. Fenran, whether ghost or man of flesh and blood, had shown him that truth; he was learning to accept it, and youth and resilience were already coming to his aid. He'd find another love, an enduring love, in time. And until then he was content to be her friend.

Indigo rose to her feet and held out a hand, squeezing his fingers lightly. 'Yes, Forth' she said. 'I'll be honoured.'